May the Road Rise Up to Meet You

Praise for Peter Troy's

May the Road Rise Up to Meet You

"*May the Road Rise Up to Meet You* is a rich look at the boiling melting pot that was Civil War–era New York."

—*The Star-Ledger* (Newark)

"A classic tale that feels equally Irish and American."

—*BookPage*

"*May the Road Rise Up to Meet You* is a generous and sweeping Civil War saga about Southern slaves and newly arrived immigrants linked by a shared desire for abolition and freedom. Ranging from the clawing hunger of the Irish Famine to the abusive captivity of South Carolina, from rough-and-tumble Five Points to the genteel streets of Richmond, Virginia, this affecting and moving tale links disparate lives of impressive integrity, suffering and triumph, and yields a deeply personal portrait of the immigrants who fought the war and the people they fought it for. A hopeful, magnanimous depiction of America at its most vulnerable."

—Robin Oliveira, author of *My Name Is Mary Sutter*, winner of the Shaara Prize for Excellence in Civil War Fiction

"The depth of Troy's characters offers compelling insights into the Civil War era." —*Publishers Weekly*

"Troy has written a heartfelt and moving saga of America's most fateful hour." —*California Literary Review*

PETER TROY

May the Road Rise Up to Meet You

Peter Troy is a former high school history teacher from New York. He is at work on his next novel.

May the Road Rise Up to Meet You

A NOVEL

PETER TROY

ANCHOR BOOKS
A DIVISION OF RANDOM HOUSE
NEW YORK

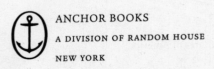

FIRST ANCHOR BOOKS EDITION, NOVEMBER 2012

 Published in the United States by Anchor Books, a division of Random House, Inc., New York, and in Canada by Random House of Canada Limited, Toronto. Originally published in hardcover in the United States by Doubleday, a division of Random House, Inc., New York, in 2012.

The Library of Congress has cataloged the Doubleday edition as follows:
Troy, Peter.
May the road rise up to meet you / Peter Troy.
p. cm.
1. United States-History—19th century—Fiction. I. Title.
PS3620.R685M39 2012
813'.6—dc22
2011019543

Anchor ISBN: 978-0-307-74357-2

Book design by Pei Loi Koay

www.anchorbooks.com

Printed in the United States of America
10 9 8 7 6 5 4 3 2 1

For my Mother and Father, with a lifetime of gratitude for Sunday drives to nowhere in particular, and bookshelves that formed a comfortable nook for exploration, and believing that normal is vastly overrated; for raising kids and not a lawn, and knowing the soul matters most of all, and going back to school when others your age were planning their retirements, showing us all that dreams are worth pursuing . . . however, whatever, whenever.

PETER JAMES TROY

1937–2010

". . . and until we meet again, may God hold you in the palm of His hand."

AUTHOR'S NOTE

The historical events and characters depicted in this novel are presented with as much accuracy as possible. Inasmuch as the fictional characters that make up this story are placed within the context of non-fictional events, creative liberties have been taken.

May the Road Rise Up to Meet You

Prologue ❧ *The Stitchin*

MARY WILKENS
RALEIGH, NORTH CAROLINA
SEPTEMBER 9, 1853

Gertie's settin in her chair, th'rickety one what makes more noise than a old sycamore tree tryin t'stay up in a storm, an she's at her stitchin again, same as she is most nights, no matter how tired she get. An there's you watchin her, same as always, only littler now, only ten years old or roundabout. Still you tired like you always is now that you gots t'work in th'fields all day long, steada th'part days you usedta work.

Gertie works more'n anyone on th'place same as ever, at it 'fore sunup, cookin oatmeal or cornbread or th'sometimes bacon Massa Wilkens gives for th'field han's breakfas'. She don' make you get up wit her no mo' t'help out, not since you started workin th'fields all day long, now that you ten. So Gertie gotta go to th'well an get th'water herself these days, then do th'cookin, then watch after th'littlest ones while she's makin th'midday an evenin meals all th'while. An still, all that don't matter none when it comes to her stitchin . . . they's always time fo' that.

Ain't but a trickle a'light comin from what's left of th'fire, first real one of th'season now that it's gettin on harves' time. Still, she's pullin that needle through, th'big needle wit th'eye fat enough so she can thread it now, now that her eyes ain't what they was. An you lay on your bed, not so tired as usual since maybe it's Sunday an there ain't been any workin in th'fields today.

So you lay there an watch Gertie insteada sleepin straight off, listnin to her hummin . . . doin her stitchin. She got her bad leg propped up on a pilla on toppa th'stool, got her bad arm, wit th'scars burnt wrist t'elbow, holdin th'circle frame of her stitchin. An you wonder 'bout how she do it, not th'stayin awake or sittin up when she's tireder than a plowmule, or even how she do it wit one bad leg an one bad arm . . . cause you seen her do too much for too long t'even think on that anymore.

No, you wonderin th'same thing you been wonderin for as long as you seen her stitchin, wonderin how she can tell what she makin outta all those little bitsa thread the Misses give her. The best of 'em ain't nothin but scraps, an the whole thing ain't nothin more'n a piece a'blank white cotton cloth gettin stitched all over wit them scrapsa thread. By a woman wit one good arm an one good leg, tired as a plowmule all th'time, stitchin wit a too big needle, 'side a fire mostly goin out. An still she pokes 'at needle through one side an out th'other, like she don' even hafta look at what she doin pract'ly. An from roun' dis side a'that circle frame, th'one the Misses give her, all you can see is a whole messa threads, wit all they diffren' colors, hangin ever which way.

The Misses give her some a'that fine silk thread what th'white folks use fo' they clothes, an Gertie mixin it in right along wit th'cotton an even bitsa th'gray wool thread what she use to mend th'sacks for th'sweet taters. Don' matter none to Gertie whatever she stitchin wit, she jus keep on stitchin.

An then, when she get done wit one a'them threads—which is plennya times, cause they ain' nothin but scraps from th'start—well, she turn th'frame 'round th'other way, sets it on her lap an ties it off best she can wit th'one good hand an th'one what's always givin her a hard time. Then she's back at it again, fiddlin a new bitta thread through that big-eyed needle, then tyin it off best she can, an pushin it through th'one side an out th'other.

You seen what her stichins end up lookin like. You seen th'three of 'em what ended up in the Misses' own dressin room in The Big House. An seen th'ones what Miss Frances an Miss Carlotta got in they rooms. Not that you seen 'em there in The Big House 'course, cause you ain't never been inside it, but you seen 'em 'fore even Miss Carlotta an Miss Frances an even the Misses got t'see 'em. Cause you seen 'em when Gertie firs' said they was done. Like you was one a'them poor ol' shepherds 'round Bethleehem 'at got to see th'Baby Jesus soon as he was born. 'Fore th'Three Wise Men even showed up. An they was th'same 'zact pictures as what ended up in The Big House, 'cept for th'fancy frame an how the Misses calls 'em embroideries when they in The Big House. But Gertie say they jus' stitchins when they out here wit you an her.

You got plennya questions 'bout this partic'lar stitchin, an they burstin out from inside, same as always. Cause, from 'round where you layin down on yo' bed, all you can see is th'messa threads hangin loose, a bitta red tied off wit a bitta blue, a bitta yellow findin its way . . . somehow . . . to a bitta green, an on an on . . . th'fine silk from th'white folks' mendin tied off wit a bitta cotton, or wool even. Like as if the Misses' dress was bein patched up wit a piece a'them sweet tater sacks. An it don' make no sense. None. Justa messa bits goin ever which way. So you ask her, interruptin her hummin, fiddlin yo'sef onta one side an proppin yo' head up wit an elbow planted inta th'pilla.

How you know whachu doin Gertie? you ask.

Been at dis fo' a looong time she says, an starts a'hummin again.

Naw, you say, I mean . . . how you know whachu stitchin when it don' look like nothin but a buncha threads ain' got nothin t'do wit each otha? All I can see is a whole buncha scraps, red an green an black an yella an blue an all. Little bits. Silk an cotton an wool an such. An justa whole messa knots an tangles all along th'back. It don' look like nothin from over here!

An den she stops hummin an stitchin altogetha. Looks at you like she does when you ask her th'kindsa silly questions you do . . . like why th'water in th'stream out back always run in th'same direction . . . or why some clouds drop all kindsa rain an some don'. She shakes her head side t'side an smiles a little. Starts hummin again, an pushin that needle through a few mo' times. An you figure you ain' gonna get a answer to this here question, th'way you sometimes don' when she know you gonna unnerstan soon enough . . . once you get growed up some mo'.

So you flop offa that elbow an onto yo' back again, listnin to her hummin. It's anotha minute or two, or maybe mo', you can't tell when it comes to layin there listnin to her hummin, peaceful as it is. Then she stops, an you look over sideways seein her tyin off anotha thread.

You cain't tell nothin 'bout whachu seein when you layin over there, she says. Cain't tell nothin 'bout nothin in dis worl' when all you seein is th'knots an tangles an ever'thin' goin ever which way, lookin like a buncha mess. How you gonna unnerstan' when you layin' dere seein jus' th'messa it all, when th'mess only one parta it, no matta how it seem sometime? Cain't see how all dese little bitsa thread be connected togetha, jus' like all th'bitsa yo' life gonna be, cause you ain' lookin at it the way it meant t'be seen.

An then she smiles. Not th'big kinda smile what comes wit laughin, but th'happy, looka what I did, sorta smile you give her first evenin you worked in th'fields all day by yo'sef. An then she turns 'round that stitchin she been workin on so you can see it straight off. An it's pretty as a picture ever was. Dey's a green field wit' flowa beds an some trees that look like they jus' wakin up at th'starta spring, an off inna distance is a nice big house, one you ain't never seen befo' like Gertie jus' made it all up in her 'magination. It's got a big ol' porch 'cross the front an looks like they's folks on it, colored an white folks it seems, some settin in chairs an some standin up too, only it's so far off 'at they's no faces on the folks a'tall, jus' they tiny little bodies like they was ants or somethin'. An 'cross th'toppa it is a sky all th'colors a rainbow eva was . . . an you smile, seein sucha pretty picture as this.

Gertie's smilin too . . . bigger now than befo'. Dis here, she says, what aaaall dat mess look like . . . when you gets t'seein it frontsways.

Exile

PART ONE

1 *The Hunger*

Ethan McOwen
COUNTY FERMANAGH, IRELAND
APRIL 25, 1847

Th'LahrdismyshepherdIshallnotwant . . . His Da had loved Father Laughton for the way he got through the Sunday Mass *like a Protestant wit' an overflowin' bladder.* That was always the kind of thing Da would have to say about the Father, even when his Mam'd go on about something the Father said in one of his three-minute sermons in the weekday Mass, Da would always say *t'ank th'Lahrd we've got de only priest in Oireland that doesn't run at th'mouth,* or something like that. Seanny and Aislinn and Ethan'd laugh, and Mam'd slap Da's shoulder and tell him, *In fronta th'children?* And he'd say, *Sure they're waitin' t'get outta there as much as meself,* and they'd laugh some more and Mam'd hit him again, only this time pressin' back a smile of her own, tough as it was for her to stay mad when her family was laughin' so.

But this service was a different matter and Ethan knew his Da wouldn't be happy about the Father's bladder today. *Fer Chroist sakes Fadder, dat's my little girl in dere,* he'd say, *wouldja slow it down a little?* Or maybe Aislinn'd say, *All due respect Fadder Laughton, but would ya please read wit' some inflection, an' make th'words come aloive?* That's what she was always tellin' Ethan to do, and she'd say it to the Father in such a way that it wouldn't be a mortal sin, and the Father'd laugh and say, *Yer right, Aislinn dear, lemme give it anudder go,* and he'd smile and pat her on the head and go back to readin', slower this time, and with more meaning. Ethan wished he could say something in his sister's place, but he'd just sound like an insolent little boy, and he didn't want to go sinning like that, placin' his immortal soul in jeopardy and givin' his Mam something else to worry about. So he stood quietly, thinkin' of what a shame it was that the last words spoken for Aislinn'd be like this.

He stared down at the hole in the ground and admired the precision of its edges, cut perfectly straight and square to one another, with the displaced earth stacked in two neat pyramids at either end of it. He knew that had his and Aislinn's places been switched, and the fever'd overtaken him instead of her, she would've appreciated the craftsmanship, too. But it was his sister's undersize coffin layin' comfortably inside the hole, not his, and he tried not to think about how they'd had to bend her legs at the knees, then fold them back behind her, so she'd fit in the four-foot-long box made for a child half her age. At least it'd keep the dogs off her better than one of those government-issue wool sacks, the ones the poorest families were left with, the ones they'd later have to see torn from the ground and ripped to shreds as the dogs and rats got at what was left of their loved one. There'd be none of that for Aislinn, because the eight and sixpence his Da and Seanny had sent from America, the money that was to go for food until the new potatoes in July, bought the coffin and the slate and the Mass to be said in her name, instead.

When The Hunger claimed the first of its victims, most of the village turned out for the services after the Sunday Mass, but now it'd just be family members and perhaps a few friends. Still, Ethan counted forty-one, not includin' Aislinn, here this mornin', a testament to his sister's gentle and encouraging nature and the dozen or so children along the Lane she'd taught to read in the past few years. Even Old Mr. Hanratty was here, standin' alone, perhaps fifteen feet behind the Bresnihans. Ethan knew this was as close as he'd been to the inside of a church in thirty years, so he nodded his head to him in confused gratitude, and Mr. Hanratty, tight-lipped, nodded back.

Aislinn's service was done in ten minutes and the two gravediggers began to spill the neatly piled dirt on top of her coffin as his Mam and Aunt Emily wept. Ethan looked away after just a moment, not wantin' the water to get in his eyes the way it was in his Mam's and Aunt Em's. He noticed how most of the older graves had tombstones that stood upright while the newer ones were marked with about what Aislinn'd have, a one-inch-thick slate, fourteen by ten inches, lyin' flat on the ground. That was all there'd be to tell anyone who might be interested that she'd been here for almost sixteen years, and that she wanted to be a teacher, and how, for the last two years, since it was just her and him and Mam livin' at Aunt Em's, she and he would put on shows every Saturday night, and oh were they gettin' so good at it. No, none of that at all. Instead all it read was . . .

AISLINN MCOWEN

1831–1847

. . . as if a few numbers said anything about her, like it was some sort of achievement how long a person lived, and when they'd died young, like Aislinn, people fifty years from now could look at the numbers and say, *Oh poor lass, just sixteen what a pity, what a tragedy, musta been The Hunger.* Most of the stones that were laid flat across the graveyard were covered over with grass and weeds, and Ethan vowed that he wouldn't let the same thing happen to her. He wouldn't let her fade away like that.

The crowd quickly dispersed, with only a few people comin' by and nodding their sorrow or placin' a hand briefly on his Mam's shoulder. Father Laughton was one of the last to approach. He may not have read with much inflection, Ethan thought, but the Father's pain was written on his face in deep creases that led to sunken eyes, and Ethan realized then that the Father'd seen more death than any of them.

Mayth'Lahrdcomfortyou, he said to the three of them, and waved his hand in a downward line and then across.

He was gone before any of them could say a word, though both his Mam and Aunt Em blessed themselves and curtseyed. And then it was just the three of them standin' beside the gravesite, with a few stragglers a little farther away.

Jaysus, me hands're just about tahrn up from all dis rocky soil, one of the gravediggers said. It's loike shovelin' bricks.

Ahh yer always complainin', the other replied. Yer hands can't be bad as me back.

They were strangers to Ethan, men who traveled constantly, earning a shilling here and there, plyin' their morbid trade like vultures in the Irish countryside. He could hear every word they said, and regardless of what a fine job they'd done diggin' the grave, he wanted to take the shovels from them and cover his sister's body himself. If his Da and Seanny were here, they'd probably want to take the shovels and bash the gravediggers over the head, he figured, so he felt a little ashamed, less of a man, for not wantin' to do so as well.

Mam and Aunt Em closed their eyes as the coffin disappeared beneath the dirt, them without an extra penny for the gravediggers and so forced to hear more about various aches and pains as the men carried out their work. Ethan felt the anger grow within him until Mr. Hanratty walked up to each of the men and handed them a coin and whispered something to them while noddin' toward Ethan's Mam. The men continued on with their work in silence, and Mr. Hanratty glanced over at Ethan and his Mam and Aunt, placin' his gray woolen cap against his heart and nodding his head slightly. Then, without a word, he was off.

When the coffin was completely covered and the tombstone set in place on the fresh dirt, the three of them walked quietly home. To Ethan, the lustrous green fields were now gray as a winter sky, and their cottage seemed as vast and hollow inside as a fourteen-by-sixteen-foot space could ever seem. There'd be no grand funeral dinner, as was the custom in the Old Days. There'd be no reveling, no cousins runnin' about in the fields as the men and women sat inside by the fire and drank a few pints Old Man McGeary'd supplied from his pub down the Lane. There'd be no stories told of the person who'd passed, no fiddle, or singing. No laughter.

Ethan realized that it was exactly one week ago, when he returned home from the Mass with Aunt Em, that they were told by his cryin' Mam that Aislinn was gone. Now, as he'd done then, he bounded up the stepladder to the loft he'd shared with his sister since they moved in two years earlier, once Sean and Da were off to America. He sat on his bed, two five-by-one-foot wooden planks raised just off the floor by corner posts. Aislinn's bed was across from it, the two of them separated by their collection of eleven books stacked neatly on a small plank, held up on either side by painted rocks used for bookends. They called it The Library. The first six volumes'd been given to Aislinn when she saw them piled beside the trash bin in the Brodericks' library and Mr. Broderick caught her skimmin' through them. Since that time he'd given her five more, and she and Ethan had read them all several times, though she generally had to help him with some of the more challenging ones like *Paradise Lost* and a collection of the Shakespeare.

Every Saturday night, until two weeks ago, the two of them took a scene from one of their books and acted it out for Mam and Aunt Em, often taking what Aislinn called *poetic license* with the tragic scenes, much to the approval of their audience. Loud applause always greeted them when Hamlet, or Romeo and Juliet, or other doomed heroes were spared in the end. But even the happy memories brought the water to his eyes now, so he left the books in their place and took a minute to fully compose himself before going back down the ladder.

His Mam and Aunt Em were busy cooking the biggest feast they'd seen since Christmas. There'd be three small turnips, a little cabbage and wheat flour bread, and as a special treat, they'd each get a few ounces of beef cut from the scraps fed to the Brodericks' dogs. Aunt Emily had cut it and stuffed it in her pocket when nobody was lookin'—she called it Aislinn's severance, whatever that meant—and he knew that this funeral supper would chase away The Hunger for at least one night. But when it was ready they ate in virtual silence, chewing everything slowly, tryin' to make it last as long as possible. Ethan felt terribly guilty and he was sure his Mam and Aunt felt so too. Aislinn hadn't eaten a meal like this for the last few months of her life, and the only reason each of them had so much now was because there were only three of them left to eat it. And so, as the food hit his empty belly, he found none of the usual satisfaction or relief, only shame.

That night, sleeplessly staring around the darkness, he could tell when Mam or Aunt Em were awake by the sounds of their sniffles. And much as he tried not to, his thoughts wandered to *that* day, just three Saturdays ago, and the last time he and Aislinn had performed one of their scenes. He'd rushed home that day with nothin' more than a quick wave to Mr. Hanratty, carryin' the usual pocketful of oats and even more of a bounty in his other pocket, four pieces of jerky that Mr. Broderick'd given him for stayin' late. It wasn't like he'd had any choice *but* to stay, what with Mr. Broderick and his daughters still out there ridin', but it was a nice thing he'd done all the same. It made Ethan feel even guiltier than usual about taking the pocketful of oats, even though Aunt Em always said it wasn't really stealin', just *doin' the Lahrds work for Him, feedin' th'poor and such, like th'loaves an' fishes in th'Bible.* But his guilt quickly faded when he reached home that evening since it was Saturday night and Aislinn'd already picked out a scene for the play.

Sure, it turned out to be the last time she'd been anything like herself, but Ethan let the thoughts press fully on him now, as if to give her the proper sort of remembrance the dead should have no matter how much it hurts the ones left behind. And this wistful recollection gave way to the dreams that linger on the edge of sleep, needing only to close his eyes to be taken fully back into the moment . . .

I was thinkin' we'd do a bit from The Odyssey, *she says as soon as you hit the top step to the loft. I think I can read for ya, but you'll havta do th'performin'.*

She seems weaker than she'd been just that mornin', but you'll not mention anything of it.

What part? you ask and even start gettin' a little worried about the idea of doing your first solo.

When Odysseus is given the bag t'contain all th'winds so dey can make it home t'Ithaca, she says. And then you remember the jerky in your pocket, and hold the four pieces up to her, proud as can be.
Where'd ya get them? she asks, smilin'.
Mr. Broderick gave 'em t'me for stayin' late, you say, like you've done somethin' important to earn them. You can have mine Ais'.
Ahhh no, Ethan, she says wavin' her hand. One's plenty.
It doesn't matter anyway since Mam cooks the jerky in the soup for supper. And you're all excited to taste the flavor of beef again, even though you're thirsty afterwards from the salt. Then Mam and Aunt Em settle in their stools and Aislinn lies in Mam's bed with The Odyssey *out and open before her. You go up to get your blanket, then step outside, while Aislinn sets the scene, talkin' about how Odysseus was given this great sack to hold all the winds of the seas. And when you come back in, you bounce all around the cottage, like a man holdin' the winds in a sack'd do. You bounce from side to side of the cabin, and they all laugh, Aislinn even, and the more you swoon, the more they laugh, so you swoon even more. After a minute or two of that, you, Odysseus, settle down to sleep. And Aislinn reads on, about how the members of his ship's crew talk of the treasure they think Odysseus is keeping hidden from them in the sack.*
So you spring up and assume the role of Odysseus' jealous crew, and Aislinn pauses as you move from one spot to another around the sack, speculatin' about whether it's gold or silver or even something better inside. You open your mouth wide, and pretend to talk, and point to the place where you'd laid down as Odysseus. And when you put your hands on your hips like you're angry at that empty spot on the floor, Mam and Aunt Em and Aislinn laugh some more, and you ham it up for as long as the laughin' lasts. Then Ais' continues readin' aloud, telling them about how Odysseus' men decide to open the sack and see what's inside.
And you open it up and bounce all around the cottage again, even

bouncin' out the door and screamin' and howling as you grab hold of the doorposts and pretend to hold on for dear life. And Mam and Aunt Em and Ais' laugh harder than ever 'til Aislinn starts coughin' and you come back in and close the door tightly.

After just a moment, when she collects herself, she finishes readin' the scene, the final lines about Odysseus going back to sleep on the deck of the ship, sad that he'll have to face more years lost at sea. And when you lay back down on the floor, playin' Odysseus again, Mam and Ais' and Aunt Em all applaud hard as they can.

There are two encores that night . . . first the part where Odysseus blinds the Cyclops, and then, when they still want more, you have another go at the bit from *Richard III*, only much better than the last time, since Aislinn'd explained to you what, Now is the winter of our discontent made glorious summer . . . and so on, really means, which starts with the fact that it isn't really about the actual winter, or summer, at all. You always need . . . needed . . . Aislinn's help with the Shakespeare.

And that's the end of that evenin's performance, but later that night you and Ais' talk about what books Mr. Broderick might give you the next time he makes a trip to England. He's sure to bring back a couple of brand-new ones with leather bindings and pages that feel like they've been pressed with a hot iron, and you and Ais'll get whichever battered old ones the new ones are pushin' off the Brodericks' shelves. Ais' hopes for another from Shakespeare, or maybe some Byron, but you're hoping for *The Iliad* to go along with *The Odyssey*.

And then you and Aislinn talk about America and what it'll be like when you ALL get there. And even though Da and Seanny are havin' a tough go of it sendin' the money to bring you over, Aislinn keeps sayin' that it'll all be different soon enough, that just because you and she and Mam and Aunt Em and Seanny and Da have been given this particular startin'-off point in life, growin' up poor and

such, that doesn't mean that's where your endin'-up point has to be.
Ya know Ais', you say after listnin' to her wonderful sorta dreams made into words, I think maybe I'd like t'be an actor when we get over dere.
Or a teacher maybe . . . a professor . . . or a writer, even.
You could do that Ethan, she says. You could do any of those things.
Sure ya could, you've got a worlda livin' left t'do . . .

And that was the end of the story he allowed to be converted into a dream, for that night at least. He opened his eyes back up to stop the flood of memories and stared at the light from what was left of the fire reflected off the thatched roof just a few feet from his face. Still, try as he might, there was no escaping one final thought about his sister . . . that, despite how often she'd told him about all the grand things he might do one day, how she filled the minds of the kids along the Lane with thoughts of the very same adventures . . . here she was, left to spend eternity without ever havin' made it more than a few miles from the place where she started out.

SUMMER 1847

The spring planting took place two weeks late that year. The ground hadn't been frozen in months, but what with the disastrous potato crops of the past two years, nobody was willin' to bet completely against the first April snow in anyone's memory. Despite Aislinn's death and the loss of her wages, Ethan's family was doing better than most of the families along the mile-and-a-half lane between the Church and the Brodericks' house. Even though the three of them earned the half-wages of women and children, it was enough to pay the rent on the cottage and their eighth of an acre. The potatoes Ethan and his Mam and Aunt planted weren't meant to make up more than half of their diet, unlike most people on the Lane. So with a little help from the occasional cabbage or chicken carcass Aunt Em'd nick from the Brodericks' kitchen, and the handful of oats Ethan brought home from the livery each day, they'd managed well enough until the fever caught up to Aislinn. Still, with a bag of flour costin' three and four times what it had just a year before, they knew The Hunger all too well.

Mam and Aunt Em worked late at the Brodericks' almost every day now, and Ethan stopped at Mr. Hanratty's most days on his way home from the stables, dreading the idea of returning to an empty cottage with nothin' but memories for company. Mam'd long before warned him about Mr. Hanratty and the trouble to be found in the old man's words. It had something to do with why Seanny'd wanted to go off to Dublin to join the Young Irelanders before Mam and Da sold everything they could and Da took Seanny off to America lest he end up on a prison ship to Australia. But that was all *before* The Hunger, and before the three of them had moved to the Lane to stay with Aunt Em. Surely everything was different now, he figured, and even if it wasn't, the old man'd become his friend, telling him stories that were almost as interesting as those in his books back home. And never once had there been a mention about the Young Irelanders except for the one time Mr. Hanratty called them *a buncha blowhards unfit t'wipe Wolfe Tone's arse for all da good they're doin'*, whatever that meant.

When Mr. Hanratty said it was safe to plant, Ethan dug up the small patch next to their cottage and put in the few healthy tubers they had from the year before. Each of the last two years people up and down the Lane had planted their potatoes as they'd always done, harvesting the new ones in July, and the full-grown ones in September. But nearly all of them had turned black in the ground or within a week after bein' harvested. For several days in a row now, they put what remained of their hope into the soil, plantin' the few sprouts they had, touchin' them with the beads while reciting a rosary and askin' the Blessed Virgin to protect this year's crop. Still, Mr. Hanratty said it didn't matter if the blight was completely gone, since the paltry amount of plants that could be put into the ground would yield far less than what was needed to feed the people through the winter. There'd be more starvation, he said, more funerals, more people sitting almost lifelessly outside their cottages, their gaunt faces stained green around the mouth from the grass they chewed to keep death at bay.

Ethan learned about far more than farming at Mr. Hanratty's. As they tended the potato field, checking for any early signs of disease just beneath the surface, the old man'd share the stories of his younger days. It was here that Ethan learned of Wolfe Tone and the Rebellion of '98. Mr. Hanratty'd lean against his wooden spade and get a far-off look on his face and tell Ethan about the late spring of that year, when the Rebels controlled pockets of territory throughout the country, and for the first time in a century an Irishman knew what it was to be free in his own land. Then Mr. Hanratty'd lose that mystic gaze and point to his left leg and tell of how he was shot by a Redcoat at Ballynahinch. Soon after that the rebellion was over in County Down, and eventually the English tied their noose around the rest of Ireland, but he always had those few weeks, Mr. Hanratty said, to recall with reverence and delight.

That was the way Mr. Hanratty could sum up all the subsequent years of his life, it seemed. Little pockets of happiness that he said were like the water cupped between two hands. You could struggle against all hope to hold on to it, watchin' it spill out and evaporate drop by drop, or you could drink it up while you had it. Mr. Hanratty'd drunk it up long ago.

He'd married Orla, whose hair was *th'speckle o' light left of a spring day five minutes after th'sun had gone to sleep* and whose eyes *th'Lahrd musta gleaned from the surface of Strangford Lough fresh o' th'morn' she was brought into th'world.* Ethan couldn't help but smile when Mr. Hanratty described her in such ways, glancin' back across the horizon for a moment or two as if that was where the memory of her was stored. After they were married he became a tenant farmer as his father'd been, and they had a son and then a daughter in the first five years together, years he spoke of as blissfully as he did those brief days of freedom in '98. They had a sow and a few chickens and a small vegetable garden to go with their potatoes, and Mr. Hanratty worked the nearly two and a half acres that paid the rent and fed and clothed his family with a little left over to save each year. Sunday mornings they'd go to the Mass, and then he'd have a visit to the pub, where he and his friends'd tell stories and talk a little treason for a while before it was home to a grand supper and a turf fire. Those five years were glorious, Mr. Hanratty said, and what made them all the better was that they *knew* they were glorious, something most folks don't figure out until long after such times are gone. But their happiness was shattered when little Brea died before she turned three, and then two years later Orla was gone from the cholera as well. Her funeral was the last time Mr. Hanratty'd set foot inside a church.

Ethan figured that his friend had pretty good reason to be one of those bitter old men who sat outside the pub most afternoons, but Mr. Hanratty generally spoke only of those happy years, and before long Ethan began to see the years Aislinn was with them in much the same way. She was the water that'd finally slipped out of their hands, and he was comforted by the thought that at least they'd *known* they were happy while she was here, despite The Hunger. Still, he hoped there'd be more happy years, never quite the same to be sure, but with some measure of what they'd once known. The idea that happiness'd be a stranger to him from the age of twelve was a frightening prospect and he asked Mr. Hanratty one day about the years after his wife's death, hopin' to hear of a new happiness.

Ethan lad, Mr. Hanratty said with a knowin' laugh. If it's a happy tale yer after, den sure you was bahrn in th'wrong land.

But there *were* good times after that, he later found out. Mr. Hanratty's son grew old enough to work the land with him and they managed pretty well for those few years, findin' bits of contentment to overcome the loss. Then Henry Munro Hanratty grew into a man himself and took after his father just a little too much.

It's me own fault fer namin' th'lad after me commander from Noinety-Eight, Mr. Hanratty said of his son's Christian and middle names. When th'lad was bahrn, I was still a young buck an' t'ought I'd be showin' me arse to d'English by havin' me son carry on dat name. What else could th'lad turn out t'be but what he did, pissin' on th'Crown like his old man'd done. They shipped him off t'Australia noineteen years ago. I've not heard worda him since.

Ethan looked up at Mr. Hanratty and wanted to console him, so he turned to the response he'd heard people use before when it came to the loss of loved ones.

Well, you'll see 'em all again in Heaven, he offered.

But it didn't have the soothing effect he sought, and Mr.

Hanratty looked sharply at him with anger in his eyes for the first time since Ethan had known him.

Any god good enough t'have a place like heaven'd never allow da t'ings goin' on down here t'continue, he said sternly. It'd be th'bleedin' *English* he wiped out wit' a blight on *dere* land, jus' like de Egyptians an' th'ten plagues in th'Bible. It'd be the damn Dukes and Lords off to the workhouse insteada the good folks that already do all the bleedin' work! It'd be Queen Vic*tah*ria herself watchin' her country's children die from Th'Hunger.

Ethan was sorry to have asked Mr. Hanratty to dig up such sad memories, and he began to wonder if it was the stories of rebellion his Mam didn't want him hearin', or if it was the sad stories of loss. Grown folks were always doin' that, he thought, tryin' to pretend that everything will somehow be better for the children than it was for them. But Mr. Hanratty's look softened when he glanced at Ethan's worried face.

Ahh lad, but don't you worry none, he said patting Ethan's shoulder. Yer Da an' brudder'll be sendin' money from over dere, and it'll be off t'America wit' ya before long. You'll be pickin' gold nuggets up off the streets an' stuffin' yerself 'til ya can't stand.

Money did arrive just about the time they dug out the new potatoes in early July. They came out of the ground without any hint of disease, just as most of them had the two years before, only this time they didn't turn black a week after harvest. Still, because so few tubers had been planted, the yield wasn't much better than the previous two blighted years had been. It was enough for Mrs. Broderick to convince her husband to take them to her family home in Scotland so their two little darlin's wouldn't be exposed to any of the assorted diseases waftin' their way up from the tenants' farms. Only a skeleton staff would work the Broderick land and maintain the house, and Mam and Aunt Em were told of their release by Mrs. Broderick. She gave Mam six shillings as a severance, and gave Aunt Emily, who'd been with them since before their daughters were born, a single pound, *a bleedin' shillin' a year,* as Aunt Em called it.

Ethan was given the chance to stay and tend the horses until the Brodericks arranged to have them shipped over in a month or two. But there was nothin' left in Ireland for them other than *scratchin' a few potatoes from th'ground a month from now, then a winter of eatin' th'Protestant soup an' watchin' each udder waste away,* as Aunt Em said. So on a cloudless summer evenin' in the middle of July, they ate their final meal in the cottage, sitting in a silence almost as disruptive as what'd filled their home after Aislinn's funeral, until, mercifully, it was broken by a knock at the door.

Evenin' Mrs. McOwen, Mr. Hanratty said when Mam opened it.

Good evenin' Mr. Hanratty, she replied, stepping back a little. Won't you come in? We've a few new potatoes left an' there's some tea from th'Brodericks'. I'm afraid we've used th'leaves a few times, but dere's still—

No, I'm not meanin' t'interrupt yer supper. But I t'ank ya for de offer, Mr. Hanratty said in a more formal voice than usual. I know yer leavin' in th'mahrnin' an' I brought this over for th'boy.

He handed her a cap similar to the one he wore, only smaller.

It belonged t'me son when he was a lad, Mr. Hanratty said. I t'ought young Ethan could make use of it.

Yes, I'm sure he'd like it, Mam said, extendin' her arm toward the inside of the cottage again. Woncha come in fer a minute, Mr. Hanratty?

T'anks, but no. When you've said as many goodbyes as I've in me life, y'get t'avoidin' 'em as much as ya can. He grabbed the brim of his cap and bowed his head slightly. My best t'ya, Ma'am, an' yer sister, an' th'boy. Safe journey.

And he was off down the path without another word. Ethan knew Mr. Hanratty wouldn't want him to run after him to say goodbye, much as he wanted to do it anyway, so he simply stood with his Mam at the door and watched as his friend disappeared over the rise. He hadn't anywhere near the experience with saying goodbyes that Mr. Hanratty had, but between seein' off his Da and brother, and then Aislinn, he knew they were something to be avoided too.

When they'd finished supper, their meager packing began. Each of them would take two extra sets of clothes, their blankets and a few other trinkets. Ethan had originally hoped to take all of the books from The Library, but when he wrapped them in the satchel formed out of his blanket, he realized that they'd be quite a burden to carry even *half* as far as they had to go. One by one he took out the books that'd been their least favorite among the collection, with the histories of England going first, since he didn't particularly care to read about their glorious conquests anymore. When he got the number down to six, the load at last felt manageable. He opened the front covers of the ones that were to make the trip, and checked the names that'd been inscribed long ago, back when two pennies for a jar of ink was a reasonable expense. Each carefully penned inscription read:

This book passes now through the grateful hands of:
Aislinn McOwen & Ethan McOwen

(though the stories contained within belong to the ages)

Of course every bit of it had been Aislinn's idea. She was always comin' up with interesting sayings like that, he thought, and from the time she'd brought the first batch of them home, she insisted that books were like the land, since no one could ever really *own* such an eternal thing. And now, as he ran his fingertips over them, rememberin' when he and his sister first proudly staked their temporary claim to such treasure, he couldn't help but think of what'd concerned him from the first moment his Mam told him they were leavin'. Aislinn was to be the only one left behind.

JULY 19, 1847

It's still night when he's awake and slippin' his way down the ladder from the loft. Mam and Aunt Em were up talkin' way after he was supposed to be asleep, and he worried that he'd not wake in time to pay Aislinn one final visit. But something wakes him when there's just the slightest hint of light on the horizon, and he gets past Mam and Aunt Em, who've yet to stir. Maybe it was Aislinn woke him up, he thinks, as he's off down the Lane to the churchyard.

The slate is still clear of any weeds or grass, often as he and Mam and Aunt Em come to visit, each of them separately, pretendin' they didn't do so, but each of them knowing every time the others'd been here. Ethan sits down beside her, careful not to touch the ground above her coffin, or the one alongside it either.

Mahrnin', Misses O'Neil, he says to the slate next to Aislinn's. He barely knew the woman when she was alive, but it's as if he's become close to her, what with all the visits and settin' down alongside her eternal resting place as often as he has by now.

Mahrnin', Aislinn, he says, sadder, the guilt of their departure heavy on his mind and in his words. We're off t'day, loike I was sayin' yesterday. Three days it'll be to Newry, Mam says. I can only take six o'the books in th'Libr'y. We each gotta carry some o' the food an' six was all I figgered I could manage. I was gonna bring th'others out here an' lay 'em alongside ya, but I figgered you'd be sad t'see 'em get rained on like dat, even if dey're mostly th'English hist'ries an' such. Better t'leave 'em in the cottage, an' maybe whoever else comes t'live here'll get a chance t'read 'em.

He's spent so much of his twelve and a half years with Aislinn as a constant presence, even in the ground like this, that his eyes can't help but fill with the water at the thought of sayin' goodbye once and for all. But he doesn't want her to be sad, and doesn't want Mrs. O'Neil to see him cry, so he opens the book he's brought with him, and turns to the page he'd marked with an old piece of shoelace.

I'm takin' th'Shakespeare along wit' me, he says. I still gotta sound out some o' da words an' I don't know if I'll ever understand him th'way you do, but I figgered you'd want me to keep workin' at it. I remembered how you liked *Much Ado About Nothin',* an' I figgered it'd be better t'read somethin' from one o' da comedies than somethin' sad. So here goes, it's from Benedick. *This can be no trick. The conf'rence was sadly borne. Dey have th'trutha this from Hero* . . .

When he finishes it, he half-expects to hear Mrs. O'Neil start applauding the way Mam and Aunt Em always did on Saturday nights. But there's just the silence of the first light of mornin'. So he talks a little more, mostly about the journey, with a few *you remember when's* . . . followed by a story and maybe a little laugh at the end of it, thrown in amongst the chatter. But there's only so much of it he can handle, and before too much longer he's off, not saying goodbye, just *s'lahng,* figurin' that Mr. Hanratty had it right when it comes to moments like these.

He's not halfway back up the Lane when he sees Aunt Em making her way toward him. And he knows just what she's doin'.

We figgered you was here, she says. She's not mad, not with the water in her eyes either, but still not her usual self, and Ethan realizes she's lived here for more than twenty years. This was the church she was married in and the churchyard where her husband, who Ethan doesn't remember knowing, was buried ten years ago. So she's got to say goodbye to him as well as Aislinn. And then he remembers that he forgot to say goodbye to his Uncle Michael, Aunt Em's husband who he doesn't remember, and is sad for the omission.

Yer Mam is back makin' something t'eat before we go, Aunt Em says. She'll be comin' t'say her goodbyes before we're off.

And she slides her hand across his hair, smilin' through her eyes squinted in the morning sun, then pats his cheek. Yer as foine a brudder as anyone could ever ask fer, she says.

Sorry, Aunt Em, he answers.

Fer what now?

I fergot t'say goodbye to Uncle Moike.

And she brushes her hand across his cheek again, smilin' broader than before and saying, I'll give'm yer best, love. And then she's off, back the way he'd just come.

The journey to Newry is nearly fifty miles, so they carry just a few pounds of raw potatoes and bits of bread with them, hoping to arrive by the end of the third day, where they can maybe take a room for the night and have a proper meal. The four pounds, three shillings they have is a fortune that could've fed them for three months, but they can't afford to buy some salted pork or even a few more potatoes for the voyage. A full three pounds of that money, the amount Da and Sean sent over, is for Ethan's passage to America. The remaining shillings'll take them on the ferry from Newry to Liverpool, then take Mam and Aunt Em as far as the textile mills of Manchester, to work and wait, maybe, for their own turn.

They leave an hour after first light, with Ethan and Aunt Em meeting Mam at the churchyard, waitin' some more for her to finish saying goodbye to Aislinn. They walk for a long while without sayin' a word, take a short rest, then get a ride on the back of a hay wagon for nearly two miles. Then it's walk and walk and walk some more, with only little rests in between. When darkness sets in, they make a small fire beside the road and cook a few potatoes, certain that they've covered twenty miles that day. But the next day they're slowed a little by a steady rain, slowed a great deal more by the soreness each of them feels in their feet and legs, and The Hunger that eats at their spirits. They cover slightly more than half as much ground as the first day, and by the time they scrounge up enough relatively dry wood to build a tiny fire, it's already dark. Watchin' three small potatoes boil while sipping water from a nearby well, each of them stares into the fire as if lookin' at it will somehow warm their aching bodies, but before long the rain returns and they're left to nibble on their dinner beneath woolen blankets that soon become heavy and wet.

On the mornin' of the third day, they twist the water from their blankets and eat the last of the potatoes. The plan was to spend that night in Newry, where Aunt Em swore she'd *eat da Protestant soup or even kiss de Archbishop of Canterb'ry square on th'lips, if it meant a decent meal an' a bed.* Ethan'd often heard people talk about the Protestant soup like it was some sort of evil witch's brew, but Mr. Hanratty told him it was regular food the same as any other, *just that the Prods're no better'n the Priests or the bleedin' English, what with how all of 'em want to grab holda yer soul b'fore they'll thinka feedin' ya.* Whatever it is, Ethan figures he could go for some of that Protestant soup just then, or English soup if there's any, or even a handful of the hosts the Father gave out at Communion, God save his immortal soul for thinkin' such a thing. And while he's full of such sinful thoughts, Ethan watches his Aunt unwrap the six ceramic plates her husband had bought her as a wedding present. They're hand-painted with different designs, and she looks each of them over before picking out her favorite.

Well, dis one'll have t'be enough to remember better days, she says, and wraps it back in her extra dress.

Don't, Em, Ethan's Mam protests. Moichael gave 'em to ya.

I *have* to, Nora, I can't carry 'em anymore.

Well I can carry 'em for a time an' den maybe you'll feel better an' can–

Nora, all I want t'do now is get to th'damn boat an' get on wit' whatever else it is th'Lahrd sees fit to test us wit'. I got enough to remember 'bout Moichael wit'out luggin' dese plates halfway 'cross th'bleedin' country.

Since at least Aislinn's funeral, Ethan's felt like he's let everyone down. Da told him he was the man of the house when he left, and even if he was just kidding about that, seein' how he was just a lad of ten when his Da said it, Ethan still feels like he's failed to take care of all of them the way he should've, the way his Da would've, or even Seanny. And to see Aunt Em leave this treasure behind, after all she's already left back home, is about all he can take of that shame without doing something drastic. So he ducks behind a tree, unwraps his satchel, and makes the difficult decision in just a few seconds. Shakespeare, Homer, Milton, and Chaucer make the cut, while Shelley and Swift are left behind. Out of sight from his Mam and Aunt Em, he places the two books side by side and leans them against a tree, hoping they'll be adopted by passersby for something more than kindling or to wipe their arses. Then he walks over to the discarded plates and begins to wrap them carefully in his satchel.

Ethan, what're ya doin'? Aunt Emily asks.

I can carry dem, he says with confidence.

Now don't be stahrtin'–

I can *carry* dem, he interrupts like he never would, somehow stumbling upon a man's sense of resolution, what with how neither his Aunt, nor his Mam, say anything more about it.

They walk slowly, coverin' maybe five or six miles through the entire mornin' before stopping for a short rest. When it's time to continue, Ethan can feel the weight of the satchel dig into his bruised and beleaguered shoulder, as he sets it in place. There are four books remaining, but he knows now that they can't possibly all make the trip with him, not if he's going to carry Aunt Emily's plates. Newry must still be ten or twelve miles off, he figures, and as they plod along, slower than ever, he begins to consider which book to leave behind next. The Shakespeare, Aislinn's favorite, will stay, of course. He'll drop his extra set of clothes before it comes to that. And *The Odyssey* is his favorite of all of them, so that'll stay as well. That leaves Chaucer and Milton–*Canterbury Tales* and *Paradise Lost.* Chaucer's the first to go, left at the base of a stone wall after their midday rest. Then, as evening arrives in the distance, he excuses himself from his Mam and Aunt, sayin' he has to visit the necessary just off the road. He places his bag against one tree, then walks to another twenty feet farther away to tend to business. When he returns to his satchel, he removes Milton and notices just a whisper of relief in the load he still carries.

They walk for another mile or so, then stop as darkness sets in with still no sign of Newry in the distance. Ethan can feel the blood collecting near the back of his shoes where blisters from the first day of walking had torn open on the second and then again today. He takes them off slowly, excruciatingly, then turns them over on the ground to let the blood trickle out. His Mam and Aunt sit exhaustedly beside one another, broken, nothin' proper or ladylike about their appearance now, and he knows that if they had the energy, they'd cry at the sight of each other. There's enough daylight left to collect wood for a fire, but there'll be no more progress today, no roof over their heads, no proper supper or even the Protestant soup. But Ethan feels a sense of pride as he sets the large wooden match to the kindlin' he's gathered in bare feet, then begins putting in the larger sticks to make a nice fire to warm their spirits. With his Mam and Aunt stretched out on their blankets, admirin' his handiwork, he unfolds his blanket and stacks his Aunt's plates neatly alongside him. She leans toward him and smiles a little while examining them.

Dey look wonderful, thank you Ethan, she says, and kisses him on the forehead.

He nods and smiles back, but then she looks at the rest of his things and a worried expression comes over her face.

Where are th'resta da books ya brought? she asks.

Ethan says nothing.

Ethan, you had what . . . six of 'em when we left? she asks, lookin' over at his Mam for a second and then back at him. Don't tell me . . . *awwww* Ethan, why'd ya go and do that? Just fer some silly plates . . .

She shakes her head and the water's in her eyes and down her cheeks, and he can't help but feel like he's done something wrong.

Et'an, his Mam asks tenderly. Where'd ya leave 'em?

He shrugs his shoulders at first, then figures it isn't much of a *man's* response. After all, it'd been *his* decision to carry the plates, what with Aunt Em doin' so much for them, taking them in when Da and Seanny left. It was the *least* he could do to carry her wedding plates.

Two of 'em I left behind right off, he says matter-of-factly. Den Chaucer somewhere 'round midday, an' Milton beside th'tree where we stopped about a mile back. I didn't know we were dis close to stoppin' fer th'night. But dat's it, Aunt Em—an' I'd do it again soon as I got da chance.

He stretches out his blanket, still a little wet from the night before, then folds his arms and lies down on it. After a final glance over at his Aunt and Mam, he closes his eyes, placing the cap Mr. Hanratty'd given him over his face, as if declaring the matter resolved. Neither of the women says anything, but he can hear Aunt Emily sniffling for a few minutes before the tiredness overtakes him and he gives in to sleep.

JULY 22, 1847

The Hunger wakes Ethan a few hours later, and he opens his eyes to the faint light of the quarter-moon. His exhaustion is gone, it seems, chased off by the sound of his stomach. Aislinn used to tell him to think of the noises their stomachs'd make as a cat's purring, softening it into something nice, the way she did with most difficult things. But this is more like the sound of some kind of African lion who's mad as hell, Ethan thinks, and he worries it'll wake Mam and Aunt Em, whose silhouettes he can see in the shadows just a few feet away.

In the morning they'll insist that *they* carry the plates, or that he leave them behind, and he'll have to refuse with the kind of force he'd summoned the mornin' before. But he knows that it'll be difficult to do with The Hunger eatin' at him this way. They won't have anything to eat until they reach Newry, and he isn't sure he'll be able to carry the plates that far, weak as he feels now. So without thinkin' much about it, he reaches one hand out across his blanket, grazing it over the grass an arm's length away. Then he pulls off the tops of a few dew-covered blades, placing them quickly into his mouth. The bitterness explodes over his tongue, and it's like tryin' to chew and swallow little bits of string. But after the third or fourth handful, he doesn't notice as much. One handful after the other he stuffs into his mouth, chewing as little as possible, until it's like a battle between the angry lion and the bits of string travelin' down his gullet to take him on. The lion almost wins as Ethan gags two or three times, feeling like the green string is all comin' back up. But then he sits up, slouching over at the shoulders and pulling his knees into his chest, and the lion gives way for now. Before he's off to sleep again, he makes sure to brush his sleeve across his mouth and teeth several times, to remove any green marks that might be left behind. Back home the people with green mouths and teeth were never very long for this world, and he doesn't want to give Mam and Aunt Em a scare when they wake in the mornin'.

He's up again not long after first light, and as he sits up, he notices that the small pile of books has grown by one during the night. Milton's *Paradise Lost* sits on top of the other two, and Ethan picks it up and brushes his hand across the cover and can't help but smile.

Aunt Em went an' found it last night, Mam whispers. She left right after ya fell asleep an' walked back an' found it.

Ethan feels a wave of gratitude toward his Aunt, and both he and his Mam look over at her and smile with closed mouths and heads that shake slightly side to side with a sense of reverence toward her for havin' walked two extra miles in the dark just to retrieve the book. But then Aunt Emily rolls slightly to her back and lets out a gargled snore, and it's all they can do to keep from laughin' so hard they wake her up. And still, it's a moment to be treasured between Ethan and his Mam, like they're *both* aware there won't be many more of them anytime soon.

They make Newry with an hour to spare, and by the time they board the ferryboat, their bellies've been relieved with a little fish and potatoes, and bread with just enough butter to remind them of better days. The crowd on the boat to Liverpool sits silently along the deck, shoulders hunched, faces gaunt, their hair disheveled, their clothes torn and dirty. Some of them're glad to leave, but others mourn like they've lost a loved one. When the boat pulls away from shore, some look back and begin to cry and a few even muster up the strength to join in an old song Ethan'd once heard Mr. Hanratty sing, about a man who's sent off to Australia for stealin' some food. As the Irish coast begins to disappear from view two hours later, Ethan stares back at the brown mass in the distance. He's always found it strange to hear men like Mr. Hanratty describe Ireland as *she* or *her* and not *it,* but at that moment of final goodbyes, he understands better and grows sad at the thought of never seein' her again.

Liverpool is another matter altogether, and when they set foot off the ferryboat, he can't imagine that anyone would ever look back at this place and grow sad at the idea of leaving. With its tall factory smokestacks spitting forth endless clouds of black coal dust until everything–the buildings, the streets, the people, even the sky–takes on a shade of dark gray, it's clear to Ethan that Liverpool's the kind of place that'll always be an *it,* never a *she.*

Of course, there's not a bit of time once they land since it turns out there's a ship leaving for New York that very mornin'. Aunt Em rushes off to buy the ticket for Ethan while Mam looks over the people standing in line waiting to board the *Lord Sussex.* She strikes up a conversation with one woman, but Ethan doesn't pay any attention to it, busy as he is lookin' over the ship and watching the men roll great wooden barrels up a gangway into the side of the vessel. And then there's Mam introducing Ethan to this one woman named Mrs. Quigley and her husband, who Mam says have promised to look out for him. Ethan's angry with his Mam for thinkin' he needed anyone to look out for him, when here's himself having been the man of the house for more than two years now.

Sure ain't he the spittin' image o' Seamus, Mrs. Quigley says, and then her husband puts his arm around her shoulder long enough for a single squeeze. We lost our boy to the fever just this winter past . . .

And her voice trails off like so many voices from back home would when they talked about such things. Mrs. Quigley looks far too old to have a son Ethan's age, and Mr. Quigley looks almost as old as Mr. Hanratty, but then she explains that their son was the sort of miracle that John the Baptist bein' born to Elizabeth in the Bible was, and Ethan can't help but feel sorry for them. He decides not to argue with his Mam for his own independence, figuring he can as much look after the Quigleys as they will after him. And it's sealed when Mam tells them about havin' lost Aislinn to the fever too, and there's all three of them, *Mister* Quigley even, with the water in their eyes.

When it comes to the farewells not even an hour later, Aunt Em hugs him and gives him a long kiss on the cheek, then hugs him some more, and smiles as much as she can force herself to do. But there's no such smile on Mam's face. Hers is a look he can't quite understand at first, worse than the one he remembers from when Seanny and Da left, and different from the one at Aislinn's funeral. Her face has the look of defeat, as if sayin' goodbye to her last child is all she can bear, and he wonders if she'll become like Mr. Hanratty now, with all the life and joy poured out through her cupped hands. She tells Ethan to *keep readin' an' be a good boy,* and tells him how much she'll miss him. It's unusual talk and he begins to suspect that maybe she thinks she's sayin' goodbye for the last time. But it's a thought he'll not allow himself to consider as she puts her hands on the back of his head and whispers in his ear.

Be happy, she says three times softly, before kissing his cheek and releasing him.

They separate for a moment, but then she quickly pulls him closer and kisses him one last time. And then it's up the gangway alongside the Quigleys, with just a final wave to Mam and Aunt Em, each of them with one arm wrapped so tightly around the other that it's impossible to tell which one is holdin' the other upright. As their free hands brush the water off their cheeks, Ethan tells himself that this isn't so much a *fare thee well* like in one of Mr. Shakespeare's plays, but rather a simple *s'lahng* that'd be uttered along the Lane back home . . . the kind that carried with it the understanding of seein' each other again. And soon.

2 *Odyssey*

ETHAN
SUMMER 1847

Numbers are cold and impersonal things, efficient, absolute. So it was no wonder then that they'd become Ethan's near-perfect refuge after Aislinn's death, what with the way he'd count everything he could to keep from thinkin' about her, about The Hunger, about everything else that was beyond his control. By the time he and Mam and Aunt Em'd left for Newry, Ethan already knew that the distance from the Brodericks' stables to Mr. Hanratty's cottage was about fifteen hundred of his normal steps, though he'd once made it in one thousand three hundred eleven, taking the longest strides he could. It took about two hundred strokes to properly groom each horse, three hundred seventy-seven horseshoe nails to fill the wooden bucket at the stables, and two hundred forty-seven dry oats were as many as he could hold in one hand.

So as he followed the Quigleys down into the cargo bay accommodations of the *Lord Sussex,* with people pushing and shoving and even fightin' each other as if staking out a claim to their own small bit of land, it made perfect sense for Ethan to turn to numbers once again. He counted the support rails set up every six feet or so, the ones that held up the long rows of planking that ran practically the whole length of the bay, two of them on each side with about four feet of space between them. There were fourteen support rails per side, and as the passengers scrambled for spaces by the bow where there was a trickle of light comin' down the stairway, Ethan walked slowly to the stern alongside the Quigleys, defeated just like they were, and counting, so as not to think of how he'd have to live here without enough light to read.

By the time they reached the fourteenth beam, they were at the dark stern at the end of the bunks and next to eight makeshift latrines. Eight latrines meant eight big wooden buckets set on the floor about two feet above three planks, with the hole cut into each one of them for doin' the necessary. They looked clean, but it was hard not to wonder what they'd be like when all these people were doin' their necessary in there all day long. It was a sad place, and Ethan wanted to go back above deck, to leave the ship altogether and go find his Mam and Aunt Em to work with them in the mills until they could all go to America together. But then Mr. Quigley told him the sliver of space up on the top level of planking would be his, and as Ethan climbed up, the old man stood there with a content smile on his face like he'd done his manly duty. All he'd really done, Ethan thought, was surrender straight off and consign them to the darkest corner of the whole ship, and Ethan placed his satchel down along the front edge and buried his head on top of it. Within an hour they were on their way, and there'd be no turning back, no findin' his Mam and Aunt Em or workin' in the mills. Just a dark corner of space next to the latrines that was to be the greater part of his world for the duration of the voyage.

It turned out life aboard the *Lord Sussex* was *all* about numbers, even if you weren't purposely tryin' to find them.

For starters there was the number sixteen, as in sixteen ounces of food per passenger, per day. Might be some stale bread or uncooked rice or potatoes, or even a bit of fish, but whatever it was, it was always sixteen ounces and never a fraction more. And though they'd never weighed their food back home, it was easy to see that the ship's ration was less than what they'd had in Aunt Em's cottage, even durin' The Hunger, even when it was four of them instead of three. On the third day, when they were fully out to sea, the bouncing ship turned Ethan's stomach in knots. He walked to one of the latrines and didn't even have time to close the door before his stomach started heaving and his mouth opened wide on instinct. But nothin' came out. Behind him was the old man Donnegan from across the aisle. And Donnegan let out a bitter laugh and said to Ethan *sixteen ounces ain't wort' de effort of throwin' back up.*

Then there was the number six, as in six pints of water per person, per day, or six paired with two, to make six feet by two feet of bunk space for each person. Of course, one of the crewmen informed them right off that the water was *for drinkin', washin', and cookin', not in that order, haha,* and that ration'd be cut unless they saw some rain on the trip. But the more rain they saw meant *the food stores'll rot faster, so there ya go, haha.* As for the bunk space, it was more like six and twenty, as in six feet by twenty inches per person, because two hundred didn't stand for the number of passengers aboard the *Lord Sussex* the way it was supposed to. Donnegan said the crewman counted out two hundred and fourteen rations of water each day for the passengers, which explained the tight fit in the bunks.

Donnegan took to callin' the *Lord Sussex* a Coffin Ship after what that same crewman told him was the common reference to these converted cargo vessels carrying desperate emigrants across the sea. The crewman said it was pretty common that such a ship sailing from Liverpool, Dublin, or Cork wouldn't arrive *wit' all its cargo intact,* and it took Ethan a minute to realize that *they* were the cargo.

More important to Ethan than sixteen or six or two, or any other number set rigidly in place, was the number that was constantly movin', constantly shrinking toward its ultimate, beautiful destination. It was the countdown of time until noon each day when sixty, as in sixty minutes above deck, became his favorite number. When noon arrived, Mrs. Quigley gathered their rations together to cook in one of the communal pots, and when it was done, she poured out a little of the used water for Ethan to wash his face and hands. The washin' and the eating took only ten minutes right in the middle of the hour, and the remainin' fifty minutes were Ethan's to wander about, exploring the ship and takin' in the spectacle of the infinite ocean landscape. It was his time to read, from *The Odyssey* mostly, thinking about Odysseus driftin' over the sea for twenty years, and comforted by the thought that their voyage would only be about five weeks.

Ethan kept the daily count waitin' for the hour above deck, and then there was an even more important count he kept, broken down into the hours and minutes 'til ten o'clock Sunday mornin' and the start of seven continuous, *glorious* hours above. By the second Sunday, nine days out to sea, the smell of the cargo bay was so foul that it lingered even after the latrine buckets were emptied each evening, and the thought of seven hours in the fresh ocean air made the anticipation all the greater.

Services in ten minutes! Ten minutes! was the call they'd all been waitin' to hear.

Then came a rush for the stairs, and within a few minutes most of the passengers and crew were assembled for services in front of a makeshift altar made from the same table used to distribute rations every day. The Father they had onboard was no Father Laughton, what with how his sermons ate up so much of their precious time above deck, but finally the Mass was done and Ethan was free for the nearly six hours that remained. Mrs. Quigley set up with the other women around the buckets full of brown water that'd been used to wash the decks. They pulled out torn clothes from satchels and dropped them in, hoping to take some of the smell out of them before hanging them over the sides of the ship to dry. But Ethan cared little about any of that, walkin' up to the bow and settling himself in his new favorite spot behind a pile of thick mooring rope.

The sun was almost directly overhead by now, its rays dancin' off the crests of the waves in brilliant flecks and sparkles. And Ethan took in the sea air with deep breaths, imagining that this must've been somethin' like what Mr. Hanratty described about the glorious spring of '98, when an Irishman could know what it was like to experience true freedom. Opening his book, he began to read slowly, stoppin' after every page or so to look up and take it all in again, reverently, thankfully. When five o'clock came, it was back down below and startin' the count until noon the next day, nineteen hours . . . eleven hundred forty minutes . . . sixty-eight thousand four hundred seconds.

BY THE THIRD SUNDAY OF the voyage, Ethan had a new number to count. Many of the people in the bow of the cargo bay got sick after drinkin' water from a barrel that'd been used to store salted fish. One seven-year-old girl seemed to take the worst of it, and for four days her fragile body rejected everything she was fed, throwin' it back up as soon as it hit her stomach. Then during the fourth night her chest heaved and she made strange noises as her mother woke everybody up with her screams. Before long it was just the sound of the mother's screams, as the little girl lay still and lifeless across her Mam's lap.

The next mornin' the Father said a few words about her before the Mass, but her Mam wouldn't go above deck for it, sayin' she didn't feel *loike a god who'd take anudder choild from me deserves any more o' me Sunday mahrnin's.* And all the ladies blessed themselves and took a step away from her when she said it. Ethan spent much of the Father's sermon thinking of the number one, as in one passenger who'd been tossed into the abyss of the ocean, one person who'd never get to see America *wit' the gold nuggets in the streets and the stuffin' yerself 'til ya can't stand.* One . . . so far, he thought.

He had *Paradise Lost* with him that Sunday, feelin' on this somber occasion that he should read something a little more religious in nature than *The Odyssey.* Ethan settled into his usual spot in the stern, but before he read a full page, he was startled by a deep voice comin' from just behind him.

Enjoy dat reading, young man. You will not have much for two, maybe t'ree days.

Turning quickly around, he saw a large black man standin' on the other side of the mooring ropes. Ethan'd seen him before, usually at the top of the mainmast, tyin' off and adjusting the sails while the captain on the bridge shouted orders. The man had very dark skin and powerful arms and stood at least six feet tall, but his smile eased some of Ethan's fear.

A storm come from de northwest, the man said slowly and clearly. It is a few days before de wedder is good for reading on deck.

A nod was all Ethan could manage for a response.

What book is dat? the man asked.

Ethan closed the book, keepin' his finger on the page he was reading, and stared down at the faded cover, as if there was anything to read there.

Para . . . he began, then cleared his throat and spoke in a voice just above a whisper . . . *Paradise Lost.*

I never hear of dat one. It is Irish?

Ethan shook his head, then murmured . . . English.

Oh. What is de story of it?

Ethan looked up from the book and at the man's face. He'd never spoken to or even seen an African before this voyage, and was surprised, seein' him up close, that there were no strange rings through the man's nose or ears. He wore regular clothes that covered his whole body. He had shoes on too, and didn't carry a spear, and Ethan decided that there must be two types of Africans, the ones he saw an illustration of in one of the English histories he and Aislinn used to read, and another group who were normal, just like Irishmen or Englishmen except for their skin and the way they talked. And out of that second group came the likes of Hannibal and Othello and this man who was askin' him the story of *Paradise Lost.*

It's about Satan's fall from Heaven, Ethan answered, his heartbeat beginning to slow from its previously agitated state.

Oh, like in de Bible, the man replied. I have read de Bible sometimes.

Me too.

What is your name, young man? he asked.

Ethan tried to respond in a firm and confident manner, but then, when the man said *E-tan?* in response, it sounded a little like the way his Mam'd drop just enough of the "h" so you'd hardly know it was missing. It was a harsher sound coming from the man, but Ethan didn't want to correct him.

I am Suah . . . Soo-ah, the man replied and extended his hand, which Ethan shook, feelin' his own hand disappear inside it while he did.

Dis is my favorite place on de ship too, next to up dere, Suah added, pointin' to the small platform atop the mainmast. I let you go back to reading now, dis storm last two, t'ree days at least, so you must make today last.

Just as the man'd said, rain and chilly wind kept nearly everyone but the crew from walking on deck for the next three days, until, on the mornin' of the fourth day, it passed completely and a warm sun began to emerge from behind them in the east. But the storm had taken its toll on them all. Several people below had the fever, and the worst news of all was that they hadn't made even a single day's progress in the last three. When the hour above came that day, Ethan carried *Paradise Lost* with him again, wondering if maybe he'd see the African Suah, who had grown in stature in Ethan's eyes, the way he'd predicted the storm would linger just as long as it had. He went right to his reading spot, leanin' against the wet ropes, and letting himself become transported into Milton's world of the Archangels and the Son of God and battles and eternal damnation.

So . . . more of Paradise, the familiar voice of Suah bellowed from behind him, just a few minutes after he'd settled into place. How did you like dat storm, Etan?

You were right, Ethan replied with a smile, becomin' more comfortable with the man's gentle nature, despite his dark-as-night skin and giant arms.

Yes. I know dis sea, the man said, sitting on a barrel next to Ethan. I first cross it when I was smaller dan you and de

Spaniards take me from my home in Africa to Coo-bah. I work in da sugar fields until I am almost a man, and den I run off and hide on anudder ship an' cross da sea again. Dis is fifteen times for me crossing dis Atlantic. Someday I will go back home.

Just like Odysseus, Ethan said, as if his previous assumptions had been proven correct.

Like *how*? Suah asked.

And Ethan spent the next half hour telling him all about the *who,* not the *how,* which was Odysseus, and the man who'd lived his favorite story ever. Then he learned more about Suah, who seemed happy to have at least one person on the ship to talk to, considering the way most of the passengers and crew steered clear of him, as far as Ethan could tell. Suah told him of how he'd learned to read from a man who used to work on this ship, and he even asked Ethan to see his book, readin' a few lines aloud as a manner of proof. When he handed it back, Ethan read a little out loud, then passed it back to Suah again to read a few more stanzas, and so on it went for much of what was left of that hour. Suah sometimes needed help with the words, which made Ethan feel good, havin' the chance to be the teacher rather than the student as he'd always been with Aislinn. And he forgot all about Mrs. Quigley and the supper and the washin' until the call for them to return below-decks reminded him how hungry he was. It was as if Suah understood what Ethan had missed, and reached into the pouch on the side of his shirt and handed Ethan a large chunk of bread.

I am sorry you miss your food, he said, nodding for Ethan to take all of it and not just the small piece he'd torn from it.

Will you be here tomorrow? Ethan asked.

I will. I have de night watch up above for some time, Suah replied.

I'll bring *The Odyssey* wit' me. I think you'll like it better'n *Paradise Lost.*

It is your favorite one you say?

Yes, Ethan said as he chewed.

Den I will like to see it Etan. I will like to read of dis man you say travel de sea for more years dan I have . . . O-dish-is, he said.

THE FEVER'S SUNK ITS TEETH into the passenger bay before the fourth Sunday arrives, and Ethan sticks to his countin' rather than listen to the moaning from the worst ones. It works pretty well until they move all the sick passengers to the stern right next to Ethan and the Quigleys, who get to slide closer to the bow. There's at least a trickle of light there but still not enough to read by, and Ethan doesn't much like this word *quarantine* everyone's talking about, which best as he can tell is a way of marking off the ones gettin' ready to die from the ones who aren't.

By the time the thirtieth day of the voyage arrives, his count of people who'll never make it to America is up to five, and the hour above becomes more of a refuge each day, as much for the chance to read with Suah as to escape the dreariness of the cargo bay. Suah generally brings some salted fish or pieces of bread, which he offers to share with Ethan, but mostly he lets Ethan eat all of it. After the first two days, Ethan feels guilty about the food since the Quigleys don't get any of it, but Suah tells him they'd want it this way, too.

Then Mr. Quigley doesn't wake up on their thirty-fifth day at sea. Ethan climbs down from the upper bunk that mornin' to use the necessary, and there he is, eyes opened and staring at the bunk above him, but not a breath to be heard from him, as Mrs. Quigley sniffles back the water runnin' down her face from her eyes and nose. He's been sick but didn't want to let on and get moved a few feet over to the quarantine section with the people gettin' ready to die. And now it'll be over the side of the boat with him, and a mention in the Father's sermon on Sunday.

Later that day, when the crewman comes down to tell them their time above has come, Ethan tries to rouse Mrs. Quigley, who's been lyin' quiet in her bunk since her husband was tossed into the ocean that mornin'. When he walks around to face her, he sees the same blank stare that'd been on his mother's face on the docks in Liverpool, and he understands now that it must be the look of a woman who's seen her whole family disappear before her own eyes. She says nothing to him but touches the back of his hand as it rests on her shoulder, then rolls over to her other side, leavin' Ethan to walk up to the top deck alone.

One of the crewmen says that they'd spotted a fishing vessel in the mornin' and that means they can't be too far from land. It's enough to cheer Ethan a little despite the death of Mr. Quigley and the fact that Suah's been shifted to the day watch atop the mainmast again, which means they can't read together anymore. When it's time to go below, Ethan hopes that the news might encourage Mrs. Quigley, but as he approaches the top of the stairway, Suah grabs his arm.

I need de boy to help me, he says to the crewman conducting the passengers back belowdecks. He leads Ethan all the way to the bow of the ship and places him into a vacant storage space behind the captain's quarters.

Stay here Etan, Suah says. It is important dat you do not move until I come back.

Ethan settles in amidst a pile of ropes tied to the rear anchor, afraid for the first time since they boarded the ship, wondering why Suah needs his help, then hopin' it'll somehow involve climbing to the top of the mainmast. It's dark before Suah returns and hands Ethan a piece of salted fish and some soft rice. Ethan swallows it down in less than a minute, licking his palms to get any final morsels, and then Suah quietly leads him across the poorly lit deck to a compartment behind the storage cabin.

You will stay here my friend, he says to Ethan, and opens the wooden flap. Stay here Etan, and do not leave until I come to see you again.

Ethan hesitates, finally asking, What d'ya need me to help you wit', Suah?

Dis right here. I need you to stay here and not to come out unless I say it is safe.

He pats him on the head and it's not much reassurance, but Ethan follows his orders, slidin' himself in between the wooden barrels stored there. He can feel that they're empty, but the smell makes it clear that they'd held supplies of salted fish. A few minutes later the flap opens again and Suah hands him two empty sacks made of very coarse fibers.

Stay warm wit' dese Etan, he whispers. I will return tomorrow.

Ethan passes a mostly sleepless night and finally dozes off when daylight comes, and he's able to read himself to sleep by the sunlight seeping through the cracks. It isn't until midday, when the passengers from belowdecks are brought up for their hour above, that Suah finally returns. He brings him two more handfuls of food—more than Ethan had on a typical day throughout the trip—and pretends to move the barrels around as Ethan eats it. When he stands up, an excruciating tingle runs down the insides of both of Ethan's legs, and it takes a few minutes before the feeling begins to return to them. He tells Suah he wants to go below to check on Mrs. Quigley, but Suah only shakes his head.

It is very bad down dere Etan, he tells him. Many people are sick with de fever. Dis is why I keep you here.

But Ethan feels all the more certain that he should go and look after Mrs. Quigley then, and he begins to step out of the storage compartment to do just that. Suah grabs hold of both of Ethan's shoulders and bends down enough to be just a foot or so from Ethan's face. There is no familiar smile to ease the sharpness of his jawline or the intimidation of his dark-eyed stare, and Ethan immediately knows that this is not a matter to be negotiated.

You go an' walk around up here for a little while, Suah says, but do not go down dere again. It is how de woman—Misses . . .

Quigley, Ethan says.

Yes . . . it is how she will want it.

So it's back into the storage compartment, where two more nights pass in the same manner. Aside from the cramped space, Ethan's life is actually better here than it'd been below. He has more to eat, what with Suah slippin' him food twice a day, and he's able to read for as many hours as the sun is up. But he becomes very lonely by the third day, and when Suah insists he stay there for what should be the final night of the voyage, Ethan begins to expect the worst.

Did more people die? he asks.

Suah shakes his head, but he's not a good liar and Ethan presses him for the truth.

Some, is all he concedes.

Mrs. Quigley? Is she one o' dem?

Suah shakes his head again, more convincingly it seems,

and Ethan's relieved. He resumes his position for another evening amidst the smelly fish barrels, and Suah promises that this will be the last night. It's dawn the next day when a crewman opens the storage bin and is startled to see Ethan.

Get outta there ya little shit, he says. Doncha wanna see America?

Strugglin' to stand up, he looks around and sees the passengers from above deck staring out across the water toward the brown mass on the horizon. It's the first time in weeks that he's seen anything in any direction except ocean. Less than an hour later the people from the lower levels begin to make their way to the main deck, with the crew saying that they'll be docking that afternoon and they'll *have to get the stink off 'em if you're to be let into America, haha.* Ethan looks around for Mrs. Quigley, figuring she must've worried terribly about him. He wants to make sure that she knows he's all right, that she hasn't lost another one. But when he doesn't see her with the people who are already above deck, he's soon a fish swimming against the stream making his way past the crowd still climbin' the stairs. She's nowhere to be found.

She's gone lad, Donnegan says from across the aisle. Sure she'll be happy t'see her family once again.

And Ethan wants to explode at the old man with a fury of swears and fists to punish him for the way he cursed them all by calling this a Coffin Ship in the first place. But he can't do that.

How many doyed? is all he manages to ask.

Dere's been a few each day since you wandered off, Donnegan says, shakin' his head. She went yesterday mahrnin', den t'ree more last night make it noineteen b'my count.

The *Lord Sussex* eventually docks at a pier that looks as if it's equipped for ships about half its size. The crewmen arrange the passengers into several rows across the length of the deck with the sickest or weakest-looking passengers all in the center, the strongest on the outside. It's mostly the passengers who'd had the tiny cabins above deck standing on the outside, and Ethan stands in the second row between them and the sickly-looking people who are squeezed into the middle of the pack. Behind him two men are talking about the Captain and the First Mate, who disembarked just a few minutes before. They go on about bribes and quarantines and how they're worried about whether they'll be allowed in the country what with all the dead from the trip. Ethan can't help but hear it, but his mind is clouded with sadness for Mrs. Quigley and now resentment toward Suah for keepin' him above deck and not letting him do anything to save her. Then the Captain and First Mate walk out of the small building with another man, who wears a uniform and has a wooden slate in his hands with a large parchment against it.

Move them along, quickly and orderly, the Captain calls to his crew, and at once the mob begins to move. One hundred ninety-five of 'em, he says to the port official. Within the regulations, and all of 'em fine and healthy.

They pass the official who stands with arms folded as if assessing the passengers for fitness. But when Ethan walks by he notices that the official stares at a point halfway up the mainmast, not lookin' at a single passenger as they set foot in their new country. The disembarkation is completed with great haste, as if covering a wrongdoing quickly before anyone notices. Members of the crew even help the frailest carry their possessions off the ship, and in a matter of minutes the pier goes from nearly empty to swarming with a hundred ninety-five people and all their worldly possessions. And as Ethan steps off the gangway and onto the dock, he is filled with more thoughts and emotions than he can keep track of all at once. He looks back at the ship to see if maybe Suah is there on deck or atop the mainmast, forgetting about his anger of just a few moments before and hoping his friend can give him some direction on where to go. But there is no sign of him, and he is pulled along with the crowd of people for a while until he walks out on an adjacent empty dock to figure out what to do next.

He's become so accustomed to being on his own that he almost forgets to look for his Da and brother Seanny, who Mam had written to before they left for Newry. But now, remembering, he can't imagine finding them in all this mess of people. Boys not much older than Ethan swarm the docks, grabbing people's bags and runnin' off with them. When they've run far enough away so that the tired and hungry men stop chasing them, the thieves rifle through the bags and toss aside the books or clothes or trinkets that are of no value to them, pocketing little bits of jewelry and whatever money they find. Determined that they won't do the same thing to him, Ethan takes out his books and the few clothes he has in his satchel, and spreads them out separately along the bit of pier that he occupies. When one of the boys approaches him and sees Ethan's feeble possessions laid out before him, he curses at him and then turns toward another victim.

Within the first hour, most of those off the ship venture one way or another into the giant city before them, and the vultures leave right along with them. But there is still no sign of his Da or Seanny, just an endless stream of buildings as tall as anything he's seen in his life. And he decides to wait for a while longer before venturing out into it in search of the place called Brooklyn, where his Da's last letter said he and Seanny now live.

When the crewmen from the *Lord Sussex* begin to dump the few remaining pieces of rotted fish and salted pork into the harbor, Ethan almost instinctively jumps in to salvage what he can, but the seagulls quickly swarm in before he can act. And he can't help but feel that New York, that all of America will be like this, swarms of people and young boys and seagulls even, waiting to grab whatever they can before anyone else has the chance. Life here, he thinks, will be faster than anything he'd known along the Lane back home.

Two even shifts now, the Captain calls out to his men from over on the deck of the *Lord Sussex.* You have three hours each shift, then back on the ship to clean the resta this filth! Get a bath, a meal, whatever you will, but if you're past the time of your shift, don't expect to be paid the resta your wages.

Some of the crewmen walk down the gangway, Suah among them, and Ethan's happy to see his friend again. Amidst such spectacle, he forgets for a moment about how angry he was just a little while ago that Suah hadn't told him about Mrs. Quigley and the fever. He waves to him as soon as he's off the gangway, and Suah smiles and walks over to the pier where Ethan is seated.

There you are Etan, he says, apparently unaware that Ethan would have any reason to be angry with him. I worry about you dis morning but I was up above and could not see you.

But quickly comforted by his friend's presence, Ethan remembers to be mad again.

Mrs. Quigley doyed, he offers, as if confronting Suah with the truth. You said she was okay, an' then when I went below today, I found out she doyed yesterday mahrnin'.

Suah just shakes his head and then says, Yes, I am sorry that she dies, Etan. When I see her last she is very sick and I think she will not make it. I am sorry for your loss.

It doesn't seem like much of an explanation, and as Suah asks Ethan about his brother and Da, and explains that the passenger ships coming into New York land on the other side of the island, which is probably where they've gone to look for him, Ethan is listenin' only halfway at best. They will come to find him soon, he assures him, but Ethan's not ready to believe another one of Suah's promises.

Well, dis is not a good place for a young boy just new to de country, Suah says, and sits down beside Ethan. I will wait wit' you Etan, and if dey do not come today, I will hide you away back on de ship for de night and we will find dem before de ship leave in t'ree days. But first . . . he says, then leaves off as he stands back up and signals to Ethan to wait right there.

Suah walks to one of the shops not far from the pier, and Ethan has time to think about Mrs. Quigley and the rest of the nineteen who didn't survive the trip, for the first time realizing that Suah might've actually saved his life. Now the guilt bears down upon him, and is worse when Suah returns with a large piece of cheese, a loaf of bread, and something that looks like a slab of cooked beef. Ethan can hardly eat any of it, choked up with shame the way he is, and as Suah talks about the city they see before them, all Ethan can think of is *how do you thank someone for savin' yer life?* Finally an idea comes to him and he reaches inside his satchel, takes out *The Odyssey,* and offers it to Suah without saying anything.

We eat first, Suah says, den we can read some.

It's *yours,* Ethan says. I wancha t'have it.

It takes a moment until Suah realizes what Ethan's saying, then he shakes his head, as if he'll have nothing of it.

You must have your favorite book wit' you on your *own* journey, he says.

Ethan's disappointed and relieved all at the same time,

and he opens the satchel again as another idea strikes him, making perfect sense to him now. He could never give away Aislinn's Shakespeare book, and it'd be difficult to lose Odysseus and Suah in the same day, but he sees how it's all connected now, and why Aunt Em walked those extra miles the night before they arrived in Newry.

Paradise, Suah says, as Ethan hands the book to him. Etan, I cannot–

Please, Ethan interrupts. I wancha t'have it fer . . . fer savin' me.

Suah hesitates, then takes hold of the book with both hands as if it's a sacred scroll.

T'ank you, my friend, he says. I never have a book of my own before.

He smiles and Ethan does too, sayin' a small thank-you to Aunt Em for what she'd done. They eat their food, and Ethan can feel his stomach fill up like it hasn't in as long as he remembers. They read a little, but mostly look out at the city, watching the people passing. An hour goes by before Suah walks back to the shop for some more bread and cheese, and when he returns he tells Ethan about landing on this side of the island so that they could get into the city without being quarantined. He talks about the South Street Port where they usually land and how busy it is, but all that Ethan can think about then are the Quigleys and the rest of the nineteen who died on the way, and even Aislinn. It doesn't matter where they landed, he still feels guilty for havin' been allowed to make it even this far when too many others never got the chance. Suah nods his head as Ethan confides this to him, as if he knows the feeling himself.

Dere were t'ree hundred on de ship from Africa, Suah says, looking off into the distance as he speaks, almost the way Mr.

Hanratty would. Da man to de right of me die, da man to de left of me die, and more dan seventy udders, but not me. On de plantation, my friend die when he is bit by a snake I walk past just a few seconds before it bite him. And up above dere, he continues, nodding to the top of the mast, dere are many times I t'ink, dis is de last storm I will see. But each time I live t'rough it. And den I begin to t'ink maybe God keep me alive for some reason. Maybe he have somet'ing he want me to do.

He looks earnestly at Ethan and says, So why is it you do not die from de fever Etan? Perhaps God have somet'ing he want *you* to do.

And then it's quiet for a while except the noise of the city, and Ethan begins to consider what that might be.

Sam, da man who teach me to read, Suah finally says. He is up in de top mast t'rough many more storms dan I ever see, an' he make it ev'ry time. He fight against de great Napoleon when he is a young man, an' still live. Den he slip on some water on deck when we dock in Liverpool a year ago. He hit his head on de metal rig . . . an' dat's all for him. He don't wake up from it. An' all anybody talk about is how strange a way it is for *such a man* to go. No glory, no storm, no battle—just some water an' metal rig, an' he is gone. Whatever it is God has keep you alive for Etan, it is best dat you do it while you can.

IT'S MIDAFTERNOON WHEN A MAN walks partly up the gangway to the *Lord Sussex* and speaks to a member of the crew. Ethan watches him the whole time while Suah's readin', and it's only when the man walks back down the gangway and toward them that he thinks he recognizes his Da. It's been more than two years since he's seen him, and the picture Ethan has of him in his mind has grown cloudier and more distant with time. As the man walks past the dock where they're seated, Ethan gets the closest look yet, and though the last two years seem to have put five or ten years' worth of gray into his hair and slouch into his shoulders, Ethan is almost certain it's him.

I think that's me Da, he tells Suah, and Suah's face lights up as if it's his *own* father he's seein'.

Yes? We must stop him. Hello! Hello! Sir! Hello! Suah whistles loudly and Ethan's Da turns around. Suah waves to him, and Ethan stands up along with Suah, as his Da walks tentatively toward them, seein' only Suah at first. He stops about twenty feet away, but then he sees Ethan and his eyes broaden with a single glance.

Ethan? he asks, but doesn't wait for an answer before walkin' quickly up to him with arms opened, embracing him and liftin' him off his feet.

Oh Son, yer here, yer here, he says, over and over.

And past his Da's shoulder Ethan sees Suah beaming with happiness. It's a strange and proud moment all at once for Ethan. He doesn't feel like the little boy who'd said goodbye to his Da two years before, but rather like a man who'd accomplished something just by surviving it all—The Hunger, the walk to Newry, the Coffin Ship. And the initial joy of having his father lift him up, for the first time in years, quickly gives way to the awkward discomfort of such an emotional display. What would Mr. Hanratty say about such a thing?

Lookit da *soize* o' ya, gettin' t'be a man, his Da says as he places him back down on the dock.

Ethan smiles at the recognition of his new stature, even extending his hand to his Da to shake as men do. And his Da takes his hand with a bit of a laugh and a nod of his head, adding only a slap on one shoulder to confirm that his youngest son is a boy no longer.

He is a fine and *brave* young man, Suah adds with a smile, and Ethan's Da turns back around to look at Suah again, this time less suspicious than before.

This is Suah, Da, Ethan says, like one man introducing two of his lads to each other. Suah, this is me Da.

And they shake hands and share a few compliments about Ethan, and then Da mentions about how he was expectin' the ship to arrive at the South Street Port and so on, Suah sharing a few details about the fever and landing on this side of the island and so forth. Ethan is quiet as he watches the men talk for maybe a minute, but then realizes that his life has just taken another leap into something new, this voyage, as always, filled with goodbyes, first Aislinn, then Mam and Aunt Em, the Quigleys . . . and now Suah. And the thought of it begins to bring the water to his eyes, just as his Da is gettin' ready to take him home.

T'anks fer lookin' after me boy, his Da says to Suah, extending his hand toward him.

Ethan wants to tell him that he'd done a whole lot more than that, that he'd saved his life and gave him food and even waited these hours with him here on the pier. But the water's pressin' on his eyelids now, and he can't say a thing, lest it escape down his cheeks and he go back to bein' a boy instead of the man he'd just asserted himself as. Suah offers his hand to Ethan and places his other on Ethan's shoulder.

Goodbye Etan, he says.

And Ethan can only respond meekly, Goodbye Suah, in kind, squinting to keep the water in his eyes from getting out.

His Da and Suah shake hands again, and as Da begins to

reach into his pocket Suah shakes his head and holds up the book.

Your son give me dis book, he says, smiling broadly. I t'ink of you ev'ry time I read from it, Etan.

And that's the end for them, with just a final wave from the distance once Ethan and his Da have made their way back to the pier and are headed off into the vast wilderness of the city. When they're far enough away, Da asks him about Suah, and Ethan starts to explain about Mrs. Quigley and the storage container and readin' and such, and it all comes out so fast that it's just a jumbled mess, and his father's expression becomes more confused.

You'll see some colored folks around here too, lad, he says. We try t'keep t'ahr own the way this place is, but you come across a good man dere in yer friend. Sometimes you can tell that about a man, straight off . . . ahhhh lad, you'll see how it is soon enough.

New York is a collection of sights, sounds, and smells unlike anything he could've ever imagined. The buildings are four and five and six stories high with one of them right next to another. In Liverpool he'd seen his first buildings this tall, but there were only a few of them. Here there are hundreds. There's a very tall church spire that stands out from all of them, Trinity Church, his Da tells him, and in the valleys between the great buildings is the strangest element of all, the people.

It's all a stunning, frightening, and oddly exhilarating assault on the senses. In the first few blocks they walk, he hears several languages, sees a few men who look like they could pass for nobility back in Ireland, and more than a few who resemble the battered masses by the docks in Liverpool. He sees women dressed in ways his mother would surely not approve of, and speakin' to passersby in ways that make him blush. On another corner, near where the well-dressed men are gathered, there's a preacher or politician of some sort standing on a wooden crate and shouting at them about the evils of slavery.

Eventually they emerge from the tall buildings and are back at the water, and his excitement grows when he sees two dark-skinned men seated against a wooden gate by one of the ships. These two men, still at a distance from him, look like they're wearin' the same sort of clothes Suah did on the ship. And as he and his father approach them, Ethan begins to think that maybe they work on the ships too, that maybe they'll know Suah and can invite him to come visit him in Brooklyn, the way he would've done before if the water hadn't been in his eyes. But that hope is quickly forgotten as they approach the two men and he sees the chains connecting their wrists and ankles together. There's a man standin' right next to them with his hands propped on his hips, watching them, then lookin' over at the ship they're in line to board. And Ethan can't help but stare at the three of them, the two dark-skinned men with the sort of expressions bein' chained up should produce, and the white man with his right hand just a few inches from the gun in his belt. After he and his Da are well past them, Ethan can't hold back the question.

Why'd those two men have chains on 'em? he asks. Were dey criminals?

His Da seems unhappy to hear the question, like it's something he'd rather not discuss.

Most loikely runaways, lad, his Da says.

Runaways? Ethan asks.

And then his Da looks and shakes his head a little.

Oi'm sorry you had t'see that on yer first day here lad, he

says. Dose colored fellas musta been slaves down sout' an' run off up here lookin' for dere freedom.

But it doesn't fit together in Ethan's mind.

So if dey made it up here, how come dey got chains on 'em still? he asks.

Well, dat fella wit' the gun next to 'em musta been a slave-catcher who's bringin' 'em back down sout', Da answers.

And Ethan worries that maybe the slave-catcher, or someone like him, will spot Suah and try to put him in chains and bring him back to Coo-bah, which he knows is south of New York. He imagines what would happen, how Suah would never stand for it and would fight the man, and maybe the man would have to shoot him. And the worry must show on Ethan's face, because his Da puts his arm around his shoulders and pulls him to his side.

Ahh, don't worry lad. Sure yer friend is safe. Now . . . dis is South Street Port, an' dat's th'East River, his Da continues, pointin' to the water. Where you landed on th'udder soide o' th'island is th'Hudson River—named after th'explorer. An' Brooklyn is over dere.

Brooklyn is much smaller, disappointing by comparison. Everything looks more spread out on the Brooklyn side of the river, and the docks are filled with mostly fishing boats and ferries, it seems, with only a few ships the size of those on this side of the river. Onboard the steamboat ferry, Ethan watches the paddlewheel propel them forward as Da tells him what the past few weeks have been like. It sounds like a grand adventure, with him up before sunrise every mornin' to take out a small boat called a *skiff* and fish for a few hours. That's his new profession, he tells him with a proud smile.

Yer Da's a fisherman just loike Saint Peter himself, he says with a laugh, before filling him in on the rest of his routine.

After sellin' the fish at the pier, it was the ferry over to South Street, where he'd checked on all the ships that arrived there. Then he'd walked across Manhattan to the Hudson River side to see if maybe Ethan had landed there.

Three cents each way on da ferry for da past t'ree weeks lookin' for you, his Da laughs. I'm glad you showed up today, because we was runnin' outta money.

At first Ethan feels guilty for having put him out so, but then is happy that his Da would go to all that trouble. They land at a place called Fulton Street amidst a flurry of pedestrians as Da continues explaining everything he can to him, saying how Brooklyn'll one day be as big as New York, but for now they get to live in a nice quiet little piece of it out in the distance more than a mile away.

That's Red Hook, Da says, pointing south along the shore.

And as they walk toward it, the buildings grow smaller and sparser, with farms spread out in the distance inland until, approaching the settlement of tiny cabins along the shore, Ethan's struck, practically dumbfounded, by a sight that's become foreign to him. He hadn't seen it in the last weeks in Ireland, nor on the long walk to Newry or in Liverpool, and certainly not in the weeks on the ship. But here it is, a strange and most welcome sight to be sure. Out in the open fields, amidst the brilliant late afternoon sunshine, are children *at play.*

They're mostly around his age, it seems, and there are about a dozen in all. The game involves a ball, a long stick and running around in the field, and everything that's happened that day and over the past weeks gets put away somewhere inside him now, until all he can think of is being a part of the game.

They call dat *Base,* Da tells him with a smile.

He stares at the game goin' on as they walk the final steps to the small shanty house his Da says is their home. It's no bigger than Aunt Emily's cottage back in Ireland and is made entirely of wood, without a stone or thatch to be seen. His Da has him put his satchel up in the loft that'll be all his now that Seanny's found an important job over in New York.

Seanny's tendin' streetlamps in da Foive Points, an' it pays a dollar a day, he tells him, so he found anudder place in dere insteada th'long walk an' th'ferry back an' fort' every day.

When they go outside to see the skiff, Da talks about how he's planning on *bringin' over Mam an' yer Aunt Em, an' someday buyin' one o' dem big brick houses we passed up in Brooklyn Heights.* But Ethan's attention quickly focuses on the nearby field again, and the game the boys are playing.

Supper's in an hour, Da says, smilin'. Why doncha play wit' da lads 'til den.

Ethan smiles back at him and doesn't have to be told twice as he trots off, amazed to feel himself running for the first time in weeks.

Is Mr. McOwen yer Da? the boy with the stick asks when Ethan approaches them.

Ethan nods.

He told us you was comin'. I'm Terrance Harrison, but the lads call me Harry, he says, extending his hand, talking and acting just like the grown men do. Then he points to the boy standing just a few feet away. This is Finny Caldwell. What's *yer* name?

Ethan, he replies, shaking the other two boys' hands as if they're about to discuss important matters.

So you wanna play Base, Ethan? Finny asks.

I don't know how.

It's easy, Harry says. Ya hit th'ball wit' this bat, an' run to the tree over there an' th'one over there an' back home if you can. Don't worry–you'll be knockin' th'ball into the bay in no time at all.

Ethan has little idea of what Harry's just explained, and doesn't care very much either. All that matters is that they play until the sun disappears behind the tall buildings of New York across the river, all the while him thinkin' just one thing, thinkin' it's good to be a *boy* again, if only for these few moments.

And then there's that night, after they'd gone to sleep. Da's got to wake up before the sun for the fishing, but not Ethan, not tomorrow at least, *maybe in a day or two lad,* Da said to him. So Ethan slips down the steps of the loft while Da snores like Aunt Em and Mam put together on their worst nights. And it's nothin' to slide the latch across the door and push it open, and then step into the late summer air, hot like Ireland never was or he imagined it ever could be. Still, in the air that feels wet without rain–*humid* as Da called it–there's something mysterious, like Odysseus arriving on a new island, still searching. And Ethan walks out toward the water, as if it'll bring him closer to his Mam and Aunt Em and Aislinn and everything he's known. He stands close to the edge of the bay, feeling like Odysseus now more than ever, safe from the ravages of the sea, but somehow . . . not *home.*

Still, thinking she can hear him, that maybe the Ever After makes such a thing possible, he talks to her, partly in his mind, but partly aloud too, so as to let her know not to worry about him and not to think he's forgotten about her.

Aislinn, he whispers . . . *I made it, Ais'.*

3 *Inheritance*

MICAH, A SLAVE

CHARLESTON COUNTY, SOUTH CAROLINA

MARCH 21, 1853

It's a birthday ritual that dates back to before Micah can remember. Every March 21, brought out to this same insignificant field. Told the same story by his Daddy. Every year, every birthday, the story grows a little bigger, same as him. And the number attached to it grows larger. This year the number's seven hundred and forty-three. As in seven hundred and forty-three pounds down. Two hundred and fifty-seven to go. And Micah just turnin' sixteen years old this very day.

His Daddy's a storyteller. Spins a yarn like no one else anywhere near *Les Roseraies* can hope to. Isabelle's just like him. Fixin' to be the same kinda storyteller when she gets to growin' up for real. But for now she just peppers Daddy with questions. Leaving Micah and his Momma standin' like bookends. Either end of Daddy and Isabelle. Doing nothin' but listening. It's all right by Momma, who told Micah same time last year what a special day it was for Daddy.

Ain't often a colored man gets to stand in a field with his family like this. Tellin' stories, and feelin' like a man, insteada a slave. She said. Still, Micah's itchin' something awful to get to work. It's *his* number, after all, and ain't he a man now too?

The day I see yo' Momma get offa that wagon's the day I know God's got marryin' in mind fo' me. Daddy says.

It's just the start of the same long story. Daddy's gonna tell all about how he was gettin' almost past the age of marrying. How he been so caught up in workin', how there wasn't more than a few women around *Les Roseraies.* How it didn't matter even if there was a thousand of them. Wasn't none of them gonna matter to him. 'Til Massa Leroux bought the place from his cousin. 'Til Massa Leroux come here from Louisiana, bringin' all his things. Bringin' twenny slaves. Bringin' Momma. An' work wasn't all it usedta be to Daddy. Not with such a woman in this world.

Then it's all about how they jumped the broom. How Massa Leroux got a good heart. How, when Micah was born, Daddy gone to Massa Leroux that night. Drinkin' they wine. 'Cause Daddy ain't like just some ol' field hand, and Massa knows it's Daddy that makes this place go 'round.

Well now, I see that Massa Leroux, he ain't got no chillen of his own. An' he sho' seem like it bother him some—that he ain't got no son to pass his lan' down to. So I ask him that night, when it seem like he gettin' that far-off look like he wisht he had a son o' his own. I say t'him that if he let me work this here ol' field on my own, I kin grow indigo like in th'old days. It wasn't nothin' more than a overrun fielda weeds an' hedgerow when I ask him, so it ain't like I'd be cuttin' into anythin' else 'at might get planted here. Last time this here field was used for anythin' was when ol' Massa Benton—two Massas ago—used to have us let them two mules graze in this here field. 'At a long time ago.

Then there's Isabelle, askin' questions like she always does. Being ten years old and gonna be a storyteller herself when she gets growed up, the way Daddy says. So Micah's gotta listen all about the mules that usedta graze here. Long before she, or Micah even, was anywhere near born. And Micah gets impatient again, but Momma calms him down with just a look. Like only she can. Smilin'. Like this is just as important as the plantin' an' gettin' at that number.

Mr. Finch an' . . . what was th'other mule's name, Daddy?

It's like Bellie's got no idea about what they're really here for. The number. The planting. Still, she's only ten years old. And Daddy's stories were something special to Micah when he was ten. Finally Daddy gets to the point. Toward the number at least.

So I get to askin' Massa what a white man'd give his first-born son. A inheritance, what he call it, even though I already know'd what it was called. So I ask him, knowin' all the while where I was goin', if he can let me work for somethin' to give my son here. An' Massa look kinda strange at me, but it was the day o' my son's birth an' the Massa a good man anyhow. Massa Leroux say that he was twenny-one when he come into his own. 'At when his Daddy give him his inheritance. So I ask him 'bout tillin' this piece of lan' an' growin' indigo like we done way back. I tell him I'll work dis here lan' after I done all the work down in the paddies. Won't nothin' be left undone. I'll work here after the work in the paddies all done—even work on Sunday if'n he an' the Misses don't 'spect it'd upset the Lawd too much. An' he jus' nod his head again. Then he ask why I wanna do all this extra work, an' I swallows hard an' tell him flat out, like I's jus' askin' yo Momma t'pass a biscuit at the supper table. I say . . . T'buy my son's freedom . . . just like 'at.

He always pauses at this part of the story. Showing what an important moment it was. And when he does start to talking again, it's not about what happened next. No, this is the point in the story when he tells Micah and Isabelle that they should never talk to a white man or woman that way. Tells them that *he* could do that 'cause the Massa a good man. And he and the Massa almost the exact same age. And that moment was somethin' more like they was just two men sittin' around sippin' wine on the day one of the men saw his first son get born. That's the only reason he could be so familiar-like with the Massa. *But don' you all do that now, y'hear?* And he waits for both of them to answer. Nod their heads, say it out loud. Makes Micah say it twice, like *he's* the one needs to know it most of all. Only then does he go on.

An' the Massa, he take a long sippa his wine an' look me square in the eye like we talkin' jus' man t'man, an' he says, okay, Samuel. This'll be yo' son's inheritance.

An' that's when you figured out the number, right Daddy? Isabelle asks. Even though she knows the answer.

Yes Mad-em-wah-sell Bellie, that sho' is. Daddy answers.

He looks over at Momma. Checking on his pronunciation of the French. 'Cause Momma spoke French back in Nawlins. An' she smiles now, shakes her head a little at Daddy's attempt at it. Like it'll have to do.

Finally they're to the point of the whole ritual. Micah's itching to get to work, but Daddy has to explain how they came to the number. How the Massa sets a price on a good field hand like Micah's gonna be. Then figures what the price of indigo is. The Massa takes out some paper and starts to writin' out all the numbers. Calls it an even thousand pounds of indigo it's gonna take to buy his freedom. Then the Massa says that a boy should have his inheritance when he turns twenty-one years old. Just like he did. Says it's gonna take between forty-five or fifty pound a year to get that done.

But we grew sixty-five last year Daddy. Bellie says.

'At's right, we sho' 'nuff did, Sugarplum. An' dat's 'cause when I

tell him 'bout that, I din' know we'd have anotha set o' hands helpin' us wit' all this here work.

Bellie's gotta say the same thing every time she hears the story. Just so Daddy'll say that and pull her close. Like she really did any of the work, Micah thinks.

But Daddy goes on about what that means, the extra they've been growin' last few years now that Micah can do some real work. Do a *man's* work, Micah thinks. It means he'll be comin' into his inheritance a year earlier. Maybe two. Might be just nineteen when he's free. Nineteen when he can go to Charleston and get a job on the docks or maybe on a boat. Start savin' money to help Bellie get her inheritance.

Only they don't call it a inheritance for a girl, Daddy. What they call it again, Momma?

A dowry. But it's not quite th'same, Honey. Ya have to get married to get the dowry, and it's not you that gets it. It's your husband.

Ohhhh, I'm gonna have to get married to get free, Daddy?

Naw Bellie. We's gonna take care o' dat. We gonna get this here field to put out sevenny eighty pound a year 'fore long, an' wit' the money Micah gonna make in Charleston, we gonna get you your dowry 'round the time you's nineteen or twenny. An' ain't no man gonna get dat. 'At's all yours, Sugarplum.

And she smiles at the thought of it. The way Micah used to when *he* was ten. Before he was getting so close to that thousand pounds that his inheritance didn't seem like a country way off across the ocean anymore. Seemed like just the next *county* now. Like he could climb to the top of a tall tree and see it somehow.

Finally, with the ceremonies complete, they set to work. And Micah starts right in cutting down the tangle of hedgerow at the far end of the field. Attacks it like it's his sworn enemy. Like it's a wall standin' between him and freedom.

Tears at it with his bare calloused hands. Clawing for another few feet of clear ground. Five maybe ten pounds more indigo this year than last. And that much closer to one thousand.

SUMMER–AUTUMN 1853

Momma was elegant like one of the white ladies in the Big House. She'd been lady's maid to Massa Leroux's Momma back in Nawlins. Said it was such a different place with plenty of free colored folks to go along with all the slaves. And then there were plennya folks with colored and white blood in them. *Moo-lah-toes,* she called 'em. So that things almost got mixed in together enough that it wasn't such a big deal that Misses Leroux taught her to read. Had Momma read to her from the Bible most every day. Had her read from the white folks' books too. Without Momma havin' to hide it from most anyone. Even read books on her own when Misses Leroux wasn't even listenin'. But that was Nawlins.

Momma always said, wasn't *any* place like Nawlins. But South Carolina was about as unlike it as anything she could imagine. And that's why Momma only taught Micah to read when he was old enough to know not to say anything about it outside their cabin. They even kept it secret from little Isabelle 'til she was old enough to keep it secret too. 'Course, with how much more Isabelle talked just by her very nature, Momma waited 'til Bellie was ten before she started in with her lessons. Micah'd been readin' with her since he was about eight or so.

So it wasn't 'til that summer that Bellie got brought in on the family secret. She didn't have to go to sleep early anymore, or out for walks to look at the moon with Daddy when

Momma was helpin' Micah with his readin'. Instead it was the three of them readin' from a little pocket-sized Bible Momma took with her from Nawlins. Said the Misses woulda given it to her anyway if she hadn't died so suddenly. So it wasn't like stealin'.

Bellie naturally took to any of the stories with animals in 'em, so long as they didn't get killed. The Creation. Noah and the Ark. Jesus gettin' born in the manger. Stories like that. And Micah had liked them when he was just ten, sure enough. But it was 'round that summer that he started gettin' more interested in something called the Psalms. Momma smiled when he told her that he liked the way the meanin' wasn't always right there on the surface. That the words were like puzzles sometimes, 'steada just bein' stories. That it only took a few words together to make up a whole lotta meaning.

That's called poetry. She said. Then told him that back in Nawlins the Misses had whole books filled with nothin' but poetry. And how they were sometimes 'bout God, like the Psalms, but mostly they were 'bout ladies or trees or the ocean. And love most of all. And Micah didn't care much for that. 'Til Momma said that it seemed fittin' that he would like them, since he was becoming a man of few words. But smart as he was, he'd have to make those words count all the more. And that sounded all right to him.

MASSA LEROUX TOOK SICK LATE in the summer. That was when Daddy and Momma set to arguin' first time ever. Momma saying how Misses Leroux wasn't any good. Saying how the only thing she ever had was a pretty face to draw the Massa into marryin' her. Saying how the *real* Misses Leroux, the Massa's Momma back in Nawlins, didn't like the second

Misses Leroux nothin' a'tall. But Daddy wasn't hearin' anything like that. Said it wasn't nice to talk that way, even if the Misses *was* up in Charleston all that summer. Didn't even come back to nurse the Massa through his sickness. Momma asked why he think the Massa ain't got no children of his own. Asked how that gonna happen when they ain't shared a bed in goodness knows how long. How they ain't shared a *house* even all this time. Even with the Massa sick.

How I got time t'think 'bout that? Daddy said. *Up 'fore sunup workin' in 'at field by torchlight, workin' all day down on the levees, an' den anotha hour or two by torchlight up in 'at field agin. When I got time t'think 'bout anythin' but work?*

It was the most cross thing he'd ever heard Daddy say to Momma. And Micah wished he'd been asleep the whole time insteada just lyin' on his bed listening to their conversation.

Sorry 'bout that, Sugar. Daddy said, after a moment. *I don' mean t'be cross wit' you. I's jus' over-tired's all.*

And that was the end of that argument. 'Til the Massa took a turn for the real bad not long after and the Misses finally came back to *Les Roseraies.* Too late to do any good. Like she come back just to watch him die. Momma'd say. And Daddy didn't like hearin' any of that, but he didn't say it wasn't true, either.

For all the things Momma said about the Misses during those days, there was no gettin' around the fact that the Misses did put on a nice funeral. Folks came in from all around. Black sheets draped over the porch railings and outside the upstairs windows. All the slaves got the day off. Got to walk past the Massa's coffin. Touched it. Threw flowers on it. Then he got stuck in the ground, and the white folks went to celebrating. The Misses most of all.

A week after the funeral was the start of the harvest. Took

in a good crop of rice that year. Took four weeks to get it all in, set it to dry out. Bundle it up. Then Micah and his Daddy walked out to the indigo field late that first night after the rice harvest was all done. Resta them back celebratin' the harvest like always. Momma and Isabelle too, 'cause Daddy said it was a *man* thing he gotta talk to Micah about. And there he was with Daddy, standing over that field, gettin' ready to harvest it. That's when Daddy told Micah how there wasn't gonna be a indigo harvest that year. How he talked with the Misses, best as he could. How she didn't know nothin' 'bout nothin' when it come to that agreement he made with the Massa the day Micah was born. How there wasn't gonna be no inheritance, least not like they'd figured.

But before first light the next mornin' Micah went out to that indigo field anyhow. Started tearing up the indigo plants. Figured he'd finish what they started that spring. 'Course, first light brought Daddy out to the field to fetch his son. Still kind of dark, but light enough for Micah to see the tears rolling down his Daddy's cheeks. First time he ever seen that. And it was like the world had got all turned upside down, then. This mountain of a man, everything Micah wanted to be someday. Left with just tears. Askin' his son to come on home back to the cabin. This mountain of a man reduced to that. *Askin'*.

So Micah walked back with him. His Daddy's great arm draped over his shoulders. And then it was Micah's tears he was tryin' to talk away through his own. Tellin' him it was gonna be okay, Son. Tellin' him maybe it weren't the Lawd's plan for him to see his son be free. That maybe that's gonna be Micah's thing to do. That someday he'd have a son. And maybe get to make him free. Give him that kinda inheritance sweeter than all *Les Roseraies* and all the plantations in Carolina put together. And when they got home Momma and Isabelle were there. Made a fire. Cooked some biscuits. And the four of them ate 'em with some of the harvest butter on top. Isabelle askin' Daddy to tell some stories from way back. Something about them old mules that usedta graze in that top field. *His* field, the way Micah saw it. The one that was about to become useless. Again.

OCTOBER 18, 1853

The auction is held three days later. *Les Roseraies* buzzing even more than it did the day of Massa Leroux's funeral. This time with visitors not dressed so well, some lookin' downright common. All morning long they walk through the Big House and the stables. Even down to the rice paddies and slave quarters, just openin' any door they please and walking in. The slaves are told to stay in their quarters that day. And it's the first time Micah can remember hearing complaints that they *won't* be workin' that day.

Don't take long to understand why. Once Mista Erlison, the overseer, comes 'round. Tells 'em all to come on out an' stand in a line. And they walk up toward the Big House. Momma's explainin' to some of the others what's likely to happen. Says she seen this sorta *controlled* auction before, back in Nawlins at the Massa's old place.

Callin' us in from the quarters mean's they either sold the whole place and the new Massa wants to talk to us all. She says. *Or it means the auctioneer didn't get the price the Misses wants and now they gonna sell parts off one by one.*

Whachu mean "parts"? Someone asks.

Furniture. Massa's piano. The silver an' the good china. Summa the horses maybe. She says, pausing for a moment. *And us.*

When Mista Erlison asks the auctioneer, man named Mista Tilton, how he should divvy up the slaves, it don't take much to figure that there ain't no new Massa wantin' to talk to them.

Bring 'em out seven at a time. Mista Tilton says. *Nine groups of seven, perfect.*

You wan' the best ones up front? Mista Erlison asks.

The strong bucks or the ones with special skills'll draw the best price. Mista Tilton says.

Mr. Erlison starts lookin' down at his sheet and shouting out names. Daddy gets called out in the first group, even though he's more'n fifty years old. And Micah feels proud of him, standin' there with men half his age. Then, when Micah gets called at the end of the second group, he feels even better. Standin' there with the cook and the liveryman and four other field hands that got ten years on him mostly.

Whatta shame. Mista Erlison mumbles, lookin' at Daddy. Knowin' the man that's done most of the real overseeing of this plantation might go up on the block soon. Momma gets put in the fourth group, and Bellie's way back in the last one. And it doesn't seem real to Micah until they get set in their groups 'round side of the Big House. And he can hear the auction goin' on up front.

Mista Tilton said the Misses wanted eighty thousand for the place. No one offered more than sixty-eight. So now comes the *real* auction. And by the time Micah can hear what's goin' on, the price is down to seventy-four thousand. Piano and a whole buncha fancy furniture got sold. And all it did was cut six thousand off. Which means it's time to sell off more *parts.* China set and silver service and more furniture only gonna do so much. An' that's all it does.

Seventy thousand. Auctioneer says.

But sixty-five's the highest bid now. So more parts. Meanin' the first batch of slaves. Meanin' Daddy. Micah can hear the auctioneer tell how he's the best levee operator in the state, probably. Great carpenter too. Loyal. And so forth. And Micah feels proud of him again. Especially when the bidding hits a thousand dollars. Folks start talkin' about how even the biggest field hand didn't go for a thousand. But Daddy does. Eleven hundred dollars, to be exact. And when he's gone, the piece-by-piece auctionin' comes to a stop again. And the auctioneer starts askin' for his new price of sixty-four thousand.

It takes a little while for Micah to let the pride go. 'Til he realizes what really just happened. What it means for Daddy. And the rest of them.

The auctioneer seems to hope that the man who bid sixty-five last go-'round will have at it again. But sixty's all he's willing to go now. With Micah's Daddy and the six best field hands gone. So it's more parts. Meanin' Micah this time.

A young field hand with much potential. Is how the auctioneer describes Micah. *Look at those shoulders, gentlemen. This boy's gonna make a fine strong hand in a few years.*

And Micah's got an angry look on his face. Not just from the idea of bein' sold. Or even from his Daddy bein' sold. But from having the auctioneer say he's *gonna* make a fine strong hand. Like he didn't already do a man's work, and then some. Then the overseer whispers something in the auctioneer's ear and his eyes open wide.

I'm told this young buck is the son of Samuel, sold not long ago. So that's a boy who knows about hard work and knows a thing or two about operating levees and locks . . . carpenterin' too. A fine investment this one is. Now do I hear four hunnerd?

After a few seconds a man near the front calls out four hundred.

Do I hear four twenty-five?

Four twenty-five. Another man says.

Very good, now I want four fifty. Do I have four fifty?

And on it goes for a minute or two. The man who bought Daddy and another man, bidding back and forth. Past five hundred. Six hundred, even. Then the man who bought Daddy starts shakin' his head when the other man bids seven hundred.

Couldn't get that much for'm in Mississip'. The man who bought Daddy says. And that's that.

Sold at seven hunnerd to Mister . . . Auctioneer says.

Dunmore.

Sold at seven hunnerd to Mr. Dunmore of . . . ?

Virginia. Charlottesville.

Mr. Dunmore of Charlottesville in the great state of Virginia. Auctioneer says with flair. And Micah gets taken over with the rest of the slaves who already got sold.

Did the man in the blue suit git ya? His Daddy asks him. *The dealer from down Mississip', did he git ya?*

It was a man named Dunmore. Micah says, shaking his head. *From Virginia.*

His Daddy takes the news like a punch to the belly. And Micah can see him half-breaking right before him. Cryin' again now. So that's twice in sixteen years, all inside the same month. And that's when this all becomes real to Micah. It ain't about the pride of his Daddy bein' put in the first group. Or him bein' in the second. Not anymore. Now it's about realizin' that Daddy's goin' to Mississipp'. And he's goin' to Virginia.

It's gon' be awright. Daddy says, putting his arm around Micah's shoulders. The same broad shoulders that put him in the second group to start with. *The Lawd's gonna watch over yo' Momma an' Bellie . . . leastways.*

They look back up at the porch where the auction continues, 'til Micah's lot gets all sold off. Then there's some more furniture and four of the best horses from the stables. And Mista Tilton consults with the man keepin' the books at the table next to him.

Fifty-six thousand. He shouts, and the crowd seems more interested than before.

Fifty-four. Someone says, and the auctioneer shakes his head.

Fifty-five. Another says. But no.

Finally, *Fifty-six.* The man from before says, and the crowd cheers a little.

Your Momma an' Bellie're safe. Daddy says, squeezing Micah to him. *They gon' stay right 'ere. The Lawd kept them togetha, at least.*

How 'bout the indigo fiel', Daddy? Micah asks. Like he's still holdin' out hope. Like maybe if he and Daddy can harvest what's there, plus what they been doin' all these years. That maybe it'll be enough to buy the two of 'em back. And it can be the four of 'em all together again.

At's done now, Son. His Daddy says. *When Massa Leroux pass, 'at deal die wit' him. We done speculated like a coupla white gennlemen o' business. Like dem men jus' bought you an' me. Only we lost. We lost dis here speculation, Son.*

Micah stands still, not entirely sure what his Daddy means.

Fifty-six thousand, five hunnerd! Another man from the crowd shouts.

Fifty-seven! Another says.

Fifty-seven! The auctioneer says, smiling bigger than ever. *Fifty-seven, five hunnerd!*

Fifty-eight!

Fifty-eight! The auctioneer repeats, giddy now. *Where were you gentlemen earlier?*

And the crowd laughs.

'At's right. Micah's Daddy mumbles. *Where was dey befo'?* He looks down at Micah and shakes his head. *Dey's speculatin' a little too late fo' us.*

And inside Micah there are no tears. Just an icy, far-off stare. Looking at nothing in particular. Not even wondering what his new world will be like. Not much caring. Just cold and dark. Deep inside.

MICAH HADN'T SPENT MUCH OF his sixteen years engaged in conversation. Not with Daddy and Bellie around to do all the talkin'. And Micah preferred to listen anyway. Still, it was one thing to hear the playful chatter of his family. And another altogether to hear the stories of such a man as Clarence Dunmore. With him chained to the bench of the livery coach. First time Micah ever rode in a covered carriage. And it was sittin' across the width of it from his new Massa. Watchin' him sip from a flask. Left to hear the man's life story. While all he could think about was how this man took him away from his Daddy and Momma and Bellie. And this man not knowin' anything about the number. 'Bout the almost thousand pounds of indigo that was supposed to be his inheritance.

Massa Dunmore was a man to be feared. Which he kept sayin' to Micah over and over. *Tough as any soul in Albemarle County—even th'entire state of Virginia.* He said. Over and over. Especially after he took a swig from that flask.

He stood five foot eight or so. Two inches less than Micah right now. And Micah with one last bit of growin' still to come. Or so his Daddy used to say. But Dunmore was powerfully built, with thick arms and shoulders. Wide in the hips and chest. Unlike Micah. And Dunmore had meaty fists and a scowl fixed on his face, too. The kind that'd make few men want to mess with him even if it was Dunmore that started it.

They pulled into the train station in Charleston and the bustle of it all was unlike anything Micah had ever seen. For a moment or two, he stopped thinking about his mother and sister back home. Or his father on his own way to Mississipp'. Just stood there mesmerized by all that he saw before him. Then Dunmore got angry at the train attendant. Began yanking on the chains that bound Micah's wrists.

Now dis here is my investment—an' I ain't gonna risk him jumpin' off when the train slows down. Dunmore shouted at the man, standing a little straighter and pausin' for a second when he said the word *investment.*

Sir, the rules say he hasta ride in the livestock car with th'other slaves. The attendant said, looking like he didn't want to get Dunmore any more upset than he already was. *We have leg irons installed there, so there's no need to worry.* He added, sweet as pie.

Well I wanna look at whachu got set up, 'fore I let you take 'im. Dunmore growled.

And they walked to the rear cars. Dunmore jabbering to the attendant about how he had outbid a fancy slave-dealer from Charleston. How he spent seven hundred dollars on Micah.

That's a lot for a field hand. The attendant said. And Micah shot the man a dirty look at the back of his head.

Well I ain't gonna USE him as a field hand. Dunmore snapped. *This boy got special skills he learnt from his father. This boy gonna be my carpenter's apprentice and he's gonna make me a lotta money.*

You a carpenter? The attendant asked.

'At's right. Dunmore responded, glaring at the attendant as if the question was meant as an insult. *What of it?*

My Pa was a carpenter. He answered. *Tried to make me one, but I wadn't any good at it, so I joined the railroad instead.*

And Dunmore smiled. Nodded his head.

Well, it takes a certain kinda man t'be a carpenter. He said. And took the metal flask from his inside pocket. *You wanna nip?*

The attendant looked behind them up the length of the platform and turned back to Dunmore.

Don't mind if I do.

He took a long swig from it and handed it back to Dunmore. Who took a swig too.

You know, Mister . . .

Dunmore.

You know Mr. Dunmore, between yer two second-class passenger tickets, you could cash 'em in an' get one first-class cabin for just a half dollar more.

But then I'd still hafta pay cargo charges for 'im. Dunmore replied, nodding toward Micah.

Well, see—I'm th'attendant in the first-class cars. Cain't take him up there, 'course, but I could probably sneak you both into one of the compartments once we get rollin'. This way you can watch'm the whole time.

An' jus' what'll that cost me?

Well . . . you got any more of that there rum? The attendant asked.

Dunmore opened his jacket and revealed another flask just as large as the first.

Been doin' this same Charleston-to-Richmond run an' back for three years now. The attendant said. *It gets t'needin' a little somethin' t'break up the boredom, ya know? 'Course, if they ever found a flask or bottle on me I'd lose my job, but . . .*

Door'll be open. Dunmore said. *Plenny more where this came from.*

Throughout the rest of that afternoon, and on late into the night, Micah got to hear Dunmore's story told all the way through. Twice, since Dunmore would say it all over again to the attendant when he slipped in to drink some of the rum. Seemed that Dunmore could sum up all his problems on this earth in the form of just one person. His older brother. Seemed their father had given all his forty-five acres and thirteen slaves to the older of his two sons.

Goddamn pre-mo-gen-ee-tore's what they call THAT. He scowled.

So Dunmore was left with two thousand dollars to begin his life. While his older brother was given everything else. Didn't help matters that his brother expanded the plantation. Got lucky enough to start growing cotton right around the time the prices for it began steadily rising. While Dunmore moved north to Virginia. Bought a few acres of land. Only didn't make it as a farmer 'cause *the bank, the sheriff, and the goddamn weather was all conspirin' against him.* Had to sell most everything but the house he built for himself. And that was when he began doing carpentry work all the time. All around Charlottesville. Built a steady income. Figured he was as good a carpenter as any man he'd come across.

Then his brother died of pneumonia. And Dunmore didn't bother going to the funeral. But he was sure to be there when his brother's will got read. Sure enough, bastard passed everything down to his wife. Holdin' it all in trust 'til his own son reached the age of twenty-one. All Dunmore got out of it was a thousand dollars. When his goddamn brother was worth fifty sixty times that much. And just to see how much that bastard had cheated him out of, Dunmore went to the auction at *Les Roseraies.*

A goddamn stupid name for a place. He said. Angry at Micah, like it was him, somehow, who came up with the name for the place he got born.

But his brother's place was almost as big as *Les Roseraies.* So Dunmore stuck around, like he wanted to feed that anger. Watching all that money get raked in at the auction. Hating his brother more with every new sale. 'Til he saw an old man get sold for eleven hundred dollars. A ridiculous amount for a man *half* his age. But then he started hearin' some of the men in the crowd talk about the old man. Sayin' he practically ran the place. Sayin' they ain't never seen even a *white* man who got his kind of skills when it comes to runnin' the levees. Buildin' them, even. Any kinda carpentry.

That was his Daddy. Dunmore said to the attendant between slugs from the flask. *An' I figger he musta taught th'boy plenny. Ain't dat right?*

Micah decided he didn't want to speak any words to this man when a simple nod would do. Which was what he gave him. But then Dunmore, with no hesitation or sign of exertion, flicked the back of his right hand hard across Micah's face. Just like he was swattin' a fly. Only Micah felt his cheek burn instantly. And his eye began to tear up from the force of the blow.

When I ask you som'nin you better ansa me. He muttered angrily.

Yessuh. Micah replied.

And the attendant laughed. Took another swig. Then stepped out of the compartment.

An' don' go thinkin' you gonna get my Daddy's name neitha. He said when the attendant was gone. *My no-'count brother done that. He gone an' give 'em all my Daddy's las' name. So now they's a whole buncha black-as-night niggas wit' the name Dunmore. Well, ain' gonna be one more. You gonna stay just what you was when you was listed in the property back 'ere. You jus' 'Micah, a slave.' Jus' like 'ey say on 'at property list.*

And Micah didn't say anything at first. Then thought better of it.

Yessuh.

CHARLOTTESVILLE, VIRGINIA
OCTOBER 19, 1853

Micah had only ever heard about South Carolina and Louisiana before. He wasn't sure if the long train ride had taken them any closer to Louisiana. Or Mississipp', where his Daddy was headed. But he knew that they couldn't be anywhere near Charleston. Not after a full day ridin' that train.

His Daddy had told him that they'd see each other again someday. But Micah couldn't find that kind of hope within him. Even from the first moment his Daddy said it. For the first time in his life, not believing his Daddy. Not believing that the Lawd was watchin' over them the way Daddy always said. And that got him to thinking that maybe he was less like his Daddy than he'd always thought. And maybe more like Dunmore. Angry. Disbelievin'. Like the folks Momma said th'Devil got holda and never let go. So maybe that's why God had sent him off to be with Dunmore. 'Cause they was two of a kind.

Charlottesville was much smaller than Charleston or Richmond had been. Still, it seemed a wild and grand place compared to *Les Roseraies.* And Dunmore reveled in his return as they walked from the train station. Down along a few major streets. Micah still chained at the wrists. Dunmore leading him by the elbow like he was showing off a prized sow. He didn't speak to many people. Only nodded sternly at a few as they passed. As if to say, that's right. This one's mine. 'Til they came upon a saloon and Dunmore unlocked one of Micah's wrist irons. Fixed it to the hitchin' post out front. Went inside and announced that he was buying a round for all his friends. To celebrate his new investment.

And for the next two hours or so, Micah sat along the storefront curb. His left arm stretched out above him, chained to the hitchin' post. While every so often Dunmore brought men to look him over. Made Micah stand up and turn around every time. And Dunmore would tell the man all about the plans he had. And how he was a man of property now. Until finally, Dunmore walked out by himself with a full bottle in his hand. Went into the butcher's shop across the street. Came out of there with a large, newspaper-wrapped packet. And they walked the rest of the way through the town. Out to an area with several small farms all connected to one another. A mile or more outside the busiest part of town. When they came upon Dunmore's single-story house. Not much bigger than the slave cabins back at *Les Roseraies.* Though this one had four glass windows and a chimney.

You know how t'cook? Dunmore asked.

Nosuh, Micah said.

Well 'at'll be the first thing I teacha. Dunmore said. *An' 'at'll be the last time I do any cookin' 'round here.*

Right around the time the sun was dropping down over the hills, Micah could hear the sound of barking dogs off in the distance. He was washing the two pans Dunmore had used to cook steak and pan bread. While Dunmore sat on the porch with a jug he had taken from inside. And as the dogs got closer, Micah looked out through a window. Saw two men approaching. Each of them holding leather ropes attached to two dogs apiece. And Dunmore stood up now.

Well s'about time you boys got 'ere. He shouted above the barking. *I thought maybe ya didn' get ma message.*

Oh, we heard all right. Heard you done a little shoppin' down in Carolina. One of the men said. And they all laughed.

My bastard of a brother lef' me a thousand dollars. Y'believe dat? He musta been worth sixty sevenny thousand, an' he leaves me a thousan'.

A thousand's still a nice bit o' change. The other man said.

Not compared to sevenny thousan', it ain't, Tom. Dunmore answered.

No, not compared to sevenny thousand.

But I'm gonna turn 'at thousand into a lot more'n 'at. Dunmore said. *Micah! Get out here!*

Micah placed down the rag he was using to scrub the pans and walked out onto the porch. Made sure to say. *Yessuh?*

Take off that shirt and give it here. Dunmore ordered.

Micah quickly complied. Then Dunmore looked at him through squinted eyes. Like Micah had done something wrong again. He tossed the shirt to one of the men holding the dogs.

See these two gennlemen here? Dunmore asked.

Yessuh.

They Mr. Tom n' Albert Embry. The fines' slave-catchers in all Virginia. You ever run off, boy?

Micah began to shake his head but then remembered better. *Nosuh.* He replied.

Well looky here what'll happen when you even thinka tryin' t'run off from dis here place.

The man holding Micah's shirt placed it by the dogs' noses. And immediately they began to lurch at Micah. While the men held the ropes loose enough so the dogs could almost bite him. And Micah stepped back toward the door. So the men let go some more of the ropes. Until Micah was pinned in by the dogs. Barking. Lunging at him.

See how fas' dey get that scent, boy? One of the men shouted over the barking. *They'd be on toppa ya 'fore ya got half a mile away!*

An' ya know what we do when we catches ya?! The other man said.

He ain't never got the whip, boys. Dunmore said. *Maybe we better give'm a little taste of it so he don' go gettin' no ideas 'bout goin' nowhere.*

The Embrys pulled the dogs back. Tied them to trees maybe twenty feet away. And Dunmore pulled Micah down off the porch, pressed him against one of the posts that supported the roof. While one of the Embrys walked over with a rope, pulled Micah's arms around that post so he was huggin' it. Tied Micah's arms together at the elbows, so he couldn't move at all. And the other one unraveled the whip that was wrapped around one shoulder.

Micah had seen one of the field hands whipped at *Les Roseraies* when he tried to run away. The man was whipped forty times in front of all the other slaves. Massa Leroux left just before the overseer performed the punishment. Once he'd spoken to the slaves about how running off was a poor way to repay his kind treatment of them. But Dunmore didn't seem like the type to shy away from any punishment. And before Micah could form the words in his head, wantin' to tell his new Massa he'd never do such a thing, he heard the whip being wound up by one of the Embrys. Then a loud hiss and the crack of it against his bare back. Like fire streaked across his skin from rib to rib. Then winding up again, and another. And another. And another. The pain of each of them worse than the one before it. Opening the previous wounds all the more, and making their own mark, too.

Feel that, boy? Whichever Embry wasn't doing the whipping said. Didn't wait for a response from Micah, who was tryin' to catch his breath. *Now mos' folks pay us two hunnerd dollars to chase down one o' dere runaways. But Mr. Dunmore here, seein' how he's a good fren' an' all, why we do it for almos' nothin' at all. We do it wit' pleasure. You unnerstan'?*

Yessuh. Micah said quickly. Hoping there'd be no more demonstrations. But he heard the whip warm up and lash across his back again. And then again.

That's six. Dunmore said, moving close up to Micah now. *Imagine what it'll be like when it's sixty—if'n you ever even THINK a'runnin' anywhere. You unnerstan'?*

Yessuh . . . Yessuh.

You my inheritance, boy. He said. *An' I'll chase you down all th'way t'Africa if I hafta.*

Then the other Embry came and untied the knot. Handed him back his shirt as Dunmore told him to get inside and finish his work. Sleep on the kitchen floor when it was done. And Micah could feel the trickles of blood stick to his shirt soon as he put it back on. 'Til it was pressed right against the wounds. Clinging to his back as the blood started to dry.

When he was done with his work, he glanced outside to see the Embrys and Dunmore seated on the porch. Passing the jug back and forth. Slowly, he slid his shirt over his shoulders. Felt the wounds open up again as he pulled it away from his skin. Then cupped his hands and dipped them into the water he'd just used to do the washin'. Carried them carefully up past his left shoulder. Turned them over and let the water drip down his back. Stinging all the way down. But then some relief. Did the same over the other shoulder. Then wiped up what had spilled on the floor.

Dunmore had made him arrange some hay in the corner when the cookin' was done. Told him that was his bed. And now Micah lay down on it. Belly first. Exhausted. The bits of straw like little pins against the bare skin of his chest. So he pushed himself up to his knees, placed his shirt down over it. And lay back down. Settling his left cheek, the one Dunmore hadn't hit, against his arms. It had been years since he'd cried. And it felt like it would almost be a relief to him now. But he refused to allow it. 'Cause that'd be a victory for Dunmore. Like he was broken.

And no.

There'd be none of that weakness. Just cold, unfeeling, survival. Through whatever might come. Like the mule he now was. And nothing more.

4 Ain't I a Woman

MARY WILKENS
RANDOLPH COUNTY, NORTH CAROLINA
SEPTEMBER 7, 1853

Gertie steps in th'crick first an smiles like it's th'most natural place t'be in the whole world, middle of the night or not. She ain't so good at convincin you the way she usedta do wit' things you was scareda at first. An maybe it'd be enough to keep you right there on the side of that crick shakin yo' head like you was still a little girl didn't wanna go an work in the fields if'n Gertie wasn't comin wit' you. But there's somethin bout the way she smilin, like she almost never do anymore, an it's funny too that she gotta be th'one tryin to get you to come inta th'water, when she's usually tellin you to get *outta* th'crick behind yo' cabin. An 'tween her smilin an how silly it all seem right then, it's like you almost forget th'hurt in yo' belly an everything what happened in the last two days. Almost.

So you take off yo' shoes an step on inta Deep River for the first time eva. It's colder than that crick behind the cabins you always playin in 'til Gertie comes t'fetch ya. But that cold is just the thing t'wash off th'hot you both been feelin from walkin all this way, farther away from you an Gertie's cabin than you ever been in yo' life.

Dat's it Chil', you doin good, Gertie says. Less keep movin now. Ain' gonna let you fall.

An she reaches out her hand to you, an the two of you start takin little steps at first, then stretchin 'em out. You can feel th'water runnin faster when you get farther away from the edge, an you wonderin why you goin backwards again, back underneath that bridge over Deep River you jus' crossed not more'n five minutes ago. It's all you can do not t'ask Gertie why you goin this way, but she told you when you started out that you wasn't allowed t'do no talkin a'tall 'til she said it was okay, an she whispered it wit' such a scoldin look that the scare's still followin you round.

When the river starts gettin a little higher, almost up to yo' sore belly now, Gertie wraps her good arm all th'way inside of yo's, an you wanna tell her it's okay, that you so usedta walkin in that crick backa the cabin that you ain't gonna fall. But then it's Gertie that slips a little, an she squeezin yo' arm tighter t'keep her standin up, an you start t'think that maybe it's you helpin Gertie up Deep River, an not th'other way round. Ain't but a few more steps 'fore Gertie's breathin gets almost as loud as the sound of the river runnin past, an you wonder why you can't talk still, just a whisper anyhow, since it'd be quieter than Gertie's breathin.

Hold on . . . Chil' . . . she whispers, an stops walkin altogetha.

You okay Ger– you start t'ask 'fore she's shushin you wit' whatever breath she got t'use.

So you watch her breathin for a while 'til it gets a little softer, like it ain't hurtin her each time she take in an let out some air. An then you start feelin the coolness of that water on yo' fingertips from th'arm Gertie ain't holdin onto, an it's like you back in the crick behin' yo' cabin almost. Driftin, almost sleepy, like you get sometimes playin in that crick, an you start noticin how beautiful this place is, wit' th'moonlight spillin through th'trees an across th'river like little bitsa magic. An you watchin yo' spread-out fingers cuttin little streams on toppa th'river, watchin the moonbeams doin they dance, an you get to thinkin that maybe this is what it'll be like for you an Gertie now. Just a little cabin near a stream somewhere, an th'two of you wit' nothin t'do but tend to th'field an maybe some chickens an a garden an lotsa time t'spend standin in a river just like this. An you smile just thinkin of it, lettin th'cool water pass over you like it's washin away th'last day an more. An it's only th'good dreams now, th'ones wit' you an Gertie an th'cabin 'longside a stream, an th'field, an th'garden, an maybe some chickens . . .

Dis ain' far enough, I knows it, Gertie says, breakin the quiet an shakin her head. We ain' no more'n two hunnerd yards pas' dat ol' bridge. Dey gonna bring 'em dogs back round dis far when dey cain't find us.

She's still breathin hard, but you walk on for a few more steps, slower'n before, almost restin after every new one. It ain't long 'til Gertie's breathin loud an heavy again, an she stops cold.

Cain't go . . . no fartha . . . in dis river, she says, an nods over to th'shore. When you both on dry land again, Gertie puts her hands on her knees an breathes in an out almos' like a dog pantin, quick as it is. An you sit on th'ground to take a pebble from th'river outta yo' shoe, 'til Gertie tells you t'get up right off in a sort of yellin, outta-breath whisper.

Don't give 'em dogs . . . nothin more to . . . smell ya wit' . . . , Gertie says, an you stand up an take off yo' shoe balancin on one foot, just to get at that pebble.

'Fore long you're off again, walkin much slower'n before, but faster'n you had in th'river. It goes on like that for hours 'til th'first signs of mornin begin lightin up th'tippy topsa th'Caraway Mountains, an for th'first time you can see how close you are to 'em now. They seem so much bigger'n they do from th'cabin, an you could stand an watch th'sun climb over Deep River 'til them mountains get *all* lit up. But Gertie won't have none of that.

Dey's Hick'ry Crick over dere, she says, pointin across Deep River at a smaller stream runnin into it from th'other side. Leas' ways I hope dat's it, she says. 'At mean we gotta cross over agin jus' up ahead.

An this time it's *you* walkin into th'river first, reachin *yo'* hand out t'Gertie. She smiles a little an says, guess yo' belly feelin better, as she locks her good arm inside yo's an steps carefully into th'water again. An it do feel better from th'not thinkin on it so much, thinkin bout th'river an the mountains and dancin moonbeams an such. Th'current's faster'n before but not so deep, runnin just above yo' knees when you right in the middle of it. Still, Gertie's breath starts gettin loud again, an she stops when you still a ways from th'other shore.

Come on Gertie, you say, figurin it's okay to whisper when the river and Gertie's breathin makin all this noise anyhow. Put yo' hand over my shoulder, you say, like you the one takin the lead now.

An Gertie doesn't say nothin, just smiles a little, an slips her good arm aroun' yo' shoulders, leanin on you for those last few steps. When you reach th'other shore, this time it's Gertie floppin to th'ground soon as you get there. She lays flat on her back, gaspin for breath wit' one arm across her chest, an you figure it's okay for you to at least sit down, dogs or not.

You okay, Gertie? you ask, an she don't say nothin, just breathes out wit' a *mmmmm* that's 'sposed to say she's okay. You don't say nothin for a while after that, lettin Gertie catch up to her breath.

What we do now? you finally say when Gertie's sittin up.

Bout haf mile up yonner dey's a spot . . . 'tween two great big rocks . . . where we kin res' some. Maybe sleep a momen', too, Gertie says 'tween breaths.

An then you up again an walkin slower'n ever as th'sun keeps climbin in th'mornin sky. There don't appear to be a cloud anywhere to be seen, an you thinkin bout what a beautiful day it's gonna be, 'til Gertie says that it ain't no good since some rain'd do real nice right bout now. You start t'ask her why, but she shushes you right off, tellin you folks gonna be bout now that th'sun come up.

You find th'rocks just 'bout where Gertie said they'd be, an she looks off in every direction 'fore you step inside. The ground's cold an damp, but Gertie sits down an stretches her arms out to you. So you sit right beside her, just like you did when you was littler.

How you know bout dis place Gertie? you whisper, figurin you safe from folks now in these rocks. How you know how t'come all dis way?

You jus' gots . . . t'listen t'folks, she says wit' a laugh while she's breathin. We ain' th'firs' ones . . . come dis way. Now . . . close yo' eyes, Chil'.

You can feel th'thumpin of Gertie's heart as you lay yo' head on her chest, but you close yo' eyes anyway, lettin sleep finally catch up to you, hopin' yo' dreams be bout th'days what'll be comin' for you an Gertie, an not the days that passed . . . least not th'last two days, anyhow.

RALEIGH, NORTH CAROLINA
SEPTEMBER 9, 1853

When Gertie used to tell you bout yo' Momma an Daddy, she'd always say they was parta th'stitchin you was makin every day, whether you know'd it or not. She'd say they was th'mos' important part, next to th'Lawd Himse'f who was doin th'stitchin in th'first place. An even though you couldn't rememba yo' Momma an Daddy none, Gertie'd tell you they was there all th'same. Big bitsa thread that'd only show up when you was old enough to unnerstan' these kindsa things fo' yo'se'f.

You knew yo' Momma had hair that was sorta straight an *dark as a midnight sky when th'moon was sleepin,* like Gertie said, an that yo' Daddy was *a determined man what hardly never smiled, but when he did, it was as fetchin as a baby's laugh.* You knew that Gertie looked after yo' Momma sorta like a big sister'd look after a youngin, an when Momma an Daddy jump th'broom, it was Gertie stood beside Momma. Then, when Momma an Daddy got sold off 'cause Th'Massa lost alotta money buyin' lan in a place called Texas, Th'Massa was kind enough t'let Gertie look after you, th'way yo' Momma asked. An that's why you spent all those years wit' Gertie, doin almost all yo' growin up wit' her.

These are th'kindsa things you'd think on when you started workin in th'fields wit' th'resta th'hands. It'd make them long days seem much shorter, rememberin all these things bout th'three of them, yo' Momma an Daddy an Gertie together, back before you was even born. Big bitsa thread in yo' stitchin, what you'd someday come t'unnerstan.

But sittin here this mornin, it's all you can do t'keep

those kindsa thoughts away, what wit' how th'bad memories from th'last few days is all round you, cuttin those threads to pieces, it seem. They won't go away, an sleep won't turn them into dreams so you at least can wake up an think for a moment that that's all they was. They just run through yo' mind over an over, th'overseer Mista Grant doin what he done, then Gertie an you runnin off so you wouldn' get sold off 'steada Massa Wilkens havin t'send Mista Grant on his way like Th'Misses wanted him to. An there's Gertie slumpin over in Deep River, an gaspin for air when you fin'ly made it 'cross onto dry lan. An then there's them dogs, th'sounda them, a *sound* somehow bein a thread in yo' stitchin, tearin up them other threads an leavin 'em all a'tangled. Then 'fore you know it, you flopped on th'backa one of th'men's horses, wit' th'saddle pressin on yo' sore belly. An there's Gertie fallin over an over as th'men drag her behind anotha horse, an then her sideways, too, on th'ground though, holdin up her good arm an sayin, *Take me Lawd, Take me Lawd, Take me Lawd* . . . three times jus' like that 'fore th'Lawd seen fit t'take her home . . . an away from you.

Th'look on Massa Wilkens's face when the men brung you back home, an the Misses shakin her head when th'men say Gertie's dead an wasn't nothin they could do bout it . . . they all partsa that stitchin somehow since they fillin up yo' mem'ries like they ain't never goin away. Th'firs' time you saw a train turned out to be th'firs' time you got to ride in one. Only there's nothin happy bout that bitta thread, th'way they chained you to th'wall like a calf, sittin there wit' a few other colored folks chained up too, angry or scared or sad looks on all they faces. An all those threads so big in yo' mind now that it's like you can't see past them to th'ones from before, th'good ones. An sleep don't come a'tall that first night away from Gertie.

Next mornin you unhooked from th'traincar an brought round backa th'buildin an chained to a long row of slaves, th'ones from th'train an others you never seen before. They's maybe twenny of you, maybe mo', all hooked to one great big chain connected to metal spikes in th'ground, wit' th'men an boys startin roun' one side an you near th'other end wit' th'women an girls. There's a slave girl who looks not much older'n you comin round tellin th'women an girls to strip off all they clothes an hand 'em to her. She don' look like she too happy bout th'job she gotta do, but she do it all th'same, an when one of th'women won' strip down like she told to, a white man walks up to her an rips off her dress wit' one great pull. An you do what you told to, straight off then, so he won' come up to you an do th'same.

Th'men an boys are strippin down on th'other side, only it's a man collectin they clothes, an then two white men comin round past 'em, one of 'em carryin a bucket wit' water an th'other dippin a sponge into it an splashin it over all th'slaves 'cept th'ones what collected they clothes. You tryin to cover yo'sef up wit' yo' hands an arms, shamed an all, thinkin how Gertie mus' be shamed up in th'Ever Afta, t'see you like this. But then you see that ain't nobody lookin at you, wit' th'resta the slaves all just starin straight at th'ground, an th'white men an th'two slaves collectin th'clothes jus' goin bout they business. An you figure that they all as shamed as you is, th'slaves leastways, an it don't make no point lookin at someone else's shame when you just as shamed too. So you stare at th'ground like th'resta them.

Th'white men wit' th'bucket an sponge come up to you an it ain't no more than two seconds for 'em to splash some water on you wit'out even noticin you there practically. You been so caught up watchin th'ground, an then th'men wit' th'bucket an sponge, that you never even notice th'other white men what follow right behind 'em. It ain't long 'fore one of them steps in fronta you an puts his hands on yo' neck, flippin yo' chin up wit' his thumbs. He spreads yo' eyes wide open an looks at 'em for a moment, then forces open yo' mouth an looks at yo' teeth some. Then he's on to th'next one, an you watch him go down th'line. But then, before a minute's up, here come two more men wit' anotha bucket, only this one's filled wit' lard, an one man holds it while th'other scoops out a hanful an smears it up an down th'lengtha yo' body wit' both his bare hands. He runs th'lard over yo' arms an legs, an you can't help but thinka Mista Grant an what he done, an how it feels too much like th'same thing. Only this man don't seem no more interested in what he's doin than if he was dressin a pig for market, an he ain't but a few seconds 'fore he wipes a little on yo' face an cross yo' lips, then opens yo' mouth an wipes some over th'fronta yo' teeth, an he's done an on to th'next one. An you left to cover up an stare at th'ground again. Shamed, an greasy from animal fat, makin Gertie cry an yell up in th'Ever Afta fo' sho' if she gotta see you like this.

Th'slave girl from before comes down th'line of women, handin you back yo' dresses, 'cept she skips th'one what had hers torn from her. Th'man what tore her dress from her in th'firs' place walks up wit' a long sack, cuts a few holes in it, an throws it at her, laughin. You got yo's on a few seconds after the girl hands it to you, time enough to look over at th'woman strugglin to get her arms an head through th'sack, an th'man what tore her dress from her laughs on an on an on.

An then you stand in that hot mornin sun 'til th'noise out fronta th'buildin increases some, an you led by that one long chain out to where a crowd is gatherin. They's a finely dressed man there shoutin out to th'crowd an smilin at all you slaves as you stretched out in one long line behind where he's standin. He points out some of th'strongest men, an yells to th'crowd bout them, then gets a look altogether different when the women come past, 'specially th'prettiest ones. When you walk past him, his eyes go wide, an he runs th'backa his fingers 'cross yo' cheek just like th'Misses did two days before, when Gertie told her bout what Mista Grant done to ya. Only th'way that well-dressed man runs his fingers over you don't make you feel nothin' like comf'table, th'way it did when th'Misses done it.

You stand all in a line, an people from th'crowd come up an walk slowly past all of you, starin at you up an down, sometimes walkin behind you all, touchin you all, observin you like you's a buncha cattle. Most of 'em walkin past are men, but they's a few women who look only at th'women slaves, askin if you all know how to cook or sew an if you ever been a Mammy or had chillen of you own. When two ladies ask you bout cookin an sewin, you say, *No'm,* lyin only partly cause you ain't never got th'chance to learn all Gertie was gonna teach you, an it's only a little lie cause you ain't sure if what you know is enough for what these fine white ladies is lookin fo'.

When they all pass, th'finely dressed man starts shoutin out at th'crowd an th'slaves are led off t'one side. One of th'men wit' th'buckets before comes up an unchains one of th'biggest of th'men slaves, while another man stands wit' a gun behind him. They bring him to th'wooden stand an th'finely dressed man points at him up an down, an has th'white men turn him round an slaps him on th'back twice before pointin at th'crowd an shoutin some more. Only this time, some of th'men from th'crowd shout back at him, an th'finely dressed man talks so fast that you can't understand any of it. An as he gets more excited, th'men in th'crowd shout back at him louder still, 'til one man shouts *nine hundred,* an th'finely dressed man repeats it a few times before slammin his palm down on toppa th'wood stand, an th'crowd cheers some. An that slave's led off an another gets brought in, an on an on it goes like that.

They's only a few slaves left by th'time you get brung out, an th'crowd's just halfa what it was at th'start. By now that lard th'man spread all over you an yo' own sweat from th'hot sun is all mixin togetha into a great flood, an you know Gertie, if she was livin still, would be as shamed to see you as you are t'be standin there. So you stand alone, lookin down at th'ground 'neath yo' bare feet, 'til th'finely dressed man lifts up yo' chin wit' his white-gloved hand an pulls yo' face toward him. He smiles at you wit' teeth th'same brown an yellow as Mista Grant's, an you scared a'him straight off. But it's like there's nothin in you to cry . . . even though you want to like never b'fo' . . . no water to make th'tears or breath to let out in little gasps, an you feel just how all alone you are, no Gertie ever comin back, no Momma an Daddy comin from that place called Texas, no one 'cept th'finely dressed man wit' th'brown an yellow teeth in a smile what makes you thinka Mista Grant.

He talks to th'crowd steada shoutin like he done in th'beginnin, an th'crowd don't have much t'say back to him. So he lifts yo' head again an smiles as he sticks th'nail of his thumb in th'corner of yo' mouth an makes you half-smile, too. But soon as he lets go, yo'smile goes away again, an it starts t'sound like he's growin angry wit' th'crowd, small as it is, an you sure it's cause of you. Mosta th'people are just millin about or walkin right past, headin one way or th'other down th'street, lookin at th'shop windows 'cross th'way more'n they lookin at you an th'finely dressed man. He got his finger back in yo' mouth, pullin at th'side of it, forcin a bigger half-smile now, an th'crowd still not sayin much to him.

By one of th'shops 'cross th'street you see a girl a little younger'n you by a few years. She's wearin a beautiful green an yellow dress an yellow gloves wit' hair ribbons t'match, an she's starin right at you, even though her Momma's holdin her hand an facin th'store window. This girl got herself turned all th'way round to face you an th'finely dressed man, an you can't help but wonder how it is that this girl's there holdin her Momma's hand an wearin a beautiful dress wit' gloves an matchin ribbons, covered by her little green an yellow parasol, while you left to stand there in th'sun wit' th'finely dressed man stickin his finger in yo' mouth. It's like God forgot all about you, like it ain't what Gertie always said bout how God's watchin out for you, not at all it seems, an that it don't matter if you offer yo' sufferin up, th'way Gertie always said t'do. 'Cause God ain't lis'nin.

An you start to think that maybe it's 'cause of th'bad things you done . . .'cause of th'business wit' Mista Grant an th'blood what poured outta you 'tween yo' legs an onta th'stable floor makin a mess there in th'hay . . . an sleepin too late when you an Gertie run off, when you know'd Gertie was dead tired, an wasn' like to wake up on her own . . . an how you still slept even afta Gertie waked up, lettin th'dogs catch up wit' you, gettin Gertie killed like that. You get to starin at th'girl cross th'street, sure she must be practic'ly an angel on earth th'way God's smilin on her so. An then, like it's th'most naturalest thing in th'world, that little girl smiles at you an lifts her free hand up, wavin to you wit' her fingers openin an closin on her palm over an over, th'way you usedta wave when you was littler. An you start to feel like maybe they's one person here for you, like maybe God sent this angel just for you, just to smile an wave at you when you needed it more'n ever befo'.

You feel yo' mouth start t'spread open, only this time it's not th'finely dressed man wit' his finger pullin at yo' cheek, but it's *you* doin it on yo' own, smilin back at th'little girl 'cross th'way, God's angel wit' th'beautiful green an yellow dress. An then th'girl starts to tuggin at her Momma's arm, an talkin to her, an pointin 'cross at you, an then she's not wavin anymore, just pointin an cryin a little. You start to worryin that maybe you done somethin wrong again, that maybe you shouldn'ta smiled at th'girl an now it's more trouble for you. An then there's a man talkin wit' th'girl an her Momma, the three of'm lookin over at you an th'man talkin to the little girl, brushin at her cheeks like he's wipin away her tears. 'Fore long he's walkin cross th'street right up toward th'finely dressed man. You sure it's more trouble 'til th'man from 'cross th'street calls out to th'finely dressed man, an it's like he ain't angry no more. He says th'same number to the crowd, looks round for a moment, an slams his hand down on th'wood stand.

Th'girl in th'pretty dress is smilin an jumpin up an down a little, an when you led away to th'table 'longside th'platform, you still don't know if it's trouble you in or maybe, maybe . . . if God's angel is happy like that . . . maybe th'nightmare's over for now. An maybe this'll be th'starta some bitsa thread you happy to see get fixed into that stichin of yo's. Like Gertie always said.

RICHMOND, VIRGINIA
MARCH 21, 1854

Miss Justinia Kittredge's what that little angel's name turned out to be. She was the daughter of Mista an' Misses Kittredge that lived way up in Richmond, Virginia, a full day's trainride from Raleigh. Miss Justinia told Mary 'bout how they was just down in Raleigh visitin' her Momma's brother, an' how they was supposed to leave two days 'fore the auction, but then her Uncle fell from his horse an' broke his arm, an' her Momma wouldn't leave him right off like that. So there they was, in town when they was supposed to be back home in Richmond, an' when Miss Justinia spotted Mary, she just knew straight off that she wanted her Daddy to buy her so she could have someone to play with. When Mary heard all this, she never said it out loud, but she started thinkin' that maybe God was watchin' out for her a little after all, goin' to that trouble of havin' Miss Justinia's Uncle fall off his horse jus' so they could be together.

But it didn't take long to understand that just 'cause Miss Justinia was like God's angel that day in Raleigh, didn't mean she was any kinda angel the resta the time. She was going on ten, almost four years younger'n Mary, and she still cried at least once a day, usually when she didn't get things her way. She took to Mary like they been best friends since they was born, an' 'fore long if Mary'd say she liked a thing, well then Miss Justinia liked it, an' if Mary'd say she don't like a thing, well then Miss Justinia don't neither. 'Course, that made Mista an' Misses Kittredge mighty happy to have Mary around, the way Miss Justinia start actin' more an' more like Mary an' not wantin' everything she sees an' not cryin' so much anymore. Mary even got her own little room right inside the Kittredges' house, downstairs by the kitchen. It was 'bout half the size of her an' Gertie's cabin back in Carolina, but it was all hers, just for sleepin' an' gettin' dressed an' such.

Just about the only job Mary had each day was to play with Miss Justinia. Sure, she had some small chores like sweepin' an' doin' some mendin' the way Gertie taught her, but anytime Miss Justinia wanted to play, well then that work just got to wait. The Kittredges had nine other slaves, an' none of 'em took too kindly to the way Mary got treated, what with havin' her own room an' not doin' hardly any other work. But the Kittredges was good to all their slaves so none of 'em had much to complain about 'cept that they didn't have as much as Mary got. Only one of the slaves seem to decide straight out that she don't like Mary, an' that was Cora. Cora was kinda like Miss Justinia's Mammy, only with how much time Mary an' Misses Kittredge spent with Miss Justinia, there wasn't too much for Cora to do 'cept cleanin' the room an' lookin' after her clothes. An' Cora didn't take to that 'rangement. She said that *when they's too much sittin' still time, 'at's when the Devil catches up to ya.* An' considerin' it was almos' the exact kinda thing Gertie'd say, Mary couldn't hate Cora all the way through, seein' how she missed Gertie still. But most days Mary'd get her sweepin' an' mendin' done straight off, 'fore Miss Justinia finish up her breakfast an' got to wantin' to play. Then they'd go off an' play with all her dolls some, or maybe move furniture around in the great big dollhouse she got for Christmas.

The Kittredges owned one of the finest stores in all of Richmond. Mista Kittredge liked to talk 'bout how he bought it when it was just a small general store that wasn't sellin' much more than flour an' chewin' tobacco to the hayseeds, an' how now they sold all kindsa goods an' how the store took up near half the block. Misses Kittredge'd even asked him to open up a dress shop over by the side of it, an' then the dress shop grew bigger an' bigger 'til they had to build an extension on it 'an put in a wall separatin' it from the rest of the store. Seemed that even though Mista Kittredge said his part of the store wasn't just sellin' flour an' tobacco to the hayseeds no more, Misses Kittredge still felt like the fine ladies they was tryin' to bring into the dress shop didn't want to see the other folks shoppin' there for common things, hayseeds or not.

Mary'd learned to sew from Gertie, so after a few months with the Kittredges, she wasn't doin' any more sweepin'. 'Stead, whenever she wasn't playin' with Miss Justinia, she was workin' in the store, mendin' an' doin' some of the smaller jobs that come in. Cora got to do the sweepin' Mary used to, an' that just made her not like Mary even more, which was kind of surprisin' since it meant the Devil'd be less like to catch up to her. And Mary almos' told her that very thing, but thought the better of it 'fore the words came outta her mouth.

'Fore long, the ache in Mary's heart got to healin' some. She'd talk to Gertie every night when it was dark an' it was just her in her bed, an' Gertie'd sometimes answer her in her dreams. Sometimes Miss Justinia would come to Mary's room an' crawl into bed with her an' they'd talk 'bout Miss Juss's new dress or how they didn't much like Cora or how Miss Juss was gonna marry when she just sixteen an' Mary'd come live wit' her an' they'd travel 'round the world together. It was nice dreamin' out loud like that, an' Miss Juss an' Mary became more an' more like sisters as time went on . . . mostly from Miss Juss's feelin's tow'd Mary, but some from Mary's, too.

Much as she enjoyed most ever'thing 'bout her new life 'cept for missin' Gertie, there was one thing that made Mary happiest of all. Ev'ry Monday an' Wen'sday an' Thursday afternoon was set aside for Miss Justinia's lessons, an' even though

Mary liked playin' with Miss Juss, she always knew when it was a Monday or Wen'sday or a Thursday, an' couldn't wait for Cora to come into the room when it got 'round noontime. This one particular Thursday'd got off to a bad start since Cora heard Mary forget the *Miss* part when she called to Justinia. Miss Juss didn't even notice it, but Cora's eyes looked like they was 'bout ready to pop outta her head. She pulled Mary outside the room, sayin' she needed a hand with somethin', but all she really wanted to do was scold Mary.

Far as these white folks concern', you ain' no more'n a little pup, a kitten o' somethin' nice for Miss Justinia t'play wit', she told Mary. You go steppin' out yo' boun's like 'at an' dey like to sell you off wit'out no mo' thought'n it take to slap a pup 'cross his hine quarters.

The thought of being sold off made Mary cry a little, much as she tried not to in front of Cora, an' the rest of the mornin' wasn't much fun since Mary was quiet as a mouse just like she'd been when she first came here. Miss Justinia was left to do most of the talkin', an' when she asked Mary what was wrong, Mary just replied, Nothin' *Miss* Justinia, careful not to offend anyone.

'At's enough of th'play fo' now, Miss Justinia, Cora said in her usual mean way 'round noontime. You gots yo' lessons t'tend to. Miss Randall here now t'learn ya.

Miss Randall walked in an' all the upset from that mornin' blew right on out the window far as Mary was concerned, an' she smiled from ear to ear, same as always 'round noontime every Monday an Wen'sday an' Thursday. Mary'd heard Misses Kittredge complain sometimes 'bout Miss Randall's appearance. She wore her hair tucked back behind her an' tight to her head, an' she always had on her thick, square-rimmed glasses an' a dress that wasn't as fancy as Mary's even. Misses Kittredge was always noticin' such things an' said more than once how she thought Miss Randall might still find herself a husband, even with all that learnin' she done scarin' most of the men off, if only she'd do somethin 'bout her appearance. But Mary thought Miss Randall was 'bout as pretty as any lady she'd ever seen, what with the way she walked perfectly straight an' took small steps that made it look like her feet wasn't movin' at all but she was just glidin' 'cross the floor instead. But even better than that was the way Miss Randall spoke. Every word was said just the way she imagined it was 'sposed to be, like when whoever thunk up that particular word they decided this is how you say it, then over the years it got twisted an' turned 'round into all kindsa things. 'Cept when Miss Randall said it. An' she could go from English to far-off languages like French an' Greek an' Latin, like she lived in those places her whole life.

Bonjour, ma petite élève, she said to Miss Justinia when she walked into the room.

Bonjour, mad-em-o-sell, Justinia said back after she got done breathin' out through her flappin' lips an' rollin' her eyes so only Mary could see, which was her usual reaction whenever it was time for her studies.

Mary smiled an' curtseyed deeply, the way Miss Randall had taught Miss Juss, and Miss Randall nodded her head an' smiled.

Bonjour, Mary, she said.

Bonjour, Mademoiselle, Mary replied, an' couldn't help but laugh a little.

Mary walked to the chair in the corner an' picked up her stitchin' while Miss Randall an' Miss Juss said some more French about the weather and what day it was an' then set down to the lessons. Ever since Mary'd come here, this was the way it went, since Miss Justinia'd made such a fuss 'bout Mary bein' told to leave the room when Miss Randall came, that Misses Kittredge set Mary in the corner wit' some mendin' to do. She asked Miss Randall if she cared, an' Miss Randall said that it was okay, an' Miss Randall became 'bout the greatest person in the world in Mary's eyes, 'cept for Gertie of course, right that very moment. Seven months later Mary still worked in the corner, only now instead of mendin' hems an' such, she worked on what Misses Kittredge called embroidery just like Misses Wilkens done, only they'd always be just stitchin's.

Miss Randall'd only been comin' to learn Miss Justinia for a few months before Mary arrived. Cora said it wasn't 'til the Kittredges start makin' lotsa money that they start thinkin' 'bout learnin' a girl how to read an' speak French an' other such silly things. The good part of that for Mary was that Miss Juss wasn't much ahead of her when they started learnin' together, Mary sittin' in the corner pretendin' not to hear what Miss Randall was sayin', an' Miss Juss sittin' at the desk, strugglin' to sound out words Mary was picturin' in her head. Mary read everything she could, titles of books on the shelves in Mista Kittredge's library, names on the labels of cans in the store, an' the signs in the storefront windows. Just a week earlier she'd picked an old newspaper out of the trash an' hid it in her dress 'til she got back to her room. An' she'd pract'ly memorized it by now, readin' by the moonlight comin' through her window on the nights Miss Juss didn't come to sleep with her.

But it wasn't just readin' Mary'd learned by now. She was even better in math'matics, memorizin' something called the mult'plication tables in just two weeks, an' learnin' to do all kinds of 'rithmetic in her head. She liked 'rithmetic an' history an' liter'ture just fine, but she *adored* French. An' she adored most of all how she kept learnin' new words, like *adore,* that she didn't ever hear from Gertie or the hands in the field back in Carolina. Still, Mary'd become a little frustrated with Miss Juss when it came to the lessons, since she was holdin' them back, the way she struggled an' all. She'd try to help Miss Juss little bits at a time when she did lessons on her own, pretendin' not to know the thing herself but askin' her what it was Miss Randall said, knowin' all the time just what it was.

This day's lessons started with Miss Juss readin' aloud from the *Cousin Lucy* book for most of a chapter, an' Mary'd picture some of the bigger words an' spell them out in her head while she sat there doin' her stitchin'. They did some history, an' then something called division, an' it was a good while 'fore they finally got to French an' somethin' Miss Randall called con-ju-gatin' verbs. The spellin' an' pronouncin' was completely different in French, Mary'd learned by now. If you had a book in French, it was called a *livre,* only it was pronounced *lee-vra* an' not like *liver,* which was somethin called an organ in the body an' had nothin' to do with books. Miss Juss was havin' an awful time with pronouncin' the French words, worse even than Mary was havin' tryin' to spell them. But Miss Randall was determined, she'd said, to teach Miss Juss to speak French so she could walk into a place called *Versailles* an' nobody'd know she was from Virginia. Mary didn't know exactly what that meant, but it sounded good to her, much as she liked French an' the idea that she an' Juss might one day go there with Miss Randall.

The day's lessons passed along quick as ever, with three hours feelin' practically like one to Mary. Cora's knock on the door brought the session to an end, an' when she walked in the room it was like clouds movin' in an' coverin' the entire sky.

Miss Randall, beggin' yo' pardon Miss, Cora said, but Miss Kittredge sent me t'fetch Miss Justinia fo' t'bring her to the sto'. Dat is if you all through wit' yo' learnin' fo' the day.

Yes Cora, we are all through, thank you. You may take Miss Justinia.

That was another reason for Mary to *adore* Miss Randall so, since she was the only person that Cora spoke to that way, polite an' curtseyin' an' all, like she didn't even to Mista Kittredge or the Misses. Miss Randall closed the books on the desk an' put her coat on over her shoulders. But Miss Justinia was slow as ever puttin' on her own coat, so Miss Randall walked to the door by herself.

Au revoir, ma petite élève, she said to Miss Justinia.

Oh re-va, ma-dem-o-sell, Juss answered.

Et Mar-ee, au revoir à vous aussi.

Mary hesitated to show off in front of Cora, but then decided she'd show her she was more than just a little puppy the Kittredges'd sell off without a thought.

Au revoir, Mademoiselle Randall. Merci beaucoup, she added, flashin' a quick glance at Cora.

Très bien, Mar-ee.

Miss Randall walked out the door an' Cora started gettin' impatient with Miss Justinia, who was rollin' her eyes toward Mary. An' that was how they ended up walkin' out the room together without anyone realizin' the chance they were leavin' behind for Mary. She waited a moment to hear their footsteps on the stairs, an' then went straight for the French book, knowin' she could practice readin' her English anytime she wanted. The leather cover was as elegant as the words in it, an' she whispered the title out loud best as she could. *Grammare ay Vo-cab-ooo-lare Frahn-sayse.* The second page of printin' had pictures of everyday things an' then the French words for them printed next to the pictures. And Mary looked at each of 'em, all words she knew, but only now could see for sure how they were spelled. *Plume,* pen, plooome. *Chapeau,* hat, shapoh. *Cheval,* horse, shu-val. She remembered Miss Randall callin' the *ch* in *cheval* soft an' different from the hard *ch* in the English word *chair,* an' how the *i* in *livre* was pronounced like a long *e* but in the English word livery it was a short *i* sound. She became so caught up in studyin' these little differences page after page that she didn't notice the heavy footsteps in the hallway approachin' the room a few minutes later. It wasn't 'til she heard the doorknob turnin' that she snapped outta her dream.

Whachu doin' near Miss Justinia's books?! Cora said, yellin' wit'out raisin' her voice like only she could do.

Mary closed the book quickly an' squeezed it back in place between the bookends.

I's jus fixin dem cause dey was crooked an' I didn' wan' Miss Randall seein' dem' in a mess, Mary replied. She was already developin' different speech patterns dependin' on who she was talkin' to an' whether she might be in trouble or not. And in this situation she decided to go all the way back to the fields of Carolina just to show Cora she wasn't gettin' uppity.

Oh, you didn' wan' Miss Randall seein' nuthin'? Chil', if you thinkin' on gettin any o' dis here learnin' in yo' head, you bes' put it outta yo' mine right now, less'n you wants t'get yo' hide whupped an' den sol' off downa one o' dem cotton plantations down in Georgia or Alabammy.

Mary said nothin', but she hated to hear Cora call her *Chil'* the way Gertie always had. It sounded so different comin' from Cora's lips.

Dese white folks might think you some kinda fool ain't

learnin' nothin' sittin' in the corner there, Cora said, but I knows whachu up to. It against the law for a nigger to learn howta read. You wanna get the Mista an' Misses an' Miss Randall throwed in jail an' get yo'sef sold to Alabammy?

Mary shook her head, starin' down at the ground by her feet.

Well den you stop wit' all this tryin' to learn, an' you fo'get what you already done learnt, or you gonna make a mess fo' the whole lotta us. Now you get yo'sef downa the sto' an' bring yo' knittin' witcha. Miss Kittredge wanna see whachu been doin'.

She walked back over to her stool and picked up her stitchin', a lady's handkerchief with a design in the shape of a daisy sewn in light blue thread. Cora walked right behind Mary as they went down through the kitchen entrance an' out across the open grass field to the store. Lilly was another of the Kittredges' slaves, an' she worked as a seamstress in the store all day long. She didn't say anything to them as they walked through. Lilly didn't like Cora 'cause of how mean she was, an' she didn't like Mary, *just 'cause,* the way Mary figured it. The dress shop was kinda quiet, but the gen'ral store part seemed busy as usual with Mista Kittredge talkin' to the customers an' three slave workers runnin' round gettin' things for them. Misses Kittredge was with Miss Justinia holdin' a bolt of fine yellow fabric up against her shoulders.

Oh, this is just lovely with your beautiful hair, she said. Oh yes, this *must* be the color of your birthday dress.

Miss Juss smiled at Mary as she and Cora approached.

Mary, look at the pretty fabric Mommy's picked out for my birthday dress, she said.

It's *almos'* as beautiful as you, Miss Justinia, Mary said.

And the Misses smiled big as Miss Juss did, but Cora just rolled her eyes standin' beside them.

Give Miss Kittredge whachu been workin' on dese coupla hours, Cora said.

Mary handed over the white handkerchief with the blue stitchin', an' it seemed like the Misses was pract'ly amazed by it.

Why Mary, the Misses said, how did you . . . this is quite good, Mary. *Quite* good. I believe even Mrs. *Fenton* would be happy to do work like this.

Mary smiled an' looked at Cora in her moment of glory, seein' how she took the news, but Cora just rolled her eyes again as Miss Juss an' the Misses ran their fingers over the stitchin'.

Mommy, I want *Mary* to make my birthday dress, Miss Juss said, an' the Misses suddenly got a worried look on her face.

Oh Justinia Dear, I've already asked Mrs. Fenton to do it, the Misses replied.

But you just said that Mary's work was good as Mrs. Fenton's.

I said . . . I *meant* that . . . well, that Mrs. Fenton would *accept* such work, but Mary has only been . . . Dear, there's a reason why Mrs. Fenton makes so many of the dresses we sell here. She's the finest dressmaker in Richmond. Mary is good, but—

I don't *want* to wear a dress from Mrs. Fenton, Miss Juss interrupted. She's old, and she smells like mothballs and Daddy's brandy.

Justinia! The Misses said like she was shocked.

Mary laughed a little out loud, then caught herself an' covered her mouth with her hand.

Whachu laughin' at, Cora said in her yellin'-without-raisin'-her-voice kinda way.

I want *Mary* to do my dress, Miss Juss repeated.

An' it wasn't long 'fore Mary, Cora, an' even Lilly in the storeroom knew how it was gonna turn out in the end. The Misses put up a fight better than usual, but a few minutes later Mary was pullin' the measurin' tape 'round Miss Juss's waist, figurin' in her head what she wanted to do here an' how she'd put some green silk ribbon there, just like she was a dressmaker herself, just like Gertie'd taught her to do.

That night couldn't come fast enough, an' Mary knew that she'd only have a little while to talk to Gertie since Juss'd almost certainly come down to spend the night wit' her. So soon as her head hit the pillow she turned her eyes toward the window an' whispered just loud enough that even she could barely hear her words . . .

> I'm a little nervous Gertie, but a whole lot more excited t'night than I been in a long time. Maybe you figure it's just what it should be, the way you always so sure of things when you put 'em in my dreams the way you do, but I ain't altogether sure I'm ready for this. Juss'll . . . I mean Miss Juss'll be down soon . . . I gotta remember that Miss part, leastways 'round Cora, since she gave me a scoldin' today . . . two of 'em . . . but that's enough 'bout Cora, since I'm gonna be makin' Miss Juss's dress for her birthday comin' up an' I'm gonna need yo' help Gertie, so maybe you can send me one of them dreams an' tell me how I'm gonna make this dress better'n one of Miss Fenton's, maybe even good as something you'd make . . .

Climbin'

PART TWO

5 The Road Not Taken

ETHAN
NEW YORK
APRIL 17, 1857

You know, I didn't think it was possible, Seanny says, but this place stinks worse'n it did when me an' Da lived here.

He looks up Baxter Street at the Five Points, standing next to Ethan who beams with a broad smile to hear such a thing from his brother and the opportunity it affords him.

Ahhhhh, maybe yer just gettin' too comfortable in your noice new place on Fourteenth Street, fahhrr away from yer people, Ethan says. *Fahhr* away from de bosom of *Oireland*. Oh, Seanny . . .

Oh don't you start again, Seanny says, knowing what's coming.

Ethan stands up straight and tall and stares at his brother, then takes off his top hat and begins to sing loudly enough that people across the intersection stop and listen:

There was a wild colonial boy
Mick-Owen was his name,
He was born and raised in Ireland
In a town called Castlemaine . . .

A few people across the way laugh a little and a man passing them picks up the lyrics from where Ethan left off . . . *He was his father's only son, his mother's pride and joy, And dearly did his parents love, their wild Sean-ny boy . . .*

Ah, leave it to an *Irish*man to go an' change the lyrics of the damn song! Seanny says, feigning indignity as Ethan laughs.

Ahhh, I like it better this way *Seanny.*

And Ethan wraps his arm around his brother's shoulder as they stare up the street. He's long since caught up to his brother in height by now, passing him even by an inch or maybe two, but Sean wears the fine suit and top hat with far greater comfort than Ethan does his, and it gives off the impression of a native son of New York showing a newcomer around the town. It'd be hard to fault Ethan for such discomfort and unease in his deportment, since it was only the night before that he was presented with the fine suit he now wears. And he's spent the years since he arrived in America following in his father's footsteps, if any at all, and certainly not in the increasingly foreign realm of Seanny and his Tammany brethren.

So brudder o' moine, you've not said a word about me *foine* new suit, Ethan says, putting on the exaggerated brogue he and his brother sometimes do when they want to make a particular point about the general nature of things. This time it's Ethan's turn to tease his brother some, and he releases his arm from around Seanny and stands before him, bowing with exaggerated awkwardness.

Pretty nice for a Mick fisherman, Seanny says. Where'd ya get it?

Ethan looks at him with a knowing smile before answering.

Mam an' Aunt Em gave it t'me last night, he says. Said dey wanted me t'look me best when I went t'see the Dean, ya know.

Sure dey musta been savin' dere pennies fer goin' on foive years t'afford sooch a suit as dis.

Oh yeah? Seanny says.

Yeah, Oi've got dat appointment ya know . . . t'see th'fella at da university, ya know . . . t'see if dey'll take pity on a *poooor* Mick fisherman an' let'm come an' study in dere foine institution–

Is that so? Seanny says. Well it's a nice enough suit, I suppose . . . for a Mick fisherman anyhow.

Ethan stands there in front of his brother waiting for him to crack, but it takes him dancing a few steps of a jig to get Seanny to smile, and then it takes some more singing to get him to acknowledge what Ethan's known from the very minute his Mam and Aunt Em'd presented him the suit the night before.

At the early age of six-teen years,
Sean left his native home
And to ol'New York's sunny shores
he was inclined to roam . . .

All right, all right already . . . yer welcome, if it's *thank you* you're trying to say, Seanny finally admits.

Yes it is, brudder of mine, Ethan says. And I do thank you for it.

Well, you wear it like yer fresh off th'boat, Seanny says, and begins to walk up Baxter Street into the heart of the Five Points, feigning disgust as Ethan takes a few more exaggerated bows before following.

By this time, ten years since Ethan'd first arrived in New York and roughly the same length of time since Seanny'd first got his foot in the door of the municipal inner-workings of the Points, the McOwen family fortunes have changed dramatically. Seanny's among the more important men to be found anywhere in New York outside of City Hall and certain firms on Wall Street, though he spends plenty of time in each of those places. He's risen up from the ranks within Tammany Hall, not big enough, or rough enough, or stupid enough to be a thug in one of the gangs, and not Blue Blood like the Wall Street and City Hall boys, but plenty smart enough to carve out quite a niche for himself with the Tammany boys.

He'd spoken of business matters only at the very beginning, when he was still on the outside looking in, but now it's impossible to get more than a glib remark about all the various endeavors he seems to be involved in, or even more, the actual title for whatever job it is he has. *I'm just a poor streetlamp tender* doesn't fit the bill anymore. But he was able to bring Mam and Aunt Em over just a year after Ethan arrived, and they got to travel on a proper passenger ship with a cabin to themselves. Within a year after that, thanks to a little help on the rent from Seanny to be sure of it, they were moved into a nice place up in the Brooklyn Heights with more space than they ever could've imagined having back on the Lane. And then just a few years after that, Seanny came by the house one evening and told them it was theirs, that the owner'd been suddenly in need of cash and gave him a great price on it. Mam and Aunt Em seemed more willing to believe that such was the nature of life in America, but Da remained skeptical. It was possibly because Seanny'd got away from him and put himself in the way of more trouble, that Da was content to see Ethan fish with him every morning and read his books in the afternoon and play ball in summer, the last ten years passing with little distinction from one to the next. But that was about to change now, Ethan hoped.

So you're goin' through with it, Seanny says to Ethan as they walk up Baxter Street.

Mmm-hmm, Ethan responds, knowing his brother has thought the idea a foolish one from the start.

But Seanny refrains from offering his opinion once again, simply pulling his brother toward him and kissing him on the side of his head before taking his arm away and looking Ethan in the eye.

Bruddera mine, 'tis a foine *dreamin'* sorta lad y'are, Sean says, as he stops in front of the *Rose of Shannon.* Come on, would th'noble young Squire deign to sip a pint or two with the unwashed?

I'm not going in to see the Dean after a pint, Seanny. Ya want me to fulfill every idea they have about us?

Why, do you mean they might think *ill* of us poor workin' men? Seanny says, taking the mocking tone Ethan had used just minutes earlier. After *all* we went through in the *Old Country* . . . wouldn't you think–

Oh shite, Ethan interrupts him, looking over Seanny's shoulder. Here's yer boy Cormac. I gotta go before he challenges me to another arm wrestle.

And Ethan's gone up Baxter Street without even shaking his brother's hand, offering just a *thanks for the suit* as he goes. Cormac calls after him, something about an arm wrestle of course, but Ethan just tips his cap to him and keeps going.

He arrives at the Dean's office at ten minutes to two and is shown into his office by a young man around Ethan's age who must be his assistant. The next few minutes are spent wide-eyed and open-mouthed as Ethan admires the vast collection of books, each of them bound in fine leather, and filling the shelves that stretch from floor to ceiling on every wall but one. It's as if the Brodericks' entire library back home was somehow squeezed into a room a third as large, and he begins to feel as out of place as he did when he was twelve and Aislinn sneaked him in to see the original.

But when the Dean arrives a few minutes later, Ethan's fears are allayed by the very look of the man. He has no flowing academic robes or four-cornered hat and spectacles, and his wrinkled white shirt seems practically held together by a tie that fits loosely around his neck. He doesn't carry any books but does have a hammer and chisel in his hands.

Mr. MacOwen, is it? he asks.

Yes sir, Ethan MacOwen, Ethan replies and extends his hand toward him, forcing a frown to the Dean's face and requiring him to move the chisel into his left hand so he can give Ethan a limp handshake. He walks around his desk and sits down, adjusting the hammer and chisel in each hand.

What is the nature of your inquiry? he asks, looking at a side drawer on the desk rather than at Ethan.

Well sir, Ethan replies uncomfortably, put off a little by the Dean's indifference. I'm interested in becoming a student here for the next term.

The Dean says nothing in response but inserts the chisel into the seam between one of the drawers and the frame of his desk. He hits the chisel twice with the hammer before hitting his finger with the third swing.

Dammit! Confounded piece of . . . Joshua!

The door opens and the assistant steps in. Dean? he asks.

Come over here and get this damn thing open.

He hands him the chisel and hammer and Joshua taps at it awkwardly.

You're chipping the wood there! the Dean shouts.

Yes, Dean. Are you sure it's not locked?

Well of course I'm sure! It's broken. Stuck.

Joshua continues tapping at it as the Dean looks on with an expression of anguish and for the minute or so it takes them to pry open the drawer, neither of them seems to even be aware of Ethan's presence. He doesn't volunteer his assistance lest they get a look at his heavily calloused fisherman's hands, so he's forced to sit quietly and watch them struggle.

Ahh . . . there. And Joshua pulls the drawer and it slides unwillingly open.

Good, the Dean says. That's it, leave it now. Good. Take those things with you. Go.

Joshua walks out of the office carrying the tools with him while the Dean fumbles through papers, as if doing an inventory to see what might've vanished while the drawer was tightly closed. After the contents apparently meet with his approval, he slowly closes the drawer almost all the way and pulls it open as a test. When it passes inspection, he closes it again without removing anything and looks back up at Ethan, seeming almost surprised that he is still there.

So what was this now? he asks.

Well sir . . . I was hoping you would give me some information on how I could enroll for the next term as a student, he says with great attention paid to pronouncing each syllable completely.

You what? You want to be a student?

Yes, sir.

The Dean looks at him full of doubt.

From where have you come? he asks.

Brooklyn, sir. Brooklyn Heights.

Originally. Where were you brought into this world?

Had he slipped? Ethan thinks. Did he pronounce something with enough of a hint of a brogue that the Dean has seen right through him, even despite the silliness of introducing himself as Ethan *Mack*-Owen?

Your accent doesn't sound like anything I'm familiar with, the Dean adds, and I am an expert in dialects.

So he's done it so far, Ethan thinks, knowing all that was necessary now was to fill in the details of a Scottish father and perhaps a German mother and accents mixed together but him born here in this country and his parents both well-to-do and educated and . . .

Ireland, sir, he confesses as if by instinct, unable to do such a thing to the memory of Mr. Hanratty and the Heroes of '98 and his brother and Da and . . . himself. But we've been here for some time now, he adds.

I see. *Ubi studebas?* the Dean asks.

Ethan's eyes open broadly before he catches himself.

I'm . . . sorry sir?

Ubi studebas? The Dean repeats a little more insistently.

Ethan recognizes the Latin he's heard in Mass since he was a boy, but doesn't know exactly what the Dean has asked.

I'm sorry sir, I am not proficient in Latin, he admits.

Yes, you Papists sit and listen to your damn priests speaking Latin all the time and you never bother to actually learn the language! Well Mr. Mick-Owen, in what *are* you proficient?

I have read a great deal sir, he begins. Most of the classics . . . Shakespeare, Milton, Chaucer, Homer, Dante . . .

Ahhhhh . . . you're a *reader,* the Dean replies, sarcasm dripping from the word.

Yes sir.

And your education? Were you tutored privately or perhaps something a bit more formal? A *school* perhaps?

I learned mostly from my sister when I was young, Ethan replies.

Ahhhh—your *sister.* And she teaches where? Or better still, how was *she* educated?

Ethan pauses. Dean or not, he thinks to himself, this man will not extend his mockery to Aislinn and come away unscathed.

She's gone sir. She died back in Ireland in The Hunger.

The Dean seems to come to his senses just in time, perhaps responding to something in Ethan's voice or the look on his face, and quickly backs off his mocking tone.

Well, that is . . . I'm sorry to hear that Mr. Mick-Owen. Terrible tragedy that.

An awkward silence fills the next few seconds.

But I'm afraid that this is not the institution for you, he finally adds. We have quite rigorous academic standards and I don't believe you are the kind of young man who would find himself comfortable here.

I don't know the Latin sir, but I learn very quickly. I—

Greek? The Dean asks.

Sir?

Have you studied ancient Greek?

No sir.

Mathematics? Natural science? Rhetoric?

Well, I have read some of Newton's work, Ethan offers, and I'm reading Kant's *Critique of Pure Reason,* and I've also read—

Yes, you've read, you've *read*—but have you *studied,* Mr. Mick-Owen? Do you know algebra and geometry? Have you conducted any scientific experiments of your own?

Well, no sir. I've only lately taken much of an interest in natural science, that is—the past year or two. But I have read all the classics sir and I—

Yes, you've read the classics, but you don't know Latin *or*

Greek. You have no formal education and now you wish to be admitted to this *university*. But this is not how it works in the world of academia, Mr. Mick-Owen. I think you can see that this is not the place for you.

I would like the chance to–

Perhaps there is a *Catholic* institution somewhere that would consider you more suited to their standards, the Dean says, although without Latin, I would say you stand little chance. He stands up and extends his hand toward the door, and with finality in his voice adds, but I know for certain that *this* institution is not for you.

BY NOW HE'D TAKEN THE ferry ride from New York back to Brooklyn maybe a thousand times, but never in a suit like this to be sure. It was officially a gift from Mam and Aunt Em, but only Seanny had the sort of money to buy clothes such as these. Seanny, who'd been against the idea from the start, telling Ethan how there wasn't room for a Mick amidst those ivy-covered walls. Still, Ethan had to try, and Seanny was a generous enough sort to spring for a suit to fit the finest Wall Street financiers, just in case it'd do anything to conceal *th'mappa d'Old Country* splashed across Ethan's face. Clearly, it didn't.

So here was Ethan left to ride the ferry back home, new suit and all, and carrying with him now the guilt and shame for having put them all through it, for having made his Mam and Aunt Em, and even Da too, go to the trouble of hoping for such a thing that Seanny'd told him was not meant for them. *Plennya jobs for smart fellas like you down at Tammany,* Seanny'd said. He'd even told his little brother that they *needed some good Micks down on Wall Street lookin' after certain of our invest-*

ments. But Ethan'd never been interested in following in his brother's footsteps.

And so the ferry ride to Brooklyn took on a different feeling than it ever had before, like a banishment of some kind, like it'd been back in the Old Country. Only there, at least people knew straight off where they stood from the moment they were old enough to tell the difference. All it took was one look at the Brodericks' manor house, with twenty servants for four residents, and then a glance at the tiny cottages along the Lane, with four or eight or twelve people living piled on top of each other, for folks to know exactly where they stood. It was all nice and organized with stone walls and iron gates to *keep* them exactly where they belonged. Back in the Old Country, that was.

But here in America, it was all a taunting, torturing mess, without enough stone walls or iron gates to keep things separated the way the Good Lahrd had seen fit to make them in the first place. Why, on his very first day in New York, his Da had marched him past the bastions of power and riches at City Hall and Wall Street, and then a few blocks away into the Five Points, no borders, no priests wagging their fingers telling a lad to mind his proper place in the Lahrd's Creation, nothing to delineate the change . . . except maybe the smell. And worst of all about it was the way newspapers were always saying that democracy meant any man could pull himself up by his bootstraps. Sure hadn't the great John Jacob Astor gone from being a lad off the boat to the richest man in America and founding public libraries and such?

Ethan'd stared at the great man's portrait in the lobby of the library named for him, trying to find the key to climbing so far in a single lifetime, and there were moments when he swore Mr. Astor almost seemed to nod his head at him, telling him that a lad could make it from the Lane back in the Old Country all the way to Wall Street. But now he knew the truth behind that nod. A man could, sure enough, and hadn't Seanny been doing the very thing with his lads at Tammany Hall? But they'd never let you in through the front door. So it was all about smashing windows the way Seanny and his lads did, the way even the great Mr. Astor must've done along the way. And Ethan wasn't sure if he had the stomach for such a thing, or if Wall Street would ever matter enough to give up the part of his soul it'd take to get there.

Stepping off the ferry at Fulton Street, he didn't even stop to look back over his shoulders at New York the way he usually did. Instead, his first steps were turned south toward Red Hook, figuring he could help Da wash the salt off the skiff, rather than go straight home to deliver the bad news to Mam and Aunt Em, who were likely to be up to their elbows making a special meal for the occasion. There were a few familiar faces along the way and some of them saying what a fine suit it was and such, but thankfully none of them seemed to know what it was for. Once he was there at the mooring dock, it wasn't much of a wait before the familiar sail came into view, and his Da smiled and waved at him as he approached the shore. They worked in efficient silence as they always did, Ethan mooring the boat as his Da folded the sail. When it was time to lift the barrels up onto the dock, Da handed him the first but didn't even bother with the second. Ethan lifted the lid off the first one and saw just three medium-sized fluke floating listlessly in the water.

Wasn't much of a day as ya can see, Da said as he climbed up onto the dock. Then the broad smile of just a few minutes earlier exploded over his face in anticipation and he extended his hands as if to touch Ethan on both shoulders, but stopped just short.

Don't wanna ruin that suit now that yer gonna be needin' it evr'y day, Da said. So tell me how'd it go at *th'New York University*?

There was a reverent tone to the last few words and a smile in his Da's eyes that Ethan hadn't seen before. It was different from the relief that was there when he'd first come over, or when Mam and Aunt Em finally made it themselves a year later. It was different than the contented glisten after a pint, or a good song of a Saturday night, or a catch to fill both barrels right to the top with no room to spare. This was more childlike than any of those, echoing the hopes that must've been somewhere inside him before life on the Lane and in the Points and all the early days here when three medium-sized fluke would count for a great blessing, before life had done its work on him. And Ethan couldn't bear to tell him straight out, letting pursed lips and the slightest hint of shaking his head side to side do the dirty work for him, as his Da's face deflated back to its normal state, like th'Good Lahrd's Natural Order of Things being restored right there on the dock in Red Hook.

Was it yer name? Da asked.

Seanny'd been the one to tell him to call himself Ethan Mack-Owen and drop his brogue, so he could pass himself off as a Scotsman. Didn't matter how he got in the door of the place, so long as he was in, Seanny always said.

I dunno Da, he replied now. The Dean did ask a few questions about where we were from an' how long we'd been over—but I dunno if that made the diff'rence.

Well didya talk about all th'books ya been readin' all these years, all th'Shakespeare an' Newton an' . . . what's th'Froggy names again . . . the–

I told'm about readin' Descartes an' Voltaire and all the rest Da, Ethan said.

So what was it lad? Is it like Seanny said how dey'll never let an Irishman go to one o' their foine colleges so lahng as dey can help it?

But Ethan couldn't hold on to that same sort of anger his Da and Seanny had any longer. So he told him the truth, about the Latin and the Greek, about how this wasn't the way things worked, much as he'd wanted to disprove what a million Irish fresh off the boat knew to be true. They'd never let you in through the front door.

I wish I coulda done more for ya lad, his Da said. If things'd only been . . .

And his voice drifted off as he squinted in a way a man would only do when there was the sun staring straight at him or when the water was in his eyes.

Ahh . . . fook 'em, Da said. And Ethan couldn't help but stand in shocked silence hearing his Da say that word for the first time.

Da walked past him and pulled loose the aft knot he'd made in mooring the skiff, another *fook 'em* or two mumbled under his breath as he did the usual work. Ethan pulled the fore rope loose and they walked the skiff up onto the shore past the high-tide line. And it *was* as if order had been restored, as Da went for the fish barrel on the dock and Ethan pulled the scrub broom out of the skiff and dipped it into the rainwater barrel a few feet away. There was his Da, back turned toward Ethan, standing at the edge of the tiny dock and looking across the water at New York like it was the Brodericks' manor back in th'Old Country, and the East

River right there serving as all the stone walls or iron gates the gentry could ever hope to build. Quickly Da brushed his palm across one eye and then the other, then kicked one foot up to the brim of the fish barrel and spilled its contents, three medium-sized fluke and all, back into the bay. Before Ethan could turn away, his Da looked up and saw his son staring at him. Da shook his head a few times and lifted up the empty barrel.

Leave it lad, he said. A day's wert' o' salt isn't gonna kill 'er.

It's all right Da, really it is, Ethan protested, and began to wash the salt water from the tiller.

But then his Da dropped the barrel right into the skiff and took the scrub broom from Ethan's hands.

Leave it lad. Yer Mam's got a steak from th'butcher an' a cake from th'bakers, too, he said, reaching his arm around Ethan's shoulders and pulling him close, new suit and all. But I could go fer a pint at Feeny's first, what d'ya say?

Sure Da, Ethan answered, and patted him on the back before his Da let the embrace go.

They walked quietly up the short slope, leaving the skiff for another day, and Ethan surveyed what was left of the fields that had been his first home in America. The cabins were mostly gone by now, replaced by more substantial two- and three-room buildings that looked like they had a much better chance of surviving a good storm than the old places did. There were a dozen brick houses across the road covering much of what had been their baseball field just ten years ago. And the oddity of a single thought came over Ethan just then, offering some consolation in the form of a warning. Perhaps it wasn't good for a man to stray *too* far from anything that he'd ever known as home, lest he be left to drift on the seas for an entire lifetime. Perhaps Brooklyn Heights, by way of Red

Hook, by way of the Lane outside Enniskillen, was enough travel for one man in one lifetime. And wouldn't there be generations to follow to carry on with the traveling, until maybe one day the McOwens would find themselves on the other side of those stone walls and iron gates? Yes, perhaps this was enough after all.

THERE AREN'T MANY LADS DRESSED in suits at Feeny's, and none of them with one as nice as Ethan's to be sure. Feeny's is the sort of place that from the inside could almost pass for any pub down any lane back in the Old Country, and almost all of its patrons have spent at least part of their lives along one of those lanes. Wearing his suit now, Ethan worries that the lads who know him'll be full of questions about how the meeting with the Dean went, and the lads who don't will take him for an uppity Mick. But he and his Da step straight to the bar and order their pints same as they would on the days when there were two barrels' worth of fish to toast. Only, minus the day's fishing to recount, neither of them seem to know what to say to each other.

So Mam's got a steak? Ethan asks by way of easing the silence.

But his Da only nods, not relieved at all, and still has that look of uneasiness when Feeny brings their pints. Ethan picks his up same as always, but stops when he sees his Da holding his glass up as if to make a toast, as if they'd just caught enough fish to turn Saint Peter green with envy. And it's awkward for him to see his Da this way, struggling to find words of consolation, when it's Ethan who feels he's the one who should do the consoling since he'd been the one to let his family down and waste a good steak dinner and a cake from the baker's.

I wish we'da come over sooner, Da says. I wish I'd done more t'get you inta that place . . . maybe I shoulda took ya over to the Father to be an altar boy an' learn th'Latin . . . maybe if Aislinn'd lived she coulda . . .

No Da. It wouldn'ta mattered, Ethan said, shaking his head definitively.

Well—here's to you lad, Da says. Sure I'm as prouda ya as a father ever was of his son.

They clink their glasses together and spill a little over the top, then take a gulp and put them back down.

And won't yer Mam cook the Devil outta dat t'ing 'til it'll be just a mem'ry of a steak, Da said, offering relief to Ethan that the conversation would return to something more accustomed to them.

Mmmm. Maybe we shoulda brought the filly knife wit' us?

Got it right here lad, Da says, patting his coat pocket, and Ethan laughs and turns his head to one side just a bit, as if in the presence of genius.

It's maybe ten minutes and the better part of a pint before an unmistakable voice bellows from the doorway and Ethan's sorry it won't be just him and his Da for a few moments more.

How the hell am I supposed to know, Finny! Harry bellows. The man just said they wanted a few respectable lads who owned a suit an' could actually play the bleedin' game!

And then Harry sees Ethan and his Da.

Perfessor! he shouts down the length of the bar, and here come Harry and Finny, two of his friends from the first day he'd arrived in America and for every day since then.

So is it a perfessor yer t'be fer real? Harry asks.

And Ethan shakes his head, telling him about how Latin and Greek had done him in, since it's a more tangible thing to focus their anger upon than the idea of having no actual proof of being an educated man. Harry's been the leader of them from the start, bigger and louder than any of them back then and even more so now. It'd been Harry who first took to calling Ethan *Perfessor* when Ethan was just a few days off the boat and got caught reading Aislinn's Shakespeare book one morning while there were ball games to be played. But Harry has a way about him, something drawn from profound loyalty, that's always made his nickname a thing of honor for Ethan.

Latin? Harry says. Christ, it ain't like you wanna become a bleedin' priest!

And then Harry's quick to apologize to Ethan's Da for saying such words, but he stops when Da starts laughing even before the rest of them do.

Lads, Da says, join us in a pint, woncha? And he nods to Feeny to set the boys up.

There's a little bit more by way of explanations, and Finny seems to be the one who's most disappointed of all. Finny, short for Fintan Caldwell, had been there the first day Ethan arrived and played ball with the rest of them down in old Red Hook. He was the shortest of them, fast as lightning on the base paths, and the primary target of Harry's jokes. But Finny's the one to offer the best line of this conversation, and it comes after all the discussion of schools and Latin and other such matters foreign to most of the lads in Feeny's is done with, serving as a conclusion to the matter altogether.

Ahh, whatya wanna go an' study with those fellas for anyways, Perfessor? Fook 'em! Those robes they wear make'm look like a buncha nancy boys!

And as Finny begins to apologize to Ethan's Da for the salty language, Ethan can only think about how glad he is that he'll still be Perfessor to the lads, the way he's been ever since he was twelve years old.

Tell Perfessor about the fella who came t'see ya Harry, Finny says after the laughter's calmed down.

Harry takes a gulp from his newly arrived pint and puts his long arm around Ethan's shoulders, smiling as if he's bursting with news.

How'd ya like to play ball fer th'Excelsiors? he asks, and Ethan jerks his head back slightly, a question on his face as to just who, or what, were the Excelsiors.

So Harry proceeds to tell Ethan and his Da about the man named Lydell who came to the South Street Port inspector's office that afternoon. Harry works for the City of New York technically, but he mostly works for Seanny and other Tammany lads who prefer not to pay the standard taxes or go through the rigors of the law when it comes to their "importing" business. He's always good for a boatload of stories anytime they meet up at Feeny's, but this one is quite different.

So this fella Lydell is askin' fer *me* especially, an' even waits 'til I get done assessin' the cargo on a steamer from Jamaica, Harry says. Oh, an' if yer Mam's lookin' for sugar, tell 'er I know a few places she can get it at half th'usual.

Jesus, Harry, Finny interjects, d'ya think he cares about the sugar? Would ya just get to the part about playin' ball?

And Harry doesn't even look Finny's way but flicks his hand back to hit him on the shoulder and continues on with his story, with the usual amount of exaggeration to be sure. It begins with a fellow named Lydell from Brooklyn, a banker from up in Greenpoint, who, along with a few of his gent friends, is getting up a ball club just like the Empires and the Eagles and the Gothams. But most especially, just like the grand old Knickerbockers from across the river. The *nancy boy*

Knickerbockers from New York, who'd codified the damn game like they'd owned it, writing down the rules they decided on and forming an exclusive club just for themselves, with nothing but gentlemen allowed in *like it was a goddamn fox hunt back in th'Old Country,* as Harry always protested. Harry'd come over with his family when he was no more than six or seven. Still, he liked saying *th'Old Country* more than any of them.

So Lydell wants to *beat* the goddamn Knickerbockers, Harry says. That is, if they'll ever play us, and he figures he's gonna need a few lads who can actually play the game, gents or not. He's heard about us all the way up in Greenpoint, and he wants you an' me an' Smitty an' Finny t'come up to a sorta tryout.

Ethan spends some time talking with Harry and Finny about the idea of taking on the Knickerbockers, and it's the chance to take his mind off the day's events for a while. But when Da says he *best be gettin' back home to th'overcooked steak,* Ethan can't possibly stay at Feeny's any longer, even though Da tells him to stay and have an evening with his lads. The walk back home is all too brief for Ethan as he tries to conjure the words that'll make the disappointment easiest to bear for Mam and Aunt Em. That morning they'd stood atop the steps at the house and watched him head off for the ferry, and that after all the fuss of making sure his suit and hat were fixed just so, after the fuss over breakfast and the fuss of telling him how they were so proud of him and how Aislinn'd . . . and then their voices drifting off and a bittersweet smile taking the place of more words.

Da's the first one to walk inside, and both of them are greeted with the smells emanating from a kitchen where two women who'd never had much more than potatoes to boil back home have imposed their will upon a steak from the butcher's. They're soon into the hallway, one then the other, smiling in great anticipation of the news. But Da's expression must do some of the dirty work for Ethan, since by the time they turn their gaze to him, some of the life has gone out of their faces.

I'm sorry Mam . . . sorry Aunt Em, Ethan says.

And there's nothing more to be said for a few moments, just the two of them taking turns kissing him on the cheek and hugging him with the same sort of energy they'd had that morning, 'til they're both telling Ethan what a loss it'll be to the New York University not to have such a fine lad as him. It doesn't take long for normalcy to return to the McOwen household, as fanciful dreams are put back in their proper place. And they eat their steak from the butcher, sliced by Da and his filly knife amidst knowing smiles between Ethan and him, as if the excitement of the last two days was something altogether out of character.

The final difficult moment comes just after dinner is finished, when Seanny arrives unexpectedly. There's no flourish to his entrance the way he often makes it, no anticipatory stare at Ethan waiting to hear the verdict and be proven right or wrong in his assessment of the matter. And Ethan thinks it must be because Seanny'd known all along that it wasn't meant to be. It's only after Mam and Aunt Em go for the cake from the baker's that Seanny tells Ethan he's already heard the news.

Ran into Harry at Feeny's, he says, and there seems to be a combination of anger and disappointment in his words.

There are plenty of things Seanny has to say to his brother, but they have to wait until the cake from the baker's is done and 'til it's just the two of them standing on the steps out front of the house.

So are you ready to finally get off the boat for real? he asks Ethan after lighting his cigar.

Ethan looks at him as if the question is a strange one but he knows the general meaning behind it.

You an' Da an' Mam an' Aunt Em're all livin' here as if all you done was move into a nicer place along the Lane back home, Seanny says. I can see that for *them,* but fer chrissakes Ethan, you've been here for almost as many years as you were back there. Are ya gonna spend the rest of yer life fishin' off a little skiff in the Gowanus Bay and playin' ball games with yer lads?

And Ethan knows that Harry must've said something to Seanny about the Excelsiors. Just that very morning his position was a more tenable one, what with the hope that an appointment with a Dean from the New York University represented. But now Ethan knows there's little in his arsenal to contest Seanny's assessment of things. He'd never imagined he'd be just a fisherman this long either.

Whenever yer ready, there's a *real* job waitin' for ya, Seanny adds. Not in th'Points or with lads like Cormac or Harry even. Something where you'll get to use that brain o' yours for more than readin'.

Okay Seanny, is as much of an answer as Ethan is willing to give.

ELYSIAN FIELDS, NEW JERSEY
AUGUST 2, 1857

It's the most highly anticipated match of the Excelsiors' brief existence, a clash with the self-proclaimed guardians and kings of the game, the New York Knickerbockers. The Knickerbockers have called the Excelsiors common, semiliterate ruffians, and the Excelsiors have called the Knickerbockers untalented dandies afraid of a little competition. Of course most of it isn't really true, since the Excelsiors have bankers and clerks and even one lawyer on their squad, while the Knickerbockers no longer exclusively play games within their own elite club. Still, it's taken most of the summer for the two teams to finally play each other, and according to the newspapers, the event promises to draw as many as a thousand spectators to the Elysian Fields across the river in New Jersey, where the Knickerbockers have been playing for some ten years now.

The crowd is still gathering around the field when the game begins at a few minutes after two in the afternoon. It's a democratic crowd to be sure, all of them dressed in their Sunday best, but their individual bests varying greatly from the humblest of the Excelsior backers to the grandest of the Knickerbocker supporters, no segregation here, but all of them mixed together in one long line that encircles the entire infield and creates its own sort of barrier across the outfield maybe three hundred feet from home base. Early on Ethan spots his Mam and Da beside Aunt Em and her new beau, a ferryboat operator named Paddy, the four of them standing along the first-base line where the Excelsiors reside. But it's not until the Knickerbockers take the field that he spots Seanny, doing a little business most likely, in the company of a few Wall Street types right behind the Knickerbocker bench, as ever infiltrating enemy territory.

The visiting Excelsiors hit first and are retired without a run scored, three batters up, three batters retired, two on ground balls in the infield, and one on a one-hopper to the right fielder—still an out, according to the Knickerbocker rules, which have become the standard of the New York game. It was the Knickerbockers who made things like foul balls and called strikes and umpires and nine innings official parts of the game, ever since they'd bothered to write all these rules down a decade earlier. They're certainly New York's most famous ball club, which makes the Excelsiors hate them all the more, but Harry, their pitcher, has a little something up his sleeve for them, something perfectly legal within the rules that the Knickerbockers themselves have created.

They only recently added an Umpire who can call strikes once he's issued a warning to the batter for letting a good pitch go by. And slowly the pitchers have stopped simply lobbing the ball underhanded to let the batters put it in play. In fact, some have even begun throwing in more of a side-armed motion, and with greater velocity than before—like they *mean* for the batter to miss the ball altogether. Catchers have begun moving farther and farther away from the batter in the interest of self-preservation, but Smitty, the last of Ethan's friends from childhood and the Excelsiors' catcher, is every bit of *fifteen* feet behind the first Knickerbockers' batter when he comes up to hit in the bottom half of the first inning. The batter looks back at him and shakes his head, as if scorning the blatant cowardice on display, but the fellows in the field are mostly holding a bare hand or their hats over their mouths, to conceal the laughter they know is about to follow.

Harry stands in the pitcher's box as the formalities are taken care of, the batter tipping his cap to him and then Harry having to do it back, and then the Umpire getting in on the show, and the replies, as if, Harry always said, they were *about to dance a goddamn reel instead of playing ball!* But then it's done and he kicks his left leg straight in the air so his foot is nearly as high as his shoulder, driving all his weight forward as he lands that left foot, and his right arm follows—overhanded!—releasing the ball as his torso bends at the waist toward the unsuspecting batter. The resulting bullet of a pitch flies past the Knickerbocker batter so fast that it crosses home base a foot above his waist and still is caught on a fly by Smitty just below his knees. There are some *oohs* and *aahs* from the assembled crowd, and at least as many hisses of disapproval at the ungentlemanly manner in which the pitch was delivered. The Knickerbocker batter stares at Harry with a look of bewildered disgust, and then looks over at the Umpire to issue a silent protest.

Sir, the Umpire says to Harry, let's remember that we are gentlemen here—and that there are ladies present.

And as Smitty throws the ball back to Harry, the pitcher lifts his cap and bows slightly toward the batter, who nods back at the apparent apology. Harry then places his cap under one arm and turns toward Finny at shortstop, as he rubs some dirt into the ball.

Steady there, Harry, Finny says with a knowing smile.

Right-oh, Fin, Harry replies in a mock English accent. Jolly good.

Then he returns to the pitcher's box and fires another pitch every bit as fast as the first one, only this time a little closer to the batter's chin. The batter takes three steps backward to get out of the way, then slams his bat down on the ground. And the crowd is mixed once again between the *oohhs* and *aahhs* and hisses, as if some of them are holding on to the gentler past while others cheer the approach of the future. Of course, Smitty does what he does best by adding a little fuel to the matter, walking up to the batter and picking up his discarded bat, flipping it once in his hand end to end, and handing it to him.

Let's remember there are ladies present, laddy, he says, and winks one eye at him.

Smitty stands nearly six feet with shoulders almost as broad as Harry's, and the batter, a full six inches shorter and forty pounds lighter, accepts his bat back without much more of a protest. The Umpire can just mutter the same nonsense about being gentlemen, but there's nothing in the rules to tell Harry to do otherwise. The next pitch follows the pattern, only this time splitting home base and crossing at the batter's waist, and the Umpire, reluctantly, issues the warning to the batter that the next good pitch will be "called" a strike. And the Excelsiors, by way of Terrance Harrison, Harry to be precise, have just done a little bit of their own innovating of the game. The next pitch is thrown with the same authority, and the batter swings late at it, hitting it feebly to the first-base side of the infield, where he is easily retired. And so on it goes, through the rest of that inning, the Knickerbockers retired in order and with similar ease, the last one even striking out!

The full measure of the moment isn't truly seen until the top half of the second, as the Knickerbocker pitcher delivers his first pitch under the intent gaze of everyone in attendance. He kicks his front leg almost as high as Harry did, driving his weight forward and bending at the waist as his arm propels the ball forward, overhanded, toward Smitty, the Excelsiors' batter. It sails high, even over the catcher's head, and the next one bounces five feet before home base. But eventually he settles into this new delivery, and the game has now become anything *but* a pleasant Sunday afternoon's activity where gentlemen may recreate and exercise all at once. This is something much more than that, with neither side willing to yield.

By the end of the fourth inning, the crowd has swelled to such a size that they now are stretched in a line two or three deep across the entire outfield, and though the game is still scoreless, the Umpire has been a more regular participant in this game than any contest anyone can recall having seen before. Already he has called out three batters on strikes, issued multiple warnings for failure to swing at fairly pitched balls, been the final arbiter on several close plays on the base paths, and fined Harry twenty-five cents for saying the word *damn* when he fouled a pitched ball off his foot. Since no one was quite sure to whom the fine should be paid, the Umpire rescinded it and Harry got off with a warning, until he said it again just a minute later, and the Umpire demanded half a dollar from him, to be given to one of the orphanages in town.

Ethan comes to bat in the top half of the fifth inning with one out and Finny on second base. Taking his familiar left-handed hitting stance, flexing his wrists and forearms made strong by years of fishing, he swings at the second pitch and sends the ball screaming back past the pitcher and out into center field. Finny races home with the Excelsiors' first run, and the less finely dressed amongst the spectators cheer loudly enough to betray their Brooklyn roots, though they don't seem to care just then. And for the first time since the inception of the Knickerbockers Ball Club, it seems that the Elysian Fields have been invaded by a hostile throng, some of them, worst of all, *immigrants.*

The score remains the same until the bottom half of the seventh inning, when a Knickerbocker batter slams a foul ball down the third-base line, scattering several spectators and striking one of them on the forehead. The victim hadn't been paying attention to the action on the field, too busy looking through his wooden box camera, and several people in the crowd laugh when they see him go down. But as he lies there, dazed on the ground, concern for him grows. Ethan's among the people and players who walk over to tend to him, until finally a physician steps forward and reassures everyone that he'll be all right. Still, at the end of the inning, Ethan walks past him on his way in from the field.

Are you all right there, sir? he asks.

Embarrassed more than hurt, he replies, though his voice sounds weak. That was some ball you struck a few innings ago, he adds

Ethan nods his appreciation, then turns toward the camera. He's seen them before, even once up close, but he's never seen the view from under the small black curtain draped over it. The man notices Ethan's interest and lifts up the curtain for Ethan to take a look. It's a wooden box about eighteen inches square in front and connected to a smaller wooden board in back by six inches of accordion bellows, and Ethan wears a boyish smile as he leans toward it and the man drapes the curtain over his head. All goes dark until he presses an eye to the viewfinder and sees the field and the buildings across the river just as they'd been all along, only now defined by the frame the lens provides. It's as if he's taking a piece of the moment, trimming out the less important surroundings, and telling the story from his own view. He watches for several minutes as the Excelsiors are retired in order.

I'd better get back out there, he says, pulling his head out from under the curtain to see Finny trotting out toward shortstop. Thanks for the view, Mr. . . .

Hadley, the man says. Come back next inning if you'd like.

Of all the lads on the team, Ethan's interests have always cast the largest net. He'd once insisted that Finny take him up to the tower of Brooklyn City Hall, where Finny worked as a doorman, so he could see the large clock from behind with all its inner workings exposed. He's placed Harry on permanent alert to let him know when ships from exotic places come into port and spend the night. So it's this kind of interest, this curiosity, that shares an equal part of his focus when he takes the field for the bottom half of the eighth inning. The Knickerbockers get two men aboard and Mr. Hadley begins moving his camera closer and closer to the foul line to get a picture of the batter. Ethan watches him adjust the tripod and focus the lens and is so engrossed that it takes the sound of the bat hitting the ball to snap his attention fully back to the game. From the look of Finny in front of him, he can tell the ball is hit in his direction, but when he looks into the sky, he sees nothing but sunshine.

Back Perfessor, back! Finny shouts from shortstop.

And Ethan turns over his left shoulder and begins drifting back, a few slow strides at first, until he finally catches sight of the ball and sees how far over his head it is. By the time he reaches it, he's at the edge of the crowd gathered in left field and it's still rolling slowly away from him. He finally picks it up and hurls it back toward the infield, but not before the two Knickerbockers score and the batter stands safely on third. Harry retires the next batter, but the damage has been done, and Ethan feels the disappointment of having let his team down. The Excelsiors trail two to one.

Nobody says anything to Ethan about the lapse. In fact, it becomes clear that nobody even saw the delay in Ethan's break on the ball, just that it was hit well over his head and there wasn't anything he could do about it. But it hangs on Ethan's mind as Harry picks up another half dollar in fines for foul language as the Excelsiors prepare to take their final turn at bat. Smitty hits a ball high and far to lead off the inning, but the center fielder catches up to it, lets it bounce once, and catches it with ease to record the first out. Then it's

Finny, and he becomes the first man in the entire contest to reach base safely two times, this one the product of a cleanly struck single over the shortstop's head. And then it's Ethan's turn again.

He takes the first pitch and the Umpire warns him that the next one like it will be a called strike. The second delivery is almost exactly the same as the first, and he launches his weight forward off his back foot, uncoiling his body as he always does, with his wrists, shoulders, and hips opening at the point of contact, driving the ball in the air toward right field. It takes off, gaining height as it travels, while the stunned Knickerbocker fielder turns and gives chase. At first the spectators, lined up along the outfield nearly three hundred feet from home base, are stunned as well and stand still as the ball approaches them. Then a lady screams and the crowd suddenly begins to scramble out of the way, with only a few of them stopping to watch with open mouths as the ball sails over their heads and lands with a splash at the edge of the Hudson River. The right fielder races through the crowd and to the end of the short bluff at the river's edge, but by the time the ball bobs up to the surface, it's twenty feet downstream and headed out quickly to the bay. He runs back through the outfield crowd and shouts toward the infield, throwing his arms above his head in disgust.

It's gone . . . it's gone down the river! he shouts.

By the time Ethan crosses home base, the crowd is as delirious as such a refined gathering can be, knowing that it's only the second time a batter has reached the river that year, and the first time anyone has *ever* reached it on a fly, so long as anyone can recall. Even Knickerbocker supporters are cheering him for the feat, and Ethan's teammates swarm him, slapping him on the back and shouting *Perfessor!* as he waves to his Mam and Da and Aunt Em and Paddy standing not too far away. Even Seanny summons up a proud smile. But the elation of the moment fades not long afterward when they realize that, as was the case with most contests, they'd only brought one ball to the game. For a moment it looks like a brawl might break out as Harry yells that the Knickerbockers were the host team and they had to provide the ball, which they of course remind him they had until Ethan went and knocked it into the water *on purpose*!

The Umpire finally decides that they should play another game in two Sundays, playing this one to its rightful conclusion first. A reporter from the *Herald* is there, and he calls Mr. Hadley over to get a picture of Ethan. There are questions to be answered and folks who come up to offer congratulations, and even a few Knickerbockers who want to shake his hand. Mam and Da and Aunt Em and Paddy are soon headed home on the ferry, knowing Ethan'll be a while here and then with the lads at Feeny's. Seanny's leaving too, but not until after he brings a few of his associates to meet Ethan and mentions that his kid brother is just now doing some work with him and the lads down at Tammany. Ethan begins to correct Seanny, wanting to tell the Wall Street–looking men that he's still just a fisherman and a ballplayer and had only told Seanny that he'd reconsider the matter when the summer ball season was done. But his attention is quickly drawn away again as he sees Mr. Hadley begin to walk off with his camera. He joins the last of the crowd walking to the ferry but lingers a few feet behind most of his teammates while talking with Mr. Hadley the whole time, even carrying the camera for the old man. Mr. Hadley wants to talk about the home run Ethan hit, but Ethan's the one peppering *him* with questions, wanting to learn everything he can about taking pictures.

You know lad, Mr. Hadley finally says as Ethan hands him back his camera to board the ferry. I've a small office in the Brooklyn Heights where I take portraits. Anytime you want to come by and learn more, I'd be glad to teach you what I know.

Oh, you can be sure he'll be there, Harry says from nearby. Ol' Perfessor won't be happy 'til he knows everything there is t'know in this world.

He knows how to hit, Smitty adds, an' that's all I care.

BROOKLYN HEIGHTS
AUGUST 3, 1857

The fishing was done by ten o'clock the very next day since it was just him without Da, and he washed as much of the smell off him as he could without taking a full-on bath. A couple of nice fluke would buy a few pints at Feeny's, or a used book in pretty good condition, but Ethan had other ideas in mind for this day. He took the dollar and a half that was his share of three dollars' worth of fish, stuffed the fifty cents in his pocket, and the dollar went in his top bureau drawer, the beginning, he decided that morning, of his own personal camera fund.

He still went out on the skiff six days a week, though Da, starting to feel the ache of arthritic bones, had begun to take regular days off. On the days when it was just Ethan, he'd generally stay out until well into the afternoon, doing the real fishing from six to noon or so, then drifting for a while without much more than a single line draped over the side and him with a book in his hands, of course. It might've been a glorious season but for the lingering question he'd managed to put off for one summer more. He was twenty-two by now, and it was time to step off the boat for real, as Seanny'd said just a few months before. But everything was all about to change today, Ethan figured, since he'd found what it was he wanted to do.

So he put on his best suit for the first time since the debacle with the Dean, and walked the three blocks to Fulton Street not far from City Hall, walking east until he found the small storefront window that read: *J. M. Hadley, Daguerreotypist.* And beneath it: *Portraits, $1.00.* Inside was a small waiting room, and there was a young man and woman seated in the corner, wearing their Sunday clothes, too. Ethan looked around for a moment, then at the young couple again.

Hello, is Mr. Hadley around? he asked them.

That's the fella what takes th'pictures, yeah? the man said, and the young lady nudged him, pointing to the glass window with Mr. Hadley's backwards name on it.

Yes, that's him, Ethan answered.

He's in back, the man said. But we're next in line.

Oh, I know, I'm just here on business.

Well what d'ya think it is *we're* here on? the man snapped, drawing a harder nudge from the woman beside him.

No fightin' on our weddin' day fer chrissakes, she said, commanding more than asking.

What'd I say? the man asked her with mild protest.

And Ethan decided to take a seat on the other side of the waiting room, offering simple congratulations to them as he passed.

It was a few quiet minutes in that room, with the two soon-to-be-weds looking like they were about to enlist in the army instead of entering marital bliss, and Ethan sat staring out the window at nothing in particular, not wanting to strike up a conversation that might lead to a fight on the day of their nuptials. Then Mr. Hadley came out from the back room with a man and a woman and two children dressed neatly, if not in a Sunday best that'd match most people's.

Tomorrow, he said to them, nodding his head and sweeping his arm in an arching motion that must represent the sun rising and setting, Ethan figured. Tomorrow it will be ready, he said again, louder this time and holding up one finger.

The woman nodded, and the man looked at her quizzically.

Amanhã, she said, and the man nodded, taking change out of his pocket as if to hand it to Mr. Hadley.

No, no, the rest you pay me tomorrow, Mr. Hadley insisted, arching his arm again, then saying, *Aman . . .* before looking over at the woman.

Amanhã, she said, and smiled. To-morrow.

Then the man smiled and put the money back in his pocket and the two of them nodded their heads to Mr. Hadley. *Obrigado. Amanhã.* The man tapped the children on the shoulder and pointed to Mr. Hadley. *Obrigado,* they said, dutifully. And Mr. Hadley nodded back and smiled as they walked out the narrow doorway.

Just off the boat from Lisbon, he said to the couple in the corner, then spotted Ethan. Mr. McOwen, he exclaimed, did you see the *Brooklyn Daily Eagle* this morning? Did you see your picture?

No, Ethan answered, a little puzzled.

Well it's there, on page eleven, next to the article on the baseball match.

We was here *first,* the man in the corner interrupted, causing his beloved to slap him across the top of his arm.

What, I'm just lettin'm know!

They were here first, Mr. Hadley, Ethan offered. I don't want to interrupt, I just–

You just came by to learn some more about the camera, yes?

Well, yes.

Listen, can you do yer learnin' a little later, the man said, trying his best to be calm and gracious. We gotta be at City Hall by one.

Of course, of course, come right in, Mr. Hadley said, fully accustomed, it seemed, to all sorts of clients. He opened his hand toward Ethan as if presenting him to them. This is Mr. McOwen, my new *apprentice.*

And much as the word surprised Ethan, he did nothing to refute it. Mr. Hadley smiled at him, tilting his head as if asking whether the arrangement would be acceptable. And Ethan nodded in reply, smiling at the idea of it, of him, no longer a man of leisure the way Seanny sometimes teased him.

That night he slipped out of the house after supper, after all the congratulations and questions from his family, and walked, still dressed in his suit, down to Red Hook. The cabin he and his Da had first stayed in was gone now, replaced by something a little larger and more permanent looking. But there was still the nook of land that stretched out just a little farther than the rest of the shoreline, the place he'd gone to on his first night in America to tell Aislinn he'd made it. Of course, since that time he'd learned that he was facing west, away from Ireland, but by then it had become their spot, and what did it matter anyway with Aislinn looking down from the Ever After?

So he went back there from time to time, always on Aislinn's birthday and sometimes on his, on every Christmas too, and always on the anniversary of the day she died. And he'd talk to her just a little, letting her know how Mam and Da and Aunt Em and Seanny were all getting on and introducing her to the important people in his life through the stories he'd tell, out loud, in a whisper. And that was where he stood again that night, dressed as he'd never been before on such occasions, feeling the pride that comes with looking like such a gent, and letting the breeze tussle his hair as he stood with his top hat off, held by his two hands behind the small of his back. He smiled a little, knowingly, waiting to tell her the news he'd wanted to tell *her* most of all ever since he'd left Mr. Hadley's shop.

I'm gonna take pictures Ais', I'm gonna be a photographer, he said, in a voice louder than he usually used when speaking to her, as if he were making a formal pronouncement.

And he allowed himself to smile for a moment or two more, basking, as if waiting for a whisper of approval bestowed from the Ever After. Then, with only the breezes for an answer, he pulled his hat into one hand and used the other to sit down on the patch of sand and grass, the way he always did, Sunday suit or not. He bent his knees out in front of him and wrapped his arms around them, hat dangling from one hand in the space between, and the whisper returned though the smile remained. It was, since the very first night he'd sat here and spoke to her, the first time he would speak mostly of himself. It was the first time he had something worthwhile to report, something he felt might one day justify the fact that it was him who'd been given this chance to come to America and not her. And the words spilled out from him, with all the once-upon-a-time exuberance of that twelve-year-old boy.

It all started just yesterday when we were playin' the
Knickerbockers over there at th'Elysian Fields an', oh

you shoulda seen the crowd Ais', there was more than a thousand of 'em, or so the paper says. And that's another thing, I was in the paper today, picture and all. But first I gotta tell ya about the game . . .

COOPER UNION, NEW YORK
FEBRUARY 27, 1860

The speech is a decidedly different thing than he could hear anywhere near the Points. And for the almost two hours Mr. Lincoln talks about the pressing issues of the day, Ethan feels as if he's been lifted from his common origins into another world altogether, the one he'd once hoped to be a part of when he'd ventured into the hallowed halls of New York University and sought to become a verified scholar. But when it's over, and Mr. Lincoln seems to have become a leading candidate for the Republican nomination for President, Ethan steps outside and it's as if the moment is lost. Anywhere familiar he goes, he realizes, will inevitably be more of the same sort of reverence for the mundane that drew him here in the first place. And he yearns to follow the well-dressed crowd spilling out of the Great Hall, hoping to find someone amongst them who will discuss Emerson and de Tocqueville and . . . Lincoln.

Ethan! he hears a vaguely familiar voice call out to him as he stands by the front entrance. There y'are. I been lookin' all over th'bleedin' place for ya!

The yelling draws attention from much of the well-dressed crowd still milling outside Cooper Union, and Ethan follows their stares as if down a funnel all the way to the imposing figure of Cormac Toomey, his brother's *Associate.* In the Points, Cormac's been known as a thug for going on twenty years, but five years ago Seanny dressed him up in an overgrown suit, tossed a derby hat on his head, and took him over to Tammany Hall where he became an *Associate* of great value. He was particularly effective at getting out the vote on Election Day, employing a political strategy that mostly consisted of free beer and physical threats, and generally produced anywhere from two to six votes from every man he'd persuaded, dead or alive. Tammany loved his effectiveness, and loved even more that Sean could keep him on a leash far away from Wall Street and City Hall.

Jaysus Ethan, whatta crowd here t'see da tall fella, eh? Cormac asks as he approaches Ethan, with the men around them still staring. Seanny said you was here, but I been standin' by th'door fer da las' five minutes an' I ain't seen ya.

Cormac had taken to him from the first day Sean introduced them, when Cormac shook Ethan's hand and was impressed with his strong grip, then challenged him to some arm wrestles once they'd had a few pints. Ethan beat him once in five tries with his right hand, and two out of five with his left, and Cormac had liked him ever since. As Seanny always said, and Ethan agreed, it was nice to have a man like Cormac on your side. But he's not the type to be here after such an important political speech as this, and Ethan's more than a little ashamed of his affiliation with him just now.

Yeah, it was some crowd in there Cormac, Ethan replies, speaking softly now, trying to diminish the attention being paid to them. I didn't know you'd be interested in the speech.

Oh, I ain't interested in what da fella's got t'*say,* Cormac answers. It's jus' dat Seanny sent me up dis way t'see if you was still here. He ahhh . . . *requests your presence at the Astor House hotel* . . . is what he told me t'tell ya, Cormac says, relaying the message from Sean by removing his hat and bowing slightly at the waist, the way Seanny must've told him to say it.

He what? Ethan asks.

He *requests*–

No, I know whacha said Cormac, Ethan interrupts. What I'm askin' is . . . Cormac, y'can stand up straight there, I got th'message. Cormac's still bowing, intent on fulfilling his mission as if he was Sir Galahad to Seanny's King Arthur, but Ethan guides him back upright.

You an' Seanny been at th'Rose all *night* Cormac, huh? Ethan asks.

See . . . now he *figgered* you was gonna say dat an' he told me t'tell you dat he was . . . Cormac doffs his cap and bends at the waist again . . . *somewhat more'n bit by a barn weasel, but not quite altogetherly.*

Ethan can't help but laughing, partly from the terminology his brother always has at his disposal, partly at seeing this ox of a man, in a suit bursting at the seams, holding his hat over his heart and remaining in a bowed position. And he knows there'll be no dodging this invite.

All right, all right, Ethan says, lifting him again. Let's get on wit' it.

Alas, Squire, Cormac begins in a formal tone again, I am *t'pass on th'invitation an' find me way home . . . for I'm more'n bit by a barn weasel meself.*

Ohhhhh no, Ethan insists. Yer just the man t'help me carry Squire Seanny back to his house. You owe me that much!

Ethan knows there'll be no danger of his brother talking politics on this night. Seanny, as a Tammany man, is by definition a Democrat, while Ethan has taken to the Republican Party and their stand on halting the spread of slavery. Seanny'd always laughed at the pie-in-the-sky ideals of Ethan and now lumped men like Lincoln right in there with him. And their debates had grown more pointed, though as inconclusive as ever, over the years. But if Seanny's in anything like the state Cormac is in, Ethan thinks, he'll mop the floor with him in a debate now, and since his brother only enters the ring with victory almost assured, there'll be no serious discussion on politics this evening. Along Broadway they pass Barclay Street and spot Seanny standing a good distance from the front entrance of the Astor and leaning up against a streetlamp.

Ahhhhh, here they are, Sean says as they approach. The Squire and his Associate.

Jaysus, Seanny, Ethan says, you leave *any* whiskey in th'Points?

Sean turns to Cormac, pretending to take offense at the insult.

Sir Cormac, he says, with as much royal diction as he can muster, my young Squire brudder here has drawn into question th'sobriety of yours truly. An' this after Oh've gone t'ahll the considerable trouble of discoverin' th'location where a certain Mr. Ayyy Lincoln, Esquire, of Springfield, *Ill-eee-noise,* will be stayin' for th'duration of his visit t'ahr fair city.

Ethan's eyes light up as Sean waves his arm toward the entrance of the Astor Hotel and Cormac follows suit. They both bow slightly and move a step to the side to allow Ethan to pass.

Yer on the straight here? Ethan asks. How'd you find out?

My good sir, Sean says, perhaps you wishta withdraw th'insults previous?

I do, Ethan says with a smile, a little too giddy for a man of twenty-five.

They wait in the elegant lobby seated around a table beside

the massive fireplace. Ethan's in a chair facing out to the front entrance while Cormac and Sean each take up occupancy of separate couches facing the fire. A waiter from the restaurant comes out and Sean orders brandy for all of them before Ethan can send him away.

We're not going up to a presidential candidate completely smashed, Ethan says to Sean.

Oh, there's no *we* to this operation, Squire, Sean assures him.

No *we,* Cormac repeats, then grimaces slightly and adds, but I do koinda *hafta* wee.

And wee you shall, my good man, Seanny says with his customary formality when he's in such a state. Sir Cormac here, who hasta wee, has completed th'task of uncoverin' Mr. Lincoln's temporary residence, and now it's all up to *you,* Squire brudder of mine, to carry out actually shakin' the tall man's hand. In th'meantime, I believe I shall do some weein' of me own.

They walk off to the necessary, and so it goes for the better part of an hour. Sean and Cormac, when they return, find considerable amusement in teasing Ethan while they drink their brandy. Just as the two of them are about to break into song, Ethan spots the unmistakable figure of Mr. Lincoln walking through the front entrance. He tips his stovepipe hat to the doorman as well as to the attendant behind the front desk, and walks toward the grand stairway. Ethan is up in a shot and Sean and Cormac stop their joking for a moment to turn around and see what's caused the reaction.

Give'm a kiss for me, Squire, Sean jokes once he sees Lincoln, and he and Cormac laugh uncontrollably.

Ethan walks across the lobby and catches Mr. Lincoln on the landing between the first and second floors. He looks remarkably tired and his shoulders are slouched, making his arms appear even longer than before.

Mr. Lincoln, sir, Ethan calls out from a few steps behind him.

Lincoln takes the final step up to the landing and turns toward him. His fatigue is evident, and his face isn't just gaunt like before, but appears sunken, like it's frozen in the middle of drawing in a deep breath.

Yes, hello, he replies while removing his hat.

Sir . . . it is an honor to meet you, Ethan says, fumbling for words. I . . . I was at your speech this evenin' at Cooper Union, and I must tell you that you have my full support for th'nomination . . . not that it's of any importance, but . . . well, it was a fine speech, sir.

Well thank you, young man. You are? Lincoln asks, and extends his hand.

Ethan . . . Ethan McOwen, sir. Lincoln's hand is bigger than Suah's even.

It's a pleasure to meet you, Mr. McOwen. Irish, yes? I thought I detected a brogue.

Yes sir. Though I've been here longer than I was in the Old Country, Ethan replies, dismayed just a little that he's so easily identified, even now.

Compared to my voice, yours is quite presidential, Lincoln says, as if he can understand Ethan's expression. Where are you from?

Outside of Enniskillen, County Fermanagh . . . in the north, Ethan says, and can see that Lincoln is not familiar with it. My family's been here since The Hunger—the famine, that is, sir.

Oh yes—a terrible tragedy. What terrible suffering your people have faced. But you're doing well now, it appears.

Yes, we are, Ethan replies. My brother's in politics . . . well, he's a Democrat.

Lincoln laughs. Even great men have their vices, he says.

Very true. Well, he does a great deal of work in the Five Points. He's a supporter of many charities there.

Good, there's plenty of work to be done there, he replies. Tell your brother for me that it's important work he does. And tell him when he's ready to come over to the Republican Party, we'll forgive all his past transgressions. And what is it *you* do, Mr. McOwen?

I'm a photographer . . . portraits mostly, Ethan says.

I had mine taken just yesterday, Lincoln says.

Yes sir, at Mathew Brady's. I read about it sir.

Well if I had known, I would have come by your studio as well, Mr. McOwen.

And with that Mr. Lincoln tips his hat and bows slightly. Ethan wants to press on with the conversation, but can see that the politician is tired of politicking, and just plain tired in general.

Thank you sir, he says, and I do hope you'll receive the nomination of the party.

Most days I do too, Mr. McOwen, and they shake hands again before Lincoln ascends the steps before him.

As Ethan walks back across the lobby he can't help but think of being back in Ireland, stealing handfuls of oats from the Brodericks' horses and feeling his family didn't deserve as much, what with how the Brodericks were a proper rich family and all. Thoughts of Seanny and Cormac and Harry and his Da run through his head, as if each of their paths was one he might've followed. But instead here he is, a struggling photographer with potential, a would-be scholar without a degree, and now, being called *Mr. McOwen* by a man who just delivered the kind of speech that might soon have him running for President of the United States.

Did ya get a locka his hair, Squire? Sean asks as Ethan returns to them.

I gotta tell ya Ethan, Cormac adds, dat's one *homely*-lookin' lass ya got dere.

But it doesn't matter, none of it, not when he's come this far. He looks at the empty brandy bottle on the table, then sees that the bar is still open across the Great Hall.

I could use a pint, Ethan says. I'm buyin'.

Oh good god, this *is* a day to remember, Seanny says, and he and Cormac are soon following behind.

6 *Should Have Been Born a Man*

MARCELLA ARROYO
SAVANNAH, GEORGIA
AUGUST 18, 1860

"Three cards for Miss Marcella?" Witt asks, with every ounce of genteel condescension he seemingly can muster.

"Three . . . oh . . . yes please, Mr. Witt," she replies, placing the cards nervously down in front of her. "Oh, wait a moment," she quickly adds, then looks at the two cards in her hand, exchanging one of them for one she has just discarded.

The men laugh, looking around at each other and back at her, acknowledging that she is charmingly out of place. Marcella giggles with embarrassment, looks at her cards again, and nods before placing them down on the table.

"I believe I'd give you *four* cards, Miss Marcella," Witt says with a giant half-moon smile beneath his finely groomed mustache. "If I wasn't afraid you'd take all my money from me, hahahahaha . . ."

Marcella smiles and bats her eyelashes some. "Well I *do* thank you, Mr. Witt. And what a charming, thoughtful man you are," she says. *Jackass,* she thinks.

The new cards are dealt, and she's wide-eyed and appearing gullible as a child as she studies each man's reactions to his new cards.

"Well . . . I'll bet *ten* dollars," van Nils announces, his voice cracking just a bit. *Bluffing again,* she thinks.

"Make it twenny!" Starling exclaims. *And thank you, Mr. Starling, for always raising so emphatically when you have the weakest hand.*

Jordan is next and he only calls. *Didn't make his straight or flush,* she thinks. *Two pair, perhaps.* And all eyes turn back to her.

"Why Miss Marcella, here I give you three brand-new cards an' you haven't even *looked* at 'em yet," Witt says. "Now why would you go and hurt my feelin's like that?"

"Oh dear, I was so caught up in all the excitement," she says. *Oh dear, it'll be a* particular *pleasure to take your money, Mr. Witt.*

Marcella pretends to be horribly embarrassed, smiles apologetically, and picks up the three new cards. While the men continue laughing, she puts them down and looks at the original two again.

"You're *allowed* to look at 'em all at once," Starling jokes.

"An' even if it *was* against the rules, Miss Marcella," Jordan adds, "why, I believe we'd make'n exception for such a charmin' young lady as yourself."

"Well I sure do thank you all," Marcella replies. "Ha, *'you all,'* I believe I'm becomin' more Southern ever' day we're here." *Try not to shudder now,* she reminds herself.

"Well we're happy t'have such a pretty lady decoratin' the room like this, Miss Marcella," Witt says. *Steady.*

"A reg'lar Spanish Southern belle, an' pretty as the moonlight," van Nils adds. *Steady.*

"An' we don' wanna see you lose any money, so . . ." Witt adds, getting to the point.

"Oh my, is it *my* turn to bet?" she asks.

"Well, Mr. van Nils already bet ten dollars, an' Mr. Starling made it *twenty,*" he replies, as if telling a child about ghosts in the attic. *Goodness me!* she orders her face to express.

"Oh my. So twenty dollars? Two red ones?" she asks.

"Well yes," Witt says, "but you don't *hafta* play, Miss Marcella . . ."

But before he can complete his sentence, Marcella throws in her twenty dollars.

"Now hold on just a second," he says. "I was gonna say you could *fold,* Miss Marcella, an' save th'twenny dollars. Now you didn't know that, so I'm sure the gentlemen won't mind if you take 'em back." He looks around at them and they're all quick to agree.

"Oh, I *see* . . ." she says. "But *that* wouldn't be very much *fun.* No—this is fine."

Witt shakes his head as if what he is about to do will wound him greatly, but it's out of his hands. *Barely even looked at his two new cards,* Marcella observes. *So three of a kind. They'd better be aces, Mr. Witt. Now, at least.*

"I'm sorry, but . . . well . . . I'll make it thirty, gentlemen," Witt finally says, looking over at Marcella as if his heart were breaking to take her money like this.

"I'm out," van Nils says, throwing his cards away with disgust.

"Forty!" Starling exclaims with a greater edge this time. *Too quick again, Mr. Starling.*

"Call!" Jordan says. *Ahhh, Mr. Jordan,* she thinks, *you'd be a very good player if you just didn't so hate the idea of losing to Mr. Starling.*

They all look condescendingly at her again.

"Now Miss Marcella," Witt cautions. "This hand's gotten richer'n we usually—"

"How much is it, fawty dollars?" she interrupts. "*Fawty* dollars, hee-hee. I'm 'bout ready to move down here with y'all." *Forgive me Mrs. Carlisle,* she jokes to herself.

"Well, only *twenny* more to you," Witt says, "but now you don' hafta . . . that is . . ."

"You can *fold* like I did," van Nils says. "Just smart poker's all that is, Miss Marcella."

"Oh—but I'd like to see this through to the end, I think. So yes, I believe I'll give it a go. There—two more red ones," she says, tossing the chips into the middle and then looking around at the pained faces of her opponents. "Oh, don't worry so much, *y'all,*" she laughs. "It's only *money.*"

Her smile seems to ease some of their suffering.

"Well, might as well see it through," Witt says, and tosses his money into the pot.

They all look to Starling, who places his pair of jacks down in front of him, announcing them with far more glee than they merit.

"Nines over fours," Jordan counters, happy just to beat Starling no matter what it cost.

"Well . . . I've been very lucky *indeed.*" Marcella says, cautiously, so as not to offend. "Three *kings,*" she says with just enough glee to make the men actually feel happy for her.

"That beats my three tens," Witt says, sounding almost relieved.

"Well, lookit that!" van Nils adds, and the men laugh as Marcella rakes in the pot of nearly two hundred dollars.

"*That'll* buy a new dress or two, Miss Marcella."

"Charmin', witty, *and* a card shark." "Don't forget pretty as a daisy." "A daisy? Pretty as a *rose.*" "A *Savannah* rose."

Steady, she urges herself.

The men fall all over themselves complimenting her, and she takes it all in with blushing amusement. *I didn't think it would be* this *easy.*

"Well . . . y'all are *fahhr* too generous in your praise," she says. "I'm just glad I had some better luck than my poor brothers did. They're the ones who taught me howta *play,* after all."

The men look at each other and laugh some more.

"Yes, well," Witt says, as if speaking for the entire table, "Miss Marcella, I believe it's safe to say that *you're* the best card player in your *esteemed* family."

"Why thank you, Mr. Witt," she responds. *I know just how small a compliment that is.*

For two hours that evening, she'd sat in one of the parlor room armchairs beside the poker table, pretending to read while she watched her brothers stumble through playing with as much subtlety as they employed in their daily lives, sons of their father that they were. They bet with the kind of bravado that was as clear a tell as Starling's exclamations or van Nils's cracking voice, but with even less sense. And then, before her brothers were completely out of money, Marcella slipped upstairs and waited in the parlor between their rooms. Bartolomé and Miguel strolled in a short while later, looking to have a few more brandies and commiserate over what bad luck they'd had, and Marcella quickly found out that they'd lost five hundred dollars between them. A half hour later she managed to charm her way into the game, declaring to the young gentlemen, "Daddy gave me two hundred dollars for new dresses, but I already have more dresses than I could possibly ever wear as it is, and—my brothers taught me all about the game—and in Europe the ladies play cards with the men all the time, for money even, and . . . well—I'm just so terribly *bored.*" And the men finally, *laughingly,* relented.

What's most difficult for Marcella is that she has to play at a level beneath these men for most of the evening, selecting only the best opportunities to win a pot. But by the time midnight rolls around, she is up five hundred dollars. It's astounding the run of *luck* she's had, and that recognition, combined with her flattery and batting eyelashes, keep the gentlemen as cordial as ever. She's only won back what her brothers had lost, after all. But she knows that things will change if she lets that *luck* continue to roll. So she bides her time, waiting for one more big splash before she'll suddenly become shocked at how late it is and excuse herself from the game. But when an hour more passes and the cards don't provide such a prospect, she begins to think of settling for what she's already won. And then the swirling tornado of a healthy dose of male vanity, mixed with a double measure of brandy, provides her with a chance.

The hand starts with Jordan dealing, and Marcella the first to bet. After she declines, Witt wagers ten dollars, van Nils squeaks it up to twenty, Starling leaps in to make it forty, and that aggravates Jordan enough to make it sixty. Marcella looks at her cards again, grins slightly, and puts in sixty dollars. By now the men have given up any remorse in trying their hardest to beat her, so Witt raises it to eighty. *No more "Poor Miss Marcella"?*

This is where the brandy comes in as van Nils makes it a hundred, Starling a hundred fifty, and Jordan, angrier than ever, makes it an even two hundred. He looks around the table as if he has settled the matter once and for all. But Marcella quickly calls the bet, and the men begin to look around at one another, shocked that she's still in, and perhaps feeling a little guilty for their bravado. Witt, van Nils, and Starling simply call the bet as well. *Scared, are we?*

Jordan makes the call for cards and Marcella looks at her hand again, then lays them down with a blushing smile.

"No thank you, Mr. Jordan," she says as graciously as possible. *Be sure to flash those eyelashes now,* she reminds herself. *That's it. Now look around and take in their . . . panic.*

The men all take one or two cards, trying to posture strength and assurance. She watches their faces again as each of them picks up their new cards, and predictably, with a pot of a thousand dollars, whatever reserve they'd had before slips quickly away. Witt quietly exhales and she knows he's missed his straight or flush. Even van Nils has to know his two low pair won't do the trick in this kind of pot and Starling bites his lower lip slightly before forcing a confident smile and sticking out his chest. That leaves only Jordan. *He couldn't possibly have hit something to go with his three of a kind . . . or perhaps . . . no, he didn't get the fourth . . . he couldn't stay that calm if he had.*

It's her turn to bet, and she knows that this is the hand of her life so far. It will either provide her with a great story to tell to all her friends back home, or assure that she'll never mention this night to anyone again. She lifts her cards up and slowly fans them out, looking at the three of diamonds, the jack and six of spades, and the two and nine of hearts, studying them as if trying to make sure that they haven't changed since she first looked at them. Then she bites her bottom lip as if holding back a smile, and places the cards neatly face down on the table, watching them all the way, then looking up with her eyes first, her head still slightly tilted downward. *Mischievous smile now,* she tells herself.

"Well gentlemen, it's been so much fun playing cards with *y'all.*"

"An' you *too,* Miss Marcella," Jordan replies, maintaining what composure he can with such a large pot at stake. "So does that mean you fold?"

"*Fold?* Oh no, Mr. Jordan—my apologies, but I mean to *wager.*"

"Oh . . . it's just that it sounded like you were done for th'evenin'," he says.

"Well yes it *is* gettin' ratha late," she agrees, "an' perhaps I *should* make this m'last hand. It's just that y'all have been such gentlemen, an' I don't want there t'be any ill feelings."

"Miss Marcella, I think I can speak for all of us when I assure you that we could *never* think ill of you," van Nils declares. *Oh, Mr. van Nils,* she thinks through her smile, *someday you'll find a woman foolish enough for you, and you'll live happily, foolishly ever after.*

"Oh, that's so kinda you to say, Mista van Nils," she replies, and blushes as much as her olive skin will allow. "Well then . . . I'll wager five hundred."

"Five hundred!" Witt exclaims as if the chandelier has just crashed to the table.

"Oh . . . well, yes, I know I'm dippin' inta all that dress money Daddy gave me," she answers. "But this is *so* much more fun than buyin' a dress!"

"Yes, but do you need to . . . that is . . ." Witt's still at a loss, and Marcella notices that van Nils and even Starling have already pushed their cards away from them. "It's a shame with this kind of hand," Witt stammers, ". . . but . . . well . . . I can't bet five hundred–not with the way *fortune's* smiled upon you, Miss Marcella."

He tosses in his cards as if he's doing her a gentlemanly deed, and then there is just Jordan and his three of a kind. Of all the men at the table, Jordan has played the best poker. *But not* that *good. Not good enough to call here.*

"Miss Marcella," he says after a long pause. "I'm not likely to sleep tonight if I don't get t'satisfy my curiosity an' see whatcher holdin'."

"Well, I sure don't mean to cause you any un*rest,* Mr. Jordan," she says amusingly.

He looks at her sternly for a moment, then returns to his former, artificial self. *Just lay them down . . . go ahead now,* she thinks.

"But then again, I'm not likely to sleep for a *week* if I lose five hundred dollars to a . . . well, no offense now, but . . . to a woman. Even one as bright an' charmin' as you."

How could I possibly be offended by that?

"So if I fold these cards," he continues, "will you go ahead an' show me yours?"

Marcella blushes as if he's asked her to show him her petticoats.

"Well Mr. *Jordan,*" she says, and looks around the table. "I . . . am I *allowed* to do that, gentlemen?"

They chime in with immediate approval, just as anxious to see her cards as Jordan is.

"Well in *that* case," she says, looking at Jordan with a wry smile, "I s'pose I could."

He thinks about it for a moment or two, then throws over three aces, shaking his head at sacrificing such a hand.

"You had the straight, Miss Marcella?" Jordan asks.

"Naw, it was a flush!" Starling insists.

"Well," she begins, "you gentlemen should know that I *never* do this . . . but I just *had* to try it one time."

She flips over her colossal bluff and it's as if they don't recognize it right away, as if they're looking closer and closer trying to figure out what they're missing. And then they collectively understand what has happened. Not very long ago she would have triumphantly collected the chips and delivered a brief lecture on the capabilities of women. But instead she maintains her mischievous grin, and a situation that might've ended with fists being thrown were she a man, quickly gives way to laughter. And then the men are fawning in their congratulations. She stays for a few moments to collect all their praise, and most of their money, then cashes in her chips and leaves, as each of the men stands and applauds her exit. Her winnings total fourteen hundred seventy-five dollars. *Oh, how they will hate themselves in the morning.*

Upstairs, she enters her room through the hallway, and hears Miguel and Bartolomé stirring in the parlor that connects their rooms. There's just enough time to stuff the money away in a dresser drawer before Miguel begins knocking.

"Marcie," he calls. "Marcie . . . *tenías suerte?*"

She opens the door and steps past him, walking to the table where the nearly empty brandy bottle is situated. She pours herself a small glass with what's left and for effect says nothing as she walks over to a nearby chair and flops down in it. She drinks the brandy down in a sip, then gazes at her brothers.

"No luck," she announces. "Couldn't get a decent hand all night."

"How much do you lose?" Bartolomé asks, deflated.

"Menos que vosotros," she says. "That's how I know you'll never say a *word* of it to Papa."

Both of them look at each other, shaking their heads as if they'd never had any intention of telling their father.

"I didn't think they can beat *you*," Miguel says in astonishment.

"*Could* Miguel," she corrects. "I didn't think they *could* beat you. *Subjunctivo*."

"We need more brandy," he replies.

THE NEXT MORNING BRINGS THE final day of the trip, and Marcella is off from the hotel before her father or brothers emerge from their rooms. Walking as casually as she can manage, she makes her way to Montgomery Street, then pauses, unsure of which way to proceed. In the distance to her left is a church steeple still under construction. Mrs. Carlisle hadn't said anything about what to do from here, but the steeple is a more promising sight than anything she sees to her right. Her heart begins to race as she nears the building, then sinks when she sees that it's made of brick instead of wood. Mrs. Carlisle had described a white wooden structure that would be nearly forty years old by now. This one is newly built, with only the steeple left to be completed, and for those next several moments she worries that the whole trip will end in failure. But then she sees a beacon of hope.

A small tapestry hangs over a wooden post beside the church, adorned with a pattern of three backwards *L*'s interlocked to form the image of a wood cabin tipped onto its side. A square yellow patch fills the inside *L*, and she knows that this is exactly the place she has sought. A minute later her hope is confirmed, as she approaches the front of the building and sees the sign out front: First African Baptist Church.

She can't help but smile, then quickly composes herself before looking up and down the street to see if anyone is watching her. There are several people along the avenue, but none of them seem to take particular notice of her. It's still quite early, but she can see that the church doors are slightly opened, and she walks up the steps and inside the building with newfound determination. The pews are empty and everything is silent, but she sees another promising sign glancing up at the ceiling and the Nine-Patch ornamentation. A man walks out from the door next to the pulpit and seems to take no notice of Marcella at first, but when he does look toward the back of the church, his smile quickly fades as soon as he sees her. And she knows this will be more difficult than she had anticipated.

"Good mornin', Ma'am," the man says, and walks tentatively toward her.

He is far too young to be the man Mrs. Carlisle had described as the pastor she remembered. *But he's dressed in a preacher's suit and he walks with the calmness of a preacher, even if I am making him nervous,* she thinks.

"Good morning, Ma'am," he says again as he stops perhaps ten or fifteen feet from her and bows slightly at the waist.

"Good morning," she replies. *Should I curtsey, or would that be scandalous down here?*

"May I be of any assistance t'ya, Ma'am?" the man asks before she can figure out whether to curtsey or not.

"I hope . . . that is . . . I believe you can. I'm looking for Mr. Marshall. Pastor Marshall."

The calmness in the man's face quickly gives way to suspicion.

"Reveren' Marshall's no longer wit' us, Ma'am," he replies. "Passed some years ago."

And at that moment the impulse hits her to just turn around and walk out, difficult as this will now be, and given all the consequences. But she couldn't possibly return to the ladies in New York, to Mrs. Carlisle in particular, and say she had made it to the actual place and not seen it through.

"I'm so very sorry," she says, and can see the surprise in his face now. Then, remembering Mrs. Carlisle's description of living in Georgia, Marcella realizes that this might be the first time in this man's life that a white woman has apologized to him.

"Thank you, Misses . . ." he replies, bowing slightly again.

"Miss," she corrects. "Miss Arroyo."

"Miss Ar- . . ."

"Marcella."

"Miss Marcella," he says with greater ease. "I'm William Campbell. I'm the pastor now since Reveren' Marshall passed."

"Oh! Oh, that's wonderful to hear. Then yes, Reverend Campbell, you *can* help me."

She looks back at the open doors and then around the church to verify that there is nobody else around them, before proceeding.

"I am from New York, well, Spain originally, but New York for the last seven years now," she begins awkwardly, then adjusts her voice down to little more than a whisper. "I am . . . I'm a member of the Ladies Abolition Society of New York, and one of its founding members, Mrs. Carlisle, lived here in Savannah for seventeen years when she was married."

He's never heard of Mrs. Carlisle, she thinks. *Of course not, it's been years since she was here. And now he's got that look you would expect when I mentioned the Ladies Abolition Society.*

"I'm sorry Miss, but I don' think I can help you none."

"You are not familiar with Mrs. Carlisle, I imagine?" she asks.

"No, Miss."

"Well, Mrs. Carlisle had the idea two years ago that we should start collecting whatever money we could in order to purchase freedom for slaves," she said. "We raised nearly two thousand dollars last year and were able to buy the freedom of a woman and her sister and two children. They live in Brooklyn now."

Nothing. He doesn't believe me. Keep explaining.

"Then my father and brothers were coming on this business trip, and I knew they would be traveling through South Carolina and Georgia, and Mrs. Carlisle mentioned that we could put the money we collected since last year to far greater use if we could get it to people who . . ."

She looks around before continuing.

". . . who were assisting with runaways on the Underground Railroad."

His expression changes dramatically now as his mouth opens, and his eyebrows are lifted as high as they can go, like he's just heard the greatest blasphemy imaginable.

"Miss, I don' know o' nothin' like that 'round here," he says. "This is a good Christian place o' worship here, firs' one of its kind, bringin' Jesus to th'colored folks, an' we don' know nothin' 'bout any o' *that* business."

"Oh, I'm sorry, I . . . I know I shouldn't *talk* about such things," she offers. "I'm very new to this."

"Miss Marcella, I don' know what your fren' mighta believed was goin' on 'round here in the past, but I been Pastor for goin' on four years now, an' I never seen a runaway anywhere 'round here," he insists. "Is there anythin' *else* I can help you wit'?"

He begins to inch his way toward the front door, and she knows she'll have to convince him she is who she claims to be.

"That's a very nice pattern there," she says, pointing up at the ceiling. "*Nine-Patch,* I believe it's called."

She looks back at him, and then continues before he has the chance to reply.

"And that beautiful tapestry outside, the one draped over the wooden post? That's the log cabin symbol, I believe. Yellow patch on the inside, signifying the light's on and it's safe to come in?"

"Miss, I don' know—"

"Reverend Campbell, I assure you I am here to offer what help we can," she insists. "And this may be my first time in the South, but I *am* familiar with the symbols used on the Underground Railroad. And Mrs. Carlisle didn't only *believe* this church was used as a hiding place, she knew it. She *assisted* in the work. She's the one who told me to come here."

"Miss, I don' know 'bout any—"

Oh enough of this now. I'm here to give you money, dammit, she thought, losing patience as she so often and so easily did.

"Are there holes in the floorboard by the sanctuary?" she asks, folding her free hand into a fist and placing it palm down against her hip in an accusing manner. *Mmm-hmm, that look means yes.* "They're cut to appear to be some sort of symbol, but they are really there as air holes for the space beneath it. That's where you hide the runaways, is it not?"

He said nothing. *Offended the preacher. Typical for you,* she thought, and realized this was surely no simple matter for him.

"Reverend Campbell, I apologize for being so blunt," she says, reaching her hand into the closed parasol she has carried with her and taking out the small canvas satchel hidden inside it. "But we are leaving for New York in a few hours, and the whole *reason* I talked my father into taking me along on this trip was to come here and give you the eight hundred dollars the Ladies Abolition Society has most recently raised."

She offers the satchel to him and he looks at it, silently, then walks slowly to the front door, closing it and sliding the latch across into its holster. Then he walks to each of the windows along the back of the church, looking in every direction from them before pulling the curtains closed. Then slowly he walks over toward her, stopping this time just five feet away.

Now we're getting somewhere, she thinks.

"Please take it, it's for you, for the work you do," she says, extending the satchel toward him. "It's for clothes and food for the runaways."

His face softens a bit and he looks around again.

"Well, we do accept donations for the buildin' o' the steeple an'such," he says. "Even been a coupla white folks kind enough ta help us."

So this is how it must appear, she thinks.

"Well, call it what you will, but know that the Ladies have collected this for the *work* you do, *not* the steeple."

She walks forward toward him, arm outstretched with the satchel in her hand. He nods and hesitates just a second before taking it from her and placing it quickly into his inside pocket, not even looking at it for more than a second.

"I understan', and thank you Miss Marcella," he says, smiling just a little for the first time since she walked in. "An' wonchu please be kind enough to thank the Ladies for us. Eight *hunnerd* dollars."

He shakes his head at the thought of it and touches his coat where the satchel is hidden inside.

"Well, it's actually a bit more than that," she says, smiling. *How to tell a preacher this?*

"More than eight *hunnerd*?" he asks, looking astonished again.

"As you are a man of God, Reverend, I suppose I shouldn't tell you about the good fortune that befell me and . . . well . . . let's just say there are a few more *donations* included in that pouch. There's nearly two thousand three hundred dollars there, Reverend, and I'll just leave it at that."

He's nervous again now. I shouldn't have mentioned anything. Would it be better or worse if I told him that I won it from four men who owned five hundred slaves between them?

And for a moment she worries that all will be lost at this final, crucial moment.

"Two *thousan'* three *hunnerd* dollars kin do a might bitta good, Miss Marcella," he says, looking as if he's considering how many runaways he'll now be able to set on their way with a real chance of making it all the way to the North, to Canada even.

"The Lawd surely works in mysterious ways," he says, and smiles.

And for Marcella it is a victory greater than even the triumph of the previous night, a crowning moment in her life to date.

"Yes Reverend, He surely *does,*" she answers. *If only you knew.*

NEW YORK
SEPTEMBER 1, 1860

It's the same pearl-handled brush she's used nearly every morning for the last eight years, but it is always on this day that it has far greater meaning, and the memories run thicker than the long black hair it professes to tame. Eight years ago, on this very morning, her Abuela gave her the brush wrapped in lace and tied with a red silk ribbon. She'd come into Marcella's room in the faint suggestion of the dawn, waking her by brushing her hand across her cheek, and Marcella could tell right away that the letter had come, and this was to be the end of their time together. Every first of September since that one, she's awoken as if by instinct at the same inviting hour, to think back—each year with fewer tears than the one before—and replay those cherished moments in her mind. And now, running her fingers over the brush rather than bringing it to her hair, her thoughts drift, though at the safe distance she's always placed between herself and her truest feelings, imagining the story as if it had happened to another person altogether . . .

Querida . . . Querida . . .

You woke to the familiar voice and the wrinkled dryness of Abuela's hand on your face, and then the look, the half-hearted smile masquerading tears, made you start to cry as well.

Querida—I bring you something . . .

And then the gifts, the brooch and hair ribbons and the brush that had been given to Abuela by her Mama.

You think of me when you are to use these and also every morning when you . . . cuando tú cepillas . . . ?

Brush.

Sí, When you brush your beautiful hair—you think of me.

You looked at Abuela and knew this was the end.

A letter from Papa? you asked.

And another smile from Abuela to hide a tear.

Sí. It come when you sleep—tu Mama receive it at the party. Señor

Higuera give it to her and it say that you Papa . . . compra . . . that he buy a house for all of you in New York. So you go now to live there—with you Papa—all of you together again.

Abuela tried her best to make the news sound as if it had been something truly anticipated. But you had only dreaded it, you dreaded every letter from Papa, sent to Señor Higuera with a fake name for fear that he would be found out and somehow brought back in shame.

When are we to leave? you asked, angry at Abuela that she would not save you from this fate.

Tomorrow . . . Querida—is good for you to—

Why I cannot live here with you?

Abuela shook her head, the way she always did when she felt powerless to act . . . when she felt the limits of being a woman.

I am sorry for the Papa mi hijo become . . . I am sorry for the things he do—pero, he is you Papa. And you . . . tú perteneces . . . ?

You would not translate, shaking your head.

Tú perteneces con tu Papa. Toda la familia pertenece juntos.

I belong with YOU. You are my family too, you said.

No soy tu Papa . . . y tu Mama? Pilar? Tus hermanos?

I want to live with you . . . I—

Ah, Querida—I know it is difficult . . . I know what it is to . . . esperar . . . ?

To wish.

Sí . . . I know what it is to wish . . . all my life to wish I am borned a man—from when I am una niña. When I am a little girl I wish this. All of life I wish this. Desde . . . ?

Until.

Sí, sí . . . until I am una vieja . . . until you Abuelo is no more with me.

And you understood a little better then. It was the men who ruined things.

I have these for you, Querida, Abuela said.
And as if it was a consolation, she handed you the three notebooks of blank paper bound in leather.
Tú escribe—you write in these—always—all the time you wish that too—write to me in these and you can . . . it is like we are here. Saberando que yo comprendo—I understand what you think. Ahhh, Querida . . . I understand . . .

And now she opens the drawer of her dressing table, taking out the jewelry box and lifting out the shelf to reveal the small key hidden beneath it, using the key to unlock the lower drawer, where the notebooks are kept. There are the three of them from Abuela, filled a long time ago, at the bottom of a pile of ten—better than one per year—and they produce the usual proud smile whenever she sees them all together like this, like it was something of an accomplishment to have endured this long, pouring her thoughts and whatever emotions she allowed herself to feel into these books, every entry in them addressed to Abuela. She takes the three, forgoing the other, more recent histories of her life, and places them beside the brush on her dressing table. And there is barely enough light to read through them in the silence of the house while even the servants are still asleep, as she carries out this ritual of every first of September morning.

The first pages tell of the journey over, of the complaints of her brothers for having to travel in the second-class cabins, of the massive plumes of smoke and steam the ship's engines produced and the way they willowed off into the infinite sea sky. And when she was gone just a few days, the entries became less about life on the ship or sharing a room with Pilar and Mama, and were instead filled with the details of the previous year, as if Marcella knew that it was a time in her life she must record now, lest it drift off like so many plumes of smoke and steam.

She began that portion of the story on *9 September 1852*, starting not with the first days at Abuela's estate, but with the events leading up to it. Marcella wrote it as she did all the ones previous, as if speaking to Abuela, only telling her what she already knew all too well about Papa's *asuntos de amor*, copying the sweetened phrase the servants used when describing his philandering ways. Marcella had overheard the conversations for years, even before she understood what any of them meant, even before she understood the inherent sadness in Mama's boast to Tía Teresa that Papa *never carried on an affair with more than one woman at a time*, and didn't have the first of them *until they were married nearly five years!* But writing those entries to Abuela then, it was clear that Marcella had come to understand all of it, understanding why Mama felt no other recourse than accepting Papa's hollow apologies, understanding why Papa's *asunto de amor* with *la esposa* of the Minister of Finance was another matter altogether, understanding why Papa's business dealings were legal when he was just another rich and powerful and philandering man, but were not so legal when he was carrying on with the *esposa* of the Minister of Finance.

And examining those pages now, thinking of Papa eight impenitent years later, she is stirred to the sort of emotion she generally seeks to contain, lest her true feelings be discovered too soon. So she flips past them, past the days when Papa fled to America, to the early weeks at Abuela's when she felt more alone than ever before or since and convinced herself she would have it no other way. She would rise with the sun and walk outside to watch the field laborers start their irrigation work in the vineyards. Then she would follow around Lela, a chambermaid who had lived in Florida for the first fifteen years of her life. Lela was bitter and surly but tolerated having Marcella for a shadow since she would ask her the English word for everything they saw and then repeat it over and over, giving Lela the chance to laugh at her mispronunciations.

Then after the midday meal and the siesta, Marcella was forced to join Pilar and her brothers and Mama in the grand parlor so they could practice their English in anticipation of being summoned to America by Papa. For the first few weeks, such gatherings were led by Abuela, who had lived in Florida for three years after she and Abuelo were first married. But by the third month Marcella had become more proficient in English than even Abuela, and by the fourth she became the teacher. It was around that time that Abuela began to take special notice of Marcella. Each afternoon Abuela summoned her to her room, and they spoke fractured English back and forth. Marcella, as always, was full of questions, and she began to understand that Abuela was far more than the *vieja* she had always seen her as. She began to see that her grandmother was perhaps the happiest woman she knew, and it seemed a remarkable contradiction to her, given what she had known of the world thus far, given that Abuelo had died just a year before.

Reading through the recollection of these happy hours, recorded when they were still fresh in her mind, Marcella is able to drift back again, to one afternoon in particular, just weeks before the fateful letter from Papa arrived . . .

Why are you such happy? you asked her.
I am happy to be with you, Querida, Abuela answered.
And you could tell that she had not understood the question.

No . . . not now, this moment—always it seem . . . with Abuelo not here . . . anymore, you said.
And she took on a more serious look then, making you worry that you had said something wrong and hurt her, that you had ruined the moment or even your relationship altogether.
But then Abuela smiled.
It is because I live for me . . . solamente for me . . . because you Abuelo no can say to me what I do or where I go, she said.
And you worried then that Abuelo had been a man like your papa.
You have love Abuelo? you asked.
Sí . . . sí . . . she answered, with no more emotion than if she were discussing a hair ribbon. But a woman . . . she can be happy . . . she can only be . . . completamente . . . ?
Completely.
And Abuela smiled and rolled her head the way she did when a translation was so simple and she had just forgotten it.
Sí, sí, sí . . . completely . . . a woman can only be completely happy when she have no papa and no esposo—nobody to tell her what she can do and what she cannot do.
And she added nothing more, as if that said everything on the matter.

The memory ends there amidst stirring from next door. Pilar is awake, and Marcella shakes her head and rolls her eyes just to herself, knowing that this is as far as she will read this morning. It is perhaps better, she thinks for a moment, since she will revisit these books again in March, stirring up the memories on the anniversary of Abuela's death that had once so devastated her just six months after she had given her the brush and the brooch and the notebooks now filled with her part of the conversations they never had the chance to say out loud. She closes the book and locks it away with the rest of them until that sad day, bracing for the onslaught, and the duties of an older sister—soon to be free of all of this—and perhaps . . . *completely* happy . . . one day soon.

THE ARROYO WOMEN, LIKE ALL women of any stature and breeding, were meant to be little more than functionaries in their own homes and ornaments outside them. Marcella's Mama had certainly fulfilled her part of that requirement, serving as loyal wife, competent hostess of even the most unendurable business-inspired dinner parties, and silent companion at all manner of social occasions. She had endeavored to make sure that Marcella and Pilar learned proper social behavior and were educated just enough to interest a young man—but not so much that they would scare him off. It was only in this matter that she could be found lacking, having long ago lost control of the reins when it came to Marcella and eventually shifting her focus to the still salvageable Pilar. By now she governed Marcella, if at all, only through a sense of guilt and pity inspired by a moment of great emotion more than a year earlier when she had confessed to Marcella how much she envied her. And Marcella, seeing a woman long ago defeated and made entirely subjugate, generally allowed herself to be guided by her Mama's appeals, except when they stood too directly in her way.

"I don't see why I cannot go with you," Pilar pleads as she watches Marcella get ready to leave late that afternoon. "You know that Papa's business friends will all be drunk by then and I will be forced to stay and listen to all their bored talk."

"Bor*ing* talk," Marcella corrects, and laughs just a little at the thought of what her sister will have to endure for hours more than she will.

"Bor*ing*!" Pilar exclaims. "Marcella, how can you not take

me with you to the recital? All those musicians which I never get a chance to meet when Papa is inviting all these bor*ing* businessmen to our house! I—"

"Whom," Marcella interrupts.

"What?"

"All those musicians *whom* I never get a chance to meet."

"O shut up!" Pilar protests, and throws a silk pillow from the couch at Marcella. "And I am sixteen now anyway, and Papa lets me go to the balls and concerts *without* you!"

"Well then you don't need me."

"That's not . . . ooohhh . . . Marcella!"

"Pilar!"

"You are the worst older sister a person can ever have."

"Could."

Pilar throws another pillow—the last one within reach—and seems genuinely upset now. She is an admiring younger sister, filled with all the foolishness of most girls who have just turned sixteen, Marcella has often reminded herself. And the distance between them in maturity and seriousness of purpose is not so much due to any deficit in Pilar as it is to the surplus of these qualities in Marcella. She had long ago decided not to hold Pilar's childish infatuations against her, realizing that *she* must be even more disappointing to have as an older sister than Pilar is to have as a younger one. Two months shy of her twentieth birthday, Marcella has never shown any interest in the young men Papa brings to the house with regularity. The American men do not generally follow the custom of arranged marriages, and Marcella never lets one get close enough to ever consider a proposal, so it has become understood that Papa will have to intervene within the next few years and find a European man whom she will be forced to marry. She has let the family believe this is what will happen, and has even laughingly discussed it with Mrs. Carlisle and Catherine, all the while knowing she will be her own woman soon enough. Still, Marcella has as tender a sentiment for Pilar as she does for anyone, and can play and laugh with her, sometimes at her, even if she has never been able to show her the error of the path her sister seems destined to follow.

"Are you coming downstairs?" Pilar asks, giving up on her sister sharing any more details of the evening with her.

And Marcella summons the will within her, rolling her eyes to elicit a laugh from Pilar, then stands up with noticeable reluctance.

"I suppose I must make an appearance," she answers, and the two of them walk down the hallway together, the previous moments soon forgotten.

Papa had bought the house when it was just eight rooms and when Sixty-Third Street was the virtual frontier of the city—a "neighborhood" of unpaved roads and grazing fields. Even Mama had been unable to contain her disappointment at first sight of it since it was less than half the size of their house in Madrid and had barely enough room for the six of them, let alone any servants. But Papa had quickly reassured all of them that it was only a temporary circumstance. He reminded them of the stench that billowed from the overcrowded slums downtown, told them that practically every boat that arrived carrying passengers—the *refuse* of Europe, he called them—only served to pack the slums tighter. And he predicted that the wealthy uptown families, those in the fashionable districts from Tenth to Fortieth Street, would soon be pushed farther north by the onslaught.

From the very beginning, he had insisted that they host a dinner party a week—limited to four or six invited guests by their early lack of space—just to show influential people what was awaiting them uptown once they grew tired of trying to hold back the waves of immigrants. And by now, just eight years after he made such a bold prediction, it has already come true in part, with the most fashionable areas of town extending north of the depots and slaughterhouses and breweries of midtown, reaching well into the Fifties blocks, with Sixty-Third Street seeming like a place to get in on quickly before it is too late. Their house has grown along with Papa's business interests, now boasting sixteen rooms and staffed by a half-dozen servants. And the dinner parties, though far less frequent than before, are now two or three times as large, with her brothers, as men of the business world now, inviting their own associates to go along with Papa's.

Among the many annoying friends of her brothers there are only two, Marshall Varrick and Peter Septon, whom Marcella finds to be generally quite tolerable. Perhaps it is because they do not call her brothers Mickey and Barto as most of their other acquaintances do. Perhaps it is because they display at least *some* intelligence and a sense of humor. But more likely than anything, it is because they have already lost more than two hundred dollars each to Marcella in the card games she sometimes manages to talk her way into when Miguel and Bartolomé bring friends back to the house much the worse for brandy and looking to extend the evening's amusements. She is equally accommodating to all of her brothers' friends when it comes to cards, but Marshall Varrick and Peter Septon at least lose with dignity.

Marcella and Pilar walk downstairs to the parlor, only to see that the two of them have already arrived, fully fifteen minutes before five o'clock—a mild social offense even for such familiar acquaintances. Both she and Pilar curtsey as the young men stand and bow, Marcella and Varrick and Septon smiling wryly through this still formal greeting, even though they have been in the house dozens of times by now. Both Varrick and Septon have, at different times, tried their hand at wooing Marcella. Septon lasted little more than an afternoon, but Varrick, being the more resilient of the two, endured for nearly an entire week, making him the most impressive of a thoroughly *un*impressive array of would-be suitors.

The proprieties taken care of, Marcella and Pilar settle into their customary seats and the conversation becomes less formal as the butler fills the gentlemen's brandy glasses. Mama looks over at Papa with as much of a corrective glance as she can ever manage, hoping to at least slow him down so early in the evening, though it has no effect. And then it is the usual sort of banter, with some mention of business between the men, a trickle about the opera season, and then, somehow, a too-healthy dose of politics that finally piques Marcella's interest, only to have the subject quickly changed by Mama just as Marcella is about to enter the fray.

"So when do you gentlemen go to Europe?" Mama asks Varrick and Septon. "It is the custom for young gentlemen to take a summer in Europe, yes?"

And Marcella can see the faint smile on her mother's face at having taken away her fun before it even has begun. It is just as well, Marcella decides, since it affords her the opportunity to leave early for Mrs. Carlisle's and the "recital" she will attend that evening.

IN THOSE FIRST YEARS IN New York, she read every book and every newspaper she could get her hands on, and became the family's resident grammarian to the point of annoyance. The servants became her closest friends and confidants, though that was very much a relative term. When they first arrived, there was just the cook, Mrs. Bridges, and Molly, the Irish maid, for Marcella to shadow. Molly did the shopping for the Arroyos in the early years, and Marcella tagged along with her whenever she could. They sometimes stopped to see Molly's sister Patricia, who worked in a house on Twenty-Third Street, and on one of those early visits Marcella met the widow who owned the house, Mrs. Carlisle.

Mrs. Carlisle was almost as old as Abuela, and of a similar disposition. She had been born in New York and was nearly thirty when she married a man from Savannah, spending seventeen years there until he died. Childless, she sold everything off and moved back home, carrying on the abolition work she had come to slowly in a decade-long conversion surrounded by slavery's inescapable cruelty. To assist her in this crusade, she hired Miss Catherine Hardwicke, an ardent abolitionist who had been recommended to her by like-minded members of Mrs. Carlisle's family from upstate New York. And the two of them, Mrs. Carlisle and Catherine, lived what seemed to Marcella an idyllic life of music and books and Friday afternoon teas with the newly created Ladies Abolition Society. Mrs. Carlisle was impressed with Marcella from the start, particularly with how proficient she had become in English within less than two years of arriving here. She told her she spoke with such an indistinguishable accent that people might easily mistake her for a native of New England or somewhere out west perhaps. As for Catherine, as she insisted on being called by Marcella, she seemed perfectly wonderful as well. Molly remarked that she was unlikely to ever marry, having reached the preposterous age of thirty-three, but that mattered little to Marcella, of course, who was instead fascinated with how Catherine had taught herself to play the pianoforte.

It wasn't long before Marcella had convinced Catherine to give her lessons. Fourteen by then, Marcella in turn convinced her father that the four dollars a week such lessons would cost were well worth it. Of course, Catherine gave Marcella the lessons for free, delighted as both she and Mrs. Carlisle were to have the company of such a bright young girl. But Marcella insisted that her father wanted to contribute three dollars a week to the Ladies Abolition Society fund, the same one that went toward purchasing freedom for several slaves every year. The extra dollar went toward Marcella's *personal* liberation fund, an enterprise no one, not even Catherine, not even Molly, not even the journal entries written to Abuela, knew anything about.

Through the intervening years Marcella grew closer to Catherine and Mrs. Carlisle, and it was generally accepted that her education be passed into their hands once her Mama had conceded to the inevitable. The contributions to the Ladies Abolition Society were then doubled as Papa insisted that he would pay the customary eight dollars a week that a personal tutor cost. And Marcella was then free to spend the better part of four days every week with Catherine and Mrs. Carlisle, though she managed to keep the two parts of her life remarkably separate from each other beyond the initial meeting and whatever Molly's sister felt qualified as worthwhile gossip. Marcella went to Mrs. Carlisle's house each day with Molly or the butler or even her Papa and brothers on their way to Wall Street. But by the time she was seventeen she was able to travel mostly by herself and always stayed for the Friday Teas of the Ladies Abolition Society. She had become an abolitionist mainly through the passion and influence of Mrs. Carlisle and Catherine, but as she grew older and understood more about the inner workings of the institution, despising how her father profited from it just as so many other men did, her devotion to the cause became fully her own, and no longer the residual effect of her friendships. Her visits to Mrs. Carlisle's house soon grew to include Saturday mornings and even occasional Sunday afternoon "recitals" or "gallery expositions," which were, as often as not, completely falsified. But above all, she was careful to keep the two worlds separate and was happy when Molly married a young man who took her out west, and any links between her own home on Sixty-Third Street, and her adoptive one forty blocks away, were diminished even further.

Catherine is by the front door and is smiling more than usual when Marcella arrives that evening. One of the temporary servants takes Marcella's coat, and Catherine leads her into the vast dining room, where the great table is being attended to by three more servants hired just for the day.

"It's beautiful," Marcella says to Catherine as they look over the room. "I don't understand though . . . why are there so many settings?"

Catherine smiles again but discloses very little, toying with Marcella now the way Marcella had with Pilar.

"Oh, are there more settings than you anticipated?" she asks with exaggerated innocence. "I hadn't noticed."

And Marcella probes now for the meaning behind Catherine's smile, a playful sort of banter not unlike that she had engaged in with Pilar that very morning, though rather than conjecture about imaginary suitors, they are instead counting off the guest list for that evening's banquet. Marcella names the women of the Abolition Society, the fourteen of them who are regular attendees and the half dozen others who are less involved in the weekly meetings, including the women with spouses who are likely to accompany them. It brings the total to thirty-one, and then thirty-four when she includes herself and Catherine and Mrs. Carlisle, of course. But there are forty-one settings in all, and Catherine mentions a few additions and husbands who will be dragged along for the first time.

"That makes thirty-nine," Marcella says.

"Oh yes. I suppose that does leave us with two extra *places* . . ." Catherine teases.

Marcella says nothing, but smiles, waiting for Catherine to finish with her fun.

"Perhaps they are for two special guests . . . people who have come from far away . . . perhaps from all the way up in *Cooperstown* . . ."

And she smiles, as Marcella quickly comes to understand. She long ago heard of Mrs. Carlisle's cousin from there, the woman who assisted on the Underground Railroad, carrying food and clothes to runaways throughout Pennsylvania and central New York and helping them make it all the way to Canada.

"Mrs. Stimson is coming?" Marcella beams.

"And Mr. Stimson as well," Catherine answers. "Mrs. Carlisle has gone to the station to meet them. They are due any minute."

And she considers what a joy it will be to meet a woman who has such inspiring stories of the cause, a woman who has not only *met* the great Harriet Tubman on several occasions, but has even had her as an overnight guest in her home! Thankfully, Marcella can share a story of her own with her, and hopes there will be time to tell her about the money she delivered to Reverend Campbell in Savannah.

Mrs. Stimson—Olivia, as she insists on being called—is in fact the *second* cousin of Mrs. Carlisle, and a few years younger than Catherine. And within minutes of meeting her, Marcella wants to hear all the stories she has to tell, finding it easier, now that she sees the small woman with determined features, to imagine her riding through the hills and woods, dashing in and out of harm's way, to help the cause. Her stories are not quite so fantastical, but they are more than enough to captivate Marcella thoroughly, as the room slowly fills over the ensuing hour.

Mrs. Carlisle has placed Marcella near the head of one table, with Mr. Stimson beside her and Mrs. Stimson directly across from them. It is Mr. Stimson's turn to entertain those seated around him, as he tells of his days on the other side of the cause, when he was hired out by town constables to help track down runaways in the county. He describes how his heart was always filled with reluctance to do the work, but his belly told him it wanted to eat, so he went along. And then he came across Olivia riding in the woods not far from Otsego Lake carrying enough food and water for half a dozen people . . .

"Well, that's when everything changed—for me," he says.

And there is laughter all around them.

"'Liv had me converted to the cause before the end of the afternoon, had me converted to the Quakers before the end of the month, and had me married before the end of the summer."

"Well, he wasn't much at first," she adds, "but he's a fast learner."

And Marcella is silent amidst the laughter, trying to imagine such a moment ever occurring in her own home, trying to imagine her father or brothers ever being strong enough to become such a man. The evening ends far too early for Marcella, but she is on her way just before ten o'clock, while there is still vibrant conversation and more than half the guests still present in the front parlor. These are the limitations of her *present* state, she reminds herself when she steps inside the taxi carriage and waves goodnight to Catherine, who stands at the front door. The Stimsons will stay for a week at least, and there will be plenty of chances for Marcella to talk with them more; still, it is difficult for her to depart knowing what she will return to.

Back home there is nothing like the atmosphere there had been at Mrs. Carlisle's. Papa has already retired for the evening, thanks to the brandy, but Miguel, Bartolomé, Varrick, Septon, and two others she has not met all linger in the parlor.

"Marcie," Bartolomé whispers to her as she makes her way upstairs.

Marcella stops and walks back a few steps.

"We going to play cards . . . you wan' . . . ?"

"I think he meant to say," Varrick interjects, "that we were just about to start a little card game, Marcella dear . . ."

How many brandies did it take for you to call me that? she thinks.

". . . and it would be entirely more memorable if you graced us with your presence."

Oh, you have *had a few, Varrick . . . dear.*

Given the circumstances and the presence of two unsuspecting newcomers, Marcella could probably add at least a hundred dollars to her coffers. But there is more important business she feels compelled to get to, and quickly, unimaginatively declines.

Pilar calls to her from behind the opened door of her room as Marcella passes.

"How was the recital, Marcie?" she asks, sounding more

like a little girl than she had just hours before, given where Marcella has spent the evening.

"It was good, Pila," she responds. *It's not her fault,* she reminds herself. *Be nice to her, poor thing.* "How was the dinner?"

Pilar shakes her head and then rolls her eyes the way Marcella had that afternoon before the onslaught, and Marcella can't help but laugh.

"Do you want to talk for a while?" Pilar asks.

And she doesn't have to think of an excuse, as their mother is soon in the hallway turning down the lamps.

"In the morning, Pila," Marcella says. "You can tell me all about it then."

A few minutes later, once she's changed into her nightclothes and glanced into the hallway to make sure that Pilar and Mama have turned their lamps all the way down, she returns to the dressing table where the day began. Uncovering the key once again, she takes out the top notebook this time and folds back its already-filled pages. The ink bottle will have to be filled again, but there is enough to at least begin to tell Abuela about this magnificent evening.

Abuela,

Tonight was the greatest of all the dinner parties I have ever been to at Mrs. Carlisle's. Her cousin, her second cousin, it turns out, was there with her husband and . . .

7 *Oh to Live in Interesting Times*

MARY
RICHMOND
NOVEMBER 3, 1860

Two well-dressed women arrived at the front door and opened it, allowing the noise from the street to invade the relative quiet of the shop. But the ladies did not step inside, hesitating for a moment as they noticed two other women behind them being led by a finely dressed livery slave. They stepped aside, curtseying slightly and allowing the far more prominent Mrs. Simms and her granddaughter Anna to enter the shop first. Mary and Mrs. Kittredge had been waiting for this moment and met the Simms ladies at the door.

"Bonjour, madame," Mary said, and curtseyed deeply before Mrs. Simms. *"Bonjour, mademoiselle,"* she added with similar enthusiasm and a curtsey only slightly less reverent directed toward Miss Anna.

Mrs. Simms nodded politely in keeping with the propriety of the situation, but Anna's response was almost as enthusiastic as Mary's had been.

"Bonjour, Mary," she said in an accent that would have met with Miss Randall's approval. *"Il me fait plaisir de vous voir. C'est une très jolie robe."*

"Oh, merci beaucoup, Mademoiselle Anna," Mary replied with equal proficiency. *"Vous êtes tellement gentil de votre part dire donc, mais la vôtre est beaucoup plus jolie."*

The two young ladies smiled broadly, the compliments on each other's dresses taking on an aristocratic air when spoken in French. Mary curtseyed again, and Anna returned the gesture, bending her right leg behind her left and lowering herself two or three inches. The two ladies who had walked in behind the Simmses looked at each other with raised eyebrows, silently commenting on the sight of a society girl like Miss Anna Simms curtseying to a colored girl, free or not. But these women were new to the store, and such reactions were to be expected after all. Mary had been playing this game for several years by now, and her artistry with a needle and thread, her impeccable manners, and her often upper-class diction made it nearly impossible for patrons to see her in the same light as a common slave. And any of the women who frequented the shop naturally treated her in the manner her elegance seemed to demand.

"Mary," Mrs. Simms said after barely acknowledging Mrs. Kittredge's presence, "I would like to talk a little about Miss Anna's wedding dress. It's only a few months away, you know, and I don't want to leave anything to chance."

"Certainly, ma'am, Miss Anna, I am *right* pleased and honored that you would trust me in this most important matter," Mary responded with another curtsey.

Then she took Anna's hand and led her to the counter with almost as much familiarity as if it were Miss Justinia beside her. Anna beamed in anticipation, and Mrs. Simms followed them, all propriety temporarily lost in the rush of excitement. The two other ladies were left to Lilly the seamstress, with Mrs. Kittredge watching both interactions but mostly Mary and the Simmses.

Miss Anna Simms was the daughter of Mr. Horatio Simms and his wife, Annabelle Curtiss, both of whom could trace their family trees back two hundred years or so to the first aristocratic settlers in the Virginia colony. When his wife died soon after Anna's birth, Mr. Simms had entrusted his mother with the care and upbringing of his daughter while he went about his business in the House of Delegates. And Anna had been raised to be as prim and proper as her grandmother was, though it only *took* most of the way.

"Well anything Miss Anna wears she makes just pretty as can be, but maybe we can come up with some ideas that'll make all the ladies positively *falling over* with envy," Mary said, sounding now like a perfect Southern Belle.

"Merci, Mary," Miss Anna replied in the tone of one who was accustomed to such compliments but never seemed to grow tired of them. *"Je suis sûr que votre robe sera la plus belle dans Richmond. J'ai dit à ma grandmère que je n'aurai aucun autre couturière. Il doit être vous, ou je me marierai portant seulement mes jupons!"*

"Oh, Mademoiselle Anna, vous êtes trop choquants! Mais je vous remercie si beaucoup!"

Mrs. Simms spoke no French at all but beamed to hear her granddaughter speaking it so well to Mary, whom all the ladies assumed was a native speaker. The ladies were soon seated in two comfortable armchairs, watching Mary mix and match fabrics on the counter, holding court as she created the dress for the bride of one of the following year's biggest social events. And Mary was perfectly at home through it all, as if she were the native French speaker, the elegant *couturière,* the *artiste.* She had played this game, or a variation of it, almost from the moment she was brought to Richmond. And though it could be quite tricky at times, she managed to straddle a delicate social high wire without much stumbling.

Mary was just twenty years old, but had as firm an understanding of the world and how things worked as people two or three times her age. She was well aware that what made Parisian lace and dresses better was the fact that they came from Paris, that in some shop over there, a poor girl embroidered her designs just like Mary did. And based on what Mary could see of the French dresses that used to come in to the store, Gertie had been every bit the seamstress that that French gal was, and Mary was pretty sure that by now she'd become at least as good as Gertie was. But Gertie's designs were *stitchin's,* not embroideries, and Mary quickly learned that the difference between the two—once you reached the talent level of that French gal, or Gertie, or even Mrs. Fenton—had everything to do with the *presentation.* That French gal and Mrs. Fenton were white, which made their work better than Gertie's by nature, the way folks—colored and white alike—saw it. And that French gal spoke French, of course, and when she was finished with a dress it was put in a big box with a fancy ribbon and carried clear across the Atlantic just so some society lady could spend a great deal of money on it and tell everyone how much it cost without coming right out and saying so, just letting it slip somewhere in the conversation with one friend and letting gossip take over from there. Mrs. Fenton's dresses might be just as nice, but she didn't speak French, and when her work was finished it was put in a carriage and brought to the store and didn't cost nearly as much, so it couldn't be as good as the one that came all the way from Paris, and it certainly wouldn't be as much fun for the lady who bought it to talk about and accidentally let slip how much it cost.

But by now many Richmond women were beginning

to forget about that girl over in Paris and sought out Mary instead. And that had everything to do with the one thing Mary had over that French gal . . . she could do her presenting *in person.* She flattered and curtseyed, spoke beautiful French, and never had to be told a lady's name or position in society more than once. She knew every social occasion and knew which ladies would want to impress or show up which other ladies and might let slip herself that *Mrs. So-and-so will be so envious when she sees you in this,* or *Mr. So-and-so will not be able to take his eyes off of you,* slipping it in of course, accidentally on purpose. And just to make sure the ladies of Richmond knew how special Mary's work was, she suggested to Mrs. Kittredge that they charge the same price as the French dress, and that was just fine with her and Mr. Kittredge, especially with how Mary made it seem like it had been their idea all along.

The white ladies who came into the shop didn't speak to Mary at all like a slave. It was part of the illusion, and they had to hold up their part. If Mary's work was to be special, she couldn't be seen in the same light as a Cora or Gertie or Lilly. She had to be unique. Exotic. Imported. And after a while nobody ever asked her where she was from—they just assumed it was from someplace fashionable and exciting because that's what they *wanted* to believe. Even Mrs. Kittredge added to the illusion, introducing ladies to Mary as "our little French gal," and never letting on that she was anything but a free colored gal who'd come over from Paris or some exotic French colony and somehow decided to work at a dress shop next to the store where the hayseeds bought flour and tobacco. Silly as it all might have seemed, everyone had somehow embraced the audacity of such a notion, and by now Mary was almost as well known amongst society ladies as any lady actually *in* society.

Still, she was aware that all of that could change quite easily if she wore her talent too proudly. Whether she was free or slave, from Paris or the fields of Carolina, she was still colored. She was always humble and accepted compliments on her work with statements such as *Well, ma'am, I'm sure ANY dress would look beautiful on you.* And she only spoke this way around the society ladies in the dress shop. There were degrees of her field-hand drawl that could be readily reinstalled into her speech when the situation called for it, such as that spring when she had first met Mrs. Simms. Mary had put on only a fraction of the airs she displayed today, but the Southern gentle lady, once upon a time married to one of the most prominent men in the state, made her displeasure quite clear by slapping her fan against the counter and opening her eyes wide. A few not-so-elegant curtseys from Mary and a momentary return to her North Carolina plantation dialect restored tranquillity.

But by now Mrs. Simms had been brought up to speed. Indeed, Mary found the toughest part of her present life to be the constant tracking of where she stood with the people around her. She was a chameleon in an ever-changing environment, one moment speaking fluent French with a woman the manner of Miss Anna Simms, then the next needing to resort to a near field-hand drawl so as not to offend the wife of some hayseed who wanted to look around the place while her husband bought the flour and chewing tobacco next door. In truth, she was busy as any field hand, practically running the store during the day and working with Lilly and Beatrice making the dresses and embroidering the tablecloths and handkerchiefs sold at the store in whatever quiet moments could be found. Then there'd be the rest of most evenings, spent with Justinia in her room, where Mary heard all about

Juss's day, then got to talk about her own, but only for a few minutes before one of them grew too sleepy to stay awake.

It wasn't all artificiality though. Her affection for the Kittredges was quite real, and she genuinely loved Juss and knew her love was returned, despite Justinia's lingering immaturity and self-centeredness. The delicate line Mary walked with them had changed over the years. There was no more "Miss Justinia," it was either "Miss Juss" when others were around, or "Juss" when it was only the two of them. But all of this constant changing made her feel quite alone despite having people around her constantly. Her fellow slaves mostly despised her, feeling that she was putting on airs and somehow getting away with it because she could sew and had learned French when she wasn't supposed to, and the Kittredges looked the other way because she was making them so much money. And the rest of the time it was always the show, the illusion. The only time she felt she could be herself was when she was alone with Juss, and now that had become the smallest part of her day. So somewhere along the way, Mary realized, she had become an island.

But that autumn afternoon, when the Simms ladies had picked out the combinations of chiffon and lace and silk to adorn Miss Anna's dress, Mary took out a pencil and long piece of blank paper and sat in between them. She sketched her ideas for the dress, as much as possible making them appear to be the ladies' own.

"Oh yes'm, Misses Simms, I know you don't want Miss Anna showin' too much shoulder," Mary said as she filled in the top edge of the gown with some lace. "But Miss Anna's got *such* a pretty face and with just the tippy-toppa her shoulders showin' . . . like so . . . she gonna look like the Venus de Milo in a weddin' dress."

From Mrs. Simms's expression, it was clear that she didn't know the first thing about the Venus de Milo, but Mary had deferred just enough to make it appear elegant and yet unthreatening. As for Anna, Mary knew she was classically trained by a tutor every bit as refined as Miss Randall. She knew Mrs. Simms would be appalled to have her granddaughter compared to a nude European statue, but she also knew that Anna would revel in it. A little French kept the matter just between them and sealed the deal for both ladies.

"Merci, Mary," Anna said with a knowing smile. *"Mais ne mettez pas trop de dentelle sur le sommet là."*

"Oui, Mademoiselle Anna. Je le laisserai juste comme cela ainsi votre grandmère sera heureuse maintenant. Quand je le fais, j'omettrai un peu."

And she smiled at Anna, having assured her that she'd sketch it higher in the picture in order to please her grandmother. But when the dress was made, it would lie off the shoulder, the way Miss Anna wanted it. Of course Mrs. Simms and Mrs. Kittredge were none the wiser for any of it, and they were soon engaged in a conversation about the future of the store. Actually, to call it a conversation was a loose sort of way of saying that Mrs. Simms was busy telling Mrs. Kittredge what needed to be done, while Mrs. Kittredge listened intently.

"You've got as talented a seamstress as there is in the state of Virginia," Mrs. Simms said, "and yet you don't have a proper fitting room or a parlor area or anything like the fine shops in Paris."

"Mmmm . . . yes, I've been after my husband telling him how we need to expand," Mrs. Kittredge conceded.

"Well Mary here is a treasure that will only take you so far."

Anna Simms looked at Mary with a closed-lip smile

beneath raised eyebrows, as if to let Mary know that such praise from her grandmother was as scarce as desert rain. And Mary reveled in it as much as she could in that moment or two, before *Mr.* Kittredge came from next door.

"Mrs. Simms, how good it is of you to come and see us," he said. "Miss Anna too—we thank you for your patronage. And what a momentous time it is."

The ladies seemed to have no idea what he meant, and Mr. Kittredge had to remind them that tomorrow was the national Election Day.

"Mr. Kittredge," Mrs. Simms said with disdain, "I do not think you realize how serious the matter is."

"Oh I do, ma'am," Mr. Kittredge responded. "The talk in my shop next door has been about almost nothing else for a few weeks now."

"Really?" She jerked her head back slightly, surprised to hear the news. "Well, I should say that at least some people have a sense of propriety. So what are you going to do about it, Mr. Kittredge?"

"Well, my patriotic duty as a Virginian, of course."

Mrs. Simms had never had much patience for anyone beneath her elevated social status, but a self-made man such as Mr. Kittredge seemed less tolerable than others who knew the station in life into which they were born. And all that disdain was summoned in her expression toward Mr. Kittredge, along with a healthy amount of confusion.

"I have no idea what the state of Virginia has to do with it, but do you intend to make the necessary renovations to the shop or not, Kittredge?"

Anna was able to laugh out loud, but Mary had to turn her face away from Mr. Kittredge's view, at least, before she could let out a few stifled chuckles. Mrs. Kittredge could perhaps have acted as interpreter, but she was content to have Mrs. Simms detail all the work she felt should be done. It was only then that Mr. Kittredge was able to get to the point of his visit in the first place, to ask Mrs. Simms what her son had heard in the House of Delegates about the upcoming election. What would Virginia do if the Republican Lincoln was elected over Breckinridge or even Douglas? But Mrs. Simms only looked at Mr. Kittredge with even greater condescension.

"A woman of any breeding does not get mixed up in politics," she said. "That is for men such as my son to conduct and . . . for lesser men . . . to discuss."

And with a single abbreviated wave of her hand, she dismissed Mr. Kittredge from the shop, banishing him to the mercantile next door. Her smile returned, however, once she rejoined Anna and Mary.

"Now Mary, it will not be just my granddaughter's dress, you know," she said. "I will need one as well."

"Oh Misses Simms, I was hopin' you might say so," Mary answered, throwing in a little extra drawl after the incident with Mr. Kittredge. "We got some fine blue satin cloth almost as blue as yo' eyes . . ."

MARCELLA
NEW YORK
NOVEMBER 8, 1860

It was as impetuous and even childish a moment as any she could remember in half a dozen years at least, and not at all the way she had envisioned her long-awaited triumph. But it certainly achieved the cold and seemingly permanent severance she had convinced herself was necessary, even deserved.

She would turn twenty-one before the month was over, and had been prepared to break away that very day. She had two trunks to carry the last of her clothes and books, the last of the things she hadn't already surreptitiously transferred to Mrs. Carlisle's over the past several months, a book here, a kerchief there, and on grander occasions, perhaps an entire dress brought along under the guise of being unable to decide which she would wear. Of course, turning twenty-one meant nothing special to a woman in general, and where Marcella was concerned, it would only mean that she would at last inherit the thousand dollars or so that Abuela had left for all her grandchildren, the sad remains of an estate her husband had left in debt. And Marcella had never been dependent on that money, having accrued a small fortune by her own guile over the years, begun with the slow trickle of Papa's unwitting contributions and exponentially increased at the expense of Miguel and Bartolomé and card games with their friends until she had amassed over two thousand dollars in all.

Mrs. Carlisle had insisted that she was welcome to move into her home anytime, of course, and had become a little tearfully insulted when Marcella spoke of having enough money to pay for room and board. The delay had nothing to do with money, she most certainly assured her, and she looked forward to the day Marcella would join them, since she could then have both her *"daughters living with her."* And they always cried a little when she said that. But there was a principle involved, and Marcella had the chance to make the sort of bold statement that women almost never had the chance to make. Men—*white* men, Catherine always inserted—came into their own when they turned twenty-one, inheriting whatever wealth they would, not unlike Marcella, but also being granted voting rights and full recognition before the law. It was the point in their lives when they were no longer a child, but a fully recognized member of society, whether at the highest or lowest levels.

"An illiterate, malingering vagrant of a man is more of a person than the most intelligent woman in the country," Mrs. Carlisle had once said, appealing to the fire she knew would be stirred in Marcella to endure the last several months in her father's house. And so Marcella had decided to stay, perhaps for even a few days past her birthday so she could make her announcement just as any young man of age would do, as if it were a cogent, unemotional decision. But then came the sixth of November, and the most fiercely contested and divisive election in the nation's history.

Men like her father and brothers cared nothing for politics beyond its impact on business. There were no enduring principles to abide by, no loyalties, not even regret for supporting a losing candidate, since their money could just as easily buy influence with the man who had won. And when it had come to that year's election, with three fully viable candidates, they had carefully mapped out which one would serve their interest most completely. There was Breckinridge, the hotheaded Democrat from the South, who wasn't likely to win more than a handful of votes above the Mason-Dixon Line. That was because the Democrats had split, putting up a second candidate, Stephen Douglas, from the North. And then there was the Republican, Lincoln, who just might slip past the bungling Democrats and on into the White House.

His election might mean hard times for the long-term future of their business, what with how he was always harping on about standing in the way of expanding slavery into the new western territories, but in the short term his election was pure gold to Papa and Miguel and Bartolomé. They had bought up a half-dozen warehouses full of cotton in the last two years, and then held on to it, waiting for the price to escalate. They surmised that Lincoln's election would bring a spike in the price that would triple their investment, so based on this factor alone, they backed Lincoln. *"We make our money when they elect him, and then the country come to its sense and elect a real President in four years,"* Papa said at the dinner table one night. And if there was anything that could make Marcella hope for Lincoln to lose, that was *almost* it.

The results of the election took two days to fully sort out, but by the eighth of November it was clear to even the most ardent Democrat that Lincoln had won. Marcella attended a celebratory tea at Mrs. Carlisle's that afternoon and then reluctantly returned home for supper at her father's house, dreading the idea of listening to him gloat with Miguel and Bartolomé about the great fortune they had just made. Perhaps it was because she had sipped wine and not tea at Mrs. Carlisle's, perhaps it was because she had forty blocks of a taxi carriage ride to work herself into a minor idealistic frenzy, perhaps it was an inevitability regardless of the circumstances, but when she walked in the front door of the house, all previous plans and all customary decorum were immediately discarded. She flung open the doors to the parlor where her father and brothers were entertaining five business associates in a cloud of cigar smoke and brandy vapors.

"Mr. Lincoln has won!" she announced, walking quickly to the brandy decanter and then to the five gentlemen guests, filling their glasses as they laughed politely or stared in bewilderment at her.

"What *wonderful* news for you, Papa," she continued. "And

for you too, Miguel and Bartolomé—and for all of you gentlemen, I suppose. Congratulations! You will be able to sell all your cotton you've been hoarding and make a real killing!"

Her father was not amused by her antics, of course, but reserved his temper.

"My daughter is very high-spirit," he said to the men gathered around. "You must know if ever you have the bad fortune to have daughters."

And the men laughed and commented about their daughters and so on, all in the usual manner of barely acknowledging her presence in the room other than to lift their glass slightly as she approached them to fill it.

Marcella could only surmise that Papa was treading so lightly now because these men were new associates, none of them the familiar faces she had seen at the dinner table over the years, and appearances were, as always, everything to him. *I have made him squirm,* she thought, smiling furtively. *Here in this very room where he has so long ruled!* And it emboldened her to pour a snifter of brandy for herself, then lift it high in the air, clearing her throat before she spoke.

"To Lincoln! To cotton! To money!" she exclaimed, and was the only one, other than Bartolomé, to drink to her toast.

"Marcella, you should go with your Mama and sister in the other room," Papa said, only slightly more assertively.

"Oh no, I want to sit with the Masters of the World and discuss the great issues of the day," she insisted, then took a cigar from the case on the decanter table and flopped down in the seat next to it. She held the cigar up to her lips, and Bartolomé laughed instinctively before catching himself beneath Papa's icy glare.

"Marcella you embarrass yourself," Papa said, staring at her icily for a moment before looking around at the other men. "Gentlemen, I am sorry my daughter is so much a high-spirit she forget sometimes how we raise her to be a lady."

And there were fewer comments than before, but still some general recognition of the difficulties of bearing daughters.

"Ahhhh Papa," she interrupted. "I know it must have been difficult to be burdened with my presence all these years. But you will not have to fret any longer, as I am moving out! This evening. Right at this very moment!"

The men laughed a little, then stopped once they realized her sincerity.

"Marcella," Papa said, "*enough* of this now! Leave us to our business."

He said it in the way that once had frightened her, squinting his eyes and tensing his mouth as if she had shattered a fine vase. But she did not know such fear anymore.

"Oh, I *will* leave you to your business, Papa," she said, standing up and dropping the cigar on the table. "I only wanted to toast your triumph and to tell you that, from this moment on, you can reach me at Mrs. Carlisle's house on Twenty-Third and Broadway."

She lifted her glass slightly, then drank down the rest of its contents.

"Farewell, gentlemen," she said, and walked out of the room, leaving them in stunned silence.

She would have walked straight out the front door and returned to Mrs. Carlisle's at that very moment, except for the few items she could not risk leaving behind. Papa could hold on to all the dresses and whatever jewelry she had, every stick of furniture, and even the sheet music and books that had made life here more endurable over the years. But then there was the brush and the brooch and the notebooks from Abuela, and those she would not let fall into his hands to be held ransom until she moved back home. And in the time it took for her to gather these in a small case, Mama and Pilar were bursting into her room, Pilar in tears and Mama with a look that surprised Marcella, neither angry nor sad, but as if she had long been resigned to such an eventuality.

"Marcie . . . no . . . you are not leaving," was all Pilar said, sitting on the edge of her bed and pulling Marcella's arm until she sat beside her.

She could not explain to them everything, of course, since Pilar didn't seem to know the possibility of another way and her mother, if she ever had, had long ago yielded her entire identity to Papa. So she left it as a matter of simple politics, telling them that she had decided to join the abolitionist cause and could no longer live in the same house with Papa. It was an act of mercy to Pilar at least, her Mama sensing far more of the truth and thus hardly assuaged by such consolation.

In the end though, her mother insisted that she take the trunks with her, even helping her pack them, while Pilar sat on the bed and plotted ways in which she would come to visit Marcella every day, announcing that she would become an abolitionist too if that's what it would take. But even with all the promises made of letters and secret visits and the like, the goodbyes she offered them seemed final. Mama had two of the servants carry down the trunks, using the back stairs of course, and placing them in their harnessed carriage waiting for her. But Marcella would not skulk her way out the servants' entrance and insisted on using the front stairs, and the front door, more than willing to confront Papa and her brothers and their guests another time. Instead it was just her Papa standing alone by the front door, his hands planted against his hips and a scowl on his face. She could hear Miguel and Bartolomé talking in the parlor, but the men were all gone by now.

"Marcella, if you leave this house you will have no more money from me," Papa said.

And she was amazed at the limit of his response, as if he finally understood that appeals to her duty, her place as a woman, even the shame she would bring upon the family, no longer held dominion over her any more than he did. *He goes directly to the money,* she thought, but held her laughter back to only a smile and short exhale, understanding the defeat she could now administer to him. *Not Abuela, not the Minister of Finance, not Mama or Miguel or Bartolomé or Pilar, none of them,* she thought. *Only* I *have gotten the better of him.*

"That's fine, Papa," she replied, calmly, coldly. "I've got all the money I need."

"You will not be my daughter anymore," he added, though with what seemed like some trepidation that his final stand would not be enough to scare her into staying.

"I understand, Papa," she said.

And then, as if sealing her triumph, she kissed him on the cheek and walked out the door, stopping only long enough to see Pilar on the landing at the top of the stairs, tears covering her cheeks, and Mama's arm wrapped around her for comfort. Marcella smiled and raised her eyebrows slightly, wanting to tell her that it could be no other way. But the time for words had passed, and so, with one final glance at her confused father, she closed the door behind her, her life, at long last, now entirely her own.

That night, in the comfort of her new room at Mrs. Carlisle's, she couldn't help but think of the finality of the evening's events. Papa was not the sort of man whose resolve and anger grew weaker with time. And despite her mother's assistance and Pilar's desperation to remain close, she knew that neither of them would be able to stand up to Papa in any real way. So she went to the only recourse she had at that very moment, taking out the most recent of her notebooks to Abuela, and writing the shortest entry she had ever written, unable to transcribe the events of the day into more words than these:

Abuela,
Today I am an orphan.

MICAH
CHARLOTTESVILLE, VIRGINIA
MARCH 23, 1861

By the time Micah was eighteen or so he'd grown into his shoulders. And he was long done being anything like an apprentice. Dunmore had taught him everything he knew about carpentry. Took all of a few months. And still it wasn't but a fraction of what his Daddy had taught him back on *Les Roseraies.* That was 'cause Dunmore was a shit carpenter right from the start. The kinda man who had a reason for every time a job didn't get done right. Spent more time explaining than it woulda took to do the thing right the first time.

But when Micah looked old enough to do a man's job by himself, Dunmore started hiring him out to work alone, sometimes. Micah tossed out all the shortcuts and patch-ups straight off. All the ways Dunmore'd taught him about how to make a job *look* done. And that's when shopkeepers and farmers took real notice of Micah. Started asking Dunmore just to send the boy over. Told Dunmore they'd only pay for Micah to do the job. And Dunmore didn't need any persuading to become a man of leisure. So by the summer of Fifty-Seven, when Micah was a man of twenty, Dunmore was as retired as a lazy country squire. The boy had turned out to be gold. But then there came a chance to really cash in on his investment. Once and for all.

For Micah the days had long run together into one indistinguishable mess. Except for Sundays. He worked just as hard, but did all his workin' on Dunmore's shit house that wasn't such shit anymore. He knew the approach of winter and summer only once the extreme of temperatures told him to put on or remove his coat. Nothing. Not even spring. Not even the autumn colors along the Blue Ridge, could make him take notice for more than a few tortured moments. Not when the rest of his days were lived in the darkness. And by the time he was a full-grown man. Twenty twenty-two twenty-four, even. Escape was not even a thought in the deepest part of his soul. Figuring that it wasn't worth the whipping just so he could be a mule somewhere else.

And just like any other day, Micah woke up before the sun. Made Dunmore's breakfast. Woke up Dunmore. Made his own breakfast with the leftover bacon drippings. Dunmore drove him to the job site, the livery on the west end of town. Then it was off to the Blue Spruce for Dunmore, to drink all day with the Embrys, who were in town. No runaways for them to hunt down this week.

Micah'd made great progress on the job the first day. Too much it turned out. Got Dunmore thinking he could finish it on the second day instead of the three they both figured it would take. 'Course Dunmore charged the livery owner ten dollars for the job straight out. After lumber. Told him it'd take a week at least. Told him he was gettin' a bargain. Which he was. But Dunmore had plans on making a real killing this week. And Micah knew there'd be trouble soon as he heard the squeak of Dunmore's cart pulling up to the livery doors.

Micah! Job done . . . time a go.

Dunmore still hadn't figured out not to yell inside the livery. Horses started kicking, whinnying, livery boy came running. 'Course, the livery boy was every bit as scared of Dunmore as Micah used to be so he didn't go to settlin' the horses down. He ran inside to get his Massa the owner. Owner came out just as Micah was coming down the bottom ladder to tell Dunmore he wasn't done. To tell him he needed another half day.

Dunmore, what the hell're you doin'? Livery owner was angry as a mule.

Wha? Oh . . . I'm callin' m'nigga boy t'come down 'ere. Job finiss now.

Only it wasn't finished. Micah got to explaining what he still had to do. Livery owner said he was happy with what he'd done already. Another day maybe to finish it.

Now ten dollars for three days work is a nice deal for you, Dunmore.

Didn't matter that the livery owner said that. Dunmore still hauled off and whacked Micah soon as he got in range. Micah felt his right cheek on fire. Could taste the blood beginning to trickle from inside his mouth. But it wasn't as bad as it might've been. Micah knew by now to stand far enough off Dunmore's right shoulder so all he could do was hit him with a backhanded right. It was too far to reach to get his real power hand, his left, to the target. Not after a full day at the Blue Spruce. Not after the Embrys were there to do their share of the buyin'.

So then it was Dunmore and the livery owner arguing back and forth. While Micah loaded the tools in the wagon.

The livery boy calmed the horses down in time to help Micah put the last tools on the cart.

Man, you in a bad spot. The boy said. Like Micah needed informing. Just looked at him, didn't say a thing. Angry at the boy for being so afraid. Thought of tellin' him it was easy enough once you let yourself become a mule. Gave up on ideas of anything better. But still, just looked at him. Didn't say a thing. Climbed up into the cart. Then it was the ride home with Dunmore. Micah sitting in the cart while Dunmore did the driving up front.

Back home there was the broken-down horse to unhitch and water. Cook the chops Dunmore'd bought at the butcher. Cook the panbread in the grease, bring it all to Dunmore, who was on the porch with the jug. Surveying his land like the country squire he was. Not the shit carpenter anymore. Then it was feed the horse and water him some more. Cook some more panbread for himself in the grease left over from the chops. Eat it without sittin' down. Check on Dunmore.

He was passed out by now. His plate fallen off his lap and the last of the three chops lay on the porch floor, mostly untouched. Just one bite out of it, and then the dirt from the floor. So Micah stuffed it in his pocket, woke Dunmore up, none the wiser about the chop. Put him to bed. Then out to the well for more water for the broken-down horse. He poured some of it over the chop and ate it down with as little chewing as possible.

And then, the evening sky got to lookin' quite nice out over the Blue Ridge. He poured a bucket of water over himself, took his shirt off and did it again. Pulled another bucket out of the well, took off his pants, dipped them and the shirt into it. Swished 'em around some. Squeezed 'em some and laid them over the side of the well. Took another bucket and poured it over himself again. Then stood there in just his bottom underbritches, looking out over the Blue Ridge. Seeing the sea of green reaching up to the edge of the sky. And a breeze came across the field, cool against his wet skin. Making him think of far-off places for just a moment. 'Til he couldn't do that to himself no more. 'Til it was time to go inside and hope sleep came all in a rush. So there wouldn't be any more thinking of far-off places.

Next day started as it always did. Making the breakfast and so on. Dunmore dropped him off, gave him a good whack with an open left hand. The kinda whack that said worse'd be coming if he didn't finish by midday. Like he needed reminding.

And then it was back to work as always. Cutting the last of the upper hayloft support joists. Then the braces. Then hauling everything up both ladders. The first joist fit so well it looked like part of the original construction and not a patch job. Still, he took a minute to look over his work. Not admiring it so much as deciding if there was anything that wasn't just like it should be. Then he moved on to the second one.

As he shifted the ladder, he could see a man in a blue suit standing by the livery doors. Watching him like Dunmore never did. Like the livery owner never did. Like no man who knew what kinda work he did ever had to. And he stayed there as Micah put in a second joist and then a third. Then he was gone, only to come back with the livery owner and stand there some more. Pointing up to the work he was doing. Nodding his head some. The livery owner pointing over to the work Micah'd done on the other side of the loft the day before. Even pointed up at the roof Micah'd patched the year before. And the man in the suit looked puzzled. Like he couldn't tell where there'd ever been a hole to begin with. And the liveryman nodding, smiling, like that was the whole idea.

Dunmore came back around midday. All kindsa pissed at havin' to leave the Blue Spruce while the Embrys was just getting started buying rounds. And the man in the suit was following behind him, the livery owner alongside. Then the men got to talking. Only Dunmore mostly shouted.

Yep, learnt from me . . . don't come cheap . . . two dollars a day . . .

The man in the suit did some talking now.

Sell off my meal ticket?

Then some more talking.

Gonna take more'n that!

Some more talking. Only Dunmore was 'bout as happy now as Micah'd ever seen him.

Turned out the man named Mr. Longley was from Richmond. Saw what work Micah'd done and paid twenny-two hunnerd dollars for him. *Twice what yer broken-down Daddy gone fer.* Dunmore was thrilled about the deal he'd made. Thrilled enough to buy three bottles of whiskey with labels on 'em. Thrilled enough to have the Embry boys come over that afternoon. Then the real fun started.

They spent the first few hours knocking off the whiskey without any trouble. Sat on that tiny front porch that barely fit the three of them. Started firing their guns at a tree out front. Then the fence post on Hinkley's place across the dirt road. Hinkley just about wet himself any time he saw Dunmore, let alone with the Embry brothers alongside him. Wasn't likely he'd do any complaining about getting his fence post shot up. Shot *at,* was more like it, drunk as they were. Never hit the damn thing once. They were well into the jug by the time it was dark. Micah'd cooked up the steaks Dunmore bought. Panbread and the trimmings too. They about licked the plates clean, then passed the jug around again. Micah came out to get the plates, ask if there was anything else Dunmore needed.

Got a lil goin' away presen' fo' ya. Tom Embry said.

And Albert Embry walked up to Micah and ripped his shirt off him. Dunmore only laughed. Then Albert wrapped his rope around Micah's wrists and pulled him to the post a few feet from where Dunmore sat. Tom walked to his horse and took the whip from his saddle. Snapped it in midair, once, twice, three times.

Get'm hitched nice'n tight. Tom said to Albert.

Then Albert laughed and stepped aside, and Tom wound up the whip, cracking it a few more times while Dunmore laughed harder.

Here we go! Tom Embry said. And Micah braced for the pain. Heard the whip winding up and then only a thud against his back. Not the harsh tearing of the leather strands against his flesh. But the blunt weight of the handle instead. Then the three of them, the Embrys and Dunmore, laughed more than they had all night.

Good'n Tom. Dunmore said between belly laughs. *He's 'spectin th'real thing, pissin' his trousers.*

I still wouldn' min' addin' a few more stripes to this'n here. Tom said. *Never did like this'n.*

Uh-uh, twenny two hunnerd dollars I got comin' tomorra. Dunmore answered. *Can't put no more stripes on'm than he already got.*

And once he was done laughing Albert Embry untied the rope around Micah's wrists. Looked him square in the eye from just a few inches away. Meaner and colder than even his brother or Dunmore could be. Then walked back to his seat on the porch. Leaving Micah to pick up the soiled plates and bring them inside. Cleaning them in the half-bucket of water left over.

How you figger that slicker pay you so much? Albert Embry said, loud enough so Micah could hear it.

Gotta be th'war. Tom answered. *Bet he's figurin' on makin' five, maybe ten dollars a day wit' all that new construction they got goin' on now 'at Richmond gonna be the capital of th'whole damn Confederacy.*

Don't care 'bout none of that. Dunmore said. *All I know is I'm gonna be a rich man come tomorra.*

And there wasn't even the anger in Micah that such an idea might've once stirred in him. Just the rest of the cleanin' on his mind. Then finally to sleep on the pile of straw in the corner.

For one more night, anyway.

And the idea of a new Massa and a new home not even something he let himself think on for long. Just hoped a dreamless sleep would come to him soon. All he ever hoped for.

Anymore.

RICHMOND
APRIL 1861

It was a strange sorta thing working for Massa Longley insteada Dunmore. Just as much work, more even, since Richmond seemed like it was growin' by the minute. But right from the start, Micah had a one-room cabin all to himself. Two sets of workin' clothes. Plenny to eat. And about forty other slaves living right there all around him in the quarters behind the sawmill.

Of course Micah didn't hit it off with them from the start. Once they heard how much money got spent on buyin' him. Once they saw how Massa Longley drove along with him on those first few jobs. Once they saw how Micah kept to himself just by his nature. Like he was better'n them, they musta figured. And not like he wasn't used to havin' people to talk to for some time now. So life stayed mostly the same for him. Work sunup to sundown six days of the week. Only now with Sunday to rest some. And be alone.

It was his fifth job that was unlike anything he'd done before. Massa Longley told the man who owned the place that Micah'd built an entire house all by himself back in Charlottesville. Which wasn't altogether true. But the man who owned the shop and the one next door to it musta believed it 'cause Micah was there very early the next morning. The shopkeeper's name was Kittredge, but he didn't do none of the explaining about what was to be done. The man just stood there alongside as his wife pointed out to Micah what she wanted. Closin' off most of the storeroom to make two smaller fittin' rooms, whatever that was. Then opening up the storeroom and adding on to it out back so it was even bigger than before.

Micah figured it'd take two weeks at least, but then Mista Kittredge explained one more thing. Said it wouldn't be appropriate for him to be workin' around the shop when all the ladies were there. Said he'd planned it out with Massa Longley that Micah'd work from sunup 'til ten o'clock, when the shop was opened. Then come back after it was closed, and work 'til ten at night by the light of the oil lamps. During the day he'd be free to rest and make whatever cuts were necessary back at the sawmill. Or so Mista Kittredge said. But Micah knew Massa Longley'd find some other jobs in town for him to do in the hours the shop was open. So he set his mind right there to three four weeks at least of workin' sixteen seventeen hours a day. At least. And that night in the cabin he thought for one minute that the one good thing about Dunmore was that he was a lazy man. Too lazy to do anything more than wait for folks to come and hire Micah out. But it seemed like Massa Longley had his mind set on riding this mule 'til it dropped.

The next mornin' was all the measuring and writing down the cuts and lumber he'd use during the first few days. He was sure to use only numbers or pictures. No words, of course. And when it was done he waited 'round back of the store and out of the way, like Mista Kittredge told him. Waitin' on Massa Longley to come and get him. And prob'ly take him to some other job to fill up the next few hours.

Then he saw her.

She walked along the cobblestone path like she wasn't walkin' at all. Such easy steps that didn't disturb her dress more than an inch to one side or the other. Straight-backed and chin held up to let the world know she was there. Graceful. And beautiful as anything he'd ever seen. Like the sun dippin' down over the Blue Ridge in the distance. Demanding, with a whisper, that a man stop and take notice at what God had done here.

And just as she reached the storeroom door she saw him standing by the corner of the alleyway where Massa Longley'd told him to wait. She did nothing at first 'til she got to the top of the steps. But then she turned toward him before opening the door. Smiled enough to make it seem like more than just good manners. And she curtseyed. To *him.* With something in the action that made him reach for his hat, take it off, and bow slightly. Forgetting for that moment that he'd ever felt like just a mule. 'Til she was gone inside. And the hundred feet or so between the house set back off the street and the storeroom door became hallowed ground to him. To think that he might see such a thing each morning for the next three four weeks. At least.

ETHAN
UNION SQUARE, NEW YORK
APRIL 20, 1861

Jesus I've never seen so many people in one place in my life, Finny says. I heard one of the Wall Streeters sayin' there was probably a hundred thousand.

He looks over at Ethan for confirmation of the estimate, as if he's an expert on such matters. But Ethan looks back at Finny with wide eyes and a shrug of his shoulders and a *how the hell am I supposed to know, Fin,* look on his face, and the two of them go back to scanning the crowd.

Can ya see the Sumter flag over there? Ethan asks, and points to the opposite end of the square.

They look over at the mounted statue of George Washington, the one that'd just been put in five years or so ago, with the makeshift flagpole and the giant scarred flag that had flown over the fort in South Carolina that none of them had even heard of until two weeks ago. Now there are a hundred thousand people assembled in Union Square just to get a glimpse of it in their fervor of righteous indignation. One hundred thousand people who were ready to secede themselves now gathered around to support the Union; one hundred thousand people who became Lincolnites the minute the guns opened on Sumter; one hundred thousand people who, for now anyway, want nothing more than to teach the Reb bastards a lesson.

I knew we shoulda got here earlier to set up by Old General Washington there, Ethan says. Now it'll be nothin' but shots of the crowd with the Sumter flag a ballfield away in the distance.

And Finny paints the metallic solution over the plate and hands it to Ethan, watching closely as he inserts it into the side of the box camera, then lowers himself beneath the curtain around back again.

I don't know 'bout that Perfessor, Finny says while Ethan focuses in on another shot. Seems to me the story's not so much about the flag . . . or about Sumter even. I mean, who gave a rat's arse about either one of'm a coupla weeks ago? Seems to me the story's 'bout the hundred thousand folks ready to string up the Reb bastards that shot *holes* in th'damn flag.

There is the click of the shutter lens and then Ethan lifting himself out from the curtain, a smile upon his face as he slides the new glass plate negative into the black cloth sleeve in Finny's waiting hands.

Fin, Ethan begins, with a triumphant sort of look, you're absolutely right! That poor old fella over there's gonna have nothing but a picture of a flag mounted on a statue. We'll have the hundred thousand who came to see it. These'll sell for five dollars apiece easily. Gimme another plate Fin . . .

And they spend the next half an hour lining up all manner of photographs to be taken from every imaginable angle along the Washington Square, with Fin counting out what twenty percent of Ethan's fifty percent of Mr. Hadley's enterprise might be. There are speeches, and bands playing, and vendors all along the square selling little flags and *God Save the Union* buttons, and such, 'til Smitty finally finds them up on the steps of this house beside the square.

I saw a line of about a hundred lads over on Sixteenth Street waitin' to sign up for their ninety-day hitch, Smitty says. Saw a coupla dozen more that looked like they were headed up to the all-Irish regiment up on Twenty-Fifth.

And Ethan and Finny know immediately what that could mean. Lincoln's only called for seventy-five thousand recruits from the entire Union, and if there are a regiment's worth of them at either of those places, they might miss out on their chance. They'd only talked about it for the first time the night before, and all of them figured they could get away easily enough from their jobs for such a cause, though Smitty was in the stickiest spot, being married and such. Still, every one of them liked the idea from the start . . . Finny and Smitty mostly for the adventure, Harry because *no Reb bastard was gonna get away with that,* and Ethan for altogether different reasons . . . thinking that there were perhaps grander principles hidden amidst the vengeance and escapade, though he hadn't been able to find the words to express them.

We better get over there, Finny says.

But there's the camera and all the glass plates already in their sleeves to consider. They'll be worth five dollars apiece if they're even a little clear, ten for the really good ones. And since the half-dozen other cameras posted around the square all seem lost in the middle of the throng, not on the edge of it looking in the way Ethan is, he might just be able to corner the market.

Fin–how're we gonna get these pictures out of here? Ethan asks.

I'll carry'm, Perfessor, he says.

It'll be nothin' at all for the three of us, Smitty adds.

Not that . . . it's just that they'll only be worth a dollar apiece if we don't develop 'em first. And then we still gotta take . . .

And his voice trails off as he realizes the foolishness of missing out on this opportunity for such a trivial matter. All right, gimme a hand here, he says, and they get quickly to it.

It's not the first time Finny has served as Ethan's *assistant* of sorts at an assignment. Mr. Hadley still ran the shop and took most of the portraits, but Ethan brought in twice as much money by taking pictures that newspapers and periodicals could convert to dot image engravings on their front pages as a means of selling more copies. And this would be as big a story as there had been in months, and as big a payday too—but first things first.

Which one are we goin' to, the one on Sixteenth or the one up on Twenty-Fifth? Ethan asks, looking at Smitty.

Harry's probably up at the one on Twenty-Fifth already, Smitty says. He told me that if he didn't show up here for the rally it's 'cause he'd gone straight to the recruitin' station.

And now Ethan and Finny stop their work and look at Smitty for the verdict. Through no fault of his own, Smitty—Walter Smythe—is mostly Scottish, with a little bit of Welsh mixed in there somewhere. He'd been their friend since he settled in Red Hook with his widowed mother a few years after Ethan arrived. And though there had been some moving about, different jobs, and even Smitty's marriage to pull the old friends apart, baseball and Saturday evening visits to Feeny's had overcome all obstacles so far. But this one was potentially the most difficult of all, and one that they hadn't resolved the night before, when they all decided to enlist.

Harry had been the one to say that they should all go up to the recruiting office on Twenty-Fifth Street, where he'd heard about an all-Irish regiment, and Smitty hadn't resisted, joking about how *I spend all my free time with a buncha Micks already, what's a few more.* But he and Ethan and Finny even were concerned that they wouldn't let Smitty in and that they'd end up in entirely different regiments. *Christ, it'll be the first time anyone got thrown outta someplace fer NOT bein' Irish,* Harry'd answered. And they'd left it at that.

You know Smitty, if you go first, and they give you a hard time, me an' Finny an' Harry can just go with you to the office on Sixteenth, Ethan says. And that finally settles the matter.

Sure enough, Harry's there waiting for them when they arrive, their arms full of glass plates and the box camera and tripod. Harry's talked to one of the corporals standing guard at the door and knows everything there is to be done, how they'll stand in the same line so they get put in the same squad, how there won't be any problem for Smitty being Scottish *but maybe it's best he doesn't mention it right off either,* how the war'll almost certainly be done before their ninety-day enlistments are even up. And it's an easy enough thing to have the doctor look at them with shirt off, listen to a breath or two, check the eyes and look at their tongues, then nod to the recruiting sergeant who tells them where to sign, and that's that. They are to report for duty in three days and that's when they'll get their uniforms, they're told. But that doesn't stop Ethan from setting up the camera across the street and taking a couple of pictures of the lads of the new Sixty-Ninth New York, *sure to be the meanest, toughest regiment in either army in this here war!* they say. And it's on to Richmond one and all, with maybe a night at Feeny's to celebrate their leaving and to talk about how they'll teach them Rebs a lesson they'll not soon forget.

If we can get these pictures developed and sold off, Ethan says, we can start th'evenin' with a steak dinner. I'm buyin'.

And Ethan and his *three* assistants, civilians for just a few more days, are soon off for the ferry. Then *On to Richmond!*

Tempests

PART THREE

8 Them Irish Devils

MARCELLA
NEW YORK
JULY 25, 1861

They had gone off on their frivolous adventure three months before to the sounds of marching bands and cheering crowds. Their departures were made as conspicuous as possible, with entire regiments sometimes marching right up Broadway in the middle of the day, just to be seen by adoring crowds. Now they came stumbling back, some by train, some by ship, but all with different looks upon their faces.

For Marcella, Catherine, and Mrs. Carlisle, it was a most depressing sight. After the debacle at Manassas Junction—what the northern press was calling the Battle of Bull Run—it had become clear that this was not going to be as simple a procedure as originally anticipated, and now New Yorkers were getting the chance to see what the face of war looked like up close. They tried to welcome the boys home as cheerfully as they had sent them off, but there was something missing in their cheers.

"So many of them are wounded," Catherine said with grave concern. "Look at all the bandaged heads and splints and crutches."

She covered her open mouth with her hand and tried to hold back her tears. Marcella put her arm around her friend and tried to comfort her, knowing that Catherine had been the most optimistic of all of them that a successful campaign would somehow encourage President Lincoln to free all the slaves. It seemed a preposterous notion now.

"These boys are at least free from their enlistments," Mrs. Carlisle added. "Their suffering is over."

And time for the next batch of recruits to take their turn, Marcella thought.

The three of them watched quietly as the exhausted men marched slowly past. Someone along the sidewalk recognized the regimental flag from a newspaper account and shouted out for all to hear: "That's the Sixty-Ninth! Those are the boys that took on that *Stonewall* Jackson!"

A cheer went out from the crowd and a few of the men acknowledged them. According to press accounts of the battle, two legends had emerged. The "fighting" Sixty-Ninth New York had shown the most courage on the field amongst the Union Boys in Blue, and the General who had led the Rebs that stopped them had picked up a nickname that papers both north and south could not resist. The men of the Sixty-Ninth—almost all of them Irish, the paper had said—seemed bolstered by the crowd's enthusiastic welcome. Their steps livened somewhat, and they marched in unison now. One of the men within the lines, a sergeant it looked like, broke form a little and shouted, "We'll be back at 'em. Right, boys?"

And the men around him shouted in approval.

"We'll be signing back up tomorrow if they'll let us," the sergeant said. "Those Rebs've not seen the last of the Sixty-Ninth!"

It was the sort of braggadocio Marcella generally despised, but there was something reassuring to it now. And as she and Catherine and Mrs. Carlisle watched the last of the regiment march past, she knew that she had to find a way to do her share as well. She broached the subject at dinner that evening, and Mrs. Carlisle's and Catherine's reactions were yet another confirmation that she'd made the right decision in leaving her father's house.

"What a wonderful idea," Mrs. Carlisle said after Marcella simply mentioned wanting to get involved in The Cause more. "What do you think we should do?"

"We could organize the ladies to write letters to President Lincoln urging him to emancipate the slaves," Catherine said.

Dear, sweet, passive Catherine, Marcella thought.

"Oh yes, you should bring that up next Friday," Mrs. Carlisle confirmed. "And I have a friend in Washington who just might be able to deliver them to the President personally!"

Marcella only smiled as the two of them planned out what they could say in the letters and how the Ladies Abolition Society might carry on this new phase of The Cause. And she could see how, in one manner at least, she had surpassed both of them. Despite the treasure that was their friendship, they were society women through and through, and too accepting of their limitations.

"I mean to become a nurse," Marcella blurted out. "I mean to volunteer to take care of the wounded."

Mrs. Carlisle's eyes went wide, and Catherine seemed frozen by the very thought of the idea. But neither of them contested what Marcella had said so much as sought to understand how she would carry it out. And she hadn't fully thought through the details in the time between that afternoon and this very moment.

"Does this mean you will be leaving us?" Catherine asked after Marcella had talked about going to the local recruiting station tomorrow to inquire about the matter of nurses. There was a look of such genuine concern for losing her that Marcella thought about the expression on Pilar's face when she left the house in November. And the thought now of leaving behind the two friends who had replaced her family seemed almost too much to bear, even for a woman of her strength.

"There will certainly be hospitals *here,*" Mrs. Carlisle said. "Look at all the wounded men who were in the carriages at the end of each regiment. Surely they'll need care."

And Marcella smiled at the thought of it.

"I will inquire about them tomorrow," she replied.

"Oh . . . the thought of all that blood!" Catherine added with a shiver.

Ah, dear sweet, Catherine.

ETHAN

WASHINGTON

1861–62

In reading Sir Isaac Newton's laws of the universe, Ethan'd always believed what was understood to be at the center of them, namely that time and space were constant: a minute was always a minute, a mile always a mile. But the more time he spent in the army, the more opportunity he had to question Sir Isaac's premises entirely.

A typical day might begin with the bugle call before dawn and some time to chow before morning drills. They'd punch their bayonets through countless effigies of dirty Reb bastards, then learn to turn about-face and quarter-left, then quarter-right and half-left and half-right and about-face again, until they'd dug half-foot holes with their feet right where they stood. They'd simulate marching in columns of four and stepping into columns of two for battle, then have another go at the Reb effigies, in case they hadn't taught the bastards enough of a lesson on the first go-round. In the afternoons they'd pack up their gear and tents and march in step, left-right, left-right, with a drill sergeant marching alongside calling out the same, in case anyone forgot which foot they were on. Five or seven or ten miles they'd cover, marching from point A to point who cares, where they'd stop and set up their tents, only to take them down again and pack up and march back to point A, left-right, left-right, all the while with the sergeant there to remind them lest anyone forget. Of course there was to be no talking along the way, what with the concentration necessary to not march left-right, left-left. And time and space seemed to alter in ways Newton'd never imagined possible, a minute becoming an hour, a mile becoming ten.

Having all reenlisted together after that disastrous first ninety-day hitch, with the Fightin' Sixty-Ninth now part of the newly formed Irish Brigade, Ethan and Harry and Finny and Smitty at least had each other to help pass the time. But after a month or two in Washington, time having faded from such puny units of measurement by then, Ethan wrote to Mr. Hadley back at the photography studio in Brooklyn, telling him that he'd be better off taking pictures than bothering with all the drilling and the marching. He'd meant it as a joke of course, but Mr. Hadley promptly sent a box camera and all the necessities with a letter explaining that he was sure he could make more than that investment back with whatever pictures Ethan could take of *The Front.* Harry and Finny and Smitty laughed as much as Ethan did to hear the training fields of Washington described as *The Front,* but he purchased as many glass-plate negatives and developing chemicals as he could find and started taking pictures around the camp during the evenings and on Sundays. Harry and Finny and Smitty found their way into most of the early pictures, but they eventually figured out that they could charge as much as a dollar apiece for soldiers to have their portraits taken, and thus came the business side of the venture.

Harry began offering a small cut to an artillery sergeant, and soon the boys got to stand beside one of the big siege guns to have their pictures taken, which was even more impressive, and would cost just a little bit more, of course. It wasn't long before a few officers got wind of it, and some paid the dollar and a half for a portrait, though most simply took it as a matter of privilege, the way officers were inclined to do. Ethan sent the first pictures back to Mr. Hadley around Christmastime, and Mr. Hadley responded with fifty dollars in a letter telling him to keep them coming. Word traveled up the chain of command, with Lieutenants soon pushed aside by Captains and Majors and Colonels in turn, and eventually the Division Commander, a Major General at that, was sitting for a portrait in full battle regalia. Ethan sent the fifty dollars back to Mr. Hadley, telling him that the enterprise had become profitable in its own right down here on *The Front,* and Mr. Hadley wrote back telling him that the camera was his and he'd put the fifty in a bank account for Ethan, with all future profits to be similarly split down the middle.

Then February brought news that would've been quite well received just a few months earlier. The Army would soon be on the move, bound for the Virginia Peninsula aboard an armada of transport ships, to land not far from where the first English settlers did in Jamestown, and from there head *north* to Richmond.

That'll be the enda th'picture crew Perfessor, Harry said when they got the news. Just when we was havin' some fun in this godforsaken army.

But two days before they were about to disembark, Ethan was called in by the Captain, who told him that the higher-ups decided it'd be good to have someone recording the march on Richmond for posterity. Ethan was promoted to Sergeant, and placed in immediate command of just three men, Harry and Finny and Smitty, who were now to be his photography crew until further notice. Of course, there'd be none of the marching and the drilling for them, not so long as there were pictures to be taken, but they'd still be amongst the ranks and get to fight with the Sixty-Ninth whenever there was action. The Captain asked Ethan, Sergeant McOwen that was, if he thought there'd be any problems with that, and Ethan had to bite his bottom lip to keep from laughing.

No sir, he answered. I believe we can do just that.

THE VIRGINIA PENINSULA

SPRING 1862

George McClellan's the name of the Commanding General this time around. He'd won some ground out in western Virginia at the start of the war and that was enough, seeing how it was more than any other Union general'd done, to get him promoted to command the biggest army this side of the Atlantic. He's taken to calling it *The Grand Army of the Potomac* by way of washing clean the shame of Bull Run, and most all the boys love him, what with how he's kept them well fed and well supplied and safely camped in Washington for the last six months or so. The boys call him Little Mac and the press has taken to calling him the Young Napoleon, though there's word that Lincoln's not too thrilled with the last six months of the marching and the drilling and the *Grand Army* not a foot closer to Richmond.

But they land on the Virginia Peninsula in late February and even a skeptic worse than Harry'd have a hard time not being impressed by it all. There's a hundred and thirty thousand Boys in Blue, plus hundreds of cannons, thousands of supply wagons, and ten thousand horses to carry it all. Then there's the cavalry, with thousands more horses, and the Navy to carry everyone and everything right to Virginia and then follow the *Grand Army* up the James River until the water runs shallow, their big guns covering every move as far as Harrison's Landing. It's easy going at the start as the boys pass Jamestown and then continue on to Yorktown, where Washington whipped the Redcoats once and for all eighty years earlier. And the *Grand Army,* seeming to be as invincible as Little Mac said it'd be, is headed for a victory every bit as significant as Washington's. But then they stop. Stop cold. And wait.

Nobody's quite sure why, since the Rebs couldn't possibly have half the men the *Grand Army* has, but stop they do all the same. There aren't too many new pictures to take once three weeks pass, but then Ethan's told to report to the rear of the column with his camera and crew. There's a Brigadier back there who wants his portrait taken and it's strange that the *Grand Army* would go to the trouble of having a supply wagon sent to carry them all the way back there, but who are any of them to ask why? It makes more sense when they get there and see that the Brigadier in question is practically commanding the supply lines of the entire *Grand Army.* He's not much older than Ethan and the boys, and they can't imagine how he's risen so far so fast even if he'd finished top of his class at West Point. Then a sergeant tells them that the Brigadier never even *went* to West Point, that he's a Harvard man just like his Daddy the Senator, and then it all makes sense. When Harry hears the story, it's all Ethan can do to keep him from crossing the line and saying the wrong thing in front of the Brigadier, though Harry does put on his mock English accent for the duration of their time there.

After they've taken a dozen portraits of the Brigadier standing beside all manner of cannons he'll never actually see fired in combat, it's time for Ethan and crew to head back to their regiment. Harry starts with his full-blown imitation of the Brigadier, combining a Hah-vahd accent with his fake English-gent mannerisms, and Finny and Smitty are in stitches. Ethan is too, until he sees something eerily familiar just thirty yards away on the fringes of the column.

Beneath a grove of shade trees is a makeshift camp, overcrowded with at least a hundred runaway slaves, probably more. He'd heard about how they clung to the Union column, thousands of them run off from Norfolk and Newport News and all the way down the Peninsula, but this is the first time he's been so close to the rear of the column that he can actually see them. It's a sight that sends a shiver down his spine. Except for the color of their skin and their straw field hats to replace woolen caps, they're the very image of the crowds he saw gathered back in Newry waiting for the ferry, then huddled together on the boat, then gathered on the docks at Liverpool. Their faces are gaunt, their eyes haunted, just like the folks back in the Old Country, yet there's the same determination in their gaze, clinging to freedom the way the skin-draped skeletons back in Ireland clung to life itself. And Ethan is frozen for a moment, overwhelmed by a sight he never thought . . . he hoped, he'd never see again.

Come on Perfessor, Harry calls out to him.

Harry and Finny and Smitty are twenty steps ahead, placing the glass-plate negatives on the supply wagon.

Hold on a minute, Ethan says, compelled by an idea, then giving as much of an order as he'll ever give. Bring everything over here, I wanna take a few more pictures.

We gotta get back fer the *game,* Perfessor, Smitty says, and Ethan remembers that a few of the lads from the Eighty-Eighth have challenged them to a baseball game with a case of the good stuff on the line.

I wanna take a few more pictures first, Ethan says, and they walk over next to him without bringing the equipment.

Come on Perfessor, Harry says, why you wanna take pictures of a buncha darkies? You think the Colonel gives a rat's ass about this lot?

But Ethan looks at Harry square in the eyes and says, They remind me of th'folks at Newry . . . th'ones on th'docks . . . an' th'ones dat never got outta dere . . . wit' da bones pokin' from dere skin an' da green lips from eatin' da . . .

And then he stops, collecting himself a little, wondering how his old manner of speaking came back with the memory. Ethan's never told Harry and Finny and Smitty about The Hunger, but they've heard plenty of stories from relatives and other refugees. And they know Ethan was there for so much of the worst of it. They know about Aislinn and the long walk to Newry and the Coffin Ship even, secondhand of course, since it was Aunt Em who'd told them about it, one time just before the war when Ethan was late coming home from Mr.

Hadley's studio and they'd all come by to fetch him on their way to Feeny's on a Saturday night. Aunt Em was there, joining the lads on the stoop while they waited, telling them more about Ethan than they'd ever heard him speak of himself in all the years they'd known him before, or since. So now Harry, hearing Ethan make even that vague reference to what he'd seen in the Old Country, responds like a greenhorn listening to a battle veteran tell him about war.

Okay Perfessor, he says, and then shouts at Smitty and Finny to come with him to the wagon to get the camera and equipment while Ethan walks to the runaways' camp and sets up the tripod.

The runaways don't trust him much straight off, but they're willing to have their pictures taken, so Ethan uses the dozen remaining negatives he has, wishing he hadn't wasted so many on the damn Hah-vahd Brigadier. He sees a pot of boiling water not far away, with leaves and tree bark floating on top, and he remembers the green mouths back home. The Brigadier gave him and the others two Virginia cigars each from the giant supply he had, and Ethan hands them to one of the runaways now, saying he can trade them with the pickets for some food. Finny quickly gives up his cigars too, and then Ethan looks at Harry and Smitty, who shake their heads a little, then reach into their pockets to hand them out as well.

Jesus, Perfessor, Harry says as they make their way back for the ball game. Didja hafta go an' give up them cigars?

Awww Harry, Finny says, that fella needed 'em a whole lot more'n we do. Plus we wouldn't never've had 'em if it wasn't fer th'Perfessor an' his camera anyways.

Who asked *you,* Finny? Harry barks. An' I *know* we wouldn'ta had 'em if it wasn't fer th'Perfessor. I'm just exercising my right as a soldier to complain, by God.

And they banter that way for most of the ride back to camp, drawing a few laughs from Ethan and pressing down the haunting memories back to where they've been stored all along. The game gets under way in the midafternoon, a makeshift field marked off in the clearing by the woods south of town. It starts as a friendly contest between lads who'd played for teams back home, mostly the product of Harry's boasting about the Excelsiors to a couple of men from the Eighty-Eighth who were of a mind to show him that they played a fine brand of baseball up in Albany, too. Then Harry teased them some more, asking why, if things were so grand up in Albany, they'd come all the way down to New York to sign up for the Irish Brigade? And so on. Of course, with maybe a hundred lads from the Eighty-Eighth and at least as many there from the Sixty-Ninth to watch along the base lines, it isn't a completely friendly game for very long.

It's nothing like the contests back at the Elysian Fields, with a tattered ball made from strips of cotton wrapped around a .69-caliber musket ball, and the field covered in rocks and tiny patches of grass scattered everywhere. There are errors and bad hops practically every time the ball is struck, and the frustration only adds to the competition. At the start of the sixth inning the score is tied at fifteen, and Finny leads off with a cleanly struck single. Then Ethan comes up, striking a line drive that lands just in front of the right fielder, a fella named Ferguson. The ball hits a rock or a tuft of grass or some other obstacle that litters the field, and it bounces over Ferguson's shoulder toward a grove of trees in the distance. Ferguson takes off after it as Ethan dashes around the bases amidst shouts from his teammates, until they are all silenced by the sound of a rifle shot. Ferguson freezes, but then a few seconds later another shot kicks up a cloud of dust just a few feet away from him, and he quickly turns and runs back toward the infield, with the other fielders following his lead and the crowd of men, confident they are out of range, laughing hysterically at the spectacle.

By nightfall, half a dozen Confederate snipers have been cleared out of the woods, and the men of the Sixty-Ninth sit around the campfires, with Harry and Smitty and Finny taking turns telling the story of when Ethan ended a game at the Elysian Fields by hitting the ball into the Hudson River, the grandeur of the occasion and the distance of the blast growing with each retelling. And there are the usual songs around the campfires, "Sweet Lorena" and "Just Before the Battle Mother," and for those fleeting moments the whole damn thing seems more tolerable than ever.

THE GRAND ARMY FINALLY MOVES forward into the Reb lines two days later, only to find that the Rebs aren't there, *skee-daddled th'night befo',* a slave who was with them tells one of the officers. This fella skee-daddled too in all the confusion, he tells them, and the Lieutenant thinks the man might provide some valuable intelligence, until he tells him that the Rebs had only about eleven thousand men all together on the other side. That's when the Lieutenant thinks the runaway's a crazy man, since there's no way eleven thousand men could scare a *Grand Army* of a hundred thirty thousand into stopping in their tracks for a whole month. But Ethan and Harry and Finny and Smitty know it's possible when a *Grand Army*'s got a Commanding General scared of his own farts, and that's the way it's starting to look with General McClellan. The night after they storm into the empty Reb camps, there's plenty of soldiers exercising their right to complain, by God, as they sit around the campfires and wonder if they'll ever see Richmond.

It's another month of creeping their way north until at last Finny climbs a tree and can see the church steeples of the Confederate capital. It won't be long now, they all figure, until Little Mac issues the order to stop and wait for the big guns to be brought up from the back of the lines, and Ethan and Harry and Finny and Smitty joke that at least the Hah-vahd Brigadier'll have to get off his arse and do something now. A week passes getting the guns up, and another week passes getting them into place, and then a third passes for God knows why, until finally it seems that McClellan is ready to act. But by then the Rebs've got a new Commander themselves, a fella named Bobby Lee, and it turns out he's not such a hospitable host after all.

Ol' Bobby sends his boys at the *Grand Army* every day for six days straight, and though the Boys in Blue hold the field at the end of each of those days, Little Mac issues the order for what he calls a "tactical repositioning," but all his soldiers know full well is a retreat. Every day they fight and hold the field. Every night they back up, farther away from Richmond and closer to the Union Navy at Harrison's Landing. By the seventh day they're farther from Richmond than they've been in a month and there's not a man in the Irish Brigade that isn't fed up with all this skee-daddlin' they've been doing, especially since the Rebs haven't whipped them once this entire campaign.

The fighting starts again on the seventh day at a place called Malvern Hill, and it's a whole morning of sitting on their arses waiting for the call to join the fight. The Irish Brigade's boiling mad when they finally get ordered up. They're supposed to simply hold the line protecting the flank of the entire Corps, but there's no holding back the fury that's built up by now. The Sixty-Ninth Regiment presses forward, firing a volley, reloading on the move, and firing again. Ten then twelve then fifteen volleys later, and they've pushed the Rebs back on their heels. But their muskets are overheating, burning the flesh of their palms and misfiring, so the Eighty-Eighth Regiment switches places with the Sixty-Ninth and takes the lead for a time. They press forward the same way 'til their muskets are hot as Dante's seventh circle, and now it's the Sixty-Ninth's turn again. Back and forth, back and forth it goes, once, twice, and a third time, and by the time the Sixty-Ninth is ready to take the lead for a fourth go-round, the Rebs've already given up all the ground they'd gained that whole afternoon, every inch of it lost back to the Irish Brigade.

Some of the boys in the Sixty-Ninth start shouting that if Little Mac'll just grow a pair, the Sixty-Ninth will lead the march all the way to Richmond. They're going in with almost no ammunition at all, but with bayonets flourishing, their lines slip past the Eighty-Eighth's and back into the fray, with the fighting closer than it's been all day. They're maybe ten yards from the wreck that was the Reb lines when Ethan takes aim and fires his last round. He sees the man he's aiming at as the bullet hits him right in the chest and his legs fold underneath him and crumble like a tent that's had its lines cut, bouncing onto his knees first, then falling backwards with his legs tucked beneath him. Ethan moves up closer and sees the blood gathering beside the man, forming a small pool, and him lying there, legs folded up like Aislinn in her too-small coffin, and with a look on his face that's saying, *Now why'd you go and do that?*

But then Harry's out of ammunition just a few feet away, and when a Reb that's as big as he is knocks the musket from

Harry's hands, Ethan thinks his friend's a goner 'til Harry hauls off and punches the fella smack in the nose, and they're down on the ground rolling around and cussing up a storm at each other. Ethan moves over to help Harry and sees another Reb running up to do the same for his friend, but Ethan gets there first, knocking the big man in the head with the butt of his musket and allowing Harry to get the upper hand. The other Reb's coming at Ethan then and he steps to one side, making the Reb miss partly but still managing to drive his bayonet into Ethan's shoulder. And he feels a fire of pain rush through his whole body. Still, he's got his wits enough about him to swing his own musket forward and drive the bayonet into the Reb's chest, seeing him start to go down the way the fella he'd shot just before did. There's no hesitation this time as Ethan drives his bayonet into him again, and he drops face-first to the ground, lifeless.

The bugle call finally can be heard over the noise of battle, and it's time for the Sixty-Ninth to fall back and let the Eighty-Eighth hold the line. First thing Ethan and Harry do, once they've seen each other and know they're mostly all right, is look around for Finny and Smitty. And as they retreat in as orderly a manner as men who've just been through such moments can do, boys all along the line are calling out the names of their closest friends, hoping to hear a response.

Ethan, you with us? comes the familiar voice of Finny, forgetting to call him Sergeant, the way he tries to do when it's the whole company together like this.

Yea, Fin, he answers. Harry's here too. What about Smitty?

Dunno.

Harry looks at Ethan and immediately breaks ranks, with Ethan soon following behind. It takes a minute or two for them to find Finny and then a little longer for them to catch up with the Eighty-Eighth. The Rebs've fallen back, but there are wounded scattered everywhere, gray and blue alike.

Smitt-yyyyy! Harry calls out, once twice and a third time. Until finally they hear a response.

I got'm over here!

They follow the voice and find their friend beside a Corporal from the Eighty-Eighth who'd played ball against them back at Yorktown. He's pouring some water into the side of Smitty's mouth, and then a little over the wounds where he's been shot in the arm and taken some shrapnel in the belly. After a minute or two, Ethan and Harry and Finny take turns carrying him back away from the lines, lying to him all the way, telling him they'll all be back playing ball at the Elysian Fields by the time next spring rolls around.

HARRISON'S LANDING, VIRGINIA
JULY 5, 1862

Three days later it was all over. The months of training and planning and marching and drilling and inching forward toward the ultimate goal of Richmond, and it had amounted to this. The Grand Army was abandoning the Virginia Peninsula altogether now, the wounded first, then the artillery, then the troops who'd won nearly every engagement with the enemy and were still being forced to retreat.

For Ethan it'd been a worse few days than the walk to Newry or aboard the *Lord Sussex,* and almost as bad as the days just after Aislinn's funeral. Smitty woke up the day after the battle and was sure that the pain he felt in his arm was the real thing, and not just the kind made up somewhere in the mind when it doesn't want to think about what'd been lost. And Ethan woke the first two mornings after Malvern Hill, unsure if the pain he felt in his shoulder and the arm, numb still, prickling with pins and needles, was really there in the corporeal sense, or if he'd become as mad as Smitty. But each successive morning he doubted his senses a little less, felt his arm a little more, and was left only to consider the two men he'd killed in the battle, or how he'd helped hold down Smitty when the doctor cut off his throwing arm, or how all of it turned out to be for naught.

Perhaps the worst part of it was the fact that Ethan'd be on a boat separate from most of the rest of the Sixty-Ninth. His wound was almost serious enough to warrant a discharge, but not quite, and he was happy for that much at least. He knew it would heal eventually, and he hated the idea of leavin' Harry and Finny behind to face what was next. Smitty was a different story . . . the war was over for him. Then just before the call came for Ethan to board the last of the ships set aside for the wounded, he saw Harry walking up to him with a shovel draped over his shoulder.

Where's Finny? Ethan asked, surprised that they hadn't both come by to see him off.

Well, now that you decided t'go an' get stuck, Harry said, that's all fer the picture-takin' crew, so we got some ditch-diggin' to do. Little Mac's worried the bogeyman Bobby Lee's still out there waitin' t'get him.

So how come you're here? Ethan asked.

Well, there's shifts t'things, ya know, Harry replied. Not my *shift* just now, the way I figure it. Besides, it ain't like my Sergeant's gonna do anything about it.

And Ethan smiled for the first time in a few days.

The ship was loaded with stretchers across the top deck, and as the Lieutenant began to make his way down to call for the last group to be put aboard, the thought finally struck Ethan that this might be the last time he saw Harry. There could be another fight before the boys got back to Washington, if Bobby Lee got impatient enough to kick them out faster than they were already going. And if Malvern Hill had taught him anything, it was that any man's time could be up whenever some stray bit of shrapnel or a well-aimed minnie ball decided to make it so.

I just . . . Harry . . . you gotta . . . Ethan started to say.

Hey, listen to this, Harry interrupted before Ethan had the chance to get even a little emotional. There's about a hundred Rebs a half a mile from here, a buncha prisoners we took th'other day. An' me an' Finny an' a half dozen of the lads were walkin' past yesterday, an' we heard one of th'Rebs say . . . now get this Ethan . . . he says, There's some o' them Irish devils . . . I wisht they was on *our* side.

Ethan smiled at the thought of it, pretending to find as much consolation in the accolade as Harry hoped to offer. But as he walked onto the gunboat that'd take him back to Washington, he couldn't help but feel how little it'd all amounted to once again, and that they'd been fools after all. As the ship's steam paddle finally started them downriver, he saw the sad image of what remained of the Grand Army's Grand Plans, strewn all along the riverfront. Even the caissons and supply wagons looked sad, resting beside countless barrels and crates still loaded with supplies that hadn't been used. And then, just a little farther down the river, beyond the last of the Union camps, there they were again, the runaways, clinging desperately to their last vestige of freedom, and soon to be left behind by the army that had seemed like their liberators for that one glorious spring.

When the ship was far enough away from the shore for Ethan not to feel their haunted gaze upon him, he took a place along the portside edge of the top deck and decided he'd have to tell her about the disappointments of the past two weeks. It'd be done with whispers amidst the clamor of the paddlewheel, lest a passing orderly take him for a man gone mad.

> We're done for now, Ais', he said, staring out at the water. Smitty's lost an arm and I got nicked some and we're all bound for Washington now like the whole last year never even happened.

And then his voice grew even quieter.

> I killed two men, Ais'—right up close. Close enough to look them straight in the eye and know something about what sorta man it was I was sendin' to the Ever After. And I know I'll see their faces in my dreams for as long as I live—like maybe I'll be mad as Hamlet one day, I dunno. And none of it was like the "once more unto the breach, my friends, once more . . ." from old King Henry—it wasn't anything like that at all. It's all just spit and blood and bullets and madness. I've grown to like Shakespeare almost as much as you did, Ais'—and I told Mam and Aunt Em about your book, and how they should find the right person to give it to if something happens to me an' all. But I gotta tell ya, Ais'—Shakespeare doesn't know shite about war.

SHARPSBURG, MARYLAND
SEPTEMBER 17, 1862

By the time the two armies meet along the Antietam Creek in this small farming town in Maryland, it's easy to see how so many of the men have become hardened by all the loss. The Grand Army's done nothing but lose, and nobody's callin it *Grand* anymore. Six months of buildup brought to a crashing halt just like that, with all the lads who've fallen having given their limbs and their lives for what seems like nothing at all. And now Ol' Bobby Lee's got his boys on the march north, taking the fight into Maryland for the first time.

Your shoulder's fine . . . fine enough to hold a rifle anyway, though you doubt you'll be knocking any baseballs into the Hudson anytime soon, war or not. But it's hard to think of anything back home these days, as you've learned to just put your head down and march in line . . . not much of an outlook for a division photographer, but essential for a soldier. And now this is shaping up to be the worst fight since Bull Run, likely a whole lot worse, since there won't be too many greenhorns on either side running away after the first taste of fire, and these two armies are each half again as large, and many times more pissed off, than the ones who met at Bull Run.

It starts as a mess, of course, as if anything else could be possible. The right flank of the Union Army bumps up against Stonewall Jackson's Corps making a bloody marsh out of the five-foot-high cornstalks. They're fighting hand to hand with artillery cutting down broad swaths of corn and broader swaths of men until both sides back off, ending it in a standoff. So then comes your turn, along the center of the lines, where the Rebs have the Sunken Road, a convenient trench at least a foot and a half deep where thousands of wagons over dozens of years have eroded away as perfect a firing position as an army could want. And it's the Irish Brigade's task to clear the Rebs out of there, all of you walking forward in formation, and the Rebs lying down prone on the ground, only the tops of their heads exposed.

Father Corby, the Brigade Chaplain, rides out in front before you all set off and offers a general absolution of your sins. You look over at Harry who's got that *Jesus, now that's a promisin' sign* look on his face. Still, you and Harry and Finny all remove your caps and bless yourselves, one last time maybe, before you set off. It's occurred to all of you fighting men that it makes no sense to march in formation against such a position. Not that you're afraid to get at the Rebs in the Sunken Road, *but for Christ sakes, do we gotta WALK all the way there?* For what? So the officers can keep track of things? Because that's how Napoleon used to do it?

But walk forward you do, in perfect formations that've become second nature to you by now, absorbing musket fire from the time you're a hundred or so yards out, not being allowed to fire back 'til you get in closer, closer, closer, 'til there aren't nearly as many of you left as what started out walking in the first place. There's a wooden cow fence about halfway there, and the lead lines have to stop to knock it all down while still coming under fire. Finally they march forward again, fewer still than just a minute before, and now the men from the back lines step forward to replace those that've fallen in the front. Then it's your turn, third line back, to step to the front position and replace the two men before you who've gone down already.

The command comes to fire when you're confronted by a Reb company out in front of the Sunken Road, poor lads they are, and the whole Brigade opens up and fires its volley.

But the greenhorn beside you panics a little, stepping to the side and dropping to one knee, and it's all you can do not to waste your shot as you're stumbling over him. When the smoke's settled a little, you can see the Reb company drawing back into the Sunken Road with the rest of their boys, except for a few fellas near a tree they use for cover. The lead man fires and has two men behind him reloading and handing him their muskets, and you stop, just as the smoke is clearing and the Brigade is getting ready to move forward again. You aim your musket. Twenty, maybe thirty yards away, you breathe out the way the drill sergeants taught you, see that Reb doing the shooting by the tree and aim right at his nose, then let go. And you see his head snap back, see the way his boys around him don't even bother to drag him along with them as they retreat to the Sunken Road. And that's three, for sure. Three you've killed, counting the two at Malvern Hill. An odd thought in the midst of all this.

The command comes to move forward again, fix bayonets on the move, and get ready to take the Sunken Road hand to hand. But you don't get more than three steps when you feel a ball of fire pop into your right leg, and before you can tumble from it, another goes through the same shoulder where you got it with the bayonet, making the same, terrible, sickening sound of flesh giving way to metal the way it did when you stuck your bayonet into that man at Malvern Hill. And you're down in a rush, collapsing upon yourself, limbs flopping aimlessly like the pages of a book thrown facedown onto the ground, and there's nothing but the noise beginning to meld into one vast pop and rumble and shout.

You can see the lines march past, then another horrible barrage coming from over by the Sunken Road, and plenty more falling around you. There's a bugle call for retreat, and another from the Brigade behind you to move forward, and then there's Harry, standing over you and cussing and calling to Finny, and you smile a little at the sight of them both, knowing they're all right. And then they're lifting you up with the pain bursting through you again as you feel everything going gray for a while . . . see your blood spilling out of your leg and onto Finny's arms as he carries your lower half. Then Harry's yelling at you, *look at me Perfessor, look at ME, Ethan,* and it's coming from behind you . . . straight above you since Harry's got you by both arms . . . and you smile halfway at him . . . not from seeing his face upside down in this odd manner, but from hearing him call you Ethan for the first time in maybe ten years, maybe more . . .

When you open your eyes you're back on the ground, only under a tree, and the fighting sounds farther off than before. Finny's saying how they *cleared out the Sunken Road at last,* and he's laughing nervously, thinking the best thing he can do is tell you this, that it wasn't all for naught this time around. *At least we showed them Rebs how to fight.* Then Harry's telling him *it doesn't matter now Fin,* and tells him to go off and get the Division Commander and see if he'll send his surgeon for the fella that took his portrait back in Washington. Harry's pulling off his belt and wrapping it around your leg just above the wound, like you'd learned you shoulda done from the Doc that had to take Smitty's arm. It hurts like hell but Harry keeps saying *sorry, Ethan, just a little tighter* . . . then pulls with all the strength he's got, and the pain makes everything go gray . . . then altogether black.

When you wake up again, Harry's kneeling beside you . . . *Yer gonna be fine now Ethan,* he says, and it worries you that he's still calling you that . . . but it's hard to get the air to tell him so. Finny's back before long and it sounds like the battle's done, or shifted over to the left part of the lines. The sky's turning dark and you remember that it must be this late by now, that you're not dying yet, that it's merely the sun setting in its universe the way Isaac Newton says it should, and at least that's still the same as ever. Finny's got a canteen and he pours some of its contents into your mouth and you swallow it down along with some of the red spit that's still forming from inside you. It burns like water isn't supposed to and you start to cough in gasps of breath.

Finny! Harry shouts. *Ya gotta water it down. You know he's not an OBJ man.*

Then you recognize the putrid taste of Oh! Be Joyful on your tongue. It's a foul concoction of potato peels and whatever else the men can ferment down to this rubbish, and you can't imagine how they love it so.

Sorry Ethan, Finny says, and you stop coughing before long, thinking, *Et tu, Fin?* not 'cause of the OBJ but because now *he's* calling you by the name your Mam gave you, too. Finny's gone for a few minutes and as soon as he's back, there's the surgeon standing over you. Fin tries again to pour some of the stuff from the canteen into your mouth, and the surgeon grabs it from him.

I watered it down Doc, Finny says, but the Doc's not happy.

He looks at your leg and shakes his head some, then pulls Harry's cap off your shoulder and seems not as unhappy as he is with the leg. He hands the canteen back to Finny and tells him to pour some on the shoulder, *just a bitta shrapnel there,* he says, *went clear through.* Finny's dripping it down in little drops that sting, 'til the Doc grabs hold of it and lets it spill out in a rush, and you feel the fire pour through you.

You boys'll drink this down like it's water, the Doc says, *but when you finally find something this shit is good for, you get scared.*

He pours even more of it into the wound in your leg and now it's on fire again, and the grayness starts setting in. It's only when he tells Harry to hand him *that instrument there* that you shake off the gray enough to try and see just what instrument he means . . . if it's the little scalpel or the saw . . .

Hold him down! the Doc shouts at Finny, who presses your shoulders back before you can see.

The Doc pours some of the OBJ on whatever it is he's fixing to operate with, then more into your leg, and everything starts to turn grayer than before.

Give him another sip of that, the Doc says to Finny, who's tipping the canteen into the side of your mouth. Then Harry's placing a stick between your teeth, and the Doc's looking right at you now, not more than a foot from your face.

Bite down on that now, son, he says. *This is gonna hurt.*

9 *Islands*

MARY
RICHMOND
SUMMER 1862

Good Lawd, dis mus' be some 'potant work we doin' here if'n they sent Yo Majesty down to do it wit' us.

Mary's heard the comments from her fellow slaves before. It's the price she has to pay for the comfort of her life and the chance to speak French, wear pretty dresses in the shop, and pretend she isn't just a common slave girl from the tobacco fields of Carolina. It doesn't get any easier when Miss Juss decides she simply *hasta* volunteer in the army hospital the way Sally Henridge does. Sally's still just seventeen and almost a full year younger than Miss Juss, and the thought of Sally havin' those boys all to herself is enough to drive Juss into fits like she used to have when she was no more than ten years old. Of course, the only way Mista and Misses Kittredge'll hear about Juss workin' at the army hospital is if Mary goes with her every mornin' and stays to walk her home again at mid-day. Juss spends some time every mornin' readin' letters to the soldiers, but with all the nurses and white ladies workin' at the hospital, there isn't much left for Mary to do. So they send her off to wash sheets and bandages down by the stream with some of the other slave gals, and that's the beginning of the makin' fun and callin' her *Yo Majesty* and all.

It starts straight off the very first day she's sent down there, with her fancy dress and the way she walks real straight, with her hair set back in pins and barrettes the way the white ladies do it. Truth is, it isn't Mary puttin' on airs so much as it's that she doesn't have any other dresses, but try tellin' the slave gals that. Besides, Misses Kittredge'd never let her walk through town lookin' like a common field hand, where some of the society ladies that come into the shop might see her, and that'd ruin the whole idea that Mary's something special. So it isn't Mary's fault that she looks so out of place down by the stream. Not that it matters much to the other women, who have their fun pickin' on her when they aren't ignorin' her altogether. Mary could tell the Misses about hangin' sheets on the line, and the Misses'd tell the people at the hospital to have Mary do something else. But she doesn't want to feel like this work is beneath her, and doesn't want Gertie thinkin' less of her, like she'd got uppity, and start scoldin' her in her dreams.

So for four hours every day it's hangin' up the sheets and bandages the women clean, and noontime can't get here fast enough when she can go and get Miss Juss from the hospital so they can walk home together. Juss spends the whole walk talkin' about this officer or that and what so-and-so says in this letter or that one, and they have just a few minutes for something to eat before Juss goes upstairs for lessons with Miss Randall. Juss was supposed to be done with her lessons once she turned eighteen, but Miss Randall kept sayin' that there was a whole lot more for her to learn, so that's another year of long afternoons for Juss. Mary'd like to still be studyin' with Miss Randall in the afternoons, learnin' more about history and literature and such. But she's in the shop every afternoon instead, meetin' with all the ladies who're buyin' dresses again, now that the Yankees've been chased off away from Richmond.

Between all the work and all the teasin', not to mention the way Juss is growin' up and seems more interested in officers than she is in her, it's a sad time for Mary. But a little more than two weeks in, things begin to change, just a little bit at first, then a little more each day. It isn't that the gals stop teasin' her, or that the shop gets any less busy, or that Juss is any less interested in officers, but that now Mary's got a distraction of her own.

There's a new work detail set up just down the stream a piece, where a few slaves are brought in to build a levee to steer some of the water off the stream for washin' the sheets and bandages. Farther downriver there'll be another levee, where the waste from the hospital can get washed downstream and out to the river once or twice a day. There's a white overseer and seven slaves doin' the work, but it doesn't take long to see that the overseer isn't there to do anythin' more than make sure six of the colored men keep up with the other one, the one who's *really* runnin' things. Mary doesn't recognize him straight off, what with him downstream a piece, but when noontime comes and she heads back past the men to the hospital to get Juss, she sees him lift his hat off his head as she passes. The six other slaves stare at her and smile and make jokes to each other, and not a one of 'em takes off his hat. Micah doesn't say anything, but that's nothing new for him, as far as she can remember.

When he worked at the dress shop the year before, he went about it like he was practically in his own world . . . nothing but sawin' and hammerin' and measurin' as far as she could tell. But he'd always stop and take his hat off whenever Mary or the Misses or Juss or even Cora walked past. Never said nothing then, but took his hat off all the same. He built that extension on the dress shop in three and a half weeks, working only in the very early mornin's and late in the evenin's. Mr. Kittredge said it was well worth the high cost Mr. Longley charged to rent out Micah since he's about the best carpenter in the city, white or colored, he said. And if there's ever another job to get done 'round the store, it'll be Micah he hires to do it.

Mary didn't pay too much attention to Micah back then, what with the store plenty busy and her tryin' to remember who she could speak French to and who she had to be that Carolina field hand with and everything in between. Besides, she still wasn't in much of a mind to take any more notice of men than she had to back then, and when she'd talk to Gertie at night, she'd sometimes wonder if maybe Mista Grant had ruined her toward thinkin' of men altogether. But that was a year ago, and seein' Juss growin' up more every day, talkin' 'bout officers like she used to talk about dresses and hair ribbons, it's made Mary start to do some changin' too. The dress shop's been seemin' more like a *job* lately than some kinda adventure, the way it used to, and soon enough Juss'll find a young man to make the most important person in her life, and Mary realizes she'll be alone as Cora . . . or like Gertie was before she took Mary in. And somehow that's got Mary wantin' for something more, somebody who might understand her the way Juss and Cora, and Gertie even, can't. Somebody who knows what it's like to be an island.

And so when she walks past the workin' men, and sees Micah take off his hat, standin' up straight and noddin' his head just ever so little, she sees him in a altogether different way than she saw him before. She looks at him with a smile she doesn't mean to make, happy to see him, happy that there's one person out here along this stream that ain't teasin' her like the women slaves or oglin' her like the overseer and the men slaves. Next day she sometimes looks up from her work washin' the sheets just to watch him. She sees how he's quiet as ever, but not cause he's broken. No, not at all that. He isn't takin' orders from the overseer but more like consultin' with him, tellin' him what needs to get done, and the overseer yells at the other men to do just what Micah says. Of course, the other gals all notice Micah too, but they notice *all* the men, and for a time they're spendin' the mornin's just talkin' 'bout them and got no time for teasin' Mary anymore.

Every noontime Mary hangs the sheets and bandages on the line 'til comes the best part of her day, walkin' past Micah and him takin' off his hat. She's ready for it on the second day and gives him a little curtsey back when she passes. The gals're just lovin' that 'cause now they got something else to tease her about, and the other men laugh and take their hats off and bow deep at the waist, hopin' she'll notice them the way she does Micah. But this ain't about none of them at all. They can tease and laugh and jump around like a buncha no-class nothin's for all she cares. It's like she and Micah are out there beside the river just the two of them. And he seems like he's thinkin' the same thing, like all this ain't about washin' sheets or diggin' a levee or anything of the sort. It ain't even about the war, no more. This is a Mary and Micah thing now, like they're doin' a little dance, movin' closer and closer to each other in little tiny courtin' steps. And Mary's thinkin' all the time about the secrets she still ain't told him, wonderin' whether maybe he's got some secrets of his own, wonderin' about what kindsa threads been makin' up *his* stitchin' up to now.

By the end of the first week with the men there, Mary

takes a minute to make sure her hair and dress are all in order before she walks back to the hospital at noontime. She smiles and curtseys at Micah, and he smiles back and bows just a little, needin' some practice at all this type of thing. By the start of the second week, he says *Afta'noon Miss Mary* when he's takin' off his hat, and she knows he remembers her, too. After that first day of bein' surprised by it and the next mornin' of the gals teasin' her some more about it, she takes to sayin' *Afta'noon Mista Micah,* right back to him.

The gals keep noticin' Micah sure enough, but they mostly only talk about the other men who pay any attention to them. Lunchtime comes, and they go over there smilin' and battin' their eyes at 'em, and there's fightin' among 'em now because there's nine women and just the six men, after Micah, who ain't interested in them at all. Micah takes his hat off when they pass, same as with Mary, but there's no smilin' or sayin' *Afta'noon* or anything to make them feel like he's got eyes for them, so after the second week is over, they leave him alone altogether. They start sayin' he's uppity and no wonder he and Mary get on so good together, and she could *have* him 'cause *th'other men's just as good lookin' an' know howta show a gal they's int'rested.*

Mary starts watchin' Micah all mornin' long, seein' how he only talks to the white overseer when he has to tell him something about the project, and none of the other men seem to like him. One of the gals says she heard that Micah's the only one there that ain't *donated* by their Massas, that Mista Longley charges what he always does for Micah to work, and the government or the hospital or whoever it is that's buildin' the levees says they'll pay it just to have Micah there. And that makes the men and the gals hate Micah all the more. But Mary starts to think that maybe he understands what it's like for her, what it's like to be all alone even with so many people around.

By the third week, Mary takes to stoppin' for a minute or two to talk to Micah when she walks past. The men set themselves down by the stream eatin' their lunch and talkin' up the gals, and the overseer stuffs himself over by the shade tree, and there's Micah all by himself like always. They get to talkin' about the dress shop, and she says what Mista Kittredge said about him and what a fine job he done. He says something about how pretty her dress is, and she says it's dirty some from hangin' the sheets and bandages *but thank you all the same.*

Mary and Juss start gettin' back to the house later and later since Mary's stayin' a little more past noon each day, and Juss ain't about to complain that she's got to spend extra time with them soldiers. Micah starts bringin' something extra for his lunch, sayin' that's a kinda special privilege he gets and that's part of the reason most of the other slaves don't like him too much. Mary starts bringin' whatever she can too, and the two of them share what they got every day, sittin' under a tree all by themselves with the overseer stuffin' himself and the other slaves busy fussin' down by the stream. The gals tease Mary that the two of 'em are just like uptight white folks with all their manners, and *when y'all gonna get to th'love makin'?* But Mary just ignores them the way she's used to doin' by now. They don't know about Mista Grant, and how he done to her before the runnin' off, way back in Carolina, back when she was just a nothin' field hand girl livin' with Gertie. They *couldn't* know, she thinks, or else they wouldn't be talkin' that way. But what's it matter anyhow, she figures.

This here is a Mary and Micah thing.

Micah

CHARLOTTESVILLE, VIRGINIA

SUMMER 1862

He still worked as much as he had with Dunmore. More even. Sometimes Sundays even. And sunup to sundown most every day of the week. Without the sometimes free days when Dunmore didn't get outta bed until past midday. Then gave Micah a wallop or two for not wakin' him up sooner.

No, with Massa Longley it was work most *all* the time. Lotta money to be made with this here war on. But Micah never minded the work, just like his Daddy. Took pride in it, like his Daddy. And with Massa Longley there wasn't any talk about making a thing *look* done, even when it wasn't. Like it had always been with Dunmore. Massa Longley understood the value of things like Dunmore never did. And working for him just this last year, Micah'd come to understand why his daddy got sold for so much back at *Les Roseraies.* And more especially, why he'd got sold for *twice* that much to Massa Longley.

This boy's the finest craftsman this side of the Atlantic, Massa Longley'd say to folks tryin' to hire him. And most of 'em would protest about paying so much for a slave to fix their stables or make them new bookshelves. But Longley knew how to deal with 'em. Made them feel like they was gettin' something special. Told them how he had ten or twelve projects lined up waiting to be done. That if they paid that much he'd put 'em right to the top of the list. *Otherwise . . . might be two three months.* He'd say, shakin' his head. And folks almost always paid to have it done now.

And with a year of that, of extra food and a cabin all his own, Micah had begun to feel like a man again. Proud. Like his

Daddy. Used to receiving compliments from white men and ladies. *Mmm-mmm, you do some fine work boy.* The men'd say. *Oh it's lovely.* The ladies'd say. 'Til they caught themselves, realized who they was talkin' to. And Micah'd just nod his head, eventually got comfortable enough to answer back. *Thank you Suh.* Or. *Thank you Ma'am.* Was as much as he'd ever say. Not like Daddy, who could talk to white folks almost as comfortable as if he was white himself. He'd spin some kinda tale about where he learned to do this. Or how he was watchin' some bluebirds buildin' a nest and got an idea for that. But not Micah. His Momma once told him that Daddy and Bellie was the talkers in the family. And she and Micah were the thinkers. And that was good enough for him. 'Til Mary come along.

He first saw her just a few months after he come to Richmond. Workin' on the store since business was so good. Didn't take more than a few days to know that *she* was the reason for it. And he full-on smiled the day Massa Longley was late gettin' there and he heard her speaking French to one of the society ladies. Like his Momma did back in Nawlins and sometimes 'round the cabin. But he was just a short time with Massa Longley then. Still walkin' around mostly with them blinders on. Still feelin' like a mule most days. And not a man who could interest a woman such as Mary.

Massa Longley hired him out to the government a few months later. Did some work on the soldier hospital and some more on the prison. Then come July and a worse job than he'd ever had with Dunmore. Digging levees so the soldier shit could get flushed out to sea without upsettin' none of the white folks' delicate noses in town. And he hated hearing about that job. Hated looking over the site that first morning. Hated having a useless white overseer he'd have to clear everything through. Hated that it'd take most of the summer to finish. Six fools there to get in his way an' laugh an' dance like fools in fronta the fool women. Then midday came that first day and Mary walked past. A breath of elegance cutting through the stink of the latrines. And there was no more hating that job. She was something to make him think beyond the shit-filled streams and working like a mule for another man's benefit. A reason to look forward to noontime every day. A reason to work slower than he ever had, just to drag out the stolen moments they'd have together. A reason to *know* there was a God.

'Cause something like her couldn't happen by accident.

As the summer progressed, they went from tipped hats and curtseys to all manner of conversation. And he was slowly restored himself. Back past the year working for Longley. Back past the nightmare of Dunmore. Back to *Les Roseraies.* Only not as a little boy anymore, but a full-grown man. Talkin' with his Momma and Daddy in some of his dreams. As a man. And them no older than they was when he was a boy. Momma reminding him about the words. Saying she didn't spend all those evenin's writing letters and words in the layer of flour on the table just for him to forget all about 'em when times got tough. Remindin' him that those letters and words was the sorta things nobody could take away. And then there was Daddy, sayin' how it wasn't such a difficult thing to tell a story. Just gotta figure how things feel, he was tellin' him. And then compare it to something else. How a sunset ain't just pretty. How it's pretty as a sweet tater pie inna windowsill at the harvest jubilation. And so on.

He'd wake from those dreams sometimes and step outside his cabin. Find a small stick, then sit on the log out front that served for a chair. His eyes straining in whatever light the moon cared to offer. And write in the dirt beneath him. Letters first. Remembering all of them. And in his head thinking what Momma said about the sounds they made. Then putting them together in words. Like so many piles of flour. 'Til it got so he couldn't seem to think any thoughts without spellin' the words out in his head. Couldn't ride from Longley's to the soldier hospital without slowing down to read every sign and every storefront in town. Smilin' to think of what his Momma would say. Thinkin' 'bout how Daddy would describe such a woman as Mary. And how she changed everything just by bein' there. More than all the sweet tater pies and sunsets and harvest jubilations there was ever gonna be.

And he passed those days with more purpose than he'd ever had before. The world, somehow, bigger now. When he wasn't with her. And tinier too. In those moments when it was just them to pass smiles and curtseys and bows and such. Whole entire conversations like Momma and Daddy used to have. Packed tight into whatever words could be fit into those stolen moments. And him deciding it was time to be a better man. The kind of man a woman like Mary might someday get to lookin' on the way Momma looked on Daddy. Who wasn't ever gonna be as refined as Momma. Just like he wasn't gonna be with Mary. But still. Maybe. With such a reason to hope. With Mary. Elegance to outshine the ugliness. Like it wasn't such a difficult thing at all.

MARY

SEPTEMBER 1862

Mary's so happy spendin' lunch with Micah that all the busyness at the store, all of Juss's talkin' 'bout this officer or that, all the gals teasin', all the everything that was wearin' her down at the start of the summer, is now all wrapped up in a bundle so small she doesn't even notice it's there most days. Instead it's like she's hearin' music in her head most all the time, hummin' along to it whether she's hangin' sheets or stitchin' dresses or just lyin' still in bed. That music's got her so caught up that she doesn't even notice that the job Micah's been workin' on is gettin' close to done as summer starts windin' down.

Then one day the overseer walks over to where the gals are workin' and says that startin' Monday they gonna be doin' their washin' in the pool over there, where the first levee is all built and ready to go. It's only then that Mary looks over and sees the second one lookin' almost exactly like the first, and she knows that they're just about done altogether. The ladies are all sad that day, and some of them cry when they go over to eat lunch with the men. Mary doesn't cry 'cause the music's still playin' some, just not as loud as before. Somehow she got to thinkin' that mornin', after the overseer came by, that even if she wasn't gonna see much of Micah, or anything at all, that somehow it'd mean something just to know he was there. That she wasn't an island after all. And that was way more than just something. It was a glory just to feel this way, what Gertie told her was the kinda love a man and a woman, *if they lucky, feel fo' each otha.*

But neither of them has much to say when they eat lunch that day. When she stands up and says she best be gettin' Miss Juss, he stands up too and reaches for his hat, diggin' around inside it. He looks at the overseer and at the men and the gals, and then takes Mary by the shoulders and kisses her. And the music's playin' so loud again that she hardly notices when he takes her hand and puts a little piece of paper inside it. It's only when she's walkin' up to the hospital that she gets to realizin' what she's got right there in her hand.

She never told him about knowin' how to read and write, and he never said nothin' about it either. It's about as deep a secret for her as the time with Mista Grant, only she knows she can't get in no trouble for the time with Mista Grant now. But readin' and writin's a different story altogether—and she starts to thinkin' about what might happen if the overseer seen the piece of paper and is maybe chasin' after her—and how she and Micah gonna get sold off a thousand miles from each other . . . and then they'd go and put Mista and Misses Kittredge and Miss Randall in prison . . . and maybe even Miss Juss too for bein' the ones that let her get all that learnin' . . . and she looks back and sees the overseer just as concerned with his lunch as ever, and there's Micah standin' with his hat off, watchin' her, smilin'. And all that worry is gone now. There's just the tingle left runnin' within her, and the memory of his kiss.

Juss is talkin' the whole walk home, about the usual things, this officer and that, this or that nurse who told her not to get too friendly with the patients, and such. And it's all so much the same sorta thing walkin' back home, that Mary drifts into her own thoughts, off'rin' the occasional *mmm-hmmm,* by way of keepin' up. But her mind drifts elsewhere, back to Carolina, and the overseer Mista Grant, the man who she's worryin' might make Micah not want to be her man once he knows about what happened 'fore she and Gertie run off. And the heat of the day . . . the worryin' about the paper in her sleeve . . . and the memories of all those years past . . . set her to driftin' more than walkin' . . . dreamin' one of those nightmares all over again . . .

You see Mista Grant's whiskered face, feelin his grip take holda your arms again, pullin you into the empty stable pen. He smells of sweat an foul breath an you can almost feel the pain of bein thrown down on the stable floor, the back of your head smackin against a wooden plank buried under a thin layer of hay still wet with horse pee. An it's like he's on toppa you again, tearin at your clothes an rubbin his rough, sweaty face up against yours, down your neck an along your body, stripped almost naked the way he tore your dress. There's the pain of violent thrusts an his animal groans an there you are tryin to offer up your sufferin to Jesus, the way Gertie always told you to. But you can see the Devil's face in his eyes, 'til, sudden as it all begun, it's over, an he lets out a deep, poisoned breath. He lays on toppa you for a few seconds more, an you can feel the weight of him squeezin the air from your lungs. With a sudden jerk he pushes himself up, standin over you, fixin his clothes, then laughin as he walks off.

An there you are, standin up when you feel like you can move again, then seein the puddle of blood on the stable floor an feelin that it's comin from you, from 'tween your legs. You sweepin straw to cover up the puddle when your head goes faint an your legs buckle, an you on the floor now with your face in the blood puddle, every breath you let out makin tiny ripples 'cross the toppa it . . . driftin . . . floatin . . . tryin to figure out what just happened an' how you gonna get in all kindsa trouble now . . .

You all right, Mary? Juss asks, as they're steppin' up to the house.

And Mary can't answer her, takin' hold of her arm instead and leanin' her head against Juss's shoulder. Juss walks her through the front door and yells at Bessie to get her some water. And then it's into Mary's room, where she sips the water and lays down on her bed, with Juss sittin' beside her for as long as she can stay 'til the Misses assures her Mary's all right now, and it's time to get to her lessons.

No work in the shop for you today, the Misses says, leavin' Mary to lay there for the rest of the afternoon.

She's layin' there with just those memories, 'til she remembers the slip of paper Micah gave her, takes it from her sleeve now and can tell right off that there's handwritin' on it. She panics for a moment, thinkin' that he knows her secret, 'til she realizes that *he's* the one that done the writin', and if anything it's him who's riskin' everything, practically trustin' her with his life. That calms her a little, and she unfolds the paper altogether and reads the words written in a thick black carpenter's pencil:

> You are the sun to me after a night three thousand
> days long

And that's it right then. Like she's melted right there in her tiny room, knowin' there's such a man in this world, who could write such a thing. To her. And she knows she'll never be an island again.

10 *Wayfarers*

MARCELLA
NEW YORK
NOVEMBER 1, 1862

It was nearly as impossible to distinguish the gray uniforms from the blue as it was to see evidence of a soul having once occupied the bodies laid in patternless rows. Limbs were intermingled and thrust outward from their torsos in unnatural forms, bent awkwardly at the elbows and knees in ways they would never be when still animate. It was an unfettered introduction to the horrors of this war, and she was only glad that Mrs. Carlisle and Catherine had not accompanied her to the gallery after all. The title below the framed photograph read, "The Sunken Road, Antietam." *Mr. Brady does love his gore,* Marcella thought.

Brady's pictures were gruesome and compelling, just as advertised. But she had found herself more impressed with the work of a man who seemed to be an afterthought in the exhibition. Moving slowly down the row, she took in each picture for several minutes before proceeding. Near the end of the display wall, she stopped completely and backed up a fair distance from yet another image of Mr. McOwen's—several sturdy-looking men standing beside a cannon. The collection of these dozen photographs was entitled "Men of the Irish Brigade." *Actual living soldiers, how original,* she thought.

But aside from the obvious distinction between McOwen's work and nearly all of Brady's pictures, she saw something captured in their faces that was quite different from the usual Brady portraits with the customary puffed-out chests and stern gazes. McOwen had managed to elicit an element from within his subjects that was more revealing of who they genuinely were. Unlike the collection of corpses or anonymous infantrymen Brady's pictures coldly displayed, these photographs told stories of men become soldiers, men who had left lives and families behind, men compelled to act, but wanting nothing so much as the chance to return to those lives and families when the work was finally done, men who were a family in and of themselves. And as Marcella stared at them, engulfed in everything their two-dimensional faces said, a pair of high-society matrons approached and walked directly up to the photograph, apparently unaware that they were blocking her view. *Oh by all means, yes, please do,* she thought.

"Oh, well look at this," one of the ladies said to her companion. "This is *classic* Brady. Just look at the brutishness of the men. They are so magnificently . . . common, so . . . vile. I suppose the Irish are good at fighting at least, and Brady just captures that disdain they have for decent society."

"Yes, only Brady could do that," her friend declared. "Oh, look at this one with the beard . . . those eyes, so dark and menacing. It's deliciously terrifying."

Deliciously terrifying? Like, say . . . your hat?

Mrs. Carlisle and Catherine were not there to restrain Marcella from engaging in the games she often liked to play on occasions such as these. It was not so much that she *liked* to play them, but rather that, despite the calming, civilizing influence Mrs. Carlisle and Catherine had on Marcella, she still needed such episodes as a release that would enable her to remain calm and civilized at all other times. And after more than a year of working in the army hospital, where some of the battered men from the war struggled to put their lives back together, she had grown even more intolerant of boorish women such as these.

"Oh what a beautiful McOwen!" Marcella said, stepping forward into the ladies' conversation as if they were old acquaintances. "He just captures their inherent brutishness. So vile, are they not? So common. And yet . . . positively *delicious*!"

The ladies did their instant appraisal of Marcella as such women always did. Their eyes started on her hat, took in her olive-toned face and dark eyes surrounded by menacing cheekbones that, minus a smile, gave way too readily to something appearing to be a scowl, still, undeniably pretty in a nonclassical way. They noticed the jewelry, of course, then continued all the way down the dress, perhaps noticing her lack of a corset, and on to the tips of her shoes and back up again, before a glance at each other to confirm whether they were in the presence of someone who merited their attention or not. It was all expertly done in a matter of two or three seconds, and then the ladies turned back to Marcella and nodded. *Oh thank heavens, I've passed inspection!*

"Yes, I was just saying . . ." The first lady paused as if Marcella's statements had actually just registered with her now. She looked down at the nameplate beneath the photo, but remarkably, *deliciously* one might say, she did not miss another beat. "Yes . . . McOwen, I've heard some *very* good things about him."

"Yes, he's quite a talent," the second replied. "I've seen several of his shows. Quite a *visceral* quality to his work. Wouldn't you say?"

"Yes, quite," the first agreed.

"*Visceral,* yes . . . quite," Marcella agreed enthusiastically. "Although . . . I be*lieve* . . ." She turned the page of her program and looked down at it—"yes, that's what it says here. 'Ethan McOwen, a veteran of the Sixty-Ninth Regiment and official photographer of the valiant Irish Brigade, makes his *debut* with this evening's opening.' "

"Ohhh . . . yes, that's right," the second lady corrected. "I was thinking of that *other* Irishman . . . you know . . . *Mac* something or *Oh* something . . ."

"Oh yes, I know exactly what you *mean,*" Marcella interjected. "They're *impossible* to distinguish. But it's nice to see that at least one or two of them have something meaningful to contribute to society."

"Yes, I suppose so," the first woman agreed.

"I hear they make competent enough servants," Marcella added. "Though Pa-*pah* would never hire any of them. Said he'd hire a *Negro* first if it came to *that.* But thankfully there are enough Chinese and respectable-enough peasants to fill out a decent staff."

She laughed loudly, tapping each of the ladies on the arm with her program, and they became uncomfortable, though it was doubtful if either of them could say why. They nodded and excused themselves, but Marcella grabbed each of them by an arm and leaned in closely as if to confide a great secret to them.

"I don't know if you've heard," she whispered, "but this McOwen has taken some pictures of the *Negroes,* too. Runaway slaves. They're along the back row way over there . . .

if you can sneak over, I *highly* recommend it. Positively, deliciously vile. Such visceral brutishness."

She lifted her eyebrows and nodded her head several times for effect, and the ladies looked at her awkwardly before practically dashing back to their husbands gathered in the corner drinking brandy. Marcella watched them all the way, then nodded and winked, pointing to the back row of pictures again when they arrived safely. Finally they turned completely away from her. *Thanks for the chat,* Marcella thought, and chuckled to herself in triumph.

"That McOwen, he is *something,* isn't he?" came a voice from over her shoulder, as she stood in her triumph.

She looked to her left and saw a man leaning on a cane and smiling at her.

"Oh yes, he is a talent," she answered.

He was dressed in a black suit, and his hair was thick and covered half of his ears. There was a hint of a beard—perhaps two or three days' worth of whiskers, the blackness of which accentuated his blue eyes—and he leaned enough on the cane he held in his left hand to reveal that it wasn't simply for show. Overall, he didn't seem a comfortable fit with most of the other men here.

"Oh, most definitely a *remarkable* talent," he continued. "Better than Brady certainly. Don't you agree?"

"He is very good," she replied. "Are you familiar with him?"

"This evening is the first time I've seen his work on display. I find him far superior to Brady."

Is that a brogue underneath I hear? she thought. *Could this be a taste of my own medicine, perhaps?*

"Oh, I don't know about that," she played along. "There's only *one* Brady."

"Yes, but he lacks McOwen's sort of . . . *visceral* quality, no?"

"Oh, I wouldn't say that," she replied.

"No . . . I believe there's a certain deliciously vile element in his work, that's nowhere to be found in Brady's. None of that brutishness, that disdain for decent society, y'know."

Confirmed.

"Frankly, I find McOwen's work to be somewhat primitive," she said, holding back her smile as much as she could. "Certainly Brady is an artist, but McOwen? Perhaps *some*day."

"Well . . . perhaps you're right. But he's quite good . . . for an *Irishman,* of course. It's good to know there are one or two of 'em with something to contribute to society."

"Oh, I quite agree. For an *Irishman,* he is surprisingly . . . competent."

He laughed and extended his hand to her. She gave him hers, and he bowed and raised her gloved hand to his lips.

"It is a pleasure to meet you, Miss . . . ?"

"Arroyo. Marcella Arroyo." She spoke with a heavy accent on purpose and amused herself with the perplexed look it produced in response.

"Miss . . . Ah-ro-go?"

"Arroyo. Marcella Arroyo."

"Miss Ah-ro-yo," he said, appearing to be proud of himself.

She pulled her hand back politely and responded without the accent this time. "And you must be Mr. McOwen?"

He laughed easily and replied, "Yes. Most certainly no Mathew Brady, but surprisingly competent all the same . . . Ethan McOwen."

He looked closely into her eyes, the way a painter does his subject, and she felt for a brief moment as if she had lost a little of the comfortable advantage she generally held with men. This one didn't seem to underestimate her from the very start, or to be threatened.

"Of course Mr. Brady isn't here this evenin'," he said. "He's set up shop in Washington, where all the important folks are these days. So you'll hafta settle for th'imitation." He smiled with easy self-deprecation. Then he glanced just over her shoulder and his eyes opened wide.

"*Here* they are," he said pointing to a man with one arm escorting a young lady. "Violet, I'm sure I have you t'thank for draggin'm out here."

He kissed the young lady and shook the man's hand.

"Are you kiddin'," Violet said. "He's been talkin' 'bout nothin' else the whole week. He thinks *he's* the celebrity. He'da worn his regimental cap if he had it his way."

"Mr. Walter Smythe, Mrs. Violet Smythe, this is Miss Ar-ro-yo," Mr. McOwen said, sweeping his arm toward her as if introducing a duchess just arrived at a grand ball. "She's a great fan of . . . *Mathew Brady's.*"

"But I am beginning to appreciate the work of a certain Irish photographer as well," Marcella joked, and extended her hand to each of them.

"Smitty's a friend from way back durin' th'humble beginnin's," Mr. McOwen said. "He was with the Sixty-Ninth too."

She couldn't help but glance quickly at the arm of his jacket pinned up against his shoulder, then, angry at herself for looking, she turned to Mrs. Smythe.

"That's a lovely hat, Mrs. Smythe," she said with the social dexterity garnered from great experience.

"Violet, please . . . and thank you," she replied, looking over at her husband as if he'd neglected to pay her any such compliments. "Borrowed it from Ethan's Aunt Emily, actually. We don't get out to many functions like these, I s'pose you could say."

"What?" Smitty protested. "Why, just last week there was dinner at the Green Onion."

"Oh, that's right—the Green Onion," she said with a laugh. "The Delmonico's of Brooklyn."

"They've got tablecloths, haven't they?" he argued with a bit of a laugh.

"Yes, for all the fine people to wipe their mouths on," she said.

"Well—there you go then."

Ohhh, I like these people, Marcella thought.

"Well, let's get a look at the lads," Smitty said, stepping forward. "Aww Jesus, lookit Harry standin' with his hand on that big siege gun . . . like he ever fired one in his life."

"Yes, but there's such a delicious *brutish*ness to him, don't you think?" Mr. McOwen asked.

Smitty looked at him with his mouth twisted to one side and eyebrows pressed down. *"What?"*

"I'm afraid it's an inside joke from just before you arrived," Marcella said, and Smitty still seemed confused. But Violet smiled and looked over at Mr. McOwen and then back at Marcella.

"So Miss Ar . . . Ar-ooo . . ."

"Marcella, please."

"Marcella. So how long have you and Ethan known each other?"

I know where you're going, Violet, Marcella thought. *Not that I mind.*

"Just a few minutes," she replied.

"Yes, but *what* a few minutes they've been," Mr. McOwen said.

Violet smiled at both of them now, her eyes twinkling the way a woman's do when she's of a matchmaking frame of mind. They looked over the pictures of the Irish Brigade, and all the while it was Smitty and Mr. McOwen sharing the inside jokes and telling the ladies stories about this particular fellow or that officer. They didn't speak of any of the battles, and given the empty sleeve of Smitty's jacket, and Mr. McOwen's pronounced limp and dependence upon his cane, she was relieved they didn't.

At one point Smitty ventured over to some of Brady's pictures taken from Antietam, and his mood changed quickly. Mr. McOwen stepped up next to him, then took a step away.

"Jesus, Perfessor," Smitty said, shaking his head slowly from side to side, "lookit that mess . . . what you lads musta gone through."

Marcella was standing next to Violet, chatting politely, but couldn't help but notice the pained expression on both Smitty's and Mr. McOwen's faces.

"Ethan was wounded at Antietam," Violet whispered to her. And as the two men grew more serious looking at Brady's pictures of the Sunken Road, Violet took it upon herself to fill in Marcella with a short biography of Mr. McOwen, saving Marcella the embarrassment of having to uncover such details herself. There were the wounds, three of them in all, and a mention of how he and their other two friends—men still in the Irish Brigade and alive, thank the Lord—had carried Smitty to the triage tent at Malvern Hill and certainly saved his life. And then Violet talked about how Ethan was a prominent photographer even before the war, and how he and Smitty and the other boys had played for the Excelsiors, and so on. *His own mother couldn't do a better job of lobbying on his behalf, Violet,* Marcella thought. But then Violet told her that since Ethan'd almost lost a leg at Antietam, it had been a difficult recovery and that his employer, Mr. Hadley, had arranged for his small part in this gallery show in hopes of encouraging Ethan to embrace his old profession again.

"What these men have been through . . . ," Violet said, shaking her head. And her words were all about loss now, describing how much joy a simple game of baseball had once brought them, or for Ethan the boat he used to fish in with his father that he now seemed unable or unwilling to sail. Then she seemed to snap to attention herself, the thought interrupted by the sudden awareness of her surroundings once again. "But it looks like you've had such a good effect on him," she said in a more hopeful tone. "Let's not let them get too deeply into it."

She draped her arm inside Marcella's and walked her over to the two men.

"Now enough of this gloominess," she announced. "Ethan, you said there were some pictures of the runaways?"

"Yes, they're along the back wall," he replied.

"So the piles of corpses are all right for the decent folks t'see," Violet said, "but the Negroes must be hidden away out of view?"

Ahhh, Violet dear, Marcella thought, *I believe we might well become friends.*

They passed through the crowd gathered around Brady's photographs, and Marcella could see the difficulty with which Mr. McOwen walked. Then Violet took her arm out from inside Marcella's and took her husband's.

"Oh, you two go on ahead," she said to her and Mr. McOwen. "I think I left something in the lobby." *Oh, well done, Violet, well done.*

She tugged at her husband's arm as he began to question what she could have possibly left, before a glance from her silenced him. They were off toward the lobby, and now it was just the two of them again. Mr. McOwen offered her his arm, and she lightly placed her hand inside it, not wanting to hurt his shoulder wound or inhibit his walking with the cane.

"I like her," Marcella said as they walked.

"Violet's great," he replied. "I don't think a lesser woman could've pulled Smitty out of it when he came home from Malvern Hill."

"I can imagine," she said. And then thought, *Who was there for you?*

His pictures of the Irish Brigade had shown a hint of humanity she felt was missing from Brady's work. But his pictures of the runaways were utterly haunting. Their eyes seemed to look directly *through* the camera, as if the wooden box were not an endpoint but a portal to stare into the eyes of all those who would see these pictures. These were not the images captured by just any technician with a camera. These were the creation of one who saw the injustice with as much clarity as she did. She gently pulled her hand from under his arm and moved up close, examining each one as if staring at a masterpiece. He stood a few steps back, no smug expression on his face, or even the pride she believed he should certainly, justifiably, feel. Instead there was tempered anguish. And she couldn't help but bounce her attention back and forth from one image to the next, looking at his face in between each one, wondering what sort of man it was she had met this evening. And most certainly glad she had.

Artists, either in spite of or perhaps *because* of her father's utter disdain for them, had always interested her. But most of the ones she'd encountered in New York were either as pretentious as some of their patrons, or as rustic and bohemian as the subjects they portrayed. Mr. McOwen struck her as being different—the artist who didn't *intend* to be one, but was almost compelled to do so by his unique vision. He could have made thousands a year simply taking portraits of the society patrons gathered right here. But that seemed not to interest him at all. Nor did he seem impressed with his own success, or the accolades Mr. Sacramore, the owner of the gallery, poured on him while Marcella was still mesmerized by his pictures. And then she could see his reluctance turn to anguish, imagining the pain of receiving such compliments for documenting the suffering of others. When Mrs. Sacramore joined her husband with equally effusive praise, Marcella walked back over to stand beside Mr. McOwen, if only to offer him the chance to change the subject. And as she approached, a tight-lipped, straight line of a smile appeared on his face, leaving his eyes to express his relief.

He introduced her to Mr. and Mrs. Sacramore, and then somehow, just as Violet had done before, the two of them spoke to her as if she and Mr. McOwen had known each other far longer than these twenty or so minutes. When Mrs. Sacramore invited them to a dinner party at their house the next evening, Mr. McOwen did nothing to correct her mistake.

"Are you free tomorrow, Miss Arroyo?" he asked, smiling mischievously now. It was the type of presumption she would normally have a witty retort for, but this offer was too intriguing to even think of turning down.

"I believe I *am,* Mr. McOwen," she replied, and the matter was settled.

NOVEMBER 2, 1862

He arrives in a taxi carriage to pick her up on the evening of Mr. Sacramore's dinner party. Mrs. Carlisle has gone beyond her old sort of looking out for Marcella, having some time ago adopted her as a daughter, in her thoughts anyway . . . and Marcella's, too. And now she fills the role of both parents, prodding and poking at Mr. McOwen with her questions. It's an interrogation designed to see if he'll crack, if he has any hope of deserving her beloved Marcella. But he holds the line quite well with a certain confidence Marcella noticed in the gallery. It's not the usual arrogance of her father or brothers or so many of the men he brought around in hopes of marrying her off.

Whatever it is about him, he meets with Mrs. Carlisle's approval, and they soon take their leave from her and Catherine, riding the taxi carriage uptown just a few blocks from her father's house. They converse politely on the drive, and when they arrive at the house, Mr. McOwen opens the door of the carriage for her and offers his arm, smiling comfortably as he does. The first guest they are introduced to is Mrs. Lydia Templeton, whom she's seen perform at the Opera House on more than one occasion, and then follows a collection of writers and abolitionists that's unlike anything she's been a part of before, even at Mrs. Carlisle's. Here in this one parlor are more truly interesting people than had attended all her father's monthly parties over all the years she was required to be a part of them.

Mr. McOwen seems very much in demand, with many of the guests wanting to speak to a man who has actually been there *in the thick of the war*, as they describe it. But when publishers, or writers, or actresses are introduced, he never lets Marcella be excluded from the conversation. And as the evening goes along, she realizes that it's the same thing she'd seen the other night, when Violet and Smitty came back while Mr. Sacramore and several other notables were still in their midst. Mr. McOwen treats them all alike, with an equal cordiality, even familiarity, which is most engaging. *Neither an ounce of snobbishness nor of crudeness in him. How positively unlike a man,* she thinks.

They eat at a table twice the size of the one in her father's house, all thirty-six of them comfortably aligned around it. The service is elegant, the meal lavish, and were it not for the far more enlightened conversation, and the complete absence of any discussion of money or business, she might feel as if they were at one of her father's parties. After dinner is through, they withdraw to the parlor again for what is, in her mind, the true test of whether this whole evening has been real or imagined. This was always the most infuriating time at her father's dinner parties, the moment the men would go off to the library to discuss truly important matters while the ladies sat around and gossiped and talked about dresses and such. She imagines Ethan with the other men, smoking a cigar and drinking brandy, and it's as if all that has been so positively impressed upon her up to that moment will be wiped out as soon as the men return. As if, having solved the pressing crises of the day, they're now ready to grace the ignorant ladies with their presence again.

But then an odd thing occurs. The men all sit alongside the ladies and Mr. Sacramore stands, and rather than requesting the men join him in the library, he requests that Mrs. Templeton sing an aria for them. And Marcella realizes then that there will be no brandy and cigars, no segregation of the sexes, no girlish gossiping and fashion talk to endure. She smiles at Mr. McOwen, Ethan, as she's finally agreed to call him.

"What is it?" he asks.

She shakes her head. "Oh . . . nothing. I'm just . . . it's nothing."

And then Mrs. Templeton saves her from having to explain any further.

"Oh look at this," she says, holding up a piece of sheet music, "*Voi Che Sapete* from *Figaro.* How I love this piece—but I'll need an accompanist."

Mrs. Templeton looks around the room and finds no one willing, or able, to play. But then, as if on impulse, and inspired by the unique quality of this moment, Marcella volunteers. Ethan stands and begins the applause for her as she steps to the pianoforte.

"Oh, wonderful. Thank you, Miss Arroyo," Mrs. Templeton says, and then Marcella finds herself removing her gloves and sitting at the piano, and Mrs. Templeton is leaning over her.

"B-flat major at the beginning, and then this arrangement gets interesting," she whispers as she points to the sheet music. "Where is it . . . oh, there, see the change to A-flat major? And then . . . here, to G minor for one, two, three, four measures . . . and then back to B-flat major . . . and, oh . . . I'm sorry to get you into this; it's such a *fright*ful arrangement to play on first sight. I've sung it a hundred times, and I *still* get lost."

Marcella smiles at her, liking this woman even more now, and says humbly, "I'll do my best."

Placing her fingers on the opening chords, she glances at Mrs. Templeton, who nods in readiness. She plays the introduction with her usual comfort, and Mrs. Templeton smiles broadly at her, as if realizing that she can indeed play, before joining in on measure. Marcella is only a half beat behind at the first key change, but quickly comes back in form. At the second change, Mrs. Templeton pauses a half beat in anticipation of Marcella trailing, but this time it's Mrs. Templeton doing the catching up. The remaining key changes are right on measure, and when the aria is complete, the guests demand an encore. They collaborate on another selection from Mozart, and then Mrs. Templeton steps aside, pressing Marcella to play a solo. Unable to slip graciously away, Marcella obliges, playing the simple adagio of Beethoven's *Moonlight Sonata* from memory. She bows politely and decides that this has been enough of a debut for her. But Mrs. Templeton is having none of that, standing back up, urging Mr. Sacramore and the guests to demand another piece.

"I know you've got a better one in you than that," she whispers to Marcella. "Show them how a woman can *really* play." And when Mrs. Templeton finds Chopin's *Nocturne* opus 9, number 2, she lets out a playful gasp and then whispers, "Will you dare tackle *Monsieur* Chopin?"

Marcella smiles at her, and Mrs. Templeton stands off her shoulder to turn the pages of the sheet music. At her father's dinner parties, when he forced her to play for the guests, she always felt as if she were being shown off like a trained china doll. He would inevitably comment about how much money had been spent teaching her to play so well or how much it cost to have the instrument shipped over from London. There was always conversation throughout her playing, always dominated by her father, and she never felt like anything more than part of the ornamentation there. But here, not a word is uttered as she plays to a rapt audience. The guests applaud loudly when she's through, and Mrs. Templeton gives her a knowing smile and a wink. Ethan is smiling and still applauding as she approaches her seat beside him. It is *her* moment to shine, and he appears to be happier for her than he'd been for his own artistic success just the day before.

"Well—I am *most* impressed, Miss Marcella," he says with a bow. "You play remarkably. I expect to hear you at Irving Hall someday soon."

"You exaggerate, Mr. McOwen," she replies, "but only *slightly*."

NOVEMBER 5, 1862

Despite the thrill of the dinner party at the Sacramores', or perhaps *because* of it, she had spent the intervening days working at the hospital and growing increasingly displeased with herself. Pilar was the sort to gush over young men, and Catherine and even Mrs. Carlisle were the sort to romanticize even the most trivial of encounters. But not Marcella. And though Mr. McOwen—as she went back to referring to him in her thoughts—had seemed like no other man she had ever met, it was an all-too-brief window into his real self to yield even a fraction of her emotional autonomy. But she had foolishly agreed to a Wednesday visit—giving up one of her afternoons free from the hospital—and two days were hardly enough to steel herself against the potential dangers of such an engagement.

He arrived promptly at noon with a thin portfolio of paper wrapped in fine white lace and tied by a red ribbon. And Mrs. Carlisle and Catherine laughed with seemingly excessive delight when he confessed to having his mother and aunt take care of the wrapping. Marcella glanced at them like the meddling matchmakers they clearly aspired to be, but they only whimsically insisted she open the gift right then and there. It turned out to be a piece of sheet music, not just any piece, but *Voi Che Sapete,* from *Figaro,* and the wonderful memories of Sunday night returned immediately.

"You brought me a copy of the piece I played at Mr. Sacramore's party," she said, attempting to muster all the indifference that would be merited by a mere bouquet of hothouse flowers.

And Mrs. Carlisle and Catherine were effusive in their recognition of what a thoughtful gift it was, prompting Marcella to add a coy evaluation of her own.

"Yes, Mr. McOwen, I suppose I *do* need to practice it."

But he turned his head a little to one side and drew his eyebrows downward into a puzzled expression.

"Quite the contrary," he said. "I . . . that's not what I . . ."

Oh, I was only teasing, she thought. *I thought you had more fortitude than that, Mr. McOwen.*

And as she smiled at his discomfort and her early victory, only then did she notice that the edges were slightly frayed and the crease had been significantly unfolded.

"Is this the *actual* copy from Mr. Sacramore's?" she asked.

He nodded and said, "He was very kind about it."

And Mrs. Carlisle and Catherine were practically beside themselves, putting their hands over their hearts. But there was more.

"If you'll turn it over to the back . . ." he said.

And she did, hesitantly, seeing a handwritten inscription that read:

To Miss Arroyo, my friend and accompanist,
With fondest regards and delightful memories

of our performance together.
Awaiting an encore,
Victoria Templeton

And that was all the confirmation Mrs. Carlisle and Catherine would ever need, practically melting with sentimentality right there in the front parlor. They insisted that Mr. McOwen stay for tea, or come for supper, and he was only able to keep them at bay by promising he would gladly do so any other day but this one.

"I was hoping that Miss Arroyo might accompany me for an excursion around the city today. It is such a fine day for this time of year."

And there was no need for him to explain any further, as Mrs. Carlisle and Catherine accepted *for* Marcella, with Catherine taking hold of her arm and insisting on going upstairs with her, as if she would need help selecting a coat and hat and gloves. Their relationship had undoubtedly changed over the years, with Catherine starting out as teacher and mentor to Marcella, then slowly becoming more of a friend on equal terms as Marcella became a woman. But lately Marcella had begun to see something new in the dynamic between them, sensing that Catherine had taken to living, in certain respects, vicariously through Marcella, often expressing her amazement at the boldness and vivacity she'd never had. And as Catherine sat on the edge of Marcella's bed, gushing in a manner more befitting Pilar, *"Oh he's so gallant,"* and, *"What magnificent eyes,"* and so on, Marcella hadn't the heart to pretend that she wasn't more than a little excited by the prospects of the afternoon herself.

"It was a very thoughtful gift," she confessed, and smiled reluctantly.

Mr. McOwen had a taxi carriage waiting outside, and they

were soon off without any instructions to the driver, as if the plans had already been discussed. He said nothing, content, it seemed, to watch the city pass outside the window while tipping his hat to pedestrians on occasion and smiling coyly for most of the ride. They turned right onto Fourth Street and rode over to the Hudson River waterfront, where the driver stopped alongside one of the piers as if on cue. Mr. McOwen stepped out of the carriage and walked around to her door, opened it, and silently extended a hand. She stepped down and stood beside him, looking at a small pier where a merchant ship was just pulling away.

"That's where the *Lord Sussex* landed," he finally said. "That's where I first set foot in America."

And she felt the need to say something nice about it, though it was a dreary sight to be sure, even in the flattering midday sunshine.

"Oh, it's—" was as much as she mustered before he jumped in to finish the sentence.

"—indescribably ugly, yes I know." And she laughed as he nodded his head up and down.

"That's where we landed," he pointed out, "and the dock next to it is where I waited with Suah."

And he began to tell her about this man Suah, who he was sure had saved his life, continuing as they climbed back into the carriage, and somewhere along the way seeming to recreate the image of that twelve-year-old boy and his first day in a new world. The carriage traveled back to Broadway and then over to the edge of the Five Points, and he explained that they were retracing his and his Da's steps from that very day. She smiled when he said *Da*, finding it so much warmer than *Papa*—probably because of the men attached to each term—as they continued on past Wall Street, and then all the way across town to the South Street Port. He pointed out the pier where his *Mam* and *Aunt Em* had arrived a year or so after him, describing the scene with such affection and relief, all these years later, that she was saddened by her own story of arrival, without Papa there to greet them, and her pressed into service to speak English and instruct one taxi carriage driver to take them to Sixty-Third Street and another to follow with their trunks piled inside. But she told him none of this, content to listen to the stories he so willingly shared. And before long they were aboard the ferry headed to Brooklyn, though only after he promised her that they were not going to meet his family.

"I want you all to myself," he said. "The rest of th'McOwens will just have to wait their turn."

It was the closest thing he had said, to that point in their acquaintance, that reminded her of something that might be uttered by one of the pretentious suitors Papa used to bring home to meet her. Perhaps it was the lilt of his lingering brogue, or perhaps it was the genuineness that seemed to be at the center of everything he had done and said so far, but for some reason she was not put off by such a compliment, as she normally would be. Instead, she smiled without intent, only catching herself after a moment or two and turning her gaze to the water and the sight of New York growing smaller in the distance. *Well done, Mr. McOwen,* she thought to herself, and summoned what remained of her resistance.

Once in Brooklyn, they passed a few minutes staring up at the Heights, with him pointing out the general direction of the City Hall and of Reverend Beecher's Plymouth Church. She told him that her only trips to Brooklyn were generally to hear the Reverend's abolitionist sermons. And he told her that he had been there several times himself.

"I even convinced Mam and Aunt Em to come along–

though we sat in the back beneath the balcony in case the *Lahrd was lookin' down on that particular Sunday an' moight see us surrounded by all manner o' Protestants.*"

And she laughed again, the defenses weakening with every reference to his family that seemed in such direct contrast to her own, and the great affection he seemed capable of, like no man she'd ever known. Then, rather than walking up toward the Heights for what she expected would be a luncheon at some restaurant or inn designed to impress her, it was instead another taxi carriage ride, this one toward the south and the village of Red Hook. There were stories of fishing with his Da, and the tiny cabin that had been replaced with something much larger years before, and games of baseball with his friends in a field that was now covered with houses and a livery stable and a large warehouse as well. And he spoke of his boyhood friends with the same sort of affection he had shown when talking about his family, and she thought now of the gallery opening, thinking of the determined expressions of the men from the Irish Brigade, and trying to remember which ones were the fellows he spoke of now, Harry and Finny, knowing Smitty already of course.

They disembarked from the carriage, and he left her to stand there by the dirt path, walking thirty or forty feet over to one of the small boats turned upside down along the shore. Leaning heavily on his cane for the first time that day, he struggled to flip the boat over with his free hand, and then, having managed the task, collected himself and with opened hand gestured to a picnic basket covered by a blanket that had been stored beneath it.

"It's a little cold for a sail," he said, "but perhaps a picnic will do?"

And for the first time that day, or in any of their moments

together to that point, she saw him as what he might have been had fortunes been only slightly altered, in that instant imagining him as one of the contorted, lifeless bodies spilled across the canvas of a Mathew Brady photograph.

Just seven weeks ago he was there at that dreadful place, she thought. *And what a loss it might have been if that bullet had found his belly and not his leg, instead.*

He stood there beside the picnic basket that represented more effort and planning and thoughtfulness than all the hothouse flowers and scripted greetings of all the men Papa had ever brought home put together. And she found herself unable, or unwilling at the very least, to remain as distant as she had been previously determined to be. A few awkward moments passed as he mustered up a hopeful smile, until his foot sank a little in the soft ground, and he had to brace himself against the boat to maintain his balance. And she remembered then what Violet Smythe had said, about all that seemed lost for him, including the joy of a sail.

He must be thinking that it is all a terrible failure, she thought. *Such a man as this.*

"Who *says* it's too cold for a sail?" she said, feigning offense, and now possessed of a plan herself. "Or perhaps you think I am just a dainty little woman and unable to brave the raging waters of the Gowanus Bay? Yes, I know your type all too well, Mr. McOwen . . ."

And a soliloquy ensued, as she walked down to the boat and began pulling at it, budging it only slightly toward the water and then growing concerned that they might not be able to manage it, even together, and he would be forced to admit his incapacity, or worse, his fear.

". . . we women are perfectly capable of a great *many* things you men will not give us credit for . . ."

Oh, please move, you damn thing. Tugging harder now, not caring about the sand and dirt pouring into her shoes.

". . . it's because you never give us the chance to prove ourselves . . ."

Jesus, Marcella, what have you gotten yourself into now? Move, dammit!

". . . but we are not so fragile, you know . . ."

And with bent back and feet entrenched in the earth to give her leverage, she looked up at him and saw a smile replacing the shock, and grew hopeful.

"Well, I didn't say we were as *physically* strong, you know . . ."

And without saying a word, he stepped toward the boat and began to push.

Such a man as this, she thought again.

"The *vote,* for example . . . one of those rights you men conveniently reserve for yourselves . . ."

And with the two of them working in unison, the boat began to slide more willingly along the sandy, grass-covered earth.

Thank God.

". . . it's all part of the grander scheme, you know . . ."

And when they reached the edge of the water, he limped back for the basket and the blanket, placing them inside the boat. By now she was ankle-deep in the water, and he extended a hand to her as if to help her in, then caught himself.

"I don't mean to patronize, Miss Arroyo," he said.

And she smiled, relieved at the return of his wit.

"Equality for women doesn't mean you can't be a *gentleman,* Mr. McOwen . . ."

And he nodded his head, bowing slightly, and offered his hand again. She climbed in and, seeing the boat sink into the sand again, picked up one of the oars, pushing it into the earth and pressing on it to help him move the boat the last few feet into deep enough water. Then she braced it in the sand below, holding the boat still as he tossed his cane in first, then awkwardly folded his torso, and finally his reluctant legs, inside.

"Too cold for a sail? Why, it's a *beautiful* day . . ."

Keep talking until he can collect himself, she thought. *Dignity—let the man have his dignity.*

And then he was in, settled on the bench across from her, removing his hat and placing it on the floor of the vessel, smiling at her as he caught his breath.

"You've been sailing before?" he asked.

"Never," she said, and handed him the oar she held as he picked up the other.

It took a few moments for him to place them in the oarlocks, and then a few moments more to find a way to row with only one leg available to anchor him. And she did her best not to watch him struggle, ceasing her imaginary diatribe now and looking out over the water. But before too long he had them under way, with Marcella offering the distraction of myriad questions about the terms for everything in the boat. She learned that it was called a skiff, learned about the mast and boom and tiller and other such things until they were far enough out to raise the sail.

He instructed her to walk around to the stern and man the tiller, then caught himself and joked that he didn't mean to use such an offensive expression and would she please *tend* to the tiller. And the great effort of just a few minutes before seemed gone then, as if, in his present condition, he could be more at home, more fluid in his movements, out on the water like this. He first pulled up the mast, raising it against the hinge at its base until it was fifteen feet high straight up and down, and he could lock it in place. Then he attached the sail and raised it the length of the mast and fixed it to the boom.

"Oh, how men like to give such *determined* names to things," she said, amidst the flurry of vocabulary.

"How *else* are we to keep women subjugated?" he said, without looking at her, tending to the business of righting the boat.

Ahhhhh . . . THERE you are, Ethan, she thought, deciding that he would never again be held at such a distance to think of him with any more formal manner of address.

Once the wind took full hold of the sail, he maneuvered himself onto the back bench, separated from her by the tiller, and she looked at him as if he would take hold of it. But he smiled at her, his comfort and confidence fully restored, it seemed, and his dignity intact, content to handle the boom line while *she* did the actual steering.

"You're doing fine. Just keep her straight on into the wakes," he said, pointing out the little waves rolling in. And they passed silently over them, Marcella focused intently on the task of keeping the tiller straight and Ethan alternately smiling at her, then allowing himself to feel the freedom of being on the water once again.

How long has it been since you've been out here? she thought, but wouldn't venture to ask, lest she stir up memories that needn't be a part of this day.

They passed several minutes this way, with him pulling the boom line closer, then letting it out again, finding what manner of wind there was to be employed on such a mild autumn afternoon. Ethan nodded every now and again, pointing out a possible direction for her to follow, and she turned the tiller toward it, eventually taking them out of the Gowanus Bay and up along the East River, with the Brooklyn Heights and Manhattan Island serving as their bookends on a glorious day.

And then he looked at her, purposefully, as if surprised by the direction this entire day had taken. He turned his head slightly to one side, boyishly almost, and stared intently at her the way he had the night he first met her at the gallery. Only now it wasn't a painter's or photographer's eye gleaning bits of her heart, but the opposite entirely, as if he were confiding something in her that would be diminished with every frivolous word used to describe it.

"Thank you," he finally said, then turned back around, closing his eyes and taking hold of a deep saltwater breath, holding it for a moment longer than usual, then letting go.

She looked at him, understanding, as if welcoming him back to these waters, to normalcy. And letting go of all her reserve, of everything she had felt was necessary by way of self-preservation just a few hours before, she smiled back at him.

No, she thought . . . *thank you.*

ETHAN

FORT SCHUYLER HOSPITAL, BRONX

NOVEMBER 20, 1862

If he wanted to think of it that way, he could, that if it hadn't been for her, he never would've even considered Mr. Prendergast's offer. Mam and Aunt Em, and even the men in his family, had so doted upon him when he returned from the hospital that he'd begun to feel that his would be a convalescent's life for whatever years might remain of it. But not her.

She'd been the first one not to ask about the leg or the shoulder every time she saw him. She'd allowed him to become a man again by not treating him as anything else, and he'd gravitated toward her for that as much as for the glisten of her eyes or the curve of her cheek or the thrill of earning a laugh from her. And they'd spent at least *some* time together every day since the sail on Gowanus Bay, as if they weren't safely tucked away in New York but were stuck right in the thick of the war and couldn't waste time with trivial hesitations since the whole world could be torn asunder at any moment. More than once she'd begun to tell him something, then stopped, smiling and shaking her head slightly as if surprised at what she was confessing. Then she'd say to him *I've never said this to anyone—no one living anyway*—and then she'd tell him the thing all the same. And he'd come to know that the nonliving person she'd shared all these things with was her Abuela who'd been left behind in Spain half her lifetime ago, which made him smile and tell her a secret of his own—about Aislinn, and how he still sometimes talked to her when he was down by the water somewhere, and his words could be carried off to her resting place along the lane back in the Old Country.

And she smiled only slightly to hear it, then caught herself and squinted her eyes closed with head tilted slightly to one side. *Well, you're far crazier than I am then,* she said, and they laughed together.

If this had been back in Enniskillen, there'd have been structure to all of this, even at their ages, with the two of them falling under the collective supervision of the village as they took late afternoon walks together or went half a mile out of their way to pass by the other's cottage on the off chance they'd meet. And she'd told him that if her father had his way, she never would have met him, and certainly *never* would have been permitted to court him without bank statements to verify his suitability. Then it would be stuffy dinner parties and stuffier visits to the opera seated in separate boxes to demonstrate sufficient chastity to all the gossip-thirsty onlookers. But the fates had freed them of all that, to somehow bring them together and leave only their own inhibitions to overcome. And he began to think of this three-week interlude as something of a happy accident in the midst of a world that, with all its wits about it—free from the unbalancing effect of war—would have conspired to keep them from ever crossing paths. But now that fortunate disruption in the natural order of things was over, and it was time for the real world once again.

This hospital's far more pristine than the ones he remembers, even the ones in Washington, where he'd had a regular sort of bed and meals three times a day and nurses to change the bandages and such. In the weeks after he'd been wounded, between all the mosquitoes and the moans of the men hit real bad, he'd never got even just a half-night's sleep straight through—'til Seanny showed up with his man Cormac and they'd practically discharged him from the army themselves right there, then took him home. And as near as all these memories are to the present day, he begins to feel most uncomfortable as he makes his way past the beds of the men still recovering from Antietam and skirmishes before and since. No moans or fever-tossed restlessness in these lads—these were the ones well enough to make it through the train ride north to ease the overcrowded hospitals down where the war was hot.

Then he sees her, tending to the elevated and thoroughly

wrapped leg of a man who looks to be almost forty years old, a man who'd gone and volunteered for such a thing at such an age. And there's the terrible conflict of his thoughts contained right there in the few seconds before and after she sees him, with him feeling the assurance of his decision knowing there were things he could still do in this cause—but then seeing her face light up just for him, smiling amidst the crowd all around her—and telling her he'd accepted Mr. Prendergast's offer seems almost worse than surgery right now. But the fates are conspiring again, as he discovers when she walks over to him.

I'm so sorry, she says with a pained expression. Agnes has come down with a fever, and there's only one nurse on the overnight shift, and I told them I'd stay . . . *sorry.* And she exaggerates a playful frown in the way she's become more and more prone to, letting her emotions reach the surface of her face the way they didn't when they'd first met, the way even she'd acknowledged when she told him that *meeting you has been the death of my poker game.* Now he's the one with the expressionless face, knowing there will be no bluffing his way through the news he has to deliver.

They slip outside the main room to a dimly lit edge of hallway, and she kisses him before he's able to even introduce the subject of Mr. Prendergast's offer, the moistness of her lips and the warm caress of her breath conspiring right along with the fates somehow, telling him to reconsider what he'd decided with what he thought was finality. But there's no talk between them here, with the entire evening's kisses having to be fit into this tiny hidden-away space and the reprieve of a moment's pause from her duties. And this minute or two seem to be mere seconds before there's the call from a doctor inside the recovery room, *Nurse . . . Nurse!* piercing the stillness, with time for just one more kiss before she's off again. This time he pulls her closer, kissing her like it will be the last one for some time, before separating enough to take in the glisten of her eye and the curve of her cheek and the smile, once more.

I'll see you tomorrow after tea, she says. Violet's coming tomorrow.

And she reaches a hand up and brushes it against his cheek, then turns away back to the main room, *Nurse, I need some clean bandages here,* hardly seeming like an urgent enough order to have ruined the chance to tell her.

The trip back to Brooklyn is a cavalcade of arguments on each side of the notion, piecing together ferries and horsecars for almost two hours and thinking of how remarkable she was to have done this a few times a week for more than a year now. But then there are the regiments preparing to go off and pick up the fight where he'd left off, several of them at Fort Schuyler drilling and marching left-right, left-right, and another at the Brooklyn Navy Yards ready to embark for points south. And it's that last reminder that clinches the decision once and for all, knowing he's got something more to lend to the cause, the way Mr. Prendergast put it, and how could he sit home and take portraits for the duration instead?

That night there's the packing of the camera and all the supplies, and *civilian* clothes this time around. And then the letter to write, wondering how he'll ever do it justice and not risk losing her altogether. Aunt Emily was the one who'd been the first to ask him about her, suspicious when he suddenly took a turn for the better right after the gallery opening and in the days following when she'd catch him whistling or kissing her and Mam for no reason at all every time he left the house. *Yer about as in love as an Irishman's ever let on t'bein',* she'd said a week earlier, and he wasn't able to camouflage his expression enough to hide it from her. Now she's the one to ask him the what for in the quiet of a late-night hour when all the others have gone to sleep.

You sure you wanta go an' do this, Ethan? she asks. Yer leg's still not right, and now you've got this girl who *sounds* lovely enough, though you've never brought her 'round here . . . outta shame fer us I suppose–

Aunt Em, that's not–

I know, I know . . . sure I was only kiddin' with ya. And then she gets more serious again. Are you *sure,* love?

And Ethan nods his head, his mouth pulled slightly to one side as if declaring that the matter's been considered enough.

I *have* to, he says.

MARCELLA
NEW YORK
NOVEMBER 21, 1862

She had never felt this way about a man. How could she, with the parade of Wall Street buffoons her father had exposed her to from her seventeenth to twenty-first birthdays like cattle barons at auction? Living with Mrs. Carlisle had liberated her from that, since the Ladies Abolition Society teas and Sunday afternoon recitals were hardly overflowing with men of any sort. But that had never been of any importance to her. She had reviled Pilar's drooling over Papa's parade of eligible bachelors, and even expressed disappointment in Catherine's lament for never having married. But now she was just as silly as any of them, counting the hours between chances to see him as if she were a giggly debutante.

After the sleepless shift from the night before, Mrs. Carlisle had sent her carriage to come get her that morning. She'd spent the rest of the day sleeping as much as she could to get caught up again, but this was to be Violet Smythe's first Friday tea with the Ladies Abolition Society and as her sponsoring member, Marcella had to be present for it, of course. She'd had the idea to invite Violet to join almost from the moment she had met her at Ethan's gallery opening. Violet was witty and unafraid to express her mind. And since all of the ladies were at least ten years older than Marcella in age—and often considerably more than that in demeanor—the fact that Violet was separated from her by only two months was a most ringing endorsement indeed.

The usual civilities were tortuously slow as Violet arrived at the same time as Mrs. Wentworth and Mrs. Bianci, and they all had to discuss the weather and each other's new hats or other such triviality. It wasn't until those ladies were settled with their tea that Marcella could sit down next to Violet. A few more ladies arrived, and the conversation shifted to that side of the room, and Marcella finally turned to her new friend and smiled.

"I have a note from Ethan," Violet said before Marcella could even speak, reaching inside her dress sleeve and handing it to her.

They had shared two luncheons since the gallery opening, and whenever the subject of Ethan came up, Violet always bore a sort of knowing grin that made Marcella naturally defensive. She was well aware of the silliness that had overtaken her amidst her affection for Ethan, but she wasn't ready to relent so completely with anyone but him—not Catherine, not Violet, not even Abuela. So she did her best to contain her surprise at

Violet's statement, accepting the envelope with as much nonchalance as she could muster.

"Perhaps you might like to read it outside the room," Violet suggested, nothing of a knowing grin anywhere to be found on her face now.

Oh, that's quite unnecessary, but if you insist, Marcella thought, hoping it would find its way to her expression despite the concerns that now filled her. She calmly walked past the recently arrived ladies engaged in their pleasantries at the doorway, turning back to signal to Violet to follow her into the library. But Mrs. Carlisle intercepted Violet before she could slip past the ladies, and the introductions and pleasantries to follow would surely take longer than Marcella could stand. So she opened the envelope, unfolded the notepaper, and read:

Dearest Marcella,

I can only begin with apologies . . . for telling you this way, for telling you this at all after the joyous interlude these three weeks have been. But spending this time with you has helped restore me after I'd come to believe I'd never again be the man I was before the war. You did that, more than any other, more than myself even. And now, restored, I must do what I see as my duty in this cause.

This morning I am embarking on the train for Washington along with several members of the Press Corps. Mr. Prendergast, an editor at the Eagle, *contacted me with a job offer just two days ago after having seen my pictures at the gallery. He talked about the fight upcoming with the Army of the Potomac on the move again, and of how he had two extra correspondents traveling south to see the struggle first hand. My role, he said, would be to take pictures of the men as well as any runaways that might cling to the Army the way they did on the Peninsula. He spoke of what I might do to further support for the war, "to make the plight of soldier and slave alike come to life for people back here." It was an exaggeration, of course, but I do know that any little bit I can do to support my brothers in arms, or to publish the brutality of slavery to those who would turn a blind eye—well, I must do what I can.*

But I am sick at the thought of you reading these words rather than hearing them from my own guilty lips. There simply was not the time, so I have employed Violet as emissary to carry this letter to you—the first letter of many, I promise.

I am left to leave you with nothing but promises, I'm afraid . . . the promise that I will write, the promise that your kiss will be the final dream of each night and the first wish of each new morning, the promise that . . .

I am,
Unmovably Yours,
Ethan

The look on Violet's face was the most difficult element of the moments that followed, as if conveying an empathetic sense of loss, perhaps even feeling a measure of sisterhood with Marcella after having gone through the experience of seeing Smitty off on two separate occasions. And Marcella could tell immediately that Ethan must have shared some of his feelings with Smitty, or perhaps Violet even. There would be abundant tears when the fullness of these words hit her, when she'd had the chance to read them again. But for now she put on the bravest of fronts, immediately seizing upon the opportunity to introduce Violet to all the ladies present and bury her wounded heart in the busy chatter of a Friday tea.

It was hard to tell exactly when sorrow gave way to anger, but it most certainly did not take long after dispensing with the formalities of initiating Violet to the Ladies Abolition Society. For Marcella, the meeting was more frustrating than any in recent memory, and she became particularly vexed at the passive nature of the women present and of women in general. Writing letters, holding fund-raisers, knitting quilts, even changing bandages at the hospital—it seemed the women were always left to such trivialities while the men went off to make their *real* mark upon the world and advance the great causes of the day. And it was only the respect she had for Mrs. Carlisle and Catherine, and the desire to not scare off Violet after a single afternoon, that kept Marcella from expressing her opinions aloud while all the ladies were still present.

But that evening, several hours and several readings of Ethan's note later, the softness returned to her ailing heart, and she took out her notebook to do some writing of her own:

Abuela,

Perhaps I should have known that once the drawbridge has been lowered and the intruder is allowed in, there is no returning to the way things were. Raising the drawbridge again only locks him inside, and forcing him out seems an impossible task. The damage has been done and there is no undoing it. But when I allow myself to be governed by better aspects than my anger or my sadness, I must confess that I have rather enjoyed the fresh air of these last few weeks. And the view of the countryside looks most inviting indeed.

11 *The Dancing Lady*

Micah
richmond
december 10, 1862

His runnin'-off plan is as tight and solid as everything he builds. He's decided on Christmas Eve, the one day of the year when neither one of them will be missed right off. The other slaves and the white folks, even the Home Guardsmen, will all be asleep or too drunk to notice by the time they are gone. And he knows just how easy it'll be for them to slip away without a living soul gettin' wise of it 'til they're *long* gone. And no place anyone 'round here will ever think of lookin'.

Christmas Eve jubilatin' at Longleys' will be the same as last year no doubt, even with the war carrying on like this. Won't be the same trimmin's as last year, but there'll be plenty to go around. Micah knows something about what kind of money Mista Longley's made offa just him alone since the war started. And he's figured out some of the things that Mista Longley does to keep his other slaves happy to stay just where, and who, they are. Decent cabins are a start. And seein' how it's a lumber mill he runs, it's not hard to make it so. And clothes too. All Mista Longley's slaves get a new set of'm every five six months. Get to use the old ones for rags or for patchin' up the new ones or for whatever they want t'do with them, it seems. But then, most important of all in Mista Longley keepin' all the slaves he's got happy as any colored man or woman's ever been, is the jubilatin'.

Three times a year, it comes. And it's almost perfect how it gets fixed up about four months apart all the time. There's the jubilatin' for when Jesus got born on Christmas. Then there's the one where Jesus got raised up from the dead on Easter. And then there's the *most jubilatin'est* day of all—every year on August the twenty-third. Which is the day Mista Longley *himself* got born, Glory Hallelujah!

And even though Micah's only been here long enough to see a little more than a year's worth of those jubilatin' days, he knows just how important they are. So come time for the next one to get under way. The day before Christmas, or so. He knows Mista Longley'll come through with the necessaries for some fine jubilatin', war or not. Sure there won't be a half side of beef like there was last year. But there'll be two pigs at least to make up for it. Maybe no ginger beer neither, but *plenty* of potato-mash whiskey. And that's not countin' what folks've been brewin' for themselves these last few weeks. There won't be any sugar, but enough molasses to make the cornbread and sweet tater pie. And anywhere else there might be something missin', Mista Longley'll have something to make up for it. So the jubilatin'll go on late into the night Christmas Eve and all the next day. Same as always.

They'll save at least one of the pigs for Christmas Day, but the first'll never make that long. And the potato mash'll get sampled somethin' fierce that first night. Enough *to take the chill off,* at first, then to wash down some of that fine meat straight off the spit. Then the fiddle playing'll start, and there'll be dancin' 'round the bonfire. And more potato mash to *cool down* from the fire and all the dancing. 'Til then comes the toasting.

Someone'll get up and toast the Baby Jesus and talk about seeing the Bet-lee-hem star this year or that. Then someone else'll jump up and say they remember that year, too. And the lyin'll grow so deep that even the one that started it will believe it in the end. Then someone else'll get up and offer a toast to Massa Longley. Another one'll jump up and do the same. Only louder, hoping that the Massa's listnin'. There'll be six, eight, ten toasts to the Massa. More than there was to the Baby Jesus even, and each one louder'n the one before it. 'Til the Massa steps out onto the porch of the Main House, long across the sawmill field from the slave quarters. And he'll shout *Happy Christmas.* And send them all into a frenzy tryin' to figure out which toast it was that brought the Massa out. There'll be some more fiddle playin' and dancin'. And some more potato mash to cool off again. 'Til someone'll say they gotta save *some* of it for tomorrow. Then they'll eat most of the cornbread to keep their stomachs from turnin' sour during the night.

The next morning they'll step outside their cabins, and Mista Longley'll have the Reverend Lattimore come and preach to them. The Reverend only preaches to coloreds, even though he's a white man. Some say he got in trouble with a few lady members of his congregations over the years, back when he still preached to white folks, but he's Mista Longley's brother-in-law. So that's how he got set up with this kinda preachin' work, here and at a couple of other places, too. Preaching to the slaves. Sayin' the same thing most every time. No matter what he's readin', always comin' around to the same message—'bout how they should be happy in their station in life. That's what he calls it—*station.* Like the Lord done stopped a train somewhere and said, *All right, all you colored folks get out now, this is your station—you gonna be slaves . . . but be happy about it!*

The Reverend'll talk about how they *got it so good to have a Massa like Massa Longley.* What with the pigs and the potato mash and the cornbread sweetened with molasses. *When plenny of white folks is practic'ly starvin'* this Christmas, 'cause of the war. And all of them slaves, prisoners in their minds much as their bodies, far as Micah can tell. They'll just sit there and shake their heads and agree with the Reverend 'bout *how lucky they is—blessed even.* Then when he's through, they'll damn near knock each other over to be the first to wish him a Happy Christmas. Sayin' *God Bless ya, Rev'run.* Like the Rev'run ain't been blessed a hundred times over already.

The fire'll be set again, and the second pig'll get roasted, alongside a soup and some greens flavored with what's left of the pig from the night before. And they'll start in on what's left of the potato mash—the stuff the Massa let them brew for the last month all leading up to this day. Of course, with all the samplin' and the coolin' off and the toastin' they done the night before, it'll run out before all the cookin' gets done. But there'll be folks slipping into their cabins for a little something extra they brewed on their own, but *shhhhh don't tell no one.* And there'll be six eight ten folks that got a little spare jug of their own. Only it won't be just them six eight ten folks that got it, and it won't be just a little bit they got. So the party'll keep on into the night with more fiddlin' and dancin' and toastin'.

Then Mista Hawthorne'll come staggering over and tell 'em, *That's all, early start inna mornin'.* 'Til someone'll toast Mista Hawthorne, say how lucky they is to have a overseer like him. Someone else'll say *God Bless ya, Mista Hawthorne,* like God ain't done that already, too. And Mista Hawthorne might say, *Haffa hour more an' 'at's all.* And that'll *be* all. 'Til there's a pig for Easter and more potato mash. Then nothin' 'til the Massa's birthday. And then all the way to Christmas again. Three days of jubilatin' . . . all it takes to keep them blinders on tight for all the other days of the year.

But Micah won't be stickin' around for the Easter jubilatin' or the Massa's birthday either. That's because come Christmas Eve, once they done with the samplin' and the cornbread and stumblin' their way back to their cabins, he'll be gone. Out behind the sawmill, to the stretch of woods that runs most of the way to downtown. And then it'll be a half-mile or so 'til he comes up on the two blocks more to the Kittredges' house. And meeting Mary by the stable out back. Then it'll be slipping past any Home Guard that might not be asleep from their own Christmas Eve jubilatin'. Then down to the James River, and the rowboat that hasn't been moved in at least six months. Like whoever'd put it there had forgot where they left it. He'd sat in it, checked it for leaks, checked the oars even, when he had the job across the James that Mista Longley let him drive to by himself. And Micah figured out that they'd use it to go *up* the James River, the way not even the best slave-catchers would ever figure. Not with half the Yankee Navy less than a hundred miles *down*river. But they weren't about to trust the Yankees, or Mista Lincoln's Proclamations about emancipation. Or anybody. Except each other. Except themselves. And he'd gone over it so many times in his mind, he was sure they'd be twenty twenty-five miles away before anybody even noticed they were missin'.

In the years he'd been with Dunmore out in Charlottesville, he'd come to know that part of the state as well as most any *white* man did. With all the jobs he did for Dunmore in every neck of the county, and him havin' to do most of the driving back from those jobs when Dunmore wasn't in any condition for it, he knew those roads as well as a native, almost. And he knew he and Mary could slip through there without anyone noticing. Within a week they'd reach the Blue Ridge Mountains. And then they'd walk up the length of them all the way to Pennsylvania, where they'd be free, according to Mista Lincoln's new law. But they wouldn't stop there, no how. Wouldn't stop 'til they made it to St. Catharines, all the way up in Canada. The place he once heard talked about back at *Les Roseraies* by a couple of field hands who run off followin' the stars to get to freedom.

'Course—he would never tell Mary how folks said it snowed six eight months outta the year all the way up there. And he'd never tell her that those two field hands that run off from *Les Roseraies* didn't make it anywhere close to freedom. How they got brought back ten days later . . . got forty stripes apiece. And sold off.

But it'd be different for them, Micah figured. Hadn't they risen all this way after growin' up working in the fields? The two of them must've been the smartest, most important slaves anywhere in the city, or the whole the state even. With all the money they took in. And hadn't they got that far, climbed that high, just by their own wits and hard work?

Mmm-hmm. He reminded himself.

Wasn't Mary a better dress designer and seamstress than any white lady inside a hundred miles or more?

Mmm-hmm.

Wasn't he a better carpenter than any man, white or not—'cept for his Daddy—than he'd ever seen?

Mmm-hmm.

And weren't they smarter than any white folks that might come runnin' after them? Or their own Massas even?

Mmm-hmm—for damn sure, mmm-hmm!

And wouldn't the dogs get stopped on their trail soon as they got to the river?

Mmm-hmm.

'Til he felt his fists clenching just a little bit. Laying there in his bed in that solitary cabin. Knowing that there would only be the matter of convincing her to come along.

'Cause this here's a Micah and Mary thing. An' ain't no one gonna stop us 'til we get to where we mean to go.

Mmm-hmm.

MARY
RICHMOND
DECEMBER 14, 1862

Gertie, you there now? I just gotta tell you this, an' I know ain't no way it can wait 'til tomorrow mornin' 'cause I'll never be able to sleep 'til I tell you.

Micah come past the store in his work carriage again today. He smiles an' takes off his hat like always, an' when he puts it back on he taps the top of it, an' that's him sayin' I love you. So I pull a little at the sleeve of my dress to say I love him back, like we worked out. But this time he points his finger 'round the corner like he wants to meet me out in the back. So I go 'round back of the store to meet him, an' right off he says we should run away together! He says I give him a reason to want somethin' more than just a few extra potatoes an' meat four or five times a week, that I make him want to steal the resta his life away an' mine too, 'steada just stealin' moments at a time backa the store like this.

He says we can have a little home somewhere up north where they's gonna be real freedom now, not like before, an' he's got the perfect plan. He told me all about it, Gertie, but my mind was swimmin' after he told me 'bout the notion. Then he says to me, the God that'd make something beautiful as you sure didn't mean for you to be locked up in this place like you was some sorta hothouse flower. An' just how'm I not s'posed to love him then?

But I was so scared 'bout what might happen, 'bout how things turned out when you an' me run off an' how I lost you forever 'cause of that. An' I can't imagine not havin' Micah now. So I tell him how I dunno, how even perfect plans got a way of not workin' out sometimes an' if this one don't, that'd be the end of even these stolen moments an' so on. I knew it kinda hurt him, but he kiss me still, tell me he love me still, tell me he ain't goin' nowhere wit'out me.

Then just a little while ago, in the middle of the night it seem, I hear a tappin' noise on my window, an' I was scared at first an' thought to get Mista Kittredge. But instead I lit a candle and looked outside . . . an' there he was, Micah! So I blow out the candle an' open the window a bit, an' he says see how easy it is, an' ain't anyone even been jubilatin' today, an' Home Guard gotta be all over the place, an' still he got all the way here no problem a'tall. An' my heart's so happy just to see him, an' when he say come out the window an' meet him behin' the stable like we would the night we run off . . . I dunno, Gertie, that scaredness I had just that very afta'noon ain't there no more.

So I throw on my coat an' shoes an' slip outta the

window just three or four feet to the ground an' then run 'cross the field to the stable. There ain't but less than half a moon, but the sky's all full of colors, streaks of white an' pink an' orange dancin' their way 'cross the heavens. An' maybe it's the sorta thing that shoulda made me scared, somethin' I ain't never seen before. But Micah say they somethin' called the Northern Lights, say he hearda them once from folks that talked 'bout the place St. Catharines way up in Canada. He say they must be there all the time if they called the Northern Lights, an' won't it be somethin' to sit out on the porch an' look up at them any night we wants to. An' he kiss me again, sayin' how he knows it's gonna be just so, an' ain't this God tellin' them not to worry the way he's sendin' those lights all the way down here where they ain't never been befo'.

But still I knew I hadta tell him 'bout Mista Grant befo' I get too excited 'bout runnin' off wit' him, since maybe that'll make him change his mind the way the men in Juss's books sometimes do when they find out certain things about the ladies they wanna marry. But he just shook his head like it didn't matter none to him. An' when I started cryin', sayin' how can it not matter?—well, he took off his jacket and opened up his shirt an' turned 'round an' dropped it down to his waist, showin' me the skin all wrinkled an' gray where his last Massa had him whipped half a dozen times for no reason a'tall. An' I'm cryin' some more at the sight of it, 'course, with these long gray scars lit up by the orange an' pink an' white lights dancin' in the sky. 'Til he turns back 'round, fixin' his shirt, an' says . . . "So we both got scars."

An' at a moment like that, how'm I s'posed to say no? How'm I s'posed to try an' think of anything that ain't him an' me together all the time? Forever. An' the lights dancin' in the sky like they there just for us . . .

ETHAN
FREDERICKSBURG, VIRGINIA
DECEMBER 13, 1862

Finny's always restless the night before a battle, and he seems deep in thought as he pokes a three-foot stick back and forth into the fire beneath the three pots of water hanging from a rack. It's still nothin' but dark in the sky, but Ethan makes just enough of a rustle as he approaches that Finny turns and sees him coming. Neither man says anything at first, but Ethan takes a seat not far from him, stretching out his wounded leg toward the fire.

The leg actin' up on you? Finny asks.

No, it just takes a little longer to get goin' on cold mornings, Ethan replies.

He rubs his thigh with both hands, mostly for show, not wanting to hear from Finny how he shouldn't get anywhere near the battlefield today. He's heard it plenty already.

Couldn't sleep, Fin? he asks, by way of changing the subject.

Nope—never do when we're getting ready to go in, Finny answers. I was just runnin' through their faces in my head, Perfessor. All nine of 'em.

Nine what? Ethan asks.

Finny turns to Ethan and looks at him strangely, as if he expected him to know something straight off and is surprised he didn't.

How many men you kill? he asks. I mean, not from forty yards away in formation, but up close, so you knew they were dead . . . an' that you was th'one who done it.

I don't know, Fin, Ethan lies.

What about Malvern Hill?

Ethan shrugs his shoulders and looks away from Finny, into the fire, uncomfortable now, preferring to talk about his leg and how he should stay away from the battlefield, instead of this.

I don't remember much about Malvern Hill, Fin, he answers.

Finny seems disappointed in him, almost angry. That true? he asks.

Ethan shrugs again. I don't know, Finny.

Nine fer me, Finny says, matter-of-factly. I remember all their faces, too. Th'sounds they made goin' down. Th'looks they give me like they're sayin' *Now why'd you go an' do that?*

Ethan looks over at him in a dash, then looks away, startled to hear that Finny'd figured their faces said the same thing to him. I know Fin, he says.

Y'do Perfessor? Finny asks with unusual irritation in his voice. I mean, I never been shot like you, or went through The Hunger, so I don't know what that's like . . . and I'd never say I did. But . . . well . . . don't say ya know about the killin' unless ya really know fer sure.

Okay, Fin . . . three, Ethan says. Three fer sure.

Where? Finny asks.

Two at Malvern Hill, like you said, Fin. Shot one from maybe twenty feet . . . through th'heart. Saw him buckle and drop. Saw that same look you described. An' he fell with his legs all bent under him, like the way they put Ais– . . . like the way they put my sister in the coffin. An' there wasn't even the time to . . . then it was just a few seconds after that . . . by Harry . . . the one I stuck a coupla times with th'bayonet—same place I'd just shot th'other one.

What about the third?

Antietam . . . fella over by the tree in fronta the Sunken Road . . . best shot of my life, maybe twenny yards out.

That was you? Finny asks after a pause, like he remembers the exact man.

Ethan only nods. Got tripped up by a greenhorn next to me, he says. Fired my shot after the rest, an' . . . well, you know what it looks like, Fin.

Finny nods at him, tight-lipped, and there is silence for a few moments.

So you *know,* Finny says, gazing back into the fire. Then a few seconds later he asks, You got one fer sure wit' th'bayonet? I never did.

You're too good a shot, Fin.

Mmmm . . . maybe so Perfessor, he agrees, not bragging at all, just accepting a fact they all knew to be true. Finny's one of the best shots in the whole Brigade. Wish I wasn't though, he says. Then I wouldn't be goin' t'hell when it's all done.

What're you talkin' about Fin? It's war. Killin' happens in war, Ethan says.

Yeah. But I figure it's gotta be a little more *even,* ya know, a little more *fair,* he replies.

What d'ya mean, Fin? There's nothin' *even* about killin', Ethan says.

Sure, but I mean—you got three, an' got stuck at Malvern Hill, then shot twice at Antietam, so there . . . three. It ain't even, sure, but that's about *fair,* Finny says. But *nine*? Just so *I* could stick around with a coupla nicks an' that's all? Why would God go an' do that? That just ain't fair.

For a moment Ethan thinks of telling Finny about Suah, about what he'd said to him of God keeping him alive for some purpose. But he knows it won't be much comfort to Finny. He's not even sure *he* believes it anymore.

I don't suppose *any* of it's fair, Fin, he says instead.

Mmmm, Finny replies, and jabs at the fire some more. Ya think God'll forgive us?

Don't know, Fin, Ethan replies. Hard to figure how He . . . I don't know, Fin.

There doesn't seem to be anything more for either of them to say, so they sit in silence for a few minutes 'til the sergeants start rousting the boys from their tents. And before any of them make their way to the fire, Finny stands up and pats Ethan on the shoulder.

Don't go *up* there today, Perfessor, he says, pointing to the Confederate lines they'll soon assault. He starts to walk away, then turns back to look at him again. I *mean* it, Ethan, he says sternly. You *done* your share. Your share an' *then* some.

Okay, Fin, Ethan lies.

ETHAN'S ABOUT THE ONLY MEMBER of the Press Corps on the dangerous side of the river when the field east of town goes hot around eight-thirty that morning. The cannons boom from both lines, belching smoke in white clouds that soon fill the sky. And Ethan makes his way over to the west side of town, where he bribed an artillery sergeant the day before to help get him up close to the fighting. He's got his camera strapped on his back when the division gets the command to go up the gentler slope west of town, and Ethan struggles to keep pace—limp, step, limp, step, limp, step he goes—using the tripod for a cane, and more aware than ever how poor a soldier he'd make now. Then, before he gets a hundred yards up the slope, the assault comes tumbling unexpectedly back toward him.

It's the oddest of sensations for Ethan, standing there with his camera and bundle of equipment rather than a rifle and ammunition pouch. He's pinned down by the weight of all that he carries and a leg that's not doing him a damn bit of good when he needs it most. The next moments seem like an eternity as shells hit all around, and waves of attackers, almost an entire division, fall to the ground for cover. Ethan flops to the earth as well, his head uncomfortably on the lower side of the downslope, until he swings around the other way. He sees a Union man, a kid really, flop just a few feet from him, and Ethan arranges the equipment bag and camera on the slope above them to offer whatever protection it can from the musket fire flying past. And then it grows mostly quiet around them as the fighting shifts to the center of the line, where the field is far more forbidding, where a three-foot-high stone wall stretches across the peak of the slope, where Harry and Finny and the rest of the Irish Brigade are all waitin' to go in.

It almost seems impossible to imagine that even the worst of generals would send ordinary men up to assault such a position. But there it is, for all to see. A first brigade climbs the slope toward Marye's Heights and is quickly repulsed by just a few rounds from the Rebs perched behind the stone wall. It's the beginning of an afternoon horror that Ethan witnesses all too clearly from his prone position, huddled behind his camera just a few hundred yards away, left to think only about how it wasn't supposed to be like this. Another brigade goes into the fury, only to be thrown back before they get as far as the first, then comes a third assault, and a fourth, with results just as predictable, just as disastrous, just the same.

But as the fifth brigade prepares to climb the hill, Ethan can see the familiar green and gold flag unfold and flap defiantly in the breeze. It elicits great pride in him for a moment, but then quickly gives way to dread at the thought of what awaits Harry and Finny and the rest of the lads. The Irish Brigade is still called a brigade, answering to the call of three or four thousand men. But ever since Antietam they've barely been twelve hundred on their *best* day. Still, Ethan knows how little that matters. He knows how a battered regiment can hold off the advance of Stonewall Jackson's brigade, how the Sixty-Ninth and the Eighty-Eighth can assault Rebel lines twice their number and push them back by the sheer force of their will. And for those precious moments before they start up the slope, he feels the surge of adrenaline within him and would join them himself if he had two good legs, or even just the one, and a musket to go along with it.

They go forward, one brilliant mass of tightly formed rows marching in step into the breach. When the fire intensifies, they step on the double-quick, still maintaining their lines, patching holes in them as men fall along the way, 'til they reach the point where the first two assaults failed, and press on, fixing bayonets as they move up the increasingly steep hill. Minutes later they pass the point of the farthest Union advance, and the cannonade from all along the Rebel lines now centers on them. And still they move forward.

In his mind Ethan can see them do it once more, the famous old Irish Brigade *smashin' inta th'enemy with ferocity unmatched,* punching a hole in the line the way they did at Malvern Hill, or shattering the resistance of the Rebs in the Sunken Road at Antietam. He thinks, he imagines, he hopes, there'll be fresh troops to exploit the hole once they make it, another brigade following up, thirsting their way forward into the breach, the way water finds its way to the hole in the dam. But by the time the boys come within twenty yards of the stone wall, they're nothing like a cohesive fighting force anymore. The green flag goes down and is raised again, only to fall seconds later. And what looked like imminent victory in his hopeful eyes just moments before now dissolves into a nightmare, a battered and bloody mass of men, his comrades, his friends, his brothers, unwilling to give way, iron-willed bastards that they are.

'Til then comes the grim, imminent reality as the Irish Brigade is washed down the hill, the lads stumbling over their own wounded as the remnants of a once-formidable force yield the field, not retreating as much as blown backward, downhill, by the Newtonian might expelled from behind the stone wall—as in *for each action there is an equal and opposite reaction,* and even the iron will of the lads who march behind the green and gold flag can't change that part of the equation. The Rebs on the other side of the wall stop firing after a while and lift their caps and cheer, not mocking the Irish Brigade but showing their deep admiration. And Ethan turns on his back now, almost breathless, staring up at the sky, wondering if he'll have any friends left to see come morning.

Jesus, that last one almost *did* it, the wounded kid next to him says. Those were the Irish Boys, weren't they?

Ethan only nods his head as the water's trying to rush to his eyes now and can only be kept back by biting hard on his lip and jerking his head to his chest a few times, then burying it in his right arm.

Hey, you okay? the kid asks.

And Ethan mumbles now, Mmm-hmm.

Jesus, they almost did it, didn't they? the kid says again, none the wiser.

Ethan opens his watery eyes toward the sight of the slaughter once again.

Mmm-hmm, he mumbles, stuffing back the gasps of air his lungs keep trying to press out, pushing them back with all the rest of those memories that have no right to see the light of day.

Almost, Ethan says.

STAFFORD HEIGHTS, VIRGINIA
DECEMBER 14, 1862

The generals must've got drunk or cried crocodile tears or spent the whole night after the onslaught figuring out how to cover their arses when the day of reckoning surely comes. Whatever it was, they didn't call for the retreat, once the shield of darkness mercifully offered the chance, just left whole brigades, divisions even, to freeze there along the slope below the Reb lines.

You huddled alongside the kid named Will from somewhere in Pennsylvania, pulling in two of Will's dead comrades from nearby to offer some cover from the wind and the snipers up above. And you and Will listened to the moaning of the wounded, the final pleas from those who didn't make it through the night, and the muffled tears of those who wished they wouldn't. Sometime just before the morning, you could see enough of the moonlight reflected off the Rappahannock below to imagine you could speak to Aislinn and somehow your desperate words would be carried off to her. But there were no soliloquies about remember whens or even the lamentations for all that had surely been lost, just a simple plea in case she had any pull in the Ever After and could make such a dream so. *Let me see her again,* you whispered, knowing Aislinn'd know who.

Then came this morning, with the sun offering the grace of warmth along with the danger of the Rebs up above having clear sight of the field again. And between you and Will there was nothing but a few bits of hardtack and some almost-frozen salt pork to make it through 'til the sun finally set again and the generals figured it was time to issue the call to retreat. And it's only then that you go back down the slope to something like safety and the warmth of a fire and something to eat.

When you finally find the camp for what's left of the Sixty-Ninth you brace yourself before going in, but it does little to fend off the news. Finny is dead . . . left up there amongst the lads shattered by the canister fire near the stone wall, the lot of them nothing more than some high-water mark of the great Irish Brigade that looked victory closer in the eye than any Union Brigade three times their size. And the thought comes to you that Fin must've *known* that morning how he'd have to face the laws of probability at some point, that there were nine dead Rebs who'd have to be accounted for somehow.

What about Harry? you ask O'Leary from your old company.

Went to the flag ceremony, O'Leary answers with disgust.

The what?

Doncha know the new flag for the regiment arrived from New York? O'Leary says. There's a celebration with General Hancock himself and all the officers—the ones *left* anyway—over by the ferry docks. Harry's ready to get himself court-martialed . . . said something 'bout takin' a crack at as many officers as he can . . .

And instinctively you head off before O'Leary even finishes. Along the way you ask whoever you vaguely recognize if they've seen Harry or know where the flag celebration is, until you hear the din of a somber fiddle playing in a building not far from the ferry landing. Harry's outside it, sitting on the ground and leaning up against the wall not two feet from a window. And inside you can see officers with faces downturned and bobbing slightly side to side along with the music.

Harry, you say.

He looks up at you, and right off you can tell that he's not all right.

Jesus, Harry, what happened?

D'you hear 'bout Fin?

You only nod your head by way of acknowledgment. Then you see the blood from Harry's chest and arm, running in a thin streak down his uniform jacket.

Jesus, Harry, you're hit!

Jus' a little shrap'el, Perfess . . . nothin' like what Fin . . . or you . . . or Smitty got . . . nothin' like what *they* got . . .

And he nods his head toward the heights.

It takes the better part of an hour to get Harry to the hospital set up on the other side of the river on the bluff called Stafford Heights. He's able to walk the whole way, but you do let him rest an arm on you when it comes to climbing the last hill. And it's a sad sight the two of you must make, pressed against each other for balance, with you limping and him with a practically lifeless arm tucked inside his coat. Inside the building a nurse takes a look at the wounds, and Harry's words are confirmed—it looks far worse than it is. There'll be no amputation or even an operation that'll be worth using what chloroform they have. There will be no discharge, either. And Harry lies down on the floor at the end of a long row of triaged men waiting to be attended to by one of the overworked doctors, a single blanket underneath him and one on top. The nurse washes the wounds a little and tells him that one of them has practically stopped bleeding all on its own, and then she leaves to tend to more serious cases.

I'll stay here with you Harry, you say. Get some sleep, and I'll stay right here by the–

And Harry interrupts you with an angry look on his face and shaking his head almost violently back and forth a few times.

Fer chrissakes, Perfessor, go home! You think I wanna see your feckin' mug here . . . to be reminded of it all . . .

And his voice trails off like you've never heard from Harry before, the toughest one of all of you from good old Red Hook, now made fragile by the torment of memory.

Just go *home,* Ethan–an' don't come back here to get yerself shot at, you goddamn cripple . . . you don't belong here, pretendin' like yer still a soldier . . .

And even though you know he's only saying such things to convince you to leave, they still hurt coming from him. You lean down and put your hand on his unscathed shoulder, and he nods at you, then turns away. And you go without another word or gesture, hoping this will not be the *last* time you see him.

For a time you thought that this was where you belonged, with the lads still, fighting for the cause in whatever way you could. But it was clear that none of the lads who were actually doing the fighting cared a damn about the cause, not Union, not victory, for *damn* sure not emancipation, not now, not after all this. This war has become about simple *put your head down and forge back into the breach* attrition, with the generals' stupidity providing an endless source of fresh corpses and shattered lives. And you're glad your camera and half the glass-plate negatives you carried with you are left smashed along the slope on the other side of the river. You'll play no part in promoting the notion of a *Glorious Charge,* played out in the headlines of the *Daily Eagle*. And as for any runaways clinging to the Army of the Potomac—well, they must've got word that it's not exactly a reliable team to hitch their wagons to, since there haven't been any of them to stick around long enough for you to take their picture.

Just outside the building there's a little bench of decorative ironwork, and you flop your beleaguered body down on it, stretching out your bad leg and rubbing it as far as the knee, trying to ease the pain a little. It's a fantastic sight out in front of you and for miles into the distance, with campfires on each side of the lines flickering like tiny stars fallen to earth and the brighter glow from houses forming constellations amidst the spectral display. You tip your head back, knocking it harder than expected on the iron bench, and close your eyes until the pain becomes dull. Then opening them, you see the flashes across the canopy of a star-filled sky, little streaks of white at first, then growing bolder and wider and colored pink and orange and yellow. And the words somehow come to you like a treasure stored away that's been waiting to breathe the open air . . . *Na Fir Chlis* . . . you whisper in the Old Irish . . . The Dancing Lady.

You close your eyes again and rub your head at the point of impact, then slowly open them once again—and there she is! No counterfeit, this sight, just the brilliance of a memory brought back to life, and you can almost feel yourself along the Lane back home, back before The Hunger, with Seanny and Da still there, with Mam wrapped in her coat and draping the edges of it over your shoulders that reach only just above her waist—and Aislinn, there beside you—dancing right along with The Dancing Lady in the sky—and it's the sort of clean you thought would never again be possible, something pure as a stream back home . . . before it all—

Huhhhhh! you're interupted by the gasp from behind you, jolting your head back upright and gathering yourself before you turn to see the silhouette in the backlight of the doorway, a nurse's bonnet atop her head and a shawl draped over her shoulders and her turning her gaze from the sky to you.

Oh sorry, she says, I didn't mean to star— . . . *Ethan?*

And she gasps again.

It's only when she steps a few feet out of the doorway, and the lights from above illuminate her face, that you see the familiar features you'd spent most of the night before reconstructing in your mind—and you smile without being aware of any waking sensation.

And there is not a word between you for the time it takes you to stand up and walk half the way to her, wrapping her inside your embrace and feeling the electric charge of that dream fulfilled, then easing her away from you far enough to look into her deepest brown eyes reflecting the dancing light as they look up at you—and you kiss her now with the breathless gratitude of being given the chance again. A minute passes, maybe more, your embrace a fit of Newtonian symmetry it seems, and for that moment all the scarred earth around feels washed as clean as the childhood memory of *Na Fir Chlis*—in all her eternal splendor—until you see the blood smeared across the arms and apron of her uniform, then slip back far enough away to see the fatigue pulling at her face, and the eyes that you know have now seen too much to ever forget—to ever be as confident as only a person who has never known the horrors can be. And seeing what has been lost, you somehow become angry with her in much the way Harry was with you just minutes before.

What are you *doing* here? you ask. Why are you . . . is it . . . because of *me*?

The words are no sooner out of your mouth than you hear the arrogance in them, and the fatigue is gone from her saddened eyes as the fire returns.

I was a nurse long before I ever knew you! she says, pushing away from what's left of your embrace. How dare you think that I would follow you around like some smitten little girl! I'm doing a damn sight more than you—writing stupid letters to announce you're going off to take more pictures! Like that's doing any good! I'm helping to save lives!

And she punches at your chest with the fleshy edge of her hand, then turns and begins to walk back to the doorway. But you find the agility to make two quick steps without a limp, enough to take hold of her hand and pull it gently toward you, slowing her progress for the time needed to walk around back in front of her.

I'm sorry . . . I . . . I didn't . . . I'm sorry.

Ethan, I have just thirty minutes to breathe something other than a room filled with chloroform . . . I just want to sit and close my eyes . . .

And you regain your senses enough to lead her over to the bench while she continues to speak.

. . . I haven't slept since yesterday. I think—I don't know for sure . . .

You take your coat off and drape it across her lap, then sit beside her.

. . . it's been *terrible* Ethan—one amputation after another . . .

And as she softens into your embrace, laying her head on

your shoulder, you whisper, I know . . . I know . . . but enough of that for now . . . let's watch The Dancing Lady.

The what? she asks.

And you take just one finger and place it beneath her chin, gently lifting her head up enough to look at the heavenly display once again.

Over here they call them the Northern Lights, but back in th'Old Country, they're *Na Fir Chlis*—The Dancing Lady.

I like that better, she says.

Me too. And the first time I can remember seein' them was back on the Lane, with all of us there—

How old were you?

Couldn't have been more than six or seven.

Just a *wee* lad, she says with as much of a brogue as she can muster, and the smile warm on her face once again.

That's right, you say. And there we all were, Aislinn dancin' right along with the Lady in the sky, and Da tellin' us about what the folks long ago used t'say about such things . . .

And the whisper of your voice is answered with the melody of her soft breaths against the corner of your chest, as you tell her all you can remember of that far-off evening, understanding, with a certainty you've never known before . . . that *she* is your only cause now.

12 *Dreams Within a Dream*

MICAH

RICHMOND, VIRGINIA

DECEMBER 24, 1862

Jeremiah's about the last person in the world Micah wants to spend most of a day with. But here he is riding right alongside him. Complaining he should be the one to hold Soldier's reins. Jeremiah's good with horses, but even better at complaining.

It's almost an hour riding in from the Barnes place west of the city. With Jeremiah running off at the mouth the whole time. Talking about how the Massa sent *him* to go and see about the filly Mr. Barnes wanted to sell. He'd complained for most of the ride to the Barnes stable, and now for most of the ride home. Talking about how that means the Massa respects his opinion when it comes to *hawses.* And his backward logic makes him somehow think that it means he should be the one holding the reins now. Driving this cart, that Micah takes every day. Driving Soldier, who goes with him every day, too. But Micah wasn't having any of that right from the start. This was the last day of two weeks working at the Barnes place. And Jeremiah was just along for the ride. Left to complain from the passenger side of things. Until.

You a nigga jus' like us. Donchu go fo'gettin that. Jeremiah says.

And Micah turns to him, stares at him with a scowl in his eyes. That maybe makes Jeremiah think twice 'bout his latest complaint. But *Mmm-hmm.* Is all Micah says, for maybe the twentieth time that day. Which makes Jeremiah even madder.

They'd gone round and round before, back when Massa Longley first bought Micah a year and a half ago. Jeremiah wasn't the biggest buck in the slave quarters. Just the most favored one, it seemed. Only one with his own little kingdom, right there in the stables. And a cabin all to himself, even if it did smell like manure all the time. Then came Micah. Massa's new prize, who got his own cabin too, back all the way at the end of the quarters. Far away from the stables. 'Cause Micah was gonna be the first carpenter Massa had to go and make all this lumber they been producin' and sellin' into actual things. Like hay lofts and chicken coops, they figured. Which was bad enough. Turned out it was porches and bookshelves and storage rooms and a nursery even. Making him more of a prize than anyone thought.

Most of the other slaves on the place let Micah keep to himself. Which was fine by him. But not Jeremiah, 'cause he'd always figured *he* was Massa Longley's biggest prize. So he never missed a chance to poke fun at Micah. And Micah just took it, not caring one way or the other. Still in his days of bein' just a mule, he figured. 'Til Jeremiah went a little too far one day. Started talking about how Micah come from nowhere and musta been a half-breed whose Momma got did by the overseer. Then it took three men to pull Micah off Jeremiah. And no one messed with him after that.

It's downright 'barrissin ridin' through town like dis, me th'Massa's liv'ry slave an' you drivin' this here cart. Jeremiah says, complaining. But not scolding, to be sure.

And then again, *Mmm-hmm.* Micah says.

Then Micah taps the reins on Soldier just to show who's doing the driving right now. Jeremiah keeps on and on, dancing up to that line he knows better than to ever cross again. But Micah's mostly turned his thoughts to other things. When he guides Soldier left instead of right on Marshall Street, Jeremiah starts laughing. Going on and on about how Micah made a wrong turn and now he's lost, and how he ain't gonna show him the way to go now. *Uppity niggas always thinkin' they knows it all.* Jeremiah says. And folds his arms in front of him for show, but only after he checks to see that Micah's still wearing that silly grin he's had on most of the ride home.

They pass the Kittredges' store, and Micah pulls Soldier in. Slows the cart to a halt, then hands the reins to Jeremiah. *Ohhh nooo, dis yo' mess! You gettin' outta dis here by yo'sef!* Jeremiah says, but takes the reins all the same. Then Micah says something about having to check on a job he did not long ago. Hops down from the cart and takes off walking up the street past the Kittredges' stores. *Whachu . . . whey you think you goin'?* Jeremiah calls after him. But there is no response.

Micah doubles back, spotting Mary now, waiting 'til she sees him too. Then walks back past Jeremiah, who's still complaining, and turns down the alley one store past the dress shop. It's a few minutes of waiting, and he pretends to examine the drain spout and his work on the outside wall of the new storage room.

I thought you'd be stoppin' by. She says, stepping outside the back of the shop, straight to the scrap bin. Opening it, pretending to sort through it, just like he's pretending to inspect the drain spout. Staring at each other, though. The two of them. Smiling.

I just hadta . . . Mary . . . I just hadta . . . He says, staring right at her. Deep into her eyes, letting her melt a little, then turning his gaze to the wall . . . *I just hadta see if this drain spout's gonna be ready for th'winter time. You know, you cain't be careful enough 'bout these things . . .*

And her laughter is a symphony.

Oh, is that so? She says. Smiling. Trying best as she can to look like she ain't sweet on him. Failing. *Then I guess I'll just be goin' on back inside.*

Now don't you go nowhere without my kiss first. He says. And takes his hands off the wall. They both look all around, then close the space between them. And she leans up onto her toes as he pulls her to him. Another of their stolen kisses, secret, like all the moments they've ever had together. Her lips dissolving onto his 'til the hint of her cheek against his face is like touching one of those silk dresses she makes. And after a few seconds they break off, look all around again. Look back at each other. And it's quiet for a while.

You all set for tonight? He asks.

Her eyes have a little moisture from the cold, glistening soft amber shades. Magic. And she stares up at him, looking more serious than usual. He kisses her again before she can even speak. No looking around first. Unable to keep away. Then after a moment, she turns her head to the side and lays her cheek on his shoulder. Whispering. *I'm ready.*

He kisses her hair, slides his hands up to her shoulders, opening a few inches of reluctant space between them. Needing to see her face again. Take some magic from those eyes to hold him over. 'Til later, at least.

Two bells I'm off. Three bells we meet by the stable. He says. And she nods, three four five times.

There's more staring, another kiss, before Misses Kittredge is calling from the storeroom. Mary grabs two or three bits from off the top of the scrap bin, looks at 'em, shrugs her shoulders as if these were just what she was looking for all along. Smiles at him. And it's his turn to laugh. Out loud. Like only *she* can make him do. Then she's up the three steps and into the store with just one more glance back. He waits for a minute or two, moving his hands along the wall again, pretending. Mostly standing with a silly half-smile on his face the way it's been through most of the day.

When he walks back to the cart, Jeremiah is climbing back up into the seat, grabbing hold of the reins. And there's no reason to take them back. Not if it means hearing his complaints instead of the echo of her voice.

Yeah, the man what knows 'bout hawses got the reins now. Jeremiah says.

And only, *Mmm-hmm.* And thoughts of this time tomorrow.

MICAH JUST GOES INSIDE HIS cabin once the first bit of samplin' the potato mash starts that night. Laughs when the toasts begin. Starts packing, layin' out on his bed the long knife, the hand ax, the hammer, the chisel, the pliers, the file. All swiped that very day. One by one he wraps them inside the sleeves and legs of the extra shirts and trousers he'll be taking along. Then two blankets wrapped around all of it. Some cornbread and pork jerky and a half-dozen turnips and twice as many sweet taters all stuffed in as well. Saved 'em up for the last few weeks. He ties it with some string around the top and lifts it up to test the weight, laughs at how light the load feels. Figures he could carry this whole *cabin* the way he feels tonight. Then puts it back down and sits on the bed. And waits.

It's a while before the church bell rings ten. The celebration outside gettin' 'bout as loud as it's been the whole night. By eleven, someone's said something 'bout saving what's left of the potato mash. So by twelve there's just a few voices from the stragglers sittin' 'round what's left of the bonfire. But the next two hours are long as anything he can remember in his life. He thinks for a while that he should've told Mary to meet him at two bells, quiet as it is now. But he leans outside the cabin at one and there are still lights coming from the Main House. So the plan's right as it is, he reassures himself.

At two bells he's up without hesitation. Peeks outside first, then walks all around the cabin to see if anyone's half passed out by the fire. Nothing. He gets his satchel, and it's straight back a hundred feet or so to the edge of the trees. Walking behind Longley's timber mill, behind his warehouses filled with lumber, and off into the real woods on the edge of town. He could make it to the Kittredges' house in fifteen minutes, walking straight as the crow flies. But this is much safer. So it's through the woods for as long as he can go, then a couple of open fields and a few empty city blocks to their place. Just a sliver of a moon to help him feel his way, much less than what he'd had ten days before when he'd done it for the first time. But it's a horse path he's following, and he's out of the woods before long. Then through a long stretch of open field and the start of city blocks on the northern part of town.

The Kittredges have one of those old city houses, the kind set back off the main street and with a nice piece of property to it. Across their stretch of field in front, just a few buildings to the west, is the mercantile and the dress shop. But he's not going there tonight. Tonight it's the stable in back of the house, and he slips behind the row of stores adjacent and is just about a hundred yards away when the church bell rings three times. Walking across the open field, he looks at the house and smiles. No lights on anywhere inside. And as he gets closer, he sees her. The faint glimmer from a street light illuminating part of her silhouette leaning against the corner of the stable. Plump like she ain't never been. And must be wearing three four dresses like he told her to do. *That's my girl*, he thinks, *right on time.*

He's seventy then sixty then fifty feet from her and smiling. Then the sound of horseshoes on the cobblestone street echoes across the open field. There are three sets at least, and they're not a simple patrol, or people making their way home late at night. They're moving quickly and getting closer, and he freezes for a moment. Tries to locate them precisely. But there's no need to wait very long since they turn up the Kittredges' block and ride straight for the house. Micah drops to the ground and sees Mary turn around the corner, flat against the wall so her silhouette can't be seen. *That's my girl*, he thinks again. He wants to call out to her but is still too far away. Wait until they pass, he thinks.

But then the clap of the horseshoed hooves against the cobblestones slows to stop. And the riders turn off the road and toward the front door of the Kittredge house. They stop there, and two of the riders dismount. One of them taking the reins of the other. And the first man walks up to the Kittredges' front door and knocks loudly on it five six seven times. Micah's shock doesn't last long before he starts to crawl along the ground, pulling himself forward by his elbows. The man bangs on the door a few more times, and Micah hears a gasp from Mary, maybe forty feet away and around the corner of the stables.

I think they sleepin', Massa. The man holding the reins calls out.

Of course they are, shitwit, it's three in the mornin', the man doing the banging answers.

And Micah's eyes grow wide at the sound of their familiar voices. It's Jeremiah and Longley.

Kittredge . . . Kittredge. I need to talk to you . . . Kittredge! And Longley bangs on the door more insistently. *Kittredge! . . . Kittredge! . . .* bangs eight nine ten times. Starts calling out to anyone inside.

Hello! Hello!

Then—*what's the little girl's name?* Longley asks Jeremiah.

Mary, Suh.

Not the one he's runnin' off with . . . the little nigga girl that keeps house! Longley shouts at him.

Oh . . . ahhhh . . . Bessy, I think, Suh, though I ain't altogetha—

Bessy . . . Bessy! Kittredge!

Desperate now. Like Micah's never seen him before. And banging on the door some more, 'til a dog across the street starts barking. Someone lights a gas lamp on the second floor of the Kittredges' house, and Mary gasps again, from around the side of the barn. Micah realizes he has to get to her, so he starts to crawl again. 'Til a few seconds later the windows along the first-floor slave quarters are etched with the faint glow of candlelight. And Mary steps back around the corner of the stable so Micah can see her silhouette again, turned this time toward the house. He's maybe thirty feet away now when she takes a few slow steps, then starts to run across the field. Not toward him or toward the open fields behind the house. But back toward the *house.* The worst thing she could do.

Mary . . . wait. Mary, it's me. He says, whispering and yelling all at once. Then louder again. *Mary!* In almost a regular voice now.

She stops for a second and follows the sound to where he is in the field. With him lying on the ground. A lifetime away from her in the stretch of no more than forty fifty feet. 'Til he lifts himself up enough for her to see him. With him still unable to see her face buried in the shadows of her coat hood, following her turn away from him, and toward the Main House. And he can't tell whether she's still ready to go or if she's too scared now. As she stands frozen there in the field.

And his mind flashes through all the possibilities. Not thinking now, in these desperate seconds, of how this went wrong. But of how much worse it will be if she goes back inside. Then pressing his mind to skip forward to the inevitable. To how he can fix it. And he stands all the way up. Begins to walk toward her as the noise and light grow inside the house. But she brushes her arm two times away from her like she's shooing him off from twenty shadowy feet away. And he can see the hood of her coat twisting from side to side. Shaking her head like she's ready to abandon everything they'd talked about. In just that instant.

Wait, Mary. He urges her. *We can still get to the river before the—*

And more bangs on the front door of the house snap her head on a pivot away from him.

Just two brushes of her arm now, urging him to go away, to go back. And then she's off again, running toward the house on the tips of her toes.

Mary . . . wait. We can still . . . Mary . . .

She's so slow that he could catch her before the edge of the light that reaches out from the windows. But something holds him from it. Like the first bits of understanding how to fix a plan gone wrong. Longley's after him, he knows. But if Mary can get back in time, she might still be safe. And she's at the house now. As his head twists back and forth. Watching her step into the low window of her room. Then back to the front of the house, where Kittredge is standing with an oil lamp. Demanding to know what the meaning of all this is.

And Micah stands frozen there in the field, his shoulders dropping from the weight of all this helplessness. Looking back at Mary's window, for a minute, maybe two. 'Til there's a light in her room, and he fears the worst. That she'll be punished, sold off maybe. And he thinks of running straight down the street to draw their attention away from her, but realizes it's too late. Stands there in the field, instead. Helpless. With more windows lighting up in the house across the street and the other alongside it. And the echoes of Kittredge and Longley shouting back and forth from inside the parlor. 'Til he understands that everything is lost now. Gone in a heartbeat. The way stolen moments always are.

Mary
December 24, 1862

Memories are funny things, how they all pile up on each other and come out at the strangest times. Gertie used to call 'em your very own scrapbook, but that was when she was talking about the happy memories, the ones you *want* to remember. It's easy enough to keep those nice ones in a neat scrapbook in your head, all decorated with ribbons and such. But it's the sad ones, the *shadow* ones, the ones that hang all around and sometimes *over* you like dreams on a winter evenin'—those are the ones that can make a real mess of things.

Micah leaves around two-thirty in the afternoon on

Christmas Eve, and the way he's smiling, and you are too, it's like the shop doesn't need any wood in the fireplace, like the glow from how you feel inside could keep everyone else warm, too. Then the Misses goes up to the house and comes back not long after that, and suddenly *she's* all aglow too. She's got her brother and his wife with her, and their daughter Ashleigh, the ones from down in Carolina who haven't been here in a few years. They just arrived for a nice long visit, and the Misses takes to showing them around the shop, talking about how things've changed since they'd been here last. And she's building you up all the while to them, saying how you practically made the whole place yourself.

Everything's Mary this and Mary that, and the Misses's brother and his wife keep saying how impressed they are, and the Misses's brother's wife hopes you'll make her a dress and one for Ashleigh, too. 'Course you say you'd be glad to but then realize that it's a lie, that you'll be gone this time tomorrow, and that's a bit of a shame. It was the Misses's brother that was the reason you got saved in the first place, since it was him they were visiting in Carolina, and him who fell from his horse and made them decide to stay a little longer, which turned out to be just when you were standing up there on that auction block, when Juss first waved to you and smiled.

Before long it's time to close up, and then it's back over to the house, and Juss is there in your room waiting for you, so you can open presents like you always do before dinner on Christmas Eve. She always wants to do the giving first, and she hands you your present wrapped up in a big piece of cloth with a big red ribbon holding it closed.

Sorry there's no paper on accounta the war, she says, but you won't care 'bout that once you see what it is.

It's long and narrow and you smile and untie the ribbon,

taking your time peeling back the cloth. First you see the curved wood handle, and you know that it's your very own parasol, it's gotta be. Juss has a smile big as a half moon, and says *keep goin', keep goin',* and you peel it back some more and see the light green and then some yellow and white and peel it back all the way, and there are green and yellow ribbons tied to the tip of it. And it's then you feel your breath stop cold inside you.

Rememba that? Juss asks, still smiling. And you can't speak, with the breath still stopped inside you, so you nod your head but forget to smile.

Doncha rememba? Juss asks, and she's a little disappointed now, seeing how you're not saying anything and not smiling either. It's the same parasol I was carryin' the day we became sisters.

She's never once described that day in any other way, never said the word *bought* or *purchased* or *auction* or anything of the sort, even when she got older and knew just what was really happening that day. And you know how she means so much for this parasol to bring back happy thoughts, and how disappointed she'll be if you can't shake the breath free inside you and get to smiling and telling her how much you like it. So that's just what you do, hugging her first and holding tight, letting her squeeze you to maybe get the air moving inside you again. Then there's some tears from her, which makes some tears in you, and she's telling you how that day's just about the most important one in her whole life, telling you everything she was wearing, including the two green and yellow ribbons that she's tied to the tip of the parasol. She's saying how her Grandmamma gave her this before she died and how that makes it a family heirloom, but her Momma said it's okay to give it to you 'cause it's like keeping it in the family after all. And then you start to crying some more, and Juss does too, and by the time you get around to giving her the long white gloves with lace and special stitching you've been working on in secret at the store for the last month, well, they're not so special anymore.

You're all twisted around inside then, thinking how nice it is to have a sister like Juss and how the Misses says how you're like part of the family, and then of course you get sad thinking how you're about to run off and break Juss's heart like that. It doesn't help that the parasol brings back those memories from standing on the auction block, and you can't explain to Juss how that day was a sad one for you and always will be 'cause of how the memory's stored up inside you. You can't tell her that, and then it doesn't matter anyway 'cause Cora's opening the door without knocking, same as she always does when it's your room she's coming into. She's surprised that Juss is there with you, and that maybe makes her a little nicer, but still she's plenty mean enough when she tells you that the Misses told her she'll be sleeping in here *fer as long as th'kin is here.* Cora says the Misses give her room to her brother's slaves, and now it's gonna be the two of you together.

Everything starts to falling apart about then. Juss goes to be with the family for dinner, and you've got nothing but time and all these memories, the scrapbook kind and the shadows alike, all rushing through your head like they're fighting over who gets heard most of all. Juss stops by before going up to her room for the night, says she won't see you 'til prob'ly supper tomorrow 'cause she's got to be with her cousin and all, but she says Happy Christmas and thanks you for the gloves, and you hug her tight again, thinking this is gonna be the last time for that. There's nothing much for you to pack except some needles and thread and gloves and socks and such, and you got it all wrapped up in a blanket next to your bed. You moved the bed over some so Cora had to set her cot up by the door, and you can still slip out the window during the night.

Then Cora comes in carrying a candle that's just about all gone, and she's angry as a cuss, more so than usual even. There's nothing like Christmas in Cora's world. It's all just one gray cloud that follows her around 'til she'll someday stop breathing and won't have to worry about that cloud anymore. And she's about the last person in the world you wanna see on this night. You're not worried that Cora'll say anything about you running off, 'cause if there's one thing Cora's especially good at, it's pretending like she doesn't know *nothin' 'bout nothin',* the way she always says it. It ain't Cora that's gonna get you found out. No, that's gonna come sometime tomorrow morning when Juss stops by before they go off to church, or maybe when they get back, or maybe, if her cousin keeps following her around the way she usually does, you won't get found out 'til the Misses sends for you about the time they sit down for the supper. She always does when there's a party or any kind of important company so she can say how you made the tablecloth and napkins and the drapes and all, and she can have you speak a little French and take a bow. You don't like doing that. Gertie wouldn't like it none, you know for sure, but you can't tell the Misses that. So it'll be around supper time *the latest* when you get found out.

You told Micah 'bout that hitch in his plan. Told him that the Kittredges were gonna know you were gone long before the morning after Christmas, like he figured. But he said it won't matter if they find out an *hour* after you're gone, just so long as you've got time enough to get to that boat and on upriver, 'cause the dogs can't sniff out which way we go then, and the slave-catchers'll figure we went south trying to catch up with the Yankee Navy and all. Besides, he said, it's city streets we're walkin' on 'til we get to the river, and no dog alive's gonna be able to sniff us out, what with all the other smells of horses an dogs doin' their business all over them. Still, it's all these things running through your mind when the door opens and a stream of light pours in from the hallway.

Whachu doin' settin' here inna dark like dis, Cora says.

You roll over and look at her but don't say anything, not with all the thoughts running around your head.

Well, Yo' Majesty ain' happy wit' sharin' her room, huh? she says. You say nothing.

Well I ain' no happier'n *you,* so don't go gettin' uppity like *you* da one bein' put out. Been wit' dese folks longer'n you, an *I'm* the one got's to stay in *yo'* room.

She puts the candle down on the table between her cot and your bed, arranges the blankets some, and then lays down on it, groaning and cussing under her breath at how uncomfortable it is and how she can't spend a week in this thing. But she's off to sleep, breathing heavy inside of ten minutes, and snoring loud enough to wake the Yankee Navy not long after that. And you've got nothing but time again, waiting on the twelve bells, then one, with forever in between 'em. You're getting about as scared as you've been since you ran off with Gertie all those years ago, and worse even, because back then Gertie just woke you up in the middle of the night and told you about running off right then. And you wish it could be the same way now, that you didn't know anything about it and Micah would simply tap on your window and tell you that you were going.

The memories that hit you over and over now, even if they're of good things like the parasol Juss gave you, keep getting turned around into bad ones, like remembering where you were standing the day you first saw it and first saw her. It ain't about how you and Micah are gonna be together now, but how Juss is gonna cry for weeks and months after you're gone, and how you'll be the one giving her shadow memories of her own that she'll always remember when she looks at this parasol, 'cause you know you can't take it with you. Instead of remembering about how far you and Gertie got that time you ran off, you think only about how you got caught. And just then it doesn't matter that Micah's got a good plan, that he's about the strongest man you've ever known and how well he knows that part of the country, or how he says he's gonna watch out for you all the way there. You know you're gonna be the one holding him back, getting him caught, just the way you got Gertie caught oversleeping that morning the way you did, even though you knew how tired she was. And besides, it was your fault the two of you hadta run off in the first place, and you got her killed for it. And then the Kittredges go and rescue you from that misery, and here you go repaying them this way, dragging Micah down, getting him caught and sold off or killed, breaking Juss's heart, making the Misses cry too, ruining their Christmas with the Misses's brother and his family here special . . . and all the nice things they said about you too . . .

And these are all the thoughts running over and over through your head when the two bells ring, and you feel time start speeding up. You know Micah's gone by now, left his cabin and is walking somewhere in the woods, on his way here. And everything's about to change, about to blow up in both your faces, you just know it. And three bells must be getting closer and closer, and you feel the time squeezing the air from your lungs like the memories did before, and the tears are falling off your cheeks before you even know they're there.

Lying there, still as can be, grabbing tight onto your blanket like you're trying to slow down time, it's like you can feel those threads in your stitchin' being sewn without you wanting them to be done. And trying to get hold of the situation, you become desperate.

Cora, you whisper, and when she doesn't answer, you roll over toward her and say it again, louder this time, then start to nudging her, not even thinking how crazy it is that you're doing this.

Wha? Who dat? she says after a little nudging.

It's Mary, you whisper. Yer in my room, rememba?

Wha? 'Course I knows dat. Whachu doin' wakin' me up inna night like dis?

I gotta talk to you.

And then you get to telling her about Micah and how you met him at the hospital and all. But you don't even get to the saying-hello-at-lunchtime part before she's interrupting, asking what this has to do with her. So you tell her straight off about Micah's plan and how you're supposed to go tonight, supposed to go *now.* And then there's no chance to do the talking after that, the way she gets to chastising you.

Why you gonna do dat Chil'? she says, not asking at all, but telling. She hasn't called you Chil' in a lotta years, and it sounds better coming from her now than it used to, sorta reminds you of how Gertie used to call you.

Ainchu got it good here? Cora says. You's 'bout the best-off colored folk in all Richmon', an' you gonna throw dat all away justa run off to them hills an get *caught.* You better'n dat, runnin' through the mud an' snow, dogs chasin' after ya, tearin' at the pretty dresses you done gone t'all that trouble makin' fo' yo'self.

It's like it's someone else altogether doing the talking.

Cora's words are soft whispers instead of the sharp daggers they usually are, and she sits up a little on the cot while she's talking. Then she's on the bed sitting beside you, talking about how she ran off once a long time ago, how she done it with a man, just like you gonna, and how they got caught and he got sold south and she got sold north and how they never seen each other again. And it's about as tender as you can ever imagine Cora being, all so confusing now, Cora sounding more and more like Gertie, and making you think back to then, and getting caught and now putting Micah in that same kind of danger, for what, so you wouldn't hafta go on stealing moments and kisses out backa the store?

Stolen kisses're better than none a'tall, you say out loud, but Cora doesn't know what you're talking about 'cause you don't put the rest of the story with it.

You still got time ta turn dis all aroun', she says. You go out there'n tell him to go on home same way he come, an' won't nobody know any diff'rent in the mornin'.

And then it's all too much, the memories, and the hurting Juss, and never seeing Micah again, and how there won't be any more stolen moments or kisses or anything but a whole lotta time to think of what you lost all over again.

I can't go out there, you say to Cora. If I see him, I'll run off with him, I just know it. And then we'll get caught, and it'll be my fault and . . .

Gimme dat coat, Cora says, and you stop for just a second, then hand it to her and watch as she puts it on, drapes the hood over her head, and puts on her shoes, too. Then she moves to the window, sliding your bed over enough for her to get out, and still you say nothing, like you're frozen there sitting on the bed.

He gonna be at the stables? she asks, and still you can't

talk, so you nod instead. I'm just gonna tell him to g'wan home 'fore dis get any mo' messier, she says. Come mornin' nobody know a thing 'bout nothin', you'll see.

She's out the window, stumbling a little when she hits the ground but catching herself and looking all round the field to see if anybody's there. You're by the window watching her, just a little ways from her, when she starts to walking across the field and all the way to the stable. You keep the window wide open, and the cold starts drifting in, and you remember you don't have your coat on the way you were supposed to. So you roll out the blanket that's got the socks and gloves wrapped in it, and putting them away is like saying it's off altogether, but you do it just as three bells start ringing. You're back at the window in a second and looking for Micah, and it looks like maybe he's closing in, coming from over across the fields. Then you get to thinking how he's not gonna just shoo on home the way Cora thinks, and he'll be at your window in a minute. But that's when everything gets all turned 'round like none of you ever expected.

You're looking out the window and hearing the banging on the front door, and there's Micah dropping down to the ground outside. The Mista and Misses start to stirring upstairs, and you can hear Bessie calling out like she's frightened somethin' terrible, and there's little bits of light coming through from under the door. Then Cora starts to running back to the window, stops, and you can hear whispers coming from the field, from where Micah's laying still, calling out to Cora like it's you. Cora waves two times and starts to running on tippy-toes back to the window now. You can see Micah standing up in the field and calling after her, and your heart's breaking, right there, shattering into a million pieces, thinking how he's left out there by himself . . . because of *you.*

Mista Kittredge is shouting from around by the front door, and the Misses is there, and her brother and his misses must be on the landing on top of the stairs. Cora's at the window now sayin', *Hep me in, hep me in,* and you pull her arms through, and she flops on the bed for a second before throwing off your coat and her shoes and stepping quick over to her cot, breathing hard and scared as you ever heard her. But you hang up the coat and put the stitchin' stuff under your pillow and look out the window, seeing Micah standing there, with his arms opened up a little on each side of him, like he's saying *Mary, why'd you go an' do that?* And your heart is breaking all over again, so much that Cora's got to get out of her cot to close the window and push you down flat in your bed.

Bessie opens the door, and she's got a candle in her hands, the light flickering back and forth because her hands are shaking so.

Mary? You awake Mary? she whispers from the doorway.

Mmm-hmm, whatsa matter Bess? you say, wiping tears out of your eyes.

You gots t'git on up, Mary, she says, still scared. Massa by the front do' an wansa see ya.

So you get up, walking past Cora's cot, where she's still breathing heavy, and you walk down the hall with Bessie filling you in on everything you already know is happening. By the foyer there's Mista Kittredge standing with a gas lamp in his hand and his nightclothes on. The Misses's brother is there too, and his wife and Misses Kittredge and Juss are standing halfway down the stairs. Mista Longley's just inside the front door, and you can tell without him saying a word that he's mad as sin. He tells the other white man with him, Mista Hawthorne, who you know is Micah's overseer, to go out and mind the horses and send in Jeremiah. And you know things're about as bad as they can be.

Mary, Mista Kittredge says as irritated as you ever heard him, Mr. Longley tells me that his boy Micah has run off. Do you know anything about this?

You try to look surprised about it, crinkle your eyes and open your mouth, then shake your head from side to side. *No*suh, you say.

She's lying! Mista Longley says, and then a colored man's coming in through the front door, and Mista Longley's looking over at him.

Jeremiah, tell Mr. Kittredge what you saw out behind his store, he says.

Well, Massa, it's like I says, I be mindin' my own binness jus' thinkin' 'bout dat filly you sent me t'see—

Get to it! Mista Longley shouts, and Jeremiah seems a little scared now.

So's I walk roun' down th'alley, an' I sees Micah an' that gal kissin' an' dey sayin' 'bout how three bells they fixin' t'run off.

Mary, is this true? Mista Kittredge asks you.

Your eyes go wide, and you shake your head and say, *No*suh! I ain't been kissin' no man. You cover your arms over your chest like the very thought of it makes you uncomfortable.

She's lyin', Kittredge, Mista Longley says. For Christ sakes, you can't trust these niggers any more than . . .

There's a gasp from the Misses's sister-in-law, who's a good Christian woman, you been told. And you hear Miss Juss start to crying way up on the landing, and then the Misses steps up to her, and Mista Kittredge gets upset with it all too, jumping in to cut off Mista Longley in the middle of him going on and on about how niggers can't be trusted.

I will not have this in my home! Mista Kittredge explodes, and everyone's upset now. The Misses and Juss and the Misses's sister-in-law are all crying full out now, and the Misses's brother sticks his chest out and steps up next to the Mista.

Listen Kittredge, Mista Longley says, calmer now. Just ask her what Micah said about where he was goin' when she saw him today.

Mista Kittredge turns to you, and you start wipin' some of your tears off your cheeks and say, I ain't seen Micah since he worked on the shop two months back.

Sho' she be forgettin' dis very aft'noon, Jeremiah says, I sees her standin' out back–

Shut your mouth in my home! Mista Kittredge shouts, and that's the end of Jeremiah sayin' anything. And then you figure on putting it all to rest.

Micah mighta been a little sweet on me back then, you say, but I don't know why anybody'd think I'd go round kissin' men an' talkin' 'bout runnin' off . . . seein' how you an' the Misses done so much fo' *me*? An t'leave Miss Justinia? I don't know hows I could *ever* bear it . . .

You start to crying, and though you lied and all, the tears are the real thing, what with all the emotions running through you at once. Then Juss comes running down the stairs, and the Misses is following after her, and they're hugging you soon as they get to the bottom.

Goodnight Mr. Longley, you hear Mista Kittredge say. And that's all you hear from the men after that.

There's plenty of crying and hugging, and even Mista Kittredge, once he's chased the men out, gives you a little hug and says how he doesn't ever want to think of you running off.

We've been good to you, Mary, yes? he asks, and you start to crying some more and shaking your head yes over and over again.

Then the Misses's brother says *Happy Christmas,* and everybody laughs, and soon you're all heading back to bed. Only there's no sleep for you. You're looking out your window 'til the sun comes up around seven bells, and there's no sign of Micah.

The next day is different from any Christmas with the Kittredges you can remember. Juss comes down to your room before they go off to church, then stops by again with the cousin following right behind her when they get back. During the day you eat with the resta the slaves, and they don't tease you any, don't seem to know what to say, and you know they all know about what you lost. Cora musta told them. Bessie tells you she heard that Mista Longley got every slave-catcher in town out looking for Micah, and you know he didn't go home. He's on the boat, you hope, heading up the James River without you . . . safe, you hope.

The Misses calls you in before the dinner, the way you'd expect, and they even drink a toast to you, with Mista Kittredge giving you a glass of wine to toast right along with them. But it's nothing like it mighta been just one Christmas ago, when you woulda loved such things. Now it's all confusion and thinking about Micah, and when it's late evening, you slink back to your room, feeling like it'll be haunted all your life now. Cora's already there, and she's had plenty of wine of her own. She's softer than normal, not so much as last night, but softer than normal all the same. And she gets to talking about the man she lost and what happened when they ran off, and then she gets mad at you for bringing up the shadows *inside her,* and it's like that little window of her heart closes tight all over again.

You's a slave jus' like me an' dat fool nigga Jer'miah an'

any otha colored folks you sees 'roun dese parts. You got it better'n most all of em. Better'n plenny o' *white* folks got it. Soons you accep' dat be when you learn how t'survive dis here life. An' dat's the bes' you can hope fo'.

You don't do any arguing with her, knowing there's not much point, and maybe she's right anyway. Then Juss sneaks down that night, opens the door with a candle half-burnt down, whispering so as not to wake up Cora, telling you to come up to her room where you can talk. So you go with her, bumping into Cora's cot and waking her, and Juss starts to laugh, tells Cora not to worry, *it's just the shepherds comin' to visit the Baby Jesus,* and then she laughs some more. Up in Juss's room she talks about the day and how annoying her cousins are and the presents she got and how she likes your gloves better'n anything her Momma and Daddy give her. Then Juss gets quiet laying there beside you.

I was so scared this mornin', Mary, she says. Just the thoughta not havin' you here . . .

Her voice trails off, and she starts to crying again.

Don't worry, Juss, you say, and then the words form sadly in your mouth, the kinda words with more meaning than it might seem straight off. I ain't goin' *nowhere,* you say. And it's about as sad a few words as you ever said in your whole life.

MICAH

DECEMBER 25, 1862

There was a bridge six or seven miles up the James. Micah did some work near it three months earlier. And it only stayed in his mind at all because he'd followed the road that led to it, figuring he could get over the James to the job on the other side. But the bridge turned out to be knocked out entirely. A Yankee cavalry raid took it out earlier in the year, and then instead of fixing the old one, they built a bigger one a quarter-mile upriver. So on Christmas Day, when all Micah cared about was left behind in Richmond, that wreck of a bridge provided a perfect place to wait. On the south side of the river. The rowboat tucked away in the brush along the shore. Him tucked beneath what was left of the bridge.

He got there around first light, after everything went wrong back at the Kittredges' house. He didn't eat any of the cornbread or pork jerky. Didn't drink from the river. Didn't do anything but think about her all day. Thought about how close he was to her. How they could've still slipped away and started upriver before Longley rousted a single slave-catcher from bed. He played those moments over and over in his head. Trying to figure how it went wrong. Trying to figure what he could have done. She was just eight miles away from him all that day. And the distance was crushing. It wasn't until the last of the sunlight began to fade that he stopped thinking about what had happened, and started thinking about what was *going* to happen, instead.

So by nightfall he was on the move again. Not upriver, but back down it to the edge of the city. He pulled the boat up onto the shore and left his satchel beside it, taking only the knife, slung through a belt loop. Then set off. It was an even longer route to the Kittredge house, coming from west of the city now. Walked along the railroad tracks for a while. Then slipped through the fields of the slaughterhouse and the textile mill and eventually to the woods along the northern edge of the city. Two hours after he'd left the boat behind, he came to the open field behind the Kittredge house again. And hid there until the lights in the house were extinguished. Waited an hour or so past that, the cold biting at his limbs. Then made the same walk he'd made the night before.

Every step was short and considered. Five minutes, maybe more, passed before he finally reached the stables. Then he dropped to the ground, pulled himself along by the elbows as he'd done before. Waited to hear horses on the cobblestones. But nothing this time. When he reached Mary's window, he was covered in mud. He looked around in every direction over the field, then stood up slowly, sliding across the wall to the edge of the window. Tried just to get his left eye across the edge of the window pane. His heart racing as he peeked inside and saw her figure in the bed beside the window. Thinking she was that close to him once again, and they could have this chance to slip away. He tapped his finger against the glass. Two three four times. Lightly first. Then a few times more, harder than before, and she started stirring. Took a few more taps to let her know it wasn't a dream, and she lifted her head up off the pillow, and all at once he and she were shocked at the sight of each other. It was Cora in the bed. But she didn't shout, and he didn't jump back with shock either. Instead she lifted the window just a little. Started explaining the whole thing to him.

She done changed her mine.

She too scared to go runnin' off with ya.

Dat's what I come to tell you las' night.

Cora said a whole lot more. Talked all about how Jeremiah was the one that turned him in. How Jeremiah heard their plans. How it didn't matter far as Mary was concerned since *she changed her mine befo' that all happen.* She told him how Mary made things all right with the Kittredges. How they didn't figure she was ever in on anything. Then Cora shook her head back and forth. Seemed genuinely sad for him. Didn't do nothin' to change nothin' though. And he stood frozen by the window 'til Cora started saying how they were out lookin' for him.

Best you got now is to make a run fo' yo'sef.

Her words were enough to make his feet unstuck. They moved slowly away from the house, back the same way he'd come. But it wasn't like he was doing any of the telling them what to do or where to go. Everything was a haze now. Didn't bother hiding from tree to tree. Or look out for anyone around him as he went. *She done changed her mine,* he kept hearing. Not Mary's sweet voice, but the scratchiness of Cora's. The tired old nag. Just like *he* used to be. Like he would become again, without the hope of her. *She done changed her mine.* And it was hours, three maybe four, way into the early morning. Not far from first light, when he emerged from the woods again.

He saw the horse first. Tied to the tree a few feet from the boat he'd left by the shore. Then he saw the Home Guardsman, digging through the satchel he'd left beside the boat. Spilled the clothes out, the tools clanking on top of each other as they hit the ground. But he ignored them, went for the cornbread instead. Started stuffing great chunks of it in his whiskered mouth. Turnips and potatoes rolled out of the blanket and the horse took some interest in them.

Then everything happened at once. All his actions nothing more than simple instinct. Spurred on by the madness growing inside him. Everything seeming like it was *someone else* doing the moving, and he was standing just a little distance away, watching it all. Watching his body dash at the Home Guardsman. Watched the man panic, drop the cornbread, and make for his horse. For his gunbelt draped over the saddle. Micah's body tackling the Home Guardsman to the ground just before he reached it. Then they were rolling around over each other and back again, 'til Micah saw himself roll on top. And reach for the knife tucked inside his belt loop. The Home Guardsman began screaming loud as he could. Bits of cornbread flying from his mouth. And then there was Micah, plunging the knife into his chest. The man gasping, trying to yell some more. Then Micah's powerful hands wrapped around the man's throat. Silencing him. Squeezing tightly until the man stopped breathing altogether.

Then Micah could see himself, hands and knees and arms all covered in blood. And his body froze for a while at the sight of them. 'Til there he was dragging the man's body to the river. Rolling it in. Watching himself watch the current take the man's body a few feet downstream. Before sinking out of sight. Then he was wrapping up his satchel and the gunbelt, and riding off on the Home Guardsman's horse fast as he could. Whatever was moving his body doing the holding on to the reins, and him just along for the ride. And they rode fast up the bank of the river, leaving the terrifying remains of those few moments. Leaving everything he cared for, quickly and completely behind. Leaving. Like it didn't matter none anyway. 'Cause *she done changed her mine.*

MARY
RICHMOND
JANUARY 1, 1863

She'd hardly ever spent much time in the kitchen before, not even on holidays or dinner parties, and especially not on the rest of the days of the year, when she was plenty busy with all manner of work to do in the dress shop or just to pass the time with Justinia. But this was something different altogether, since the Misses decided to close the dress shop for a whole week on accounta her brother and his family being here. And Juss was forced to spend most all her time with her cousin Ashleigh, who not Mary or Cora, or Juss most of all, could much stand for more than a few minutes at a time.

That chil's what Miss Juss was fixin' on bein' if *you* never come along, Cora said after about three days of Ashleigh.

And Mary couldn't help but laugh a little to hear it, one of those little bits of kindness Cora'd been throwing her way sometimes at night when it was the two of them sleeping in her room. Of course, those little bits of kindness only ever came at night, with the candle blown out, and just about the time Mary was ready to start crying about what'd happened on Christmas Eve. The resta the day Cora was her old self, a chubby old bitta meanness with the wrinkles collecting along her cheeks and chin like they were conspirin' to make her face into a permanent sorta scowl. And every time Cora mentioned the man she was gonna run off with way back when, then said *like your'n,* like both her and Mary's man were the same sorta man, and both her and Mary's situations were the same sorta situations, well then . . . Mary spent an hour at least crying herself to sleep, thinking about how her face was gonna soon enough take on that same permanent sorta scowl.

So by the time the New Year came around and the Misses's brother and his family were just another day from traveling back home, Mary couldn't help but feel relieved. She'd have her room back to herself, have Juss back to herself, and her work most of all, to help someday push these terrible memories back down inside enough 'til one day it'd all be just another set of shadows. But there were still these two days to get through, even more so now, now that she'd picked up Mista Kittredge's paper he left in the library, where she was dusting just the day before, wanting something to do, and glanced through it until she came upon the notice that terrified her and gave her hope all at once:

> **REWARD: $1000 Gold!** For the safe return of Micah, a slave, run off from Richmond on 24 Dec. Dark brown skin, square broad shoulders, five feet eleven inches tall, strongly built. Some whipping scars on back and traveling with tools. Well spoke. Left handed. Reward will be paid only if returned in good condition. Contact: J. M. Longley, Longley Timber and Construction Co., Proprietor. Richmond, Va.

And it was the last part of that notice that she liked the most—*Reward will be paid only if returned in good condition.* Micah wasn't likely to go easy, she knew. He wasn't about to let some slave-catcher throw a rope around him and prop him on the back of a horse and ride him back to Richmond. But at least that slave-catcher wouldn't shoot him or whip him anymore, not with a thousand dollars gold being offered. It was at least twice as much as she'd ever seen offered for a runaway, and there was that odd sense of pride attached to it, to know that he was that valuable, her man . . . well, once her man.

She told Cora that night about the notice, forgetting to wrap it in the usual lies, like she heard such-and-such at the dress shop, or the Mista said this, but instead just coming straight out and saying that she'd read it in the newspaper. But Cora didn't get mad at Mary the way she used to when she was stealing lessons from Miss Randall or standing too long around the bookshelves she was supposed to be dusting.

Instead she just let out a frustrated laugh, like she'd done her best to learn Mary some sense and a merciful Lord wouldn't hold it against her for how she'd turned out. But then after a little while in the silence, Cora'd said another one of those little sideways kinda compliments she'd been paying Mary every now and again in their week together.

'Magine what that reward a'been if you'da gone wit' him, she said. And then let out a whistling sorta *whooo,* thinking about so much money.

And Mary went to sleep that night thinking if she woulda been worth a thousand dollars too, even though she was a woman. Of course, that only made her dream about Micah all the more that night and do nothing but think of him all the New Year's Day, one minute thinking maybe he'd let himself get caught if it meant coming back here to see her, then the next minute thinking he'd get killed by some slave-catcher or the Boys in Gray or the Yankee Army even, and she'd never see him again. And the hoping had a tough time trying to find its way through all those sad possibilities.

By the time the New Year's dinner was ready to be served, Mary propped herself on a stool over on the wall not far from the oven, figuring that watching Ginny do her work, and watching Mabel and Cora and Bessie doing the serving, would help take her mind off of Micah. None of them had mentioned Micah since Christmas morning, but she could tell they all knew what their plans had been. And it was strange the effect it had on them, like Ginny and Mabel and Bessie were almost her friends now, like they'd been softened a little to hear of her loss and didn't look to poke their finger into the wound the way they woulda before, like somehow losing a love like that was something they could all relate to.

And when Mary asked Ginny what she could do to help, Ginny didn't snap at her and tell her it was *her* kitchen, but just told her to sit over by the stove where it was warm and she'd let her know if something came up. So Mary watched quietly as Ginny took one dish after another out of the oven, always complaining about how this wasn't gonna taste the same without enough butter, or how could she make this dish without any vegetables and such. Mary just nodded her head at Ginny the first few times she turned to her and complained how the war was getting in the way of her cooking, but then mentioned that it was the same for them in the dress shop. Ginny thought about it for a moment, and Mary worried that it might turn Ginny against her again, not wanting to go back to her room and have to be alone. But then Ginny musta figured trying to make a dress without silk was about the same as making a cake without sugar, and that was all right with her then. Then Ginny let Mary help with some of the little things, like putting out all the serving dishes on the counter before Ginny filled them, or holding the gravy bowl while Ginny scraped the last of the drippings into it.

Bessie was quiet as ever, but Cora and Mabel seemed to be having more and more fun as the night went along. It wasn't until they served the sugarless cake for dessert that Mary understood why. Mrs. Kittredge asked for Ginny to come out and enjoy a small toast with them to celebrate the meal, and while she was out of the kitchen, Mabel poured some of Mista Kittredge's claret into an already-used glass, then looked at Cora, who held out her glass to be filled, then looked over at Mary with wide eyes asking if she wanted some too. Mary just shook her head, and Mabel and Cora swallowed that one down, and then each took a little more before Mabel poured the rest of it into the crystal decanter and handed it to Cora.

Boy, they sure drinkin' lotsa wine tonight, Mabel said to Cora with a nod into the dining room. And Cora laughed like Mary'd never seen her do more than once or twice in all the years she'd known her.

Then Cora smoothed down her apron and walked back into the dining room. Mabel looked over at Mary and made a pretend frown.

Aww cheer up, Mary. Donchu know this here's our 'Mancipatin' Day!? Mista Lincoln done said we all free! Dinchu know that?

And she laughed the way Cora had before, more from sadness than actual joy, and went back into the dining room herself.

There was the usual talk in the darkness of her room that night, and Mary grew a little sad when she realized that it would be the last night with Cora and probably the last time they ever spoke to each other for this long, with this much kindness. And hearing Cora talk about her man from back almost thirty years ago, she realized that this was what Cora could hold on to just to survive. Most of the year she spent closed up and mean and forging that scowl ever deeper into her face, but then there might be a few dirty glasses of wine on New Year's or a piece of half-eaten cake on one of the Kittredges' birthdays, or the chance to relive some of those memories from all the way back for a few moments in the safety of the darkness.

And Mary, feeling closer to Cora than ever, brought up the notice in the paper from the day before, hoping Cora might be of a mind to tell her it was worthwhile hoping Micah'd come back.

He ain' th'sorta man like to give up wit'out a fight, Cora said.

I know, Mary answered. I just thought that maybe, once they caught up to him and weren't gonna shoot him, maybe he'd figure it was worth coming back so . . . so he could see me again.

Now why he gonna go an' do that when he know 'bout how you changed yo' mine on goin' wit' him?

The words were a jolt to Mary.

You told me he thought you were me right to th'end, she said in a voice above a whisper now. You told me you didn't say anything to him, just shooed him off an' ran back to the house.

And Cora was silent.

What did you say to him that night? Mary asked.

Nothin'.

So why would he think I changed my mind? He saw Mista Longley there by th'door. Why would he—

'Cause he come back th'next night lookin' fo' you, afta you gone up wit' Miss Juss, Cora said, a little stern but still like it was a confession. That's when I told him 'bout you changin' yo' mine.

And she wanted to yell at Cora then, wanted to demand that she somehow fix this thing that she knew was beyond repair. Even if Micah did get caught, even if he was brought back here, there'd be no detours in the wagon to the front of the shop and lifting his hat to tell her he loved her. There'd be no kisses behind the store or little notes passed in secret.

Why would you do that? Mary said. Why didn't you tell me about that?

And Cora's explanation was all the same sortsa things she'd been saying to Mary all along, her recipe for how to live life closed up tight, every day building that scowl on her face, looking forward to the next dirty glass of wine or half-eaten piece of cake or the memories in the tiny doses they could be taken. None of it interested Mary, though, and she said nothing more to her through that whole night or even the next morning, preferring to be an island once again, than to have Cora for a confidante.

MICAH
CHARLOTTESVILLE
JANUARY 1, 1863

You're all in a daze again. The way you've been most of the time since you left Mary's window. That horse from the man you killed did all the riding. All the figuring out where to go, it seems. He rode you far and fast out of there. Like he wanted to get out of Richmond more than you did. Like he wasn't leaving anything behind the way you were.

You rode all that day, rested at night for a while. Rode some more that night and all the next day. It went like that for three days 'til you reached the turn in the river. The place you and Mary were gonna leave the boat, and head northwest to the Blue Ridge. You came to life for long enough to chase that old horse off. Didn't kill him for a few meals' worth of meat. He'd done you too good for that. Plus you got a soft spot for things that live only to serve their masters.

So you walked the rest of the way from that turn in the river. Only it wasn't straight to the Blue Ridge. No, you were headed more north somehow. Like it was that horse still carrying you there, only it was your own feet this time. You knew the way. You'd been all around these roads with him before. You knew the way to his house as much as you knew the line of Mary's cheek. Or the shimmer of her eyes. And you were thinking on Mary some of the time. Wondering why God brought her into your world only to take her away. It only stirred up more of that anger. Fed the daze. And you walked along country roads in the broad light of day. Not caring if anyone came by. Ready to take that Home Guard's pistol and put a bullet in the first white man that looked you in the eye. Those were the thoughts you sometimes had. But mostly it was just mindless walking. Like a broken-down nag with blinders on. Not so much you moving your feet as something, someone, else.

Whatever that something or someone is, it brought you here. Beside the familiar stable where you used to feed and water his horse. You can tell straight off by the look of things that he's still here. Place doesn't look abandoned, just neglected. Like a shit carpenter lives here. Making his excuses to himself about why the place looks like it does.

It's a while, maybe six eight ten hours that you wait. Hard to tell about something that matters so little as time. All day passes anyhow, and then it's dark again. You know it must be cold 'cause you can see your breath. You should be hungry 'cause you can't recall eating that day. But you don't feel either thing. 'Til sometime in the dark come the squeaking wheels. And he's home. You can hear him inside the broken-down stable. Unhooking the carriage. Cussin' the broken-down horse for needing water and hay. He walks out to the well, and you can hear him breaking the thin layer of ice on the water line. Drops the bucket onto it three four five times. When he comes back to the stable, cussin' at the water he's spilling out of the buckets he's holding, you know this is why you came here. This is the moment.

Water's over there, Tom. You carry your own buckets.

Only then do you realize another man is riding up to the stable. When you see who it is, you can feel a strange half-smile form on your face. He pours his buckets into the trough and hands them over. Starts pitching some hay into the pen. It's a few minutes before they're both in there together, and you get ready to act again.

Albert's stoppin' t'get the dogs.

He's bringin' 'em here?

Three miles closer'n our place. If we headin' inta the Blue Ridge, save us an hour in the mornin'.

And that strange half-smile returns. One perfect thing in all this mess. The three of 'em all together, like you couldn'ta planned it. You wait until they're inside, walk up to the back window. Look inside through the caked-on dirt. You see them sitting on opposite ends of the fire in the front room. Passing the jug back and forth, smoking their cigars. Fat country squires. Talking about where they're going in the morning.

Albert wadn't too happy you brung me in on 'is one, I guess.

Needed some convincin'.

Dunno why he had t'go all th'way t'Richmon'.

How th'dogs gonna know the scent if we ain't got a piece o' his clothes?

I gotta old shirt a'his right in th'room there.

Tom laughs.

That thing's almost two years old. How ya 'spect the dogs t'pick up a scent from that?

All right, all right.

You know how he hates to look like a fool. But there's no punching his way outta this one. Not with Tom.

But I tell ya, Tom, you boys won' regret takin' me in wicha for partner. I know'm, an' I tell ya he's comin' this way up th'Blue Ridge.

He's 'bout as smart a nigga as I ever know'd. He's goin' up th'Blue Ridge all th'way t'them Yankees up in Pennsylvania.

You smile a little now, and it's a strange feeling. He does know you after all. You come out of the haze for a minute. Can feel the cold for the first time. Look around the place where you spent seven years of your life. But looking around only makes you madder. Thinking now about the time that's been taken from you. The haze returning now. And it seems forever before Albert arrives with the dogs.

They're barking like crazy, pulling him in your direction. You get the pistol out of the holster, keep the ax in your left hand for the dogs. But he stuffs them in the stable. Tells them to shut up. Then it's the three of them together again, drinking from the jug, smoking cigars. Talking about how they're gonna hunt you down tomorrow morning. How the thousand dollars gold is just a bonus. How they'd do it just to put a few more stripes across your uppity shoulders. And you smile. A thousand dollars gold. Making for that same strange kinda pride you felt gettin' sold in the first place. But there's a different kinda reward these fellas got coming. One perfect thing. In all this mess.

Tom's the first to step outside. Gotta do his business, the whole thing, so he can't just lean off the end of the porch. Walks back to the outhouse with cigar in hand. And it's easy enough to be there waiting for him when he comes out. Your knife does the job of keeping him quiet right off. Slash across the throat, then finish the job with the ax. Stuff him back inside the outhouse. Stand alongside it, your heart settling again now. Waitin' to see who'll come looking for him.

Twenty minutes later it's his brother calling out from the back door. Starts walking over to the outhouse and stops. Maybe thinks about getting the dogs, from the look on his face. Then shakes his head like he can't be bothered. Cusses his brother and stomps his way straight toward you. Doesn't seem to notice the puddle of red you tried to cover up with fresh snow. Just goes right on and opens the door. It's not as clean now, the way he yells before you can make him quiet. Two, maybe three good shouts before the job is finished. Dogs start barkin' a storm now.

And then it's the reason you came here in the first place. He's out the back door with the shotgun in his hands, stumbling and loading it as he goes. Calling for Albert and Tom. Who won't be answering him back anytime soon. You got the pistol to take care of things now. Let go with two shots straight off. And he's on the ground, rolling over to his side, shotgun knocked from his hands. 'Til all that's left is to stand over him and watch his face. That strange half-smile you can't hold back now. Him with that look on his face. Trying to figure out how you got the best of him after all.

You a dead nigga now . . . shot a white man. He says.

For his last words in this life.

And you just keep smiling. Watch him struggle to say something more. But he can't summon the breath for it, the life draining fast from his body. You could make it faster with another shot, but this seems about right.

And the haze starts lifting again. You can hear the dogs howling. Decide it's their time, too, with how many folks like you they hunted down. Three shots take care of them. And it's quiet again. Across the way, you can see a light on in the front room. Hinkley's up. Probably pissing himself, figuring his neighbor and his friends are shooting at fence posts again. Wouldn't dare come outside, you figure.

So then it's just the matter of dragging all the bodies into the outhouse. Covering the blood best as you can. Taking what food's there in the house. The frying pan, too. And the shotgun with two dozen rounds.

Albert Embry's horse looks the best of the three. So you pack your things onto him and set off. Pull the other two horses behind you. Not racing now, like on the Home Guardsman's horse. But easy. Like nothing matters much. Deep into the woods you let the other two horses go. And then it's on to the Blue Ridge. Only now it's you making your own way. No something or someone else doing the riding. No haze, no fog. Only memories.

Clarity

PART FOUR

13 *Emancipation Days*

MARCELLA

STAFFORD HEIGHTS, VIRGINIA

JANUARY 1, 1863

It's another amputation, maybe the third or fourth you've assisted in during just that morning alone. For Dr. Wyler it's maybe his tenth, and you marvel at how he manages it, a man pushing sixty and with the worn face to prove it. But there he is, asking you for the hacksaw again, this time to take a leg, which will certainly be more gruesome than the arms you've seen cut on this shift so far. None of the wounded have faces anymore. They just keep pouring in, carried to the operating tables by exhausted orderlies, and then it's bandage this shoulder, remove this piece of shrapnel, stitch this leg, or just cut it off entirely. They're lined up row by row now, those waiting for an operation, those already operated upon, those who have died and haven't been taken away yet. Be ready with the bandages, the Doctor says, looking intently at you as he cuts away what's left of the patient's trouser leg and pours some water over the wound. Then he starts to cutting, and it's the nauseating sound of him sawing at flesh the way a carpenter cuts a piece of wood, and you apply the first of the bandages, holding it there until it's saturated with blood, then grab another, and then a third. He's at the bone now, but the patient starts to stir. He's waking up, and you rush over to the head of the table, taking the chloroform-coated rag and pressing it against his mouth and nose again, calling out for one of the greenhorns nearby to soak up the blood, as the Doctor keeps sawing . . . slower now . . . breathing heavily himself, then stopping altogether before his eyes close and he drops to the ground. And you hold the patient down best as you can, considering how there isn't but a drop or two of chloroform on that cloth and the ether is long gone by now. But the patient's still moving, and the chloroform rag drops to the ground. You yell at the greenhorn to take your place and hold the patient still . . . then you pick up the saw . . . beginning to move it back and forth, wanting to faint just like the Doctor did, from the chloroform and the fatigue and the sickening sensation of saw grinding through bone, made even worse when you're the one doing the grinding . . . but you keep sawing, feeling like you're cutting through rock . . . and the greenhorn is wrestling with the patient, who's waking up more and more . . . and it's no longer a straight line you're cutting back and forth . . . with the screeching sound of the bone being cut . . . and the Doctor's awake on the ground now, yelling at you to keep the damn saw straight, but it's screeching louder still until the patient breaks free of the greenhorn's grasp and bolts upright at the waist, glaring at you with eyes that shout WHY ARE YOU DOING THIS TO ME?!

She wakes up in a shiver, her heart racing and her hands wrapped one around another, gripping a piece of the blanket that's been gathered in a bunch like the handle of a saw. Her eyes try to take in what light can be offered in this predawn waking moment, but it's nothing more than the trickle of moonlight through the window and the flicker of the oil lamp in the hallway glowing faintly around the seams of the door. So she lies silently in her cot until there is enough light from outside to suggest that dawn will soon be here. And comforted by it somewhat, she pushes herself up, taking her shoes and her coat, then navigates the maze of cots, most all of them occupied, until finally she is at the door. It's then just a matter of pulling it open deftly enough to minimize the creak of the hinges, and she is safely out into the hallway, where the lamp offers a comfort of light and warmth far beyond what its tiny flame would otherwise seem to yield. And she lingers beneath it, leaning up against the wall, even after she has put on her shoes and coat, even after those too-familiar images of not long ago can be placed firmly in the past, and the realm of dreams.

Ethan is always up early, with first light most days. He says it's from being in the army, and being a fisherman before that, and even back to working in the stables of the . . . *What was the name of that aristocratic family back in Ireland?* she thinks, *back in th'Old Country?* And then she smiles to think of the way he says it, like it's a long-lost love he'd left behind . . . aahhh the Old Country. *Why don't I ever think of España that way?* she thinks. *Only Abuela would I ever think of in that way, and I spent as much time in España as he spent in Ireland . . . maybe because we never suffered from The Hunger.* And she laughs to herself a little now to think of the funny way he has of calling things—The Hunger, the Father, the Old Country, the Penance, and of course, Mam and Da and Aunt Em and me brudder Seanny, and dear Aislinn rest her soul . . . And she starts to amuse herself now by forming sentences from the words and phrases that have warmed her own heart in these past few weeks, imagining him saying *Back in th'Old Country, before The Hunger, when it was just me and Da and Mam and Aunt Em and me brudder Seanny and dear Aislinn rest her soul, I once told a lie and had to go to the Father for the Penance, and sure didn't he tell me t'say two Hail Marys and t'ree Ahhr Fahthers . . .*

And now she laughs loud enough to be aware that she could be heard if there were anyone else in the hallway. But there's no one, of course. It's still well before five, and aside from the few nurses standing night shift in the wards, and the guards outside, there will be no one stirring for another hour at least. She walks to the end of the hallway, admiring as always the elaborate design of the woodwork, thinking about what a nice place this must have been before it was turned into a hospital. *Before it became haunted,* she thinks. Ethan said he'd heard a rumor that this was the place where General Lee once courted his wife. *Well, they're welcome to have it back.*

She could go and find Ethan in the orderlies' room, where he's packed in every bit as tight as the nurses are in theirs, only with plenty more snoring and far worse smells, from what she's heard. But even if he is awake, lying there in the cot right beside the door, the one the men insist he take because he's always up before them, she'd rather let him at least rest his leg for a while longer. And she'll see him soon enough besides, at the morning service—the one to celebrate the momentousness of this day.

What will Mrs. Carlisle and Catherine be doing today? she thinks. *The Ladies Abolition Society will be in all its glory.* But still, she'd rather be here. For now.

She walks into one of the wards, the beautiful dining room that must have held some grand parties in the days before the war, and there is Kerry, fighting to keep herself awake so late in her shift.

"Good morning, Kerry," Marcella whispers. But it's loud enough to wake her from a half slumber in a start.

"Good mahrnin! . . . aahh fer Chroistsakes, Mahrcella—I t'ought you were Nurse Av'ry," Kerry says, and the lilt of her brogue is enough to make Marcella more comfortable in an instant. "What're ya doin' here—it's still an hour before I'm t'be relieved. And not by you, as I recahll."

"I couldn't sleep," Marcella replies, and sits in the chair beside Kerry, who was once a greenhorn, not four weeks ago, but has the sort of confidence of a woman who's done plenty of nursing without the formality of being called a nurse.

"Care for some company?" Marcella asks, knowing better than to volunteer to take the rest of her watch, something that would be most frowned upon by the Nurse Averys of the world.

"Aahhh, Mahrcella, sure yer an angel—and how's yer man Ethan?"

HE HAD STAYED IN THE only way he seemed to know how, not off on the fringes of the encampment with the rest of the press corps in warm, whiskey-filled cabins, but in the middle of it all, volunteering as an orderly right there in the hospital. The nightmares had grown more frequent for her as the exhaustion of those early days after the battle abated enough to allow such a thing as dreams, but each morning there he was, unharmed and wearing the brave exterior of a smile despite all that had been lost.

One late afternoon some days after the battle, he walked her out to the bluff along the river, playfully telling her to cover her eyes as he led her by the arm, and only when she opened them did she realize that it was Christmas Eve. He would later explain, when greatly pressed, that he had used the glass from his remaining photographic plates, chiseling at them with a nail to create the long shards, then affixing them to white thread and hanging them carefully from the branches of the evergreen shrub. The ribbons were torn from red and white cloth one of the supply sergeants had liberated from Fredericksburg before they were chased back across the river. And the star was formed of branches he had woven together and affixed on top, accentuating it with shards of the glass as well. All of it, shimmering in the fading light of sunset and nestled in a thin blanket of snow, was the closest thing to Christmas she could imagine in such a haunted place as this.

Down below them the campfires were soon lit. The entire army was safely back across the river by then, and what remained of their spirits was poured into bittersweet strains of *God rest ye merry gentlemen, let nothing you dismay* and the like. And he lit the fire he had arranged, as they sat on the chairs he had set up beside the tree, sipping the watered-down coffee made more tolerable by the sugar he had somehow bartered for along with the cloth for the ribbons. And she knew then that she was stuck, that there'd be no escaping this love unscathed–short of yielding to it. Only somehow she didn't seem to mind.

But there's something different on this New Year's Day, and it's only in the late afternoon, while walking with Ethan along the rise beside the river, that they understand the magnitude of it. Every January 1 for the last eight or so, she had welcomed the New Year at Mrs. Carlisle's, where they would toast to the coming year, *and may it bring an end to this abomination called slavery,* Mrs. Carlisle would say. And now, with Lincoln's Emancipation Proclamation actually taking effect, the hopes of such a toast seemed real. Still, all along the river was the evidence of what a hollow document it was, freeing the slaves in the states of what seemed more and more like a foreign power–"like Ol' Bobby Lee across the river isn't going to have something to say about that," Ethan says more candidly than usual. And when he doesn't try to offer her a more optimistic outlook on the chances of Union victory, their walk turns silent but for the sound of scattered regiments preparing for the inevitable retreat back to Washington. She can tell that his thoughts return to the death of his friend Finny and so many more, and seeing the army ready to skulk away after yet another defeat is perhaps the worst sort of medicine of all.

"Let's go back to the hospital," she says. "It's getting colder, I think."

And he looks at her for a moment with the same frustration she saw the night she first met him at the gallery, a distant sort of gaze that doesn't end at her eyes but drifts on through into the illimitable distance.

"It's just difficult to see all the loss," he begins, as if she had said something else entirely just seconds before. "All the loss with nothing to show for it—like there ought t'be some sort of reckoning, like Finny said—some sort of balancing it all out."

She doesn't have the words of comfort for him, just an arm to slip inside his, as they begin to walk back along a slightly different path, farther away from the river this time.

"It did bring *us* together," she finally says after a while.

And he turns to her with the signs of a smile he struggles to hold back, becoming mischievous in the twist of that single moment.

"So I suppose I'll have to speak to Mrs. Carlisle when we return to New York," he says.

"About what?"

"Well, from all you've told me, I don't imagine your father would be the one to offer permission."

And now she knows precisely where he is headed, though true to form for the two of them, she will not swoon the way her sister might or most women would.

"Permission for what?"

"Well, to marry you . . . that is, if the dowry is acceptable," he says.

"*I* am the only one who can grant *permission* for that," she says, pulling her arm from his and jokingly bracing her fists along her hips.

What follows is a *negotiation* of sorts, her telling him that she is sure she will be a terrible cook and housekeeper, but will not employ servants in her house all the same, and *whichever* man she *chooses* to marry will just have to accept that. He replies that he will still fish as much as once or twice a week and whichever woman he marries must limit her complaints about the smell to the time between his return from such excursions and his ensuing bath. And there is plenty of *Oh, is that so?* and *Well, I will* . . . thrown about amidst the building laughter, until they have seemed to whittle down their future lifetime together—with these as-yet-to-be-determined spouses—to such essential details as his future wife accompanying him to one baseball game for every time he took her to the ballet or the opera . . . or her future husband accepting the fact that she now intended to turn her attentions to the cause of women's suffrage and how there would be meetings every week in the parlor—and so on. Until, just as a deal seems somehow imminent and can be sealed with a kiss, once one of them actually proposes, she makes one more demand, framing it with such sincerity that there is no counterpoint being offered.

"I want to get married here and not in New York," she says. "I don't think my family would come to the wedding, and quite honestly, I don't wish to give them the opportunity to decline . . . I . . ."

"I think Father Corby would do it," he interjects, mentioning one of the Chaplains of the Irish Brigade, and bringing the smile back to her face. "I think my Mam and Aunt Em'd keel over on the spot if it wasn't a Father that married us . . . myself and the future wife, that is."

She smiles and has to agree with him.

"I think my mother might, too," she says, and the negotiations seemingly draw to a close. "Now, if only there was *such* a man . . ."

"You know . . . I believe I'd be willing to give it a go."

She steps back from him and looks him up and down, then curls one side of her mouth slightly and shrugs her shoulders a little before responding.

"Well—I *suppose* I would grant you permission . . ."

And finally the kiss to seal it—that which has seemed inevitable since the day they found each other again. The cold seems less of a foe than before, and they change their path now, walking to the edge of the fields perhaps a mile behind the hospital, strolling slowly, silently, with her arm draped inside his and her hand slipped inside his coat pocket. She knows it won't always be like this. *How could it possibly?* But she had never imagined it could come so easily, or that she would surrender so readily.

No, surrender's not the word for this, she thinks, *this is more like an admission. Perhaps the most mature thing I have ever done. Nothing little girlish about this, no tantrum against the world—no blame, no refusal to fall, to be vulnerable. What joy just to consent to these gifts.*

And she looks up at him again with sentimental eyes that must seem foreign to Ethan, and wordlessly wonders for the first time how she has merited such a fate—until her thoughts are interrupted by the far-off strains of song from the edge of the field. They walk toward them as if by instinct and soon can make out the words, sung with the collective mournful voice that seems the perfect accompaniment to this place, to this day, singing of all that has been lost and gained too:

We've come a long way, Lord, a mighty long way
We've borne our burdens in the heat of the day
But we know the Lord has made the way
We've come a long way, Lord, a mighty long way

There, perhaps thirty yards away from them now, is a small encampment of what must be slaves from Fredericksburg itself, *former* slaves now that it is the first day of a New Year of hope and now that they have crossed over the river to stake their claim to freedom. And Marcella cannot help but cry at the sight as she and Ethan stand in silence, watching and listening.

"Oh, if only Mrs. Carlisle and Catherine could be here to see this," she says. And seeing the smile on Ethan's face, she pulls his arm tighter and places her free hand against it.

"How's *that* for something to show for it all?" she says.

And he allows himself an even broader smile.

"I believe that will do."

That night, as she watches over the dimly lit recovery room while everyone but sentries and sinners are asleep for miles around, she finds time to write for the first time in all these harrowing weeks.

Abuela,

I will always recall the morning you told me that the happiest years of your life were the ones near the end, when you could live only for yourself–no Abuelo, no Papa or any little ones to worry about. And it has been my intent to live my life in just that way, as much and as long as it was possible. But that is done now. I cannot undo the last two months with Ethan—nor would I want to. I have fallen as I never imagined possible—yet I am made all the better for it, stronger, more hopeful, thankful for the smallest of treasures.

I find contentment in knowing that there is nothing of the juvenile in what I feel for him (and what he expresses to me). It is not a matter of people once incomplete now becoming completed. Perhaps this is where you and Abuelo went wrong, where Mama and Papa went wrong—seeking completeness when we can only ever make each other better, more joyful, more grateful—but never complete. I intend to go right on bothering him as much as he bothers me, each of us disturbing the laissez-faire right out of the other so long as there is breath to form the words and heart enough between us to carry on. And I will love him too, with all the heart that such a man merits. And we will so disturb each other and love each other, and work for what justice may yet be possible in this world, for all the years it will have us.

Oh dearest Abuela, at last I allow myself to hope for such a great gift as this—to never again be forced to live *only for myself.*

MICAH
BLUE RIDGE MOUNTAINS
WINTER 1863

The night was the hardest time. He was haunted every day by the faces of the four men he'd killed. But when he closed his eyes at night it was Mary's face he saw. As if she'd seen everything he'd done since he left. Like she'd just changed her mind about running off, but he'd changed his mind about what kind of man he was altogether. The sorrow in her expression, every night he saw her, told him how far away he was from her. More than just miles could ever accomplish. Like he'd betrayed her.

The morning after leaving Dunmore's house began an endless stream of days. Blended together in anonymity. Up before first light, like he always was. Riding Albert Embry's horse now. Still riding the horse of a man he'd killed, with guilt his constant companion.

The horse would graze on whatever it could find, and Micah would hunt some. Come back with mostly nothing. Then it was riding all day, dismounting for long stretches to lead the horse through the most difficult parts along the jagged spine of the Blue Ridge. Some days they might cover eight ten twelve miles. Others it might be just two. And every afternoon, long before the sun disappeared over the western ridge of the mountains, he'd search for a cave. Some indentation in the mountains where he could build a small fire, not be worried it'd be seen for miles around.

Most nights he was forced to scrape out a place to sleep in a bed of snow covered over with pine branches. Some nights he was warmed by a fire. Every night he was haunted by memories. And he gauged his bearings by remembering the words to a song the slaves used to sing in the rice fields when he was a boy. *Follow the Drinking Gourd,* they sang. A coded name for what his Daddy said was the Big Dipper. Its end star was the North Star. Pointing the way to freedom. He could remember the first lines of it, and would repeat them over in his head from time to time. *When the sun come back, When the firs' quail call, then the time is come, Follow the Drinking Gourd . . .*

And in the aching solitude he felt at night, he'd often find a clearing and look up into the sky. Try to hear those childhood voices again. And the hopeful strains from the rice paddies of Carolina. 'Til all was inevitably silent, and he'd pick up a tree branch and bury one end of it in the snow. Angle the upper end toward his guide. Like the mountains themselves weren't pointing the way.

It wasn't long before he *had* to kill Albert Embry's horse. It wasn't about any hatred he still had inside for the man. Or even because he was near starving himself. But the horse was dying a little each day. Even though he'd stopped riding him altogether days ago. Even though he carried all the tools and his blanket on his own back. And left the saddle buried in the snow-covered brush miles back. He tried pulling him along for a whole day, trying to get him to keep up. But he was starving even more than Micah was. So he had to kill him. So he didn't have to suffer anymore. The horse.

Then, in a late afternoon a few days after the kill, he came upon what looked like the tallest peak in the whole world. He was stronger now, thanks to the horsemeat. So he decided to climb the peak. There was a wooden sign set near the top, *Stony Man Mountain, approx. 4000 ft.* And he figured it was as good a place as any to have it out with God. Once and for all. 'Cause God's gotta answer for putting Mary in this world. Making something that precious in the first place. Then leaving her locked up in fear 'cause of all the mess he'd made in the world to go right alongside everything precious.

Micah figured that he killed four men. Bastards every

one of 'em. At least the last three for sure. And sure he's got to answer for that. Fair enough. But God's got to answer for Mary, he figured. So it was time to have it out. Time to settle the accounts, the way Dunmore used to say when he was of a mind of collecting a debt.

It took more to get to the top than he figured. He was out of breath like he hadn't been since he was hauling Albert Embry's horse behind him. Still, when he got to the top, it was a magnificent scene. To the west was the setting sun, slipping down behind the hills. The way it used to each night back at Dunmore's. Taunting him. And now, for the first time, he could look to the east and see far off into the distance. Imagine Washington, the Yankee capital, out beyond his view. And freedom, whatever that might mean. There he was atop the whole world, as far as he could tell. Wondering what any of it, freedom, killing horses and men, getting killed even, mattered. After all.

He took a piece of paper from the hidden pocket inside his coat. The one he was fixing to give Mary somewhere along these mountains. Sometime when she got tired of the walk. Sometime when she figured it wasn't worth it anymore, maybe. He'd stolen a real pencil from Longley's parlor and wrote the note on something like a real piece of paper. The kind a man uses to write such a thing to a woman. And then it was just him to read it, instead of her. Him to be taunted by his own words then. Reading still, all the same . . .

Through these mountains there's home for you and me, and your smile brings strength inside me to carry you every step of the way. But I'll never have to. Cause God don't let flowers die before the Spring. Cause you're like the prettiest rose, that somehow blossomed on the stem of an oak tree. Cause we're gonna carry each other home.

It practically suffocated him to read it now. Alone as he was, but sad enough that he was looking for more sadness instead of steppin' outside it. That's what made him reach back inside his secret pocket again and pull out the note she gave him. A week before they were supposed to run off.

Knowing you are in the world is knowing that I belong here,
that God did not drop me to the earth as a single tear.
I loves you.

It was the first note she wrote like it was a poem. Like the ones she read in Miss Justinia's books. The kind of words she said he wrote without thinking of making them poetry. Like that's what he was just by nature, a poet. And he read her poem over and over again, there on top of *Stony Man Mountain, approx. 4000 ft.* Remembering back, months before, when she first told him she loved him. The afternoon she referred to in the poem. Back behind the dress shop in the early morning, when he was still building the new storeroom, just a few weeks before they decided to run off together. And how she walked across the field between the house and the store. Looked all around like she always did, seeing if there was anyone watching. Then she walked right up to him. Him setting up his tools beside the lumber pile like always. She stood right in front of him, silent. A smile all over her face like she knew something he didn't. And then she kissed him. Strong enough to let him know it was her idea. Soft enough to remind him there was magic in the world. And she went up the steps to the store before stopping. Turned toward him, playfully. *I loves you,* she said. Then kicked back one foot just a little. Dancing in the half-seconds of stolen moments. And walked inside the shop. With him left to stand there, out in the yard with his tools all about him. And his jaw hung low. Wondering how he'd breathe an all-together breath again. Hard as it seemed to imagine just then, knowing such moments were in this world. And such a woman. Who *loved* him. Loved *him.*

So he sat atop that rock on *Stony Man Mountain, approx. 4000 ft.* And waited until the sky turned through every color until it was just black all around. Waited for an answer. *Waited* for God to tell him it all meant something, the suffering. Waited for him to tell him that he'd see her again. Or tell him just enough to understand a little, just enough to keep going. He waited. Raised his open arms toward the blackened sky, hoping to summon a thing greater than him. A reason to go on.

But still, he felt only the cold, tearing at him now like it hadn't done before. Ever. Mighta been six seven eight at night. Mighta been midnight or later. Didn't matter. Wasn't an answer coming. So he went back down from the peak. No dying horse to even give him the lick of company he needed *so* much just then. Instead, just him. No Mary. No answers. Alone.

Not even God.

BY THE TIME HE REACHED the Potomac River, he'd been gone eight nine ten weeks. Couldn't tell for sure. Never bothered counting days at the start, in the lingering haze. Certainly couldn't figure them out counting backward. Until, not that far in, it didn't matter anyway. As the peaks began dwindling north of *Stony Man Mountain.* Strong from the horsemeat, he'd walk all day long. Partly from the strength, partly not to have so much time to think only of Mary. He'd build a fire at night and eat some more horsemeat. Then, exhausted sleep.

Get up the next day, and eat some more, and walk all day. Like he was a nag, a mule with blinders on. Again.

Not having seen more than a few people in all that time, and those only at a great distance, the contingent at Harper's Ferry seemed like the whole Yankee Army. He dumped the Home Guard's pistol. Strapped the shotgun to his back and took his chances. Walked right up to the sentries up the road from the main bridge across the river. Like he hadn't done a thing wrong. Certainly hadn't killed four white men.

Jesus Mickey, it's a nigger! The first sentry said as soon as he saw him.

In the weeks since he'd left Richmond, there was one thing he'd been happiest to leave behind. It wasn't the work. Climbing the mountains was harder than building chicken coops and fixing barn roofs. It wasn't Longley or any of the other slaves. All of them could be tolerated at least. No. What he'd been happiest to leave behind was the subjugation. Of himself. The need to present himself as less than a man. He'd learned, like every colored man had to learn, how to be non-threatening to the white folks. Everything was Nosuh, Yessuh, Yes'm, No'm. Ignorant. Broken. Tamed. Like a dog lowering its head and tail to a more dominant one. Only it wasn't enough to do it that once, upon meeting, like the dogs did, then go about business. Like the fact had been acknowledged, and that was that.

No.

This subjugation was an *every*day thing. Played out over and over again, even to shit excuses of a man like Dunmore. *Especially* to shit excuses of a man like Dunmore. But for these last eight nine ten weeks that was the one thing he didn't have to do. And it'd just about made the hunger, and the cold so deep inside him he'd forgotten what normal was. Just about made it all worthwhile. Not to have to bow like that. Until now. Again.

Don' shoot, please Suh. I's just a . . . a runaway Suh. He says.

What he learned right off was that just 'cause they were wearing blue uniforms didn't make them any less than what they were first and foremost. More than any nation, religion, anything else. They were *white* men. And they didn't take kindly, runaway or not, to a colored man with a shotgun slung across his back.

No Suh, 'at's jus' for scarin' off bears—maybe do some huntin'. It was enough of an explanation to get him brought to the Lieutenant instead of shot right there.

Got us a runaway, Lieutenant.

A runaway with a shotgun?

That's what we was sayin'—go an figger that!

It didn't take much to slip right back into it. The subjugation of himself. Something carved that deep into everything he was couldn't go away with eight nine ten weeks in the mountains. Wasn't likely to ever go away. So they were properly appeased before long. Confident that he was harmless. Ignorant. One helluva lucky nigger to traipse all the way up the Blue Ridge. Not get shot by Johnny Reb *or* Billy Yank. Not freeze to death. Or starve. Lucky. Couldn't be smart, of course. Just, *lucky*.

But when the Lieutenant dismissed the men, and it was just Micah and him now, he started askin' how he did it. So Micah told him just enough. Told him he'd been coming up the mountains all the way from Carolina. Left a couple of weeks before Christmas. Lied, in case word had made it this far about the dead men he'd left in Virginia. Just in case something as comparatively small as the war could be put aside to find a colored man who'd killed four white men. The Lieutenant brought him over to the giant map stretched over the wooden table. Asked him more questions. And Micah tried pointing out what he thought his route was, acting ignorant. 'Til the show and the story altogether were enough to earn him a hot meal and a pot of coffee. And a tent for the night.

Next morning the Lieutenant set him up with more hot food and coffee. And Micah could feel some of the frozen layers begin to thaw, from the inside out. The Lieutenant brought him back to the big tent from the night before. Only this time, waiting inside, was a Captain. The Lieutenant presented Micah, and the Captain looked him over without saying anything. Looked him up and down. Appraised him.

What's your name, son?

Son. Captain couldn't be more than twenty-five, like Micah. Still. Son.

Micah, Suh.

Ahh, from the Old Testament. Those Rebs often do that. They figure if they name their slaves after Biblical figures, that it makes it all right in the eyes of God.

Captain looked at the Lieutenant like he was conducting a class or something. Then it was more of the same from the night before. Lieutenant asked Micah to point out the route he traveled. Went through the whole thing on the map, playing dumb again. Not that it mattered. The Captain didn't seem to care at all what he had to say. Started talking about his Daddy the preacher up in Connecticut. Talked about what an abomination slavery was. How it was the white man's burden to look out for the inferior races, not enslave them. The Captain spoke with the righteous indignation of a preacher himself. Seemed to have a very clear understanding of the Natural Order of Things.

Let me ask you now, Micah. Did you boil bark and make that Negro soup along the way?

Micah looked at him. Unable to speak. After all that with the map, here he was asking about soup. Lieutenant didn't seem too pleased by the question, either, but had to stand quiet.

Suh?

You know, stripping the white birch bark and boiling it up into one of those primitive Negro soups. The runaways on the Peninsula did it all the time.

Didn't have no pot, Suh. Jus' a fryin' pan.

The Captain seemed very unhappy to hear that answer. *But you would've. If you had a pot, you would've, yes?*

Micah looked over at the Lieutenant, whose eyes seemed to instruct, give the man what he wants. *Yessuh, Cap'n, I s'pose so.*

Mmm-hmm, mmm-hmm. See, that's what many of these Negroes are accustomed to. It's an instinctive thing in them from back in Africa. They're like the Indians that way. Not as cunning, but the same primitive instincts. Best to free all the slaves and put 'em on ships back to Africa. Back in their natural habitat.

From the entirety of his life thus far, it was hard for Micah to imagine hating a man more than he'd hated Dunmore. But he believed, just then, that he could come to feel that way about the Captain, given a little more time. Maybe an hour or so. 'Cept that was the end of the interview. Soup, and such.

No *wonder* they're losin' this war, Micah thought.

Then the Lieutenant gave him another warm meal and some rations to take with him. Made sure he got back the shotgun and all the ammunition that was left. Gave him an extra blanket, walked with him across the pontoon bridge to the other side. Lieutenant told him that they were in Maryland now. Started explaining what waited ahead for him, just like Micah'd told him about what stretched out south of here. Told him how the mountains kept getting smaller and smaller as he kept on north. Told him he could stay off the peaks, walk on the crest along the valley. Nobody up in these parts owned slaves, and no slave-catchers'd make their way past the Union Army. Lieutenant told him he could make Pennsylvania day after next. And that would mean freedom altogether. Said it like it'd mean something to Micah. Then shrugged his shoulders when Micah said nothing. Still, he wished Micah good luck. Turned out to be one good man in a whole army of 'em, after all.

He walked all that day and the next until it was too dark to see three steps in front of him. The mountains were smaller, like the Lieutenant said. The streams were easy to cross in the places he'd told him about. And except for a few farms that looked more like frontier homesteads than something permanent, he didn't see much sign of anyone. On the third day he knew he'd made Pennsylvania. Didn't know where Maryland let off and Pennsylvania picked up. Just knew he was there. And free, like the Lieutenant said. Built himself a big fire that night. Big, like the one on Christmas Eve back at Longley's old place. A free man should have such a fire, he figured. But it wasn't nearly warm enough. Not without Mary. Or Daddy and Momma and Bellie. To see that he'd made it this far. Got himself free, indigo field or not.

'Stead it was just him and the not-warm-enough fire.

And freedom. Mostly empty, after all.

MARCELLA
BROOKLYN
MARCH 23, 1863

There were fifty or sixty people there at least, Ethan's family of course, and some of his friends—Smitty and Violet—and some men who were later introduced as *business* associates of his brother Seanny—and a few people from the neighborhood including Mr. Hadley—and then, as they made their way through the crowd, she saw Catherine and Mrs. Carlisle, and five members of the Ladies Abolition Society and three of their husbands too! . . . and she burst forth to greet all of them, elated somehow, even though she had spent hours since her return with them . . . Catherine and Mrs. Carlisle *of course,* and the other ladies even—and yet still, somehow, she was filled with such great joy that they were here!

Marcella would later shed more than a few tears to hear how the whole thing had been arranged, how Ethan's Mam and Aunt Em had visited Mrs. Carlisle's just the day after she and Ethan had returned so they could start making plans . . . and how Sean—Seanny, as she promised to call him before the evening was through—had insisted upon arranging all the carriages for Mrs. Carlisle and Catherine and the ladies from the Abolition Society . . . and how Uncle Paddy, who she had learned was Aunt Emily's second husband, had arranged for a special ferry just to take them back and forth . . . and the food from the Clinton Hotel . . . and Feeny closing the pub altogether that night, just so he could be here to administer the spirits by way of a tribute to his son who had fallen at Fredericksburg along with all the rest of the lads . . . and the music, a virtual symphony of fiddles and hand drums and even a piano brought into the parlor . . . with voices loud and mostly on key—and oh!—it was as if she'd arrived in a foreign country altogether!

Then in the late evening hours, after the guests had almost all gone home, she was summoned by Mam and Aunt Em to accompany them to the front stoop, where Violet Smythe was already seated. Marcella sat along the ledge of the top step and listened to the clanking of chairs and dishes and glasses inside, where the men, including Sean and Smitty, seemed quite busy.

"What are they doing?" she whispered to Aunt Em.

And Aunt Em laughed a little before answering, "Well of course, they're doin' the cleanin' up!"

She tried to imagine her father and brothers doing anything of the sort, then laughed out loud at the idea.

"What is it dear?" Ethan's Mam asked her.

"It's just . . . well . . . in my father's house the men don't do much cleaning—or anything, really."

"Ah sure, they don't here either," she laughed.

"'Tisn't anything more than the chance to sneak in an extra pint before callin' it an evenin'," Aunt Emily added.

"Cigars and brandy," Marcella said with a smile.

And almost as soon as she'd said these things—allowing herself to be too comfortable amongst these women she was still getting to know after just a few days of living here—she wished she could have the words back.

Catherine had pulled her aside early on and told her that the McOwens had so dearly wanted to invite her family and all her friends to celebrate their marriage, but having no addresses other than Mrs. Carlisle's, they came to call on her first. Mrs. Carlisle had discreetly suggested that a *family* gathering might best wait for a future date, but that there were several dear friends of Marcella's who would no doubt be happy to attend, and Marcella felt more beholden to Mrs. Carlisle than ever before. Still, the disparity in guests from each respective side of this new union had lent itself to a few awkward moments for her. Friends far enough along the periphery of the McOwen side of things had asked Marcella where her family lived in Spain–meaning it in the present tense–and it was only thanks to Ethan or Catherine or Mrs. Carlisle being beside her at each of these occasions, that she had managed to make it through the evening without having to tell anyone that her family had been living just across the East River for going on eleven years, and wouldn't dream of coming to a party such as this, even if she *were* in their good graces.

But here on the front stoop, with the guests all gone, there would be no escaping the full disclosure of things, and it was her own fault for having opened the door to it all. Marcella was unusually reserved after the slip.

"How's that, love?" Ethan's Mam asked.

And Marcella looked at her, hoping for a way to avoid the inevitable.

"You were sayin' cigars an' brandy an'–I wasn't quite followin' ya–did ya want some brandy? I don't know if we've got–"

"Oh no, Mrs. McOwen. It's just that in my father's house, the men would slip off at the end of the evening, too–only into the library for cigars and brandy after the supper, and the women would be left in the parlor."

Then she thought of all that Ethan had said of their time in the Old Country, and how they all had worked for an aristocratic family called the Brodericks. And at that moment her heart sank to think that they might count her as one of that class–until Aunt Emily broke the brief silence.

"Well, it looks like we got the better o' that arrangement then," she said. "At least they do a pretty good job with th'cleanin' up. And it's only fer the cost of a pint."

"Could you imagine that lot drinking brandy?" Violet asked.

And they *all* laughed, Marcella even.

Then almost on cue came Ethan's Uncle Paddy booming out the first line of a song, with the rest of the men inside joining up for the second:

There was a wild colonial boy
Jack Duggan was his name,
He was born and raised in Ireland
In a town called Castlemaine
He was his father's only son
His mother's pride and joy,
And dearly did his parents love
This wild colonial boy.

And the women spoke in a songlike manner of their own.

"Oh Jaysus, there dey go," Aunt Emily said. "Four bleedin' Irishmen—"

"And a bleedin' Scot," Violet added.

"And not a one of 'em who can sing on key," Mam said.

And Marcella, feeling a little more at home with these women now, offered the finishing touch.

"What are the odds of *that*?" she said.

Violet laughed straightaway, but Aunt Emily and Mam looked at each other with wide eyes first before smiling and joining in.

"Ahh, Mahrcella dear," Mam said, touching her knee, "sure it'll be nice to have ya 'round."

"Amen to that!" Aunt Emily added, opening the front door and waiting for a break between verses to call inside to the men, "Mind the neighbors! Sure they've got ears that have to listen to ya, too!"

"And the dogs as well, poor creatures," Violet said.

And they laughed and listened to the men sing the next verse more quietly, though *far* more noticeably off-key, without being able to mask their musical inadequacies now by shouting. The four ladies looked at each other, cringing and shaking their heads.

"Just how important *are* the neighbors to you?" Marcella asked.

And they laughed in unison this time.

"Sure, you'll fit right in here, love," Aunt Emily said.

And on a night she wanted to spend with her husband and not the memory of her grandmother at all, she felt compelled to write just a few words all the same.

Abuela,

More than once tonight I was told about the memory of Ethan's sister Aislinn, rest her soul. Aunt Emily told me that I would've loved her as a dear, dear sister, and my new father-in-law said it was a joy to have a daughter again, and Seanny confessed that he could never forgive himself for her death, but he was glad that Ethan had picked such a woman as me to make the family as complete as it has been since The Hunger. I'm sure it is all the sort of pressure I would have been terrified of just a few months ago, but there is a certain symmetry to it I think now—to have lost my own family so completely, and to find a place so completely waiting to be filled within another. And so, I am an orphan no more.

Ethan
COOPERSTOWN, NEW YORK
JULY 6, 1863

She opens the familiar sheet music for only the second or third time since they've been here, and spreads it out across the display, and he considers it a small miracle that he's somehow stumbled his way up the front steps undetected, to see her there, unfettered by news of the world outside, and looking like the Venus de Milo—if ever the Venus de Milo had long black hair and arms, such arms, with graceful fingers at the end of them to play the piano. And then, with her still not knowing he's there, or choosing not to let on, she places her fingers on the opening chords and plays without hesitation.

She bobbles slightly at the first key change, and he has to smile, thinking of how she'd done the same thing when she played with Mrs. Templeton. But then she backs up and plays over the key change again, and a third time, and then the fourth sounds just right, and she allows herself a little smile while playing on, coasting through three minutes' worth of fondest memories. And he stands there taking in the music, certain that she's aware of his presence the way she exaggerates playing some of the bolder chords, and lifts her hands far off the keys in long draping lines accentuated by downward pointed fingers. So it's more of the dance that it has always been between them, and he's glad the day can at least begin this way, and the world outside can be put off for a few moments more.

Now *that* time sounded perfect, he says once she's finished, and he walks through the partly opened front door.

She turns around on the piano bench and pulls the blanket up from her hips and back over her shoulders, smiling easily at him, confirming that she'd been aware of his presence all along.

I still need to work on that first key change, she says. How was the lake?

Beautiful, but tomorrow I think . . .

And she offers an exaggerated frown at the mention of another day of waking up to find him gone from their bed.

. . . well, *next* time I go, I'll take pictures of the sunrise—and perhaps *Mrs.* McOwen will accompany me for a morning picnic?

She smiles, then asks, a *late* morning picnic?

Well, I s'pose the sun'll just have to wait until Mrs. McOwen is ready to watch it rise, he says, and she smiles her best Cleopatra sort of approval at the handling of such trivial details.

He sits down beside her on the piano bench and she opens the blanket to allow him to slip inside it. His left arm slides around her waist and they share the same long, slow, breathless kiss that has become the morning custom.

Ooh . . . you need a shave, she says, breaking away for just a moment before returning.

And then, as if satisfied that he's made up for his absence that morning, and the effrontery of thinking a flower and a note could serve as a replacement, she pulls her lips from his and stares at him with an interrogating gaze. He knows that the folded newspaper protruding from his pocket is a violation of their agreement, but the outside world seems ever more determined to find its way to Cooperstown, to this house even, and what has seemed an Eden-like interlude compared to the rest of their brief marriage. And she slips her hand down his shoulder and lifts the newspaper slowly, staring at him in an accusing manner.

You just couldn't resist, could you, she says.

And he knows he's got to tell her then.

I passed the Stimsons' store on my way back, he confesses, and Olivia was by the door talking with a few other people—and she called me over.

And she *insisted* you buy a copy of *The Freeman's Journal*! Marcella jokes, but her smile doesn't linger once she sees the more serious look on Ethan's face.

Gettysburg . . . it was more terrible than Fredericksburg . . . than Antietam even. The Rebs've gone back south, it looks, but it was bad.

Oh God, Henry Stimson came by not half an hour ago with a telegram for us, she says. I didn't read it—I didn't think it was . . . it's on the mantel over there.

She's up from the bench and at the mantel, then carrying the small folded paper reluctantly back to him. And as soon as she says it's from Seanny, Ethan knows what it says.

You read it, he says with a nod.

She opens the fold, and soon as her eyes take in the words on the paper, her hand goes involuntarily to cover her mouth. Dropping the hand with the telegram in it down to her side as if wanting to get it away from her sight, she turns her head slightly with saddened eyes reaching out to him.

Ethan, she whispers. Harry's dead . . . Gettysburg . . . the second day.

And as the news hits him, his thoughts seem strangely transported back to Fredericksburg, to the hospital on Stafford Heights, where they fell in love amidst such violently shifting emotions, a tiny oasis of tenderness draped in the misery of every day. Only now it was the reverse, these past six weeks of glorious refuge pierced by the mournful news from far off, the two experiences like photographic negatives, light as dark and dark as light. But it's not a description worth explaining when there is his wife's tender embrace for consolation.

It was Mrs. Carlisle who was primarily responsible for these past glorious weeks, since it was her home they were in after all, and she'd insisted that they'd be doing her a great favor by getting some use of the place for the first time in years. Marcella had taken to it straightaway, delighted by the scenery and the solitude. When they wanted for company, there was Mrs. Carlisle's cousin Olivia Stimson, and her husband, Henry, and stories of the Underground Railroad days. And Ethan enjoyed the place for all these reasons, too.

But it had become something more to him than it was even for Marcella. There were far too many trees, and the afternoons grew far too warm for it to remind him very much of the days back on the Lane. And yet he found these to be most welcome additions. Henry Stimson told him to use the rowboat whenever he pleased, and Ethan would fish sometimes on Lake Otsego for as long as he could stand to be away from Marcella, sometimes for two or three hours even. But mostly they'd take it out midday, drifting with whatever tiny current the wind wanted to create, and he'd sometimes read to her, or she to him. And such moments had stripped away so much of the previous months, allowing them to know each other without the march of history pressing at their backs. For him, it was the refuge of feeling that he could somehow protect her, ensure her happiness, like he'd never been able to do with Aislinn and Mam and Aunt Em.

And when Marcella wrote to Mrs. Carlisle how much they loved the place and how grateful they were for the use of it, Mrs. Carlisle replied with a lengthy letter telling Marcella that it was hers now. It turned out that she had planned to leave it to Marcella all along and leave the New York house to Catherine—her only children, as Mrs. Carlisle described it. And Marcella, much to Ethan's surprise, seemed rather easily convinced that she should not bother to protest the matter.

Then came word of Gettysburg, and a Fourth of July that was spent with nowhere to escape the discussion of the worst carnage the war had yet produced. That evening he brought Aislinn's old Shakespeare book out on the lake with them, but they mostly just drifted and tried not to think of what so many of their friends were going through down in Pennsylvania right then. Until, as if attempting to rally themselves from any manner of gloom, Marcella picked up the book and insisted that they act out a scene. She picked *Romeo and Juliet*, and gushed out the words of the balcony scene with every ounce of juvenile fawning she could muster before passing the book to him for his line. By the end they had turned it into Shakespeare's grandest comedy of all and in the space of those few minutes had restored much of the luster of this place.

But now, amidst the news of Harry, it's as if they both know there'll be no restoration to be found in a mere play. It's later that afternoon, after a visit to the Stimsons' to find out the latest news, that they walk down to the lake, and he silently begins to say goodbye to this place. Marcella is the first to broach the subject of returning home, asking Ethan if he'd like to visit Harry's mother. And he only nods, conceding the inevitable.

We made a good go at it, he says.

And the water's in her eyes as she squeezes his hand more tightly.

You made a wonderful go at it, she says.

And he's confused for a second, before realizing that she meant the lads in the Brigade.

I meant you and me, he says. *We* made a good go at it, you and me, up here, I mean. It was nice . . . it was better than nice . . .

And suddenly he's overtaken by a wave of ineloquence, 'til she laughs and sniffles a little, placing her head inside his shoulder, donning her ever-improving brogue for a reply.

Sure, we've only just *stahrted* t'make a goh've it up here, Mr. McOwen. Or don't you recahll marryin' a woman of *property*?

He recovers his humor amidst the echo of her words and replies, That's why I *married* her of course.

Well then, Squire, she says, knowing how Seanny teased him with that very title, I'll go back t'Brooklyn wit' ya, but only for two weeks. There's plentya work t'be done if we're t'live in this house all th'year 'round.

And he realizes then that this is maybe the greatest thing they do for each other, not the humor or the way they can playfully tease in even tender moments, but the fact that their love always seems to act as a gravitational force, pulling each other back from the edge of great sorrow.

Well then, Misses McOwen, he says, 'tis quite th'hard-drivin' businesswoman y'are. Two weeks it shall be.

MICAH
SUMMER 1863

When the mountains turned into hills somewhere in Pennsylvania, he worried at first. There was no more cover from the small towns along the way as he headed north. Gettysburg, Fairfield, Mechanicsburg. But in each place he saw something that he'd only ever seen once at the rail depot in Charleston. Free colored men. Men who didn't seem worried that the whole Confederate Army wasn't too far away. And even though he kept on goin' north, each of those places made him feel something more like what must have been *free.*

He even ventured into the grand city of Harrisburg. Got some work there building storehouses alongside the rail station. Kept to himself mostly, but did make one friend. First white man he'd ever think to call that. And only 'cause this man Ezekiel called him friend first, the way Quakers did it. First time a white man ever *invited* him into his house. Asked him to supper at his table. Let him stay in the spare room, for all those few weeks. And his Misses, Sarah, even knitted him a blanket with the verse from the Bible. From the Book of Micah itself:

> *They shall beat their swords into plowshares, and their spears into pruning hooks; nation shall not lift up sword against nation, neither shall they learn war anymore.*

And he took that with him as a treasure when the job was up in May. And Micah headed north again. Following the Susquehanna River, which Ezekiel told him would take all manner of turns and twists. But it'd take him all the way to New York. And without Mary. With the blood of four men still staining his memory. He wasn't in such a rush to get anywhere in particular. Long as it was north.

So that was the path he followed. Up the Susquehanna. Free. Not running from anything or anyone. No haze, no fear, no coldness deep in his bones, like the last time he traveled the long, lonely road. And he reminded himself of all that, every time he could feel those memories trying to overtake him. He fished on occasion, hunted some, traveled some, rested some. Free as any man *ever* was.

'Til the river began to slither to the east and then the west and back north. Then side to side again. And south once, even, for the better part of two full days. 'Til there was no outrunning those memories then. 'Til moving forward began to feel like he was doing a penance for the man he'd been. The man who killed four other men. Not thinking any more about how three of them deserved it for sure. Not thinking how the first most likely did, too, Home Guard that he was. Thinking just about how he'd taken four men out like that. Like it was up to him to do God's work. And worst of everything he thought about, on this long lonely road, was how he'd walked up to the top of Stony Man Mountain like he was gonna take on God. Make him accountable for what he done. For what HE done. Like God gotta explain anything. Like Micah wasn't raised by the Momma and Daddy he was, that'd taught him better.

Sometimes he thought of Mary. *Many* times he thought of Mary. Hours every day, at least. But it wasn't the sort of pained yearning it had been along the Blue Ridge. This was the sort of thinking that made him wonder how he could change the man he had become. The man who had killed four men. The man who had challenged God. The man who had gotten so far away from what he always thought himself to be that he wondered if there was enough walking to do on this earth to make up for it.

When the Susquehanna took to getting all twisted around after that. West, then east, then south again, for hours instead of days, this time. He didn't question it. Like it was a test from God. Like all these twists and turns were meant to see if he could accept the challenges he'd been given. And overcome them. He wasn't even following the *Drinking Gourd* anymore. 'Cause this wasn't a slave thing anymore. This wasn't a running-off thing anymore. This wasn't a Mary thing, or a Momma and Daddy and Isabelle thing. This was about Micah gettin' right with Micah. Gettin' right with God. And he'd follow that river for as long as it would take him. Long as God wanted him to. Long as it took for him to turn them swords into plowshares.

He became a decent fisherman and an even better hunter. Grew a beard long past his chin. Fancied himself a pioneer, on better days. And then, just when he felt like he was getting in good with things, he began to run out of Susquehanna. About midway through the summer by then, best as he could tell. The river just kept shrinking as he walked on and on. 'Til it ran into Otsego Lake. At a place called Cooperstown. And that was it. No more Susquehanna for him to follow.

He came upon the town first, thinking maybe it would be just another stopping-off point. But then what was left of the river trickled into as large a lake as he'd seen in some time. And he knew that this was all for now. Still with something left over in the way of being angry with God for not finishing the job. For not making this Susquehanna flow all the way to Canada where he was meant to go. To irrefutable freedom. And the Northern Lights.

And he stayed by the lake through much of the morning. Watching all manner of white men come and go and not bother him at all. Not ask for traveling papers. Most of 'em not even suspicious of him. 'Til one came up in a small fishing boat and pulled it onto the shore. Stepped out of it and took a fishing rod from it and three *big* ones hooked on a line. Proud.

Like he'd done a man's work this mornin' and brought back the supper for a day or two to come besides this one.

And he held them up to Micah, maybe thirty yards away, and smiled like a man would at such a moment. So Micah smiled back at him, nodded his head two three times. Then turned back to the lake, lookin' at what God had done to his byway. But it wasn't more than a few seconds before he could feel the man with the fish staring at him, closing the distance in meaningful steps.

Hello. He said. *I see your fishin' pole there . . . didya have any luck?*

Nosuh. Just got here, act'ally, Suh. Micah said, making sure to be safe.

And the man seemed uncomfortable with Micah's response.

Ethan. He said. And extended his hand.

14 And Not to Yield

Micah

COOPERSTOWN, NEW YORK

SUMMER–FALL 1863

Their friendship began over a discussion on fishing. Just like two men would do. With nothing like slavery or war or even *Yessuh, Nosuh,* to stand in the way. Each of them just a man, straight up. And Micah ate at their house that very first night. Ate the fish Ethan had caught, overcooked something awful by his wife. But still, he told them some of his story about runnin' off. The safe parts.

Mrs. McOwen—Marcella, like she kept insisting—talked for one solid hour about everything she wanted to do to that house. Making it ready for winter first. Fixin' windows and such. Patching that roof some. And such. But then the thing that brought a real smile to her face was talkin' about the porch she wanted built. And Ethan laughed some at first, then a little bit more as it went on. Not in a mean kind of way but like he was wonderin' how old he'd be before he got the half of it done.

I can do that. Micah said, matter-of-factly.

Marcella looked at Ethan, then the two of them back at him. And it didn't take Micah much explaining to them how to build such a porch, before that was that. Room and board plus twelve dollars a week and the set of tools to keep when it was done, Ethan offered. More than Micah ever would've even thought to ask for. More than Longley or Dunmore could get on their *best* days hiring him out. They just offered it like that, straight up. A place to stay and be settled for a while. Cash to walk around with, like a *free* man *should* have. And a chance not to be alone for a while. All that from one overcooked fish supper.

Ethan worked with him most of the time. He wasn't much of carpenter. Said something about how back in Ireland the English had long since cut down most of the trees and brought them back to England. So there wasn't much wood to work with. Then Marcella laughed and said to Micah. *Typical Irishman, he'd blame the rain on the English, if he could.* And Micah smiled at it, though he didn't know much about the English or the Irish. They'd always just been white folks to him. Turned out some of them weren't much better to their own kind than they were to colored folks. And that took some time gettin' used to.

Some days Ethan took pictures of the rich folks over at the hotels along the lake. And sometimes at the Stimsons' general store too, where he was hopin' to start a business. They even used some of his pictures in the newspaper in town. And then there were some days, usually when Marcella was in town, when they both cut out early from everything. Went fishing out on the lake in Henry Stimson's boat. Talked some, fished some. Read some too, since Ethan'd been reading on boats since he was a boy. Only instead of the Bible, which was the only book Micah had ever read, they'd read all manner of other things. Books from men named Shakespeare and Homer and others. But Micah's favorites were Emerson and Thoreau. Men who didn't go for any of this *be happy with your station in life* business he'd got used to hearing from white men. These were men who spoke of being *Self-Reliant,* above all.

Then there were the Stimsons, Olivia and Henry as they insisted upon, too. And Micah couldn't have ever imagined calling so many white people by their Christian names. Or having them for friends. But that's what happened. Dinner parties at the Stimsons' house were always full of stories from the Underground Railroad. And Olivia loved to have Micah tell every person who hadn't heard yet. 'Bout how he came all the way up from Virginia. With two armies standin' in the way.

But the quieter dinners at Ethan and Marcella's were better. Even if the food was never quite all the way right. Something always a little short of cooked through, or just a little burnt maybe. But not having to tell his story for folks he'd just met. Just talkin' about whatever things came to mind. And laughter, too. Plenty of that.

It was the start of October when things were close to done on that porch. And Micah had to think of what was next for him. Cold as the last winter'd been traveling up the Blue Ridge, he wasn't thinking 'bout wandering north some more. And besides that, for the first time since Mary, he felt a sense of hope. Like maybe he belonged somewhere.

So he told Ethan and Marcella over dinner one night. They told him to stay with them, of course. And he felt good that they would make the offer. Like they were his real friends and not just employers. But he had his mind set on a nice room at the boardinghouse in town. Getting as much carpentering work as he could. And Marcella said he should put a small advertisement in *The Freeman's Journal.* So folks would know what he could do. Only one hitch to that.

All the advertisers have a surname too. She said. Knowing that they'd talked about the very thing some weeks before. And her telling him that it was a thing to take pride in, the chance to decide for himself what he'd be called. Not something to be ashamed of, certainly. Said she'd had her Daddy's name, then got her husband's name. Without anybody ever asking her how she felt about it. And he'd often thought about it since then, taking some pride in the chance to choose for himself. Figured that the name he chose would be something from the man he was. And represent the man he was still workin' on becoming, too.

And so he smiled at Marcella and Ethan to let them know he'd figured it out.

Well, I was figurin' on doin' that very thing, puttin' a notice in the newspaper, he said.

Is that right? Marcella asked. And did you choose a surname?

Mmm-hmm. He said. Waited a second for effect. I like the sound of Micah Plowshare.

And from the looks on their faces he could see that his friends did too.

In the weeks that followed, Micah Plowshare would stop by most days to help out with little patching-up jobs around their house. After he was done with whatever chicken coop or hayloft or stable door he'd worked on someplace else. He'd finish those jobs as fast as he could. Always with the usual quality though. And then he'd pass by their house, just outside the main part of town. Maybe say that he'd noticed last time he was there that the back-door steps needed some mending. Or the stable stalls, even though there weren't any horses inside them.

And he'd fix it with Ethan, talking about the books Ethan had given him to read.

Marcella would always insist that he stay for supper. Her cooking wasn't improving as fast as Ethan's carpentering, but Micah enjoyed the company a great deal. Two three four times a week, Micah'd come by. Just like that. Through the rest of October. Always with his tools at first, 'til Marcella told him that if he insisted on doing all this work they'd have to start paying him again. Said she knew her cooking wasn't much in the way of compensation. And Ethan was quick to agree with that, then got himself slapped on the shoulder with an oven mitten. And all three of them smiled.

So that started a regular thing of Micah going to their house for supper a few times a week. Sometimes they'd have other folks over too. The Stimsons mostly. And he'd listen to Marcella speak her mind like no woman he'd ever met, even more than Olivia. On abolition. Women's rights. Or just the proper way to set the dinner table. Didn't matter, she had an opinion on all of it and wasn't shy to speak it. And then Ethan might argue a little, or make a joke. And she'd come right back at him. And it reminded him of what he and Mary had back in Richmond. The playfulness Mary liked so much, and he did too. 'Cause it had made him playful for the first time since he was a little boy. Or maybe ever.

And at night back at the boardinghouse. When he wasn't reading to keep his mind from such things. His thoughts would drift south, to Richmond or Charleston or wherever it was his Daddy had ended up. Only different now from the mournful nights along the Blue Ridge. Not all alone like he was then. Not a mule either. A free man. Mister Micah Plowshare, carpenter.

Ethan
GETTYSBURG, PENNSYLVANIA
NOVEMBER 19, 1863

Da had been the one to suggest it to Mrs. Harrison, and it seemed strange indeed for him to say such a thing, and even stranger for him to volunteer himself to come along with Ethan. But there was no refusing, not when Ethan heard how Harry's mother had lit up at the idea of it, and not when his Da seemed so anxious to come along.

Ethan had received Da's letter just a week earlier saying how Mrs. Harrison would come to visit far more than she used to and they could hear the sadness in her voice. And it was never sadder than when she mentioned the dedication of the Gettysburg cemetery that was soon to take place, and her far too old and with the bad feet and all, unable to see such a thing, to see where her only boy would be buried. And Ethan could hardly refuse Da's offer to go in her place. Besides, Marcella wanted to tell them the news in person, of her being *in a family way,* as she figured Mam and Aunt Em would want to hear it.

So she's in Brooklyn while Ethan and his Da are both here for a day that seems to be turning into far more than a simple dedication of a battlefield cemetery. They'd arrived the day before, and that was when Ethan took the pictures of Harry's tiny tombstone, smaller even than the one Aislinn had and laid flat on the ground just like hers, though it was hard to hold such a thing against the government, considering how many there were of them to be made. And then he'd taken several more of the view in every direction, knowing Mrs. Harrison would want to know what her only child would have to look at for as long as it took him to get to the Ever After.

That night they'd had to travel twenty miles out of town, back toward New York, just to find a hotel room for themselves. Ethan'd suggested that they just stay on the train and go all the way back home that night, but Da wouldn't hear of it. And then there was this morning, with masses of people packed onto every railcar, and this tiny farming town overrun for the second time since July. The President will be in attendance, and Ethan tells his Da to go and watch the parade without him since he'd like to set his camera up by the podium where he'll soon address the crowd. After all, he'd met the man those years before, but still has no picture of him.

As the parade begins to close in on the cemetery, he can see another photographer setting up more than thirty feet away, back behind the crowd quickly swelling into the thousands. There's no sign of Da amidst such a throng, and he smiles to think he's lost his assistant after all. When the ceremony finally begins, it moves with all the haste of the Army of the Potomac approaching Richmond, which is to say, it hardly moves at all.

There are songs from the band and greetings from the master of ceremonies, and an invocation, and more songs, and then the featured speaker, Edward Everett, who trudges on for nearly two hours, pressing patience to its limits, until at least half of the vast crowd dissipates into the surrounding areas while he's still speaking. Da manages to slip his way up to the front beside Ethan, and they roll their eyes at each other every time it appears Mr. Everett is about to wrap up but then is moved to further eloquence.

Until at last he's done and the band does what it can to stir some life back into the survivors. The President's introduced, and the crowd offers enthusiastic applause as he walks to the front of the platform and begins to speak in a voice still familiar to Ethan from a few years before at Cooper Union, but firmer now, deeper, with the resonance of all that he, and the Nation, have endured.

Four score and seven years ago our fathers brought forth upon this continent a new nation, conceived in liberty, and dedicated to the proposition that all men are created equal . . .

Ethan can tell right off that this is a speech destined for far greater things than Mr. Everett could hope to achieve, and he's mesmerized by the poetry Mr. Lincoln, President Lincoln, has added to his searing prose of nearly four years ago. And he freezes for a moment, not a photographer, just an admirer, as he was back at Cooper Union.

But in a larger sense, we cannot dedicate, we cannot consecrate, we cannot hallow this ground. The brave men, living and dead, who struggled here, have consecrated it far above our poor power to add or detract.

And in the midst of these dignified words, it takes his Da to rally Ethan from his stupor, handing him a glass-plate negative from the satchel. After a few seconds to get the camera ready and the lens focused, Ethan takes the picture, just as the President looks out over the crowd, as if beseeching them to something more than just the rah-rah of a fine band and a blustery speaker.

. . . that we here highly resolve that these dead shall not have died in vain, that this nation, under God, shall have a new birth of freedom, and that government of the people, by the people, for the people shall not perish from the earth.

The crowd pauses, perhaps surprised that this speech of less than three minutes is all the answer the President has to the two hours that preceded it. When they do break into applause, it's first as if they're expressing their relief for his brevity, but it builds in a steady crescendo, becoming jubilation, as they begin to understand just how good it was.

The band begins to play again, and then there's closing remarks and a prayer and more music, but for Ethan there is one line from Mr. Lincoln's speech that reverberates through his guilty thoughts, until it grows into a haunting.

It is for us, the living, rather to be dedicated here to the unfinished work which they have thus far so nobly advanced.

The crowd soon disperses in every direction, some to tour the battlefield, some back into town following the President to the rail station. But Ethan and his Da stay there for many minutes more, his Da listening to one of the militia guards describe how the battle proceeded. The way the man speaks to his small admiring audience, Ethan knows he's either a General or wasn't anywhere near the damn battlefield. And when one of the young boys listening asks where he was stationed during the battle, Ethan's suspicions are confirmed.

Over in that direction, the militia guard says.

On Little Round Top? the boy asks.

No . . . not quite there—back behind the ridge . . . guarding the supply lines.

Ethan shakes his head, then smiles to think of what Harry might've had to say at such a moment. And then he's reminded of the four of them, once together, with only himself and Smitty left now, and Smitty minus an arm, and he feels ashamed to think that he's been the one to come through it with just what lingers of a hitch in his step and a shoulder that sometimes tells him a few hours ahead of time when it will rain. And the haunting of Lincoln's words, to serve as judge and jury . . . *to be dedicated here to the unfinished work which they have thus far so nobly advanced* . . . 'til he begins to think that there's still more he could do, supply lines he could guard or caissons he could drive or . . . even bedpans to empty and stretchers to carry . . . *the unfinished work . . . the unfinished work . . .*

And every manner of foolishness drifts through his embattled mind until Da comes up beside him unseen, wrapping an arm around Ethan's shoulders and pulling him tight to him for a moment.

What you lads went t'rough, he says, shaking his head. I thank th'Lahrd for sparin' ya, son. Sure I do . . . now more than ever . . . and I will for all my days remainin'. But now let's go home, lad. You've done enough.

IN THE DARKROOM AT THE back of Mr. Hadley's studio the next afternoon, Ethan develops the glass negatives as methodically as ever, making large imprints of Harry's tombstone, and a panoramic collage of the view all around it, seamlessly pressing the landscape photos one beside the other, and Harry's stone beneath them, until the picture is nearly three feet long side to side and two feet high, and creates the effect of actually being there on the hill outside of Gettysburg in a way that only a true artist and master craftsman could elicit from the limits of two dimensions. He stands a few feet away from the great drying image before him, and allows himself just a hint of a smile, thinking that this will be a fitting tribute to his great friend and, somehow, to all the lads as well.

Then there is the final picture he took, the one of Lincoln, and he holds the undeveloped negative between his fingers for several long moments, pondering what best to do with it. But the words do not haunt him as they did just the day before, and he smiles with greater satisfaction than he'd even allowed himself at the sight of the masterpiece he'd just created. Carefully, he slides the plate back into its thick cotton sleeve, to be stored away with all the other negatives that actually became pictures. And he allows himself to believe, at long last, that maybe he *has* done enough.

And sure isn't there plenty of other unfinished work that needs lookin' after . . .

MARCELLA
COOPERSTOWN
MARCH 21, 1864

For the longest time you thought you would've been better off to have married as an orphan. Surely there wasn't anything in your heritage, nothing tangible to the living, to represent you in any sort of presentable way to your in-laws. Even Abuela could hardly redeem your family line, since she had admittedly come to her senses only in her fading years, and even then only after a lifetime of submission—and luxury. What manner of woman was she, or Mrs. Carlisle even, compared to a mother-in-law and her sister who were veritable mountains of fortitude in comparison? And still they had accepted you, willing somehow to overlook such a blemished family line as if they believed you were still salvageable.

You knew there had been times when Miguel and Bartolomé accosted Seanny when they saw him on Wall Street, always asking after you but then turning quickly to business before Seanny could even answer them. You had only learned anything about these meetings when you overheard a Christmastime conversation between Ethan and his brother, with Seanny confessing, *"I don't know what to tell'm, Ethan. None of the men I work wit' trust that man or his sons."* And later, *"I told'm Marcella was expectin' and they didn't so much as bat an eye, just asked whether I knew anything about the contracts on the Navy Yard."*

A week after that you received a response to your Christmas letter to your mother, mentioning only that it would be a fitting tribute to name the child, if it was a boy, after Papa. *"Maybe then he will be happy to receive you here again,"* your mother wrote, and then spent two more pages talking about Pilar's upcoming wedding. You had often heard Ethan's Mam talk about how protective she was of her children, and you realized that day that you would have to protect this child from your family, quarantining them as best you could like the deadly fever they would surely be. And all it took was to simply stop trying to include them in your life.

Then as the inevitable day approached, you found yourself grown oddly frightened, not so much of the pain of labor, but by the thought of whether you would measure up in how you made it through, and even more so, whether you would measure up as a mother. But then you saw the two of them, Mam and Aunt Em, step off the livery wagon in front of the house and Mam saying how *"no woman should go through the last month of expectin' wit' only a well-meanin' man to foul things up insteada helpin' even a little bit."* And you knew that he'd written to them, since they would not think to impose themselves upon you.

It was in those final weeks of expecting that they truly became your *own* Mam and Aunt Em, with their roles quite reversed, it seemed. Mam was the one who had been through it, and she would politely chastise Em whenever her sister started to bring up matters that didn't need to be discussed, things like miscarriages back in the Old Country or how Ethan and Seanny and Aislinn had had another brother for the space of two days "*'til the Lahrd'd seen fit to take'm.*"

And Mam would wave her hand or tap Aunt Em on the arm if she was close enough, and tell her, "*Oh Em, she doesn't need t'hear any of that . . . why wouldja . . . oh love, don't you worry about those stories from th'Old Country, where there wasn't a doctor fer ten miles at least.*" And Aunt Em would catch herself and apologize for the rest of the day, herself becoming the soft one as never before. "*Awww love, sure I didn't mean . . . Nora's right, there wasn't a bleedin' hospital or a doctor or a clean sheet t'be found in dat . . . ohh don't you worry none . . . sure you'll be fine.*" Somehow it was a comfort to you to see Aunt Em like that, as if affirming that your own blemishes could somehow be overlooked. And your fears were allayed.

There was a day when you thought this would be it, and Ethan sent off a telegram to Da and Seanny to tell them the news. But then the doctor said it'd be a few days more at least. Still, Da and Seanny were steppin' off the livery carriage the next morning, having traveled all night to see the new addition to the family. And they stayed, of course.

Until, on the day itself, it was Mam holding your hand and Aunt Em off in the corner talking up a nervous storm. For the first few hours it was just them, with the doctor coming in whenever he heard you calling out from the pain and staying until it passed. Then he'd go out of the room and reassure Ethan and Da and Seanny that everything was fine. And when the breaks in between the pain started getting shorter, Aunt Em started talking faster, getting more nervous and telling random stories from back in the Old Country or from just last week. It would have been funny to hear her if there weren't knives jabbing at you from the inside, but then Mam was somehow calmer the more nervous Em became, and she let you squeeze the color out of her hand completely while whispering to you, *"Easy, love . . . yer doin' foine, love . . . that's it, love."*

Then finally Em stumbled upon a story that genuinely interested you, describing how Ethan got his name, but started out by talking about the two miscarriages her sister had in the years after the difficult birth of Aislinn, and there was Mam chastising, *"Jaysus Chroist, Em, d'ya think she needs t'hear about that just now?"* There was something in hearing her use the Lord's name that way that rattled Em out of her nervous frenzy and offered you a few more ounces of fortitude in the form of abbreviated laughter. But the knives were back soon enough, and plenty of screaming, and Mam whispering and losing the color of her hand, and Em in the corner in stunned silence . . .'til there were the last few pushes and the knives . . . and the whispers . . . and then it was done . . . the breath returning soon after . . . and the exhilaration of the absence of such pain overcame the fatigue for just a little while.

There was the cleaning up of your little girl to do once the doctor finished his work, and Mam was there wiping the sweat from your forehead as Em stood in tears in the corner looking at you and the little girl back and forth, with both hands covering her mouth. And there was something that made you aware of wanting to include Em in the moment, so you asked her to tell you more of the story of how Ethan got his name, nodding to her to come and sit beside you, and her face lit up at the idea. Mam helped the doctor with the cleaning up, and you watched them while Em began to speak more calmly than before. *"Well, Nora went to the Father an' asked him fer a name that she could attach to th'little one while it was still in her womb,"* and she looked at Mam, who didn't seem to object to such a story then. *"Well, ya know, she was hopin' maybe the right name'd give'm a better chance of makin' it out alive. An' th'Father said that Ethan was a name from th'Old Testament, an' that it meant strong and enduring. An' dat was good enough. Nora didn't even wait for th'Father to suggest a girl's name."*

And the three of you laughed a little in those next few moments, talking about what it would have been if he had been a girl—little *Ethania* . . . *Ethany* . . . and so on, until your daughter was wrapped in the clean blanket and nestled across your chest. The three of you were in tears then until Ethan was brought into the room, with his Da and Uncle Paddy and Seanny trailing behind, and Aunt Em, seemingly restored to herself, started saying, *"Not the whole bleedin' lotta ya all at once wit' what the poor girl's been through, Jaysus,"* and you laughed and said it was fine . . . as they gathered up closer to you, with Ethan on the other side across from his Mam, fumbling his hands nervously along your arm and cheek like a boy maybe half his age.

The doctor poured some water into the glass on the table beside you and asked, *"So what's the pretty little one going to have for a name?"*

Whenever Ethan had brought it up, you told him it made you more nervous to think of such things before the child was born. But you knew all along, almost from the very start. You looked at Da and thought to yourself, *Maybe next time it'll be a boy and you'll get your tribute, but I'm so glad she's a girl.* Then you brushed your finger across her forehead and looked over at Ethan for just a second, then back up at the nurse.

"Her name is Aislinn."

And then there was only to bask in their joy . . . this adoptive family of yours.

Micah
COOPERSTOWN, NEW YORK
OCTOBER 15, 1864

When Micah was just seven or maybe eight years old at most, his Daddy explained how a plank of good wood was a strong thing of itself. Might be a very strong thing, if it was made of good enough wood. But it'd only hold so much pressure by itself. And he took a good plank and set it on two rocks and told his son to walk out onto the middle of it. Made him feel the thing bend under just his weight. Then started walkin' out on it himself. And made Micah feel it all the more. 'Til he thought it'd break and jumped off.

Then his Daddy took another rock and set it under that plank somewhere near the middle. Told him to come out on it again. Started jumpin' up and down on it when he wouldn't come. Showing how much stronger it got just by that one rock. 'Til Micah walked out on it. Jumped on it too after a while. And from then on he understood what it meant when his Daddy talked about how levees and houses and roofs and things got stronger by the fixin' together of them.

Somehow that memory comes to him now, to see Ethan walking along the roof of that porch the two of them built. Thinking back to when he wouldn't set a single foot upon it. Sayin' it was his leg that made him worry. When Micah knew different. A man who'd walked into gunfire plennya times. Wouldn't step on a roof. 'Til Micah showed him what his Daddy proved to him all those years ago.

And now there he is, walking along it like it's just the regular ground beneath his feet. And he's pouring that hot tar up along the seam against the house just like Micah showed him. Which means Micah gets to stand on actual ground, keeping the fire going under the tar pot. Then walk up the ladder instead of Ethan. Since it's faster this way, with his leg to get in the way. And Ethan thinks what he's doin' is more important than keeping this tar going just the right way. Which ain't so, but who needs to know.

Olivia and Marcella are there on the porch. With little Aislinn tucked away inside, napping. And Micah's busy keeping that tar just hot enough, hearing the two of them talking but pretending not to hear. These two women who never talk about the usual women's sorta things. Instead it's always about what the Congress down in Washington is doing. Or how the war is going, only then in quieter voices when Ethan is around, so as not to remind him of all that's been lost.

But lately, these last two weeks, when Micah and Ethan have been sealing up every seam in the place with that tar, Marcella and Olivia have been talking about nothing but suffrage. Sounded like a terrible way to describe something that was supposed to be so good. But women like Marcella and Olivia, and their Mrs. Carlisle and Catherine down in New York, are all working for suffrage. The Movement, they call it. For women *and* Negroes. And Micah couldn't help but think how most of the colored folks he knew would settle for a whole lot less than that.

This particular afternoon Olivia gets to talking about Mrs. Tubman again. Harriet, she calls her. Since she's had her at the house twice, back before the war started. And met her half a dozen times at least, outside of that. They even send letters back and forth still, though Mrs. Tubman's, Harriet's, only come every six months or so. But she'll be a great supporter of the suffrage movement once the war is done. And stirring that tar and keeping the fire hot, not a bit of all this is lost on Micah. He keeps thinking how these two women, and this man on the roof with only one leg of much use, have done more for the cause of making his people free than he'd *ever* done. 'Cept when it came to liberatin' *himself.* That he'd done just fine.

'Til he hears Marcella's voice get that sort of excitement to it, the way it does when Olivia talks about Harriet. With Olivia tellin' about how Harriet spent the first two years of the war down along the islands of South Carolina. How she led a couple hundred slaves to the freedom of the islands where the Union Navy was stationed. Went up the Edisto River and rescued them damn near herself. With the help of a couple of Union boats tryin' to stir things up down there.

Olivia and Marcella start getting back onto how Harriet is just the sorta woman who can help folks see that this new suffrage movement is all connected to the abolition movement. But Micah starts getting some ideas that got nothing to do with suffrage. And he lets that fire cool some, while he's thinking about what Olivia just said. First time he's ever heard her talk about such places. *Edisto Island. Port Royal. Charleston.* All of 'em places he'd heard plenty of talk about back home. Back at *Les Roseraies.*

And it's enough to make the tar in that pot grow hard, before he notices Ethan looking down at him from the roof. Looking down at him leaning up along the wall at the edge of the porch. Listening, too. And watching Micah. And a smile in that mischievous sorta way. Like he's maybe. Just maybe. Thinking the very same thing.

MICAH

NEW YORK

DECEMBER 1864

So Micah, there's a merchant ship leavin' in a week that'll get ya there, Seanny says. But I don't know th'Captain personally, only through a friend of a sorta friend. But if ya can hang on for a while longer, there's a supply steamer headin' outta th'Brooklyn yards on the twenny-first that's captained by a personal friend of mine. A fella rose up from th'Points . . . with a bitta help.

He nods his head to Ethan like he knows the man he's talking about. And Ethan nods back.

Cormac's brother? Ethan asks.

Yep, Seanny says. And Cormac's goin' along for th'ride.

Ethan seems relieved to hear that. Though Micah's wary of trusting anyone outside of Ethan and, maybe, Sean.

Micah, Cormac's a man I'd trust to watch out for my own daughter, sober or otherwise. Ethan says.

With Cormac it'll most likely be the otherwise parta that, Seanny adds, laughing a little by himself. But you don't strike me as a man needin' any lookin' after, Micah.

And that's enough for him.

He's spent the past two months waiting for the telegram from Seanny. Started feeling like maybe he'd be better off just going on his own, but Ethan convinced him to wait. 'Til the day finally arrived. Olivia and her oldest boy stayed with Marcella and the baby at the house back in Cooperstown so Ethan could come down and see Micah off. And it's been a long two days with the goodbyes leading up to it. From folks he knows understand that he might not be coming back.

'Til at last it's just Micah and Ethan and Seanny, standing there alongside the supply ship headed for Port Royal Island. Seanny says his usual sorts of things, bitter kinda wit about how it's not too late to change his mind. Not as tiresome to Micah when he thinks how he'll be forever indebted to him. Then it's just Ethan, with a stern face unusual for him, as he reaches inside the satchel and takes out a leather billfold. Hands it to Micah. But Micah hands it right back without even looking inside.

No . . . Ethan, I've got plenty–

Now hold on. Ethan says, not insistent but asking for him to understand.

Ethan shakes his head a few times. And Micah waits for him to explain. Figures he's earned at least that much.

You an' I know a thing or two about tryin' to get right . . . about tryin' . . . to make things right. With God . . . with whoever. Ethan says. An' sometimes when things're all just this kinda mess . . . sometimes it's nice just to be able to start to make some of it right.

And Ethan's got some mist in his eyes Micah's never seen there before.

Ethan, I got enough–

No you don't Micah. You know this isn't gonna be th'sorta thing where men do what's right just 'cause it's right, Ethan says. Yer gonna have to pay fer everything, and pay more than I'd havta. You know that. Not too many men left anywhere with more than a specka common decency. Not in all this mess.

Then he places the billfold into Micah's hands. Closes his fist around it.

That's fifteen hundred dollars there from the Ladies Abolition Society of New York, he says, as if making an announcement. They're good people, tryin' to make some of this god-awful mess right, somehow. And you're helpin' them do it.

And Micah smiles just a little at him. Takes the billfold and stuffs it inside his coat. And knows that it's his turn. To fix whatever he can.

Then Ethan reaches inside his satchel and takes out something else. A battered, leather-bound book, held together by a bit of string tied around it. Micah takes it and looks at its cover, unable to see anything like a title engraved on it anymore. Still, he holds it with two hands like it's a thousand-year-old Bible. Suspecting. 'Til Ethan tells him to turn the cover open, and it's confirmed.

The Odyssey, Micah says, reverently. Out loud. I can't take this with me, Ethan. He protests again. I don't know if I'll ever be able to return it.

But Ethan only responds with a signal to flip one more page. And Micah does, reading the inscription aloud:

This book passes now through the grateful hands of:
Aislinn McOwen & Ethan McOwen
& Micah Plowshare

(though the stories contained within belong to the ages)

Ethan, I can't accept this, Micah says, shaking his head. This is—

Not mine to hold on to anymore, Ethan interrupts. Books aren't a possessing kinda thing, my sister always said. It was her idea to put that line there at the bottom.

Then this should be Aislinn's someday, Micah argues.

It already was.

I mean . . . you know, little Aislinn, Micah says.

Oh, I've got another one I think she'll like a whole lot better, Ethan answers with a smile. And it's one that her namesake used to especially treasure. But that one there—that's meant to travel with a man on a grand adventure.

What about your son? What if you and Marcella have a son someday? He asks.

Read the inscription again, Ethan says. It's yours now. You can pass it on to whoever you want to, but it's your turn to have it now.

And then, as Micah begins to muster up a final protest, Seanny comes back.

They're getting ready to head off, he says. And Ethan shrugs his shoulders and smiles a little. Like they'd planned it all along.

MICAH
SOUTH CAROLINA
WINTER 1864–65

Port Royal and the surrounding islands are like little droplets of Union in an ocean of Confederacy. But now there's word of General Sherman marching all up and down their hindquarters with more than sixty thousand Union soldiers. And how he made it to Savannah a few days before Christmas, fixing to head this way through South Carolina. Mad as hell to get his hands on the place that started this whole damn mess. With nothing in between but a few old men and young boys with their muskets. And Micah listens to all the bits of information he can get, thinking that this will either be a whole lot easier than he thought. Or a whole lot harder. If the fight's coming this way.

The merchant ship sets back off for New York the day after Christmas. And Micah stays behind. But Sean's man Cormac introduces him to the Quartermaster Sergeant before he leaves. And then it's just a matter of five dollars every day Micah wants to sleep in the back of the storehouse. Another five dollars if he'd like to eat. And Sean's man Cormac just looks at Micah like this is how the world works.

But there is one thing that's free. On Christmas night, Cormac comes to the storeroom where Micah is alone. Hands him a rifle. Not just any rifle, a Spencer Repeater.

That can fire seven rounds before reloadin'. Cormac says. Sergeant says a man handy wit' a gun can fire twenny thirty rounds a minute if he's gotta.

And Micah half-smiles. Asks him what it costs.

Ahh, call it a Christmas present from me an' Seanny . . . an' yer man Squire Ethan.

And he offers Micah a slug from his whiskey bottle, but Micah declines.

Well, shovin' off in the mornin', besta luck t'ya, Cormac says, and gives him a slap on the shoulder. Happy Christmas too.

It's two weeks before Micah's on his way. Bribes his way onto a little supply boat headed to Edisto Island fifteen miles north. Corporal there, twenty dollars later, tells him about a rowboat. Where it's hidden. How to get it to the mainland. Where to stash it. Tells him about the place called No Man's Land.

Where th'Reb inland batteries an' Union Navy gunboats beat hell outta ever' now an' then just to remind everyone we're still here, he says. Mostly just us doin' the firin' now. Just for show, 'cause ain't anybody there anymore.

And Micah hits the mainland in the late afternoon, stashes the boat. Walks a few miles inland. Figures he's covered all there is of No Man's Land, so he stops. Waits for dark. Then he's on his way again. Ten miles or so along the Edisto River to Penny Creek. Which he reaches by the next morning. Hides himself for most of the day, sleeping some, then it's back at it when darkness comes. And on to *Les Roseraies.*

When he gets there, he walks right toward the cabin where he and his Momma and Daddy and Isabelle lived. Got his Spencer Repeater in his hands, loaded. Case whatever overseer they got running the place gets any ideas. But the slave quarters are practically abandoned. Just a tiny puff of smoke coming from their old cabin. It's gotta be way past midnight, but he knocks anyway. Then a little louder. Then pushes open the door a little.

Whoosat?

He doesn't recognize the voice.

Who you? Micah says. Cocks the Spencer Repeater to let the man know what's what.

Thomas. Dis my cabin, Suh. Man says. Suh, Micah thinks. First time he's been called that. Laughs a little. Laughs more when he starts remembering Thomas. One of his Daddy's old friends, if he's the same one.

Micah steps forward a few feet. The fraction of light from what's left of the fire catches his face. And he can see Thomas, too.

Hello, Thomas, Micah says.

Micah? Man asks, after squinting for a while. And Micah nods, half-smiling. Saving the full-on smiles for Momma and Isabelle. But happy enough to see a friend again.

They sit down once the shaking hands is done. Micah's got to explain a little bit about how he got here, but asks right off where Momma and Isabelle are. Thomas tells him they're all right. *Better'n most since they both workin' in the Big House.* Isabelle's a pretty young lady now and works in the kitchen. His Momma does some cleaning and all the taking care of Massa's Momma. *Who ain't altogetha right inna head, no more.*

Then it's the long road of filling in how things've been here. How they were for Micah. Backtracking all those years.

Oh, yo' Daddy be proud as ca'be t'see ya now, son, Thomas says. What a fine strong man you done turned outta be. Mmm-hmm.

And that brings up the point of Daddy. Ain't likely, but Micah asks if there's any word on him. Thomas's face goes cold. Sullen. And it's like Micah knows somehow. Knows it can't *all* be this easy. Thomas shakes his head.

He gone, son, Thomas says. Folks say he jumped 'at train 'long th'Savannah-Charleston line. Th'one takin' him south wit' that dealer what bought him up at th'auction. Musta been tryin' t'get on back here to his fam'ly, what I figger. He jump as they comin' on the riva crossin'. Kilt him, it did.

And Thomas's words take the air out of Micah's lungs. Make him purse his lips tight and shake his head some as he stares at the fire.

Some folks say he done it on purpose-like, Thomas goes on. Knowin' he wasn't gon' see his fam'ly no mo', he jus' couldn' take it. But that ain't th'man I knowed for thirty years. Nosuh. He was comin' back t'find y'all. That's what it was. Sho'nuff. Don't you go listnin' to none a'that.

There's nothing more said about his Daddy after that. Nothing more said about much anything. And Micah sleeps for only minutes at a time, lying there beside the smoldering fire, a few feet from where he slept as a boy. He knew he wasn't gonna see his Daddy here. But he didn't know he was *never* gonna see him. And what bothers him most is knowing his Daddy ain't gonna get to see his son a free man after all. And that anger fills him again. Like he wants to take that Spencer and walk up to the Big House right then and start taking out the white folks. Just 'cause. Don't matter that these particular white folks got nothing to do with his Daddy and him getting sold off. 'Cept that they didn't buy the place fast enough. Before so many pieces got sold off first.

Next morning Thomas is getting set to go off to work. Only twenny-two slaves left on the place, according to him. What with some getting sold off, some running off. They plant only what they can, corn, sweet taters, beans. Just a fraction of the rice they used to. Micah asks about the indigo field, and Thomas shakes his head.

Summa the fiel' han's growed sweet taters there, he says. But it ain't nothin' but a patcha overgrowed shrubs now. You an' yo' daddy's work . . . like it ain't . . .

He stops. Well now, he says, nodding his head like he's trying to convince himself of a thing. Well now, I s'pose it did 'mount to somethin'. You a free man. 'Bout as free as any colored man I ever know'd. Comin' back here wit' a fancy rifle like you meanin' t'do somethin'.

It's later that afternoon when he sees Isabelle. Thomas gets word to them both, and Isabelle's the first one that can slip away from the Big House to come an' see her brother. First time in more'n eleven years. And it's like Thomas said. She's grown up into a pretty young thing. Got Daddy's color. Got Momma's high cheeks and full nose and eyes. Taller than her, though. Just a few inches shorter than Micah. And they hug. And she cries. And he does all he can not to let himself do the same. Not at all like it was eleven years ago, no snippin' at each other. None of her getting under his skin, talking all the time. He couldn't ever feel that way again, he knows.

They get just a few minutes. And then it's late that night before Momma can slip away. And it's nothing but tears then, even from Micah, Thomas even, choking up before he leaves to give them some time. There's crying over Daddy. Momma doing most of it, but joyful like, like he'd be so proud to see his son. But she's got to be proud for both of them now.

His time with Momma is so short, he doesn't even make plans for when they gonna run off. But when she's gone back to the Big House, Micah and Thomas get to talking. Micah tells him about how he got here, and how the Union Navy ain't more than twenty miles away. Micah figures him and Momma and Bellie'll leave the next night. Make the river by the morning after that. Then hide out just like he did. Next night it's on down the river 'til they in No Man's Land and free, mostly.

Then Micah asks Thomas if he wants to come with them, and for a very short moment he sees Thomas's eyes light up with the thought of it. But then it's all the reasons why he hasn't run off before this. The dogs. The Home Guard. The long walk with little food. And Micah explains it all to him, like he's got it all worked out, and 'sides, with Sherman comin' this way, it ain't like they gonna bother running after a couple of women and a fifty-five-year-old man. But when they go to sleep, he can tell he hasn't convinced him. And he thinks what a sad thing it is to have been worn down to such a point. So many years of being a mule that he can't even lift his head high enough anymore to see what's right in front of him.

MARY

RICHMOND

DECEMBER 24, 1864

No matter how much she tried, there was no gettin' around the fact that it was two years to the very day since her world changed forever. She had stopped being a little girl long before that, on that day with Mista Grant and all the stuff runnin' off with Gertie and on the auction block. She'd become somethin' like a woman in those few days, leastways in how she saw the world, no longer wide-eyed and figurin' things might be different than they were just by wishin' them to be so. Then when she came to live with the Kittredges, she still held on to hopes, dreamed a little even, enough at least to make herself into what she became. But two years ago, when Micah ran off and she got too scared and confused to go with him, she stopped bein' something else altogether.

It took her a while to figure out what it was that got changed that day. She wasn't a girl then, so it wasn't that sort of amusement with things, the kind Justinia still sometimes had, that Mary lost that day. No, for Mary it was something altogether different. It was like she stopped waitin' for life to unfold itself to her, like she stopped expectin' things, anything, stopped expectin' altogether. And not expectin' had its good points, in that year after Micah was gone. It helped her steel her heart enough to just get up in the mornin' same as always, an to listen to Justinia dreamin' 'bout her great big future without thinkin' much of her own. But not expectin' was a sad sort of thing, too, an that first year without Micah was about the best actin' she'd ever done, pretendin' all she could that things were just wonderful all around, pretendin' she was just as happy as Justinia, almost anyway, to see her fall in love with Lieutenant Farnsworth.

They were a pretty couple, what with how Justinia'd grown out of that little-girl face and the little-girl ways and become a gold-haired beauty. She had her father's long face and her mother's green eyes and, more than anything else, a smile she took to wearin' almost all the time. And she was gettin' all her twenty years around her, with how she'd seen plenty of things in these last years of war and workin' at the hospital. And still she smiled. That hadta have more than a little to do with Lieutenant Farnsworth.

Seeing Juss and the Lieutenant together, when he was gettin' over his wounds from Gettysburg and she was walkin' to the hospital to see him all the time, made Mary think of the sort of love she'd had with Micah. Then the Lieutenant was gone again just after Christmas that year, just like Micah'd left her, gone without Justinia knowin' whether she'd ever see him again. Only difference was that Justinia didn't have a chance to go with him, like Mary did, and when he was gone, Juss still kept her smile about her almost as much as she had before. And that was the time Mary got to changin', seein' how Juss still let her heart get all warmed up by that love she had for the Lieutenant, even worried as much as she was that she'd never see him again.

That was when Mary decided that she'd been blessed after all, to love someone the way she did . . . the way she always *would* love Micah. And not expectin' grew into something else entirely then. It grew into anticipatin'. And that was something altogether different, like a healthy dose of knowin' the ways of the world, soberly, practically, but wrapped up in an equal dose of hope. That's when she started makin' the mournin' veils, one a week for the last forty-two weeks. 'Cause maybe they'd come in handy for her someday.

The war kept gettin' worse all through 1864. The Yankees had a new general, a man named U. S. Grant, and the name alone was enough to scare Mary something awful. Mista Kittredge hated this General Grant like he never hated a Yankee before. Said this General Grant was nothin' but a cold-blooded murderer the way he kept pressin' on Richmond, even after gettin' whupped. General Lee beat'm at a battle called the Wilderness. But General Grant didn't run back to Washington like the Yankees'd done all along after gettin' whupped. General Grant kept headin' south, closer to Richmond, and got whupped again, then came south again, only to get whupped even worse. Then kept on comin', all the way past Richmond even, to Petersburg, twenty miles south, where he got whupped again, then set in for a long siege. That was end of June. And General Grant and the Yankees'd been here ever since, diggin' in with trenches that matched General Lee's trenches, stretchin' thirty miles all around Petersburg and on up to Richmond like two great big slits in the land with men livin' every day inside them, waitin' for the next battle.

It'd been six months since then, and Mary'd got past General Grant's unfortunate name and come to think of him and his men as something else altogether—like they were Crusaders, Liberators, comin' to help her get outta Richmond and go find Micah if he was still alive. It'd been two years, and maybe he'd found another, she sometimes thought, when her thoughts got to racin'. Maybe she'd missed her chance after all. But still she made those veils, in her room late at night, with whatever slivers of light the moon would offer, waitin', hopin', anticipatin' . . . which was a whole lot better than just not expectin'.

Every Saturday afternoon since before the siege even, Mary would carry out the scrap bucket to the lint bin, then leave it for Robert to pick up. Like so many things in Richmond, the dress shop wasn't what it used to be. There wasn't a scrap of fresh silk anyone had seen in over a year, and not a woman lookin' for a new gown or embroidered tablecloth in almost as long. The business they did now was mostly in black—black curtains, black dresses, black veils and gloves, for all the ladies in mournin'. It'd gotten so Mary had to dye all the other colors of thread and cloth they had black. And in all the confusion, she'd been slippin' a spool or two into that scrap bucket just before fixin' to empty it every Saturday afternoon. But since this particular afternoon also happened to be Christmas Eve, two years since everything changed, she decided to give herself something like a present and put six spools of black thread into the bin, knowin' nobody'd notice since it was Christmas. Six spools would yield almost four mournin' veils, getting her closer to one hundred, which she was sure would be more than enough to get her all the way to St. Catharines, and Micah, she hoped.

By about three in the afternoon what little business they'd had was gone. And Mary dropped in those six spools, then slipped out with the scrap bin, out behind the store same as always. There wasn't any real scrap bin these days. Back when Micah was still here, Mary'd fill up that big wooden barrel out behind the store with pieces of material almost six inches square, like it wasn't worth bein' even a patch in a quilt. Now anything bigger than an inch in any direction wasn't a scrap, and there wasn't a big wooden barrel, just a tin bucket about the size of the one in the store to hold whatever didn't make the grade. Robert came to pick it up every Saturday and carry it to the hospital, where they shredded those scraps back into cotton lint and made bandages from it.

Robert was new to the Kittredges' store. He was supposed to be a slave, same as Mary, but he walked all over the place freer than any slave she'd ever seen, and Mary knew he was deep in Mista Kittredge's new business of buyin' barrels of flour outside of what the government said they could. Robert came three months before along with Mista Hughes, the first overseer Mista Kittredge ever had. And ever since then Robert'd been goin' with Mista Hughes to the depot every week, to buy up everything the stationmaster could set aside. Government prices said that a barrel of flour should go for a hundred twenty dollars Confederate, but the stationmaster would set ten or twelve of them aside, and Mista Hughes would pay the man a hundred sixty or seventy for it every week. It made perfect sense, since Mista Kittredge kept it tucked away in the old slave cabins and waited until all the flour in Richmond was gone in two or three days. Then he'd sell it to *special* customers for two hundred fifty, three hundred dollars a barrel, dependin' on how desperate things were. Then he started demandin' gold for it instead, or Yankee dollars even, since the war wasn't goin' too well for the Confederates.

With no sign of anyone on this Christmas Eve afternoon, Mary brought the scrap bin out back, then looked all around before reachin' in for the spools of thread. She pulled her dress high as her knee, rolled up her left-leg bloomer, and stuffed three spools into it, tyin' it off with a strip of cloth she'd set aside for just that purpose. Then she looked all around again and started in with the right leg, doin' just the same. When she had all three of them up in that bloomer, she took the strip of cloth to tie it off, but the bottom spool slipped out and rolled a few feet away. She hobbled to it, bent over holdin' that bloomer closed so the other spools didn't drop out, walkin' stiff legged over to that missin' spool. When she got to it, she could see someone comin' from around the corner by the alley, but didn't look up, pickin' up that spool and tyin' off that bloomer, gettin' just a single knot tied in it before he started talkin'.

Well, well, well, what has we here? he said gleefully, an Mary knew straight off that it was Robert come early to pick up the scrap bin. If it ain't da lovely Miss Mary, so special the white folks treats her like she one of 'em, an' here she is tyin' up her bloomers jus' like she a common ol' streetwalkin' gal. What'd Massa Kittredge an' the Misses say if dey saw you showin ol' Robert all 'at?

He walked slowly up to her, and she had to decide between double-knottin' that cloth and givin' him more of a show, or riskin' that it'd come loose. She stood up.

They'd ask what you were doing sneaking around corners and watching ladies fix themselves, she said, putting on that in-the-shop voice she knew irked him no end.

Well, Miss Mary, jus' you an' me now, he said, walkin' up to her, just inches away.

She tried steppin' past him to his right, but he put his arm up against the wall and stopped her. Now where you goin', Miss Mary? You gonna git all uppity on Robert now? When you's jus' like all th'resta us?

He took his other hand and wrapped it around her waist, pullin' her close to him, and kissin' her hard on the mouth, pullin' her in altogether now with his other arm wrapped around the back of her head. She got her two arms between them while he was pushin' his tongue against her squeezed-tight lips, him pryin' his way with his tongue while she was pryin' her way with her arms, 'til she could push enough to get some space between them and get her mouth free. He laughed and looked to pull her in close again, but she'd had enough of that, spools of thread do what they might. She lifted her right leg hard into him, right between the legs, then did it again and a third time, as he was fallin' down away from her, hard to the ground. And she felt the spools of thread slidin' down her leg now, with the cloth all untied, but it didn't matter, like she'd stuff them down his throat if he said another word.

But he was just rollin' on the ground when she could hear a commotion from over on the porch at the Kittredge house. A man rode up on a horse, with a Confederate uniform and a sword danglin' from his side, and when Justinia burst out onto the porch before he could dismount, Mary knew it was Lieutenant Farnsworth, and he'd got that Christmas leave after all. But still there was this matter to tend to, and Mary used her left leg to give Robert another kick, to his stomach this time, and he curled over, away from her, turnin' his back and rollin' himself up tight like he was tryin' to protect himself from any more kicks. And she had plenty of time to tie everything in her bloomers just right, lookin' at the porch as Lieutenant Farnsworth dropped to one knee, with entirely different intentions than the knee Robert was tryin' to prop himself up on just then. And Mary knew that this would be a night, and a Christmas, when Justinia'd have plenty of smiles to go around. And maybe it wouldn't be such a bad Christmas after all.

MICAH

LES ROSERAIES, SOUTH CAROLINA

JANUARY 18, 1865

The next mornin' the war practically walks right into *Les Roseraies.* Thomas sets off to work, but ten minutes later he's back askin' if you heard the gunfire off in the distance. 'Course you did. And know exactly what it means. Sherman. Which means everything's changed just overnight.

You see Thomas looking at you like he's waiting for instructions. Scared a little, like a man his age shouldn't be.

But then you start to see a chance to do more than just take care of your own. You see the chance to be a little like Mrs. Tubman was those years before. The chance to lead a whole buncha folks to freedom. And that'd be somethin' to make your Daddy proud, to be sure.

Time to go, Thomas, you say.

I'll see 'bout gettin' word to yo' Momma an' Bellie, Thomas says.

But you shake your head. Look him square in the eye, commanding this time, not asking like you did the night before.

We're ALL goin', Thomas, you say. You, me, Momma, Bellie, an' ev'ry hand on the place.

Thomas looks at you getting that Spencer Repeater ready. Knowin' you mean business. And with the determination in your voice and the shots he'd heard that morning, it's almost like he's too scared *not* to go with you now. But you don't give him a chance to say no. Ask him about where the overseer is an' where the Massa keeps his guns.

Massa gotta shotgun he ain' use in a long time, he says. Overseer's gone, they was sayin'. He lef' las' night t'join wit' some militia up the river. That's it far as I knows.

And the instructions follow. Commanding again. Telling Thomas to get word to all the slaves. Bring what food they can carry, and that's all. Meet at the creek inside an hour. And then you goin'.

What about yo' Momma an' Bellie? Thomas asks.

I'll take care of gettin' them.

Thomas sees you grippin' that Spencer tight and maybe thinks you still got revenge on your mind.

Massa's a old man like me, an' he ain't fired that shotgun in years, he says. Nobody got to die today, son.

And you look close at Thomas just so you can be sure it

ain't your Daddy doin' the talkin'. Much as it sounds just like him. Same tone, same kinda thing he'd say. Then you smile.

Don't worry. I got nothin' against this here Masta. He ain't a Masta no more, so he got enough to worry 'bout. An' maybe the Lawd wants him t'have some more time gettin' usedta that, you say. Smile at him before setting off.

Momma and Isabelle are on the front porch. The Massa's standin' there with his shotgun. Old, just like Thomas said. Done for this world of bein' anything like a Massa. Don't matter if Sherman's coming or not. He sees *you* comin', and he knows what it means. You point that Spencer Repeater at him. Tell him put down that shotgun, 'less he's fixin' to get dead. And he puts it down straight off. Turns to your Momma and starts pleadin'.

Don't let'm do us any harm, Corrine. Don't let'm kill us. Tell'm how good I was to my slaves . . . tell'm . . . please . . .

She looks at him like she's disappointed. Like she give him the benefit of a doubt more than such a man ever deserved. 'Cause she's been a slave for all her fifty years on this earth. And it'll take time to get to know something like freedom. Like she'll never be the woman she coulda been. And you feel sad at that moment. To see your Momma placin' what hope she got in such a man. Then she goes and surprises you.

That's my Son. And he's no murderer. He's a better man than you, for sure, she says. Picks the gun up from where he placed it down. We'll be on our way now.

And she and Isabelle walk off that porch like it was their own place, and they're just goin' to the Harvest Ball. Momma carries that shotgun like it's a rotted side of beef she can't wait to get outta her hands. She gives it to you, and stands with her arm over Bellie's shoulders. A half step behind you. Like you're the man of the family.

It's no surprise when the twenty-two of them, Thomas and Momma and Bellie alike, are jubilatin' when you all gather down by the creek. Like they're free already. Some of them got all their clothes and things strapped on their backs. Some of the women got blankets rolled up on their heads, carrying things inside the blankets. Making them look six seven feet tall. And you shake your head. Thinking of the foolishness. Knowing you got a ways to go yet.

One of the young boys brought a hammer and a chisel and an ax. Nothing more. And you smile at him, thinking he's just like you was when you were his age. Twelve thirteen, maybe. You call him over while everyone's jubilatin'. Ask him what other tools he can get. Send him off for the saws and a couple more things. Send Thomas along with him.

They're back with a good haul while you're still getting the crowd all together. And then you tell them about where you come from. And how you gonna get them to freedom. They listen like you was Mrs. Tubman, and you figure it's 'cause you the man with the Spencer Repeater. Then you realize Thomas still got it, from when you gave it to him to go back with the boy for the tools. And you think maybe there's something more than havin' the Spencer that makes them listen to you.

It's an hour before you get them all to the railroad bridge over the Edisto River. Where the Savannah-Charleston line crosses. And you know straight off that this is where your Daddy made his jump. Thomas looks at you. So does Momma. 'Cause they know. You shoot a glance at Bellie, but she's smilin' and talking to folks, like the place means nothin' at all. And you nod. Knowing that she doesn't need to know. Doesn't need to think the way you do, the way Thomas and Momma do, too. That maybe your Daddy picked out this place to jump that train 'cause he knew it'd do just the job it done. And oh—how you wanna *do* something about it. How you wanna shoot something. Someone. But you can't let yourself drift back into that fog that led you to kill Dunmore and the Embrys. This ain't just about *you* now.

There's some Union soldiers walking along the rail line, in something like formation. Twenny thirty of 'em. A patrol, most likely. But the shots you heard that morning came from upriver of *Les Roseraies,* not down. And you know that means Sherman an' his army must be all around this place. Farther west maybe, the way this patrol is walkin' with their rifles at the ready. They halt and look at you an' your crew of twenty-two runaways. Women and a couple of old men'n boys. And one or two men around your age. But they focus on you. Focus on that Spencer Repeater strapped to your back.

The leader, a Lieutenant, stares down at you from just that thirty forty feet above. So you nod. Like you the man he's dealin' with, if there's need for dealin'. But he just turns to the back of his line and hollers some orders. Only he's not instructing his men, but the fifteen twenny runaways he's got following at a long safe distance. Tells 'em to follow you. And then there's forty-one of you, counting yourself. And now you're *really* like Mrs. Tubman. Moses. Leading 'em out of Egypt.

It takes a while to assemble everyone together once the new ones are with you. Turns out there's another twenty or so not far off that couldn't keep up with the soldiers, these folks say. And you tell the two best men from the new ones to go back an' get 'em. Meet you on this side of the river. And they go, straight off.

You give Thomas the shotgun and tell him to take Momma and Bellie and all but the boy that took the tools and three other good men. Tell him to lead the rest on down the river far as they can go 'til they're ready to fall over. And you'll be there by nightfall. Momma and Bellie are the only ones that don't do just as you said. Feeling like they finally got to have you in their lives again, after they thought you were gone forever. And now you gonna leave them again. *So, no.* They say. But they go eventually. When Thomas tells 'em you're only doin' what his friend woulda done, what Samuel, your Daddy, woulda done.

Thomas gets them moving, and you smile just a little to see him like this. Like that fear got so built up that it just spilt out and onto the ground and now he's back to bein' a man. Not a mule. Or maybe it's 'cause he ain't just thinking for himself now either. But you don't waste any time trying to figure these things out. Instead you get the boy and the three other men and tell them to cut every short tree they can find to make into rafts. You go too, and when the first buncha branches and small tree trunks gets brought back, you stay with the boy. Show him how to set the thick ones on the bottom. Make a frame. Then the small ones on top. You and he finish the first one and get the frames for five more all set. And it's getting late in the afternoon now and no sign from the ones who fell behind the troops. So you leave the boy behind to finish the rafts, and set off with the Spencer.

You're not more than a mile from the railroad when you hear a few shots. Sound like tiny snaps, and you know they're not from the Union soldiers or any local man with a shotgun. A pistol probably. Maybe a twenny-two. Somebody in over his head, considerin' your Spencer. And that's just what it is. An overseer from one of the local plantations got a six-shooter he's using to try and corral the stragglers back. Like they're cattle gonna get spooked so easy. And there they are laying down on the ground, kids, old folks, and the two good men you sent off to find them. You pull out that Spencer and start firing. Seven shots go like nothin', even though you don't aim at nothin' but sky. Just to create some noise.

You reload, easy as can be with this breechloader. Then he fires one, and you know where he is. An' you let go, seven more shots almost right where he's standing. But not exactly. Feeling somehow that you can't kill this fool. Feeling like you don't want to kill anyone unless you have to. And it's all quiet as you reload, wondering how that hate's not there anymore. 'Til the runaways start percolating. Stand up, watching the overseer ride off south. And then they jubilate some. Before the men you sent to get them tell'm to come on.

You're back to the meeting place as it's getting on sundown. And the boy and the three other men you left got four more decent-size rafts ready to go. You figure the math in your head. More than sixty of you and five rafts means twelve or thirteen for each one. So you get fourteen onto the weakest one, just to be sure. When it doesn't sink, just getting the passengers a little wet is all, you smile at the boy. Who reminds you of yourself more than ever.

It's well past dark when you get to No Man's Land. See the ones from *Les Roseraies.* Announce to everyone that they'll be safe just a few miles more down the river. And then it's everyone onto the rafts, and all the stuff they carried is left behind. 'Cause it don't matter when you that close to freedom. And floatin' down those cool waters starts some of 'em singin' in low, humming voices. And you don't do anything to stop 'em.

You spend that night on the beach, two men standin' guard to the west in case anyone followed you. And you telling them about Edisto Island where there's a school for colored folks and whatever they're gonna need. Just waitin' for them, that close. Next mornin' you go in that rowboat across the inlet with Thomas and a few others. Find that Quartermaster Corporal that gave you the rowboat in the first place. Tell him about the folks on the mainland. Only there don't seem to be any more boats available. Not with Sherman coming this way. 'Course, a hundred dollars makes them boats reappear. And by the early afternoon every one of them folks, all sixty-three of 'em, are off the shore. And on Edisto Island. Free.

Takes another fifty dollars to buy food from the Quartermaster Corporal. At least something more than the hardtack and some half-rotted potatoes he usually gives out to runaways. And then a sort of feast breaks out. 'Cause these folks ain't breathed this sea air, or anything like freedom, ever. And you think, seeing them like this. Jubilatin'. That it makes up for the disappointment your own freedom was. 'Cause this ain't just about you now. When one of the strays you went back for, a preacher of sorts, gets to praying, they all join in. Thomas and Momma and Bellie do, too. And soon they're asking the Lord to bless you in a *special* way. Like you're their Moses. Like the Lord sent you here to find 'em.

And in the middle of all the jubilation, you walk off just to be on your own, for a few moments. Breathing deep, thankful breaths. Thanking your Daddy for everything he taught you about being a man. Preparing you for this very day. And you say goodbye to him, like you never got to, years ago. Telling him your inheritance, that indigo field . . . thousand pounds or not. Has come in at last.

15 *To the Shores of the Ever After*

MARY
RICHMOND
APRIL 2, 1865

So it turns out that everything's falling all at once, instead of the slow crumble it's been these last nine or ten months. Mista Kittredge has been all out of sorts with the Misses ever since February, when the dress shop got closed down altogether. And with how Mista Kittredge sold off all the slaves except Cora and Ginny and Mabel in the kitchen, and Mary, of course, it looks like the Mista and Misses'll be startin' off down in Carolina with nothin' like the household they had just a year ago.

Richmond's become a corpse. And saddest of all is that there's all these people still around to watch it get buried, Mary included, watchin' it whimper to a sad end while most folks are still holding on to memories of its past glory. The whole South is gettin' to be a memory, too, and slavery right along with it, and now it's just the hardest part left. Mista Kittredge has his sources in the war department, he always says, and they told him the end wouldn't come 'til early June at best, late April at worst. There isn't any more money to be made from the folks of Richmond anyway, since any flour and cornmeal has been requisitioned directly by the war department for months now, and it only ever trickles its way down to the soldiers and civilians in little bits not anywhere close to filling any of their bellies. Mista Kittredge still has a few barrels left from months back, but nobody's got much of anything to buy them with.

Still, what bothers Mista Kittredge, and the Misses especially, is that they won't be able to take most of their best things with them on that last train out of Richmond. It'll just be those two trunks full of silver tea sets and picture frames and gold jewelry wrapped in silk-laced curtains that they managed to slip out already on a train bound for Danville, Virginia. The Misses's brother was supposed to pick that up when it arrived a week ago, but they have no way of knowin' if it got there or not, since the telegraph is for military communication only now, and there hasn't been any mail in at least a month.

So Mista Kittredge announced just the day before that by the end of the week they'd be leavin'. It'd be Mista Kittredge and the Misses and Justinia and a few more trunks of picture frames and linen and clothes and such . . . and Mary, all gettin' on a train to Danville. He said it to Cora and Mabel and Ginny like it was the worst news they could ever hear in their whole lives, that they'd be left behind. And Cora and Mabel and Ginny did their best not to break out in laughter and celebration right there, savin' it for a minute later when they walked in the kitchen. When Cora saw Mary not long after that, she just nodded her head up and down with her lips pursed tightly and her hands perched on her hips.

See that now, she said, you jus' like a little pup to them what they figure they can take wit' 'em wherever they goes.

And Mary looked sternly at her, using every bit of anger

she could find within herself to keep from crying in front of her. She'd thought the same kind of thing, too, wondering why she'd be the one to go and not Ginny or Mabel who at least knew how to cook. But she offered Cora her own explanation.

Juss wants me to go with them, she said, purposely not putting the *Miss* in front of her name and then walking out of the room.

So Miss Juss wants her little pup t'come along, Cora said, and walked away with a look on her face as if she'd been right all along.

But then the morning of April 2 brings news of a Yankee victory south of Petersburg, and Justinia and Mary are sent to her room to pack *one* trunk, that's all, 'cause they may be leavin' as early as the next morning. Of course, Justinia has no interest in packing, wantin' only to talk to Mary about what, or more especially *who,* she's leavin' behind.

I can't leave him here! Justinia says, talking about Lieutenant Farnsworth. What if he's wounded? What if he's been captured? When this is over, he won't know where to find me.

Aww, Juss he'll find ya, Mary answers. Lieutenant Farnsworth knows about your Momma's brother down in Carolina. He'll be comin' lookin' for ya, Juss.

He knows about them livin' in *Raleigh.* He doesn't know that they've moved to *Greensboro*! I haven't seen him since we got that letter from Uncle James last month.

Mary's been able to see Justinia growin' up fast these last few years. And the tears Juss cries now are not the sort from the spoiled child she used to be but a woman's, filled with the sadness of everything that's beyond her control. Mista Kittredge wouldn't give his consent on their gettin' engaged back at Christmas, but he did let them leave off with a sort of *understandin'*, like they were engaged *to get* engaged once the war's over. Still, Mary knows that having an understandin' is as good as bein' engaged in a woman's eyes, and she feels something awful for Juss. She wants to at last tell her about Micah, and tell her how much she knows exactly what she's feelin'. But there's no time for any of it, 'cause the Misses bursts into the room, frantic.

Today! We're going today, she says breathlessly. Right now! The final train is leavin' in an hour. The Yankees broke the lines at Petersburg and–oh, it's awful. Your father says we can take one trunk for all of us, an' even that he's not sure of–so you'll have to wear as much as you can. One dress over another. Wear your jewelry, but cover it with a shawl–oh–hurry Justinia. Your father says this is the only train he knows for certain we can get aboard. The troops are retreatin' through the city right this moment. Hurry!

And with that she's out of the room and off to her own. But Mary and Justinia have nothin' like her sense of panic.

Did you talk to your Momma about stayin'? Mary asks, as if all that news hasn't sunk in.

Of course not. Do you see her? She'd never allow it.

Maybe if I–

But then they can hear her father's footsteps in the hallway approaching the door to her room, and both of them bounce up off the bed and over to her closet. Mary pulls a few dresses out and pretends to be sortin' through them with her as her father knocks loudly on the door.

Justinia!

Don't come in Daddy! I'm not decent!

We hafta go! Immediately!

We'll be downstairs in two minutes, she replies, then looks desperately at Mary.

Now, Justinia! her father shouts.

Help me put these dresses on, Justinia mumbles to Mary with a look of surrender.

She picks two of her plainest dresses out and hands them to Mary. Mary's surprised at the random choice but says nothing. She helps her pull one then the other over her head, then asks what jewelry she wants to take.

Oh anything, Justinia replies. I don't care anymore.

Mary goes to the vanity table and opens up the jewelry box, still thinkin' about what's going on in Juss's mind, and not thinkin' of how she needs to be packing for herself. She holds up a necklace that her father gave her years before.

You wanna take this? Mary asks.

Fine.

Then she sees the brooch that Lieutenant Farnsworth gave her for Christmas. She holds it up as well and asks again, You wanna take this?

Fine.

You gonna be all right? Mary asks.

Justinia only shrugs her shoulders and falls into a defeated posture.

I know what you're goin' through, Mary says.

And Juss looks up at Mary with sad eyes that turn doubtful.

How *could* you? Juss says.

Mary looks back at her, hurt by the realization that the closest person in the world to her these last twelve years doesn't know anything about the man she loves. She thinks of how she's heard every detail about every boy or officer Justinia ever batted an eyelash toward. Shouldn't *sisters,* the way Juss always calls the two of them–shouldn't they know all about *each other*?

Justinia! her father yells again from the bottom of the stairs.

We best be goin' before your father comes back up here, is all Mary says.

Justinia! The scream is from halfway up the staircase now.

They open the door and walk quickly downstairs, and it isn't until they're standin' by the front door that Mary realizes she has nothin' of her own packed, and worst of all, the fifty-seven mourning veils she's made over the last year are still stuffed inside her mattress.

Oh, Misses Kittredge, Mary says quietly to her, trying not to let Mista Kittredge hear. I only got dis here dress. Can I run an' fetch anotha?

I had Cora pack you a bag to take, the Misses replies reassuringly. Of course, it isn't reassuring at all to Mary.

Then Cora walks up behind her and presents her a big cloth bag that bulges at the seams with its clasp barely shut.

I didn't know which dress you'd a like the mos', so I throwed a buncha dem in there, Cora says in an unnaturally sweet tone. Perhaps freedom will make her a different person after all, Mary thinks, and takes the bag. Then Cora carries on like none of them have ever seen from her.

Ohhh, ol' Cora's gonna miss you all. You sho' been good to Ol' Cora, she says, talking in a way she never did before and looking at the Kittredges, who stand with confused looks on their faces. An' Mary, she continues, I knows we had our mischief 'tween us, but Ol' Cora's gonna miss you, too, somethin' fierce.

It's about the strangest thing Mary's ever heard from her, callin' herself Ol' Cora like that. And she thinks that maybe Gertie was right all along about how Cora saw her like she was a daughter somehow. But then Cora walks up to Mary and hugs her, placin' her head on Mary's shoulder away from the Kittredges. *I know all 'bout them veils you been makin'. Don' worry, dey in dere too,* she whispers in Mary's ear. *'Cept for five or six I kep' for myself. Ol' Cora's gotta eat, too.*

She pulls back from Mary and holds her at arm's length. You take care o' you'sef', an' you take care of de Kittredges, too, now. Dey's the bes' Massas you eva gonna hope fo'.

Mary nods at Cora, doin' all she can to suppress a smile, and Cora doesn't help matters when she winks at her. But then the Misses, overcome with emotion at Cora's short speech, begins to cry again.

Oh, we'll miss you too, Cora, she weeps, and throws her arms around her.

Cora looks over the Misses' shoulder, rolling her eyes for only Mary to see. Mary can't hold the laugh back completely now and lets forth a snort as she exhales, then quickly pretends to sniffle as if it's tears she's fightin' back.

Let's go, the train's leavin' in fifteen minutes, Mista Kittredge says.

They walk down the sidewalks carryin' the small bags themselves, with the family trunk sent ahead. The Misses is still sniffling back tears, and Juss seems like she's about to faint right there on the walkway. But Mary's thoughts aren't caught up with them for long, turnin' instead toward her own situation. She gets to thinking about how this is no *trip* they're takin', like the one at Christmas a few years before the war. They're moving, fleeing, and not likely to see Richmond anytime soon.

Almost lost in the noise of the train boiler building up steam, and the wagons moving quickly down the street, comes a low *rat-a-tat-tat* noise from a block away, the march-step of soldiers, moving toward them, gettin' louder as they approach. People stop their carriages and step off to the sides of the streets, clearing a path for what might've once been a brigade or even a division but now looks like a broken-down regiment retreating through the city. The men are all in tatters, with clothes that are hardly anything that can be called uniforms—or even *clothes,* for that matter. At least a quarter of them have "shoes" made of strips of cloth tied together with string. Maybe half have no shoes at all. And as Mary and the Kittredges watch them go past, it's hard to imagine that these men have lived through winter in the trenches dressed that way. They're shadows of men, still marching in good form from habit, but otherwise lookin' nothing like an army. There are no shouts from the civilians cheering them and urging them on again, and the men don't even look from side to side, just straight ahead at the road before them, nothing about their appearance makin' anyone believe that they can rally and beat back the Yankees once more.

It's done, Mista Kittredge says quietly after they pass, shakin' his head in sadness. They're not an army anymore . . . only delayin' the inevitable now. Just wastin' more lives.

The Misses elbows her husband, but it's too late to keep Juss from cryin'.

I'm sure the Lieutenant's fine, Mista Kittredge says. Those fellas weren't officers.

And then Mista Kittredge goes off to find the railroad official he made arrangements with, as the Misses comforts Juss. Mary stands beside them on the platform, and now, finally, the reality of the situation sets in for her. As of that very moment, she thinks, Cora and the rest of the Kittredge slaves are free. No runnin' off required for them. All they have to do is stay in Richmond until the last Confederate soldier marches out and the first Yankee soldier marches in. And they're free, not in the runaway sense, but accordin' to Mr. Lincoln's law.

It's not anywhere near the first time Mary's considered such things. But considerin' a thing and havin' it stare you in the face are different matters entirely. And it produces some strange thoughts in her mind, like, *Why am I the only one not getting my freedom? Why am I dragged out of Richmond like that trunk filled with tea sets and lace curtains that I made?* And she begins to feel that she *deserves* to be free, that any obligation she might've had toward the Kittredges for rescuing her off that auction block has been repaid many times over. She'll always feel a sense of gratitude toward them and genuine love for Juss. But now she feels that she should have the chance to see if Micah's still waiting for her. She wonders if he might be thinking of her now that Richmond is falling, that maybe he won't have married another or turned bitter toward her because she didn't run off with him. Then when she thinks about how it's been more than two years since then, she figures that maybe a second chance with him is too much to ask for. But her freedom is not.

I found Oates, Mista Kittredge says when he rushes back. We're ridin' in the eighth car, an' Mary, you'll be ridin' with the cabinet minister's slaves up in the third car.

He says it with a sense of prestige connected to the very idea of riding with slaves who belong to such high-ranking men. And Mary knows Ol' Cora'd be rollin' her eyes something fierce if she was here.

Oates says we need to get aboard this instant. The minute th'government ministers are aboard, the train'll be pullin' out.

He lifts their two large bags and turns toward the train,

and the Misses is right beside him. But Justinia is slow to follow, and Mary wraps her arm inside hers and leans her head toward her ear.

Y'know, Juss, you don't *hafta* get on this train, she says. *We* don't hafta get on this train.

And Juss looks at her as if she's spoken French to her.

What? she says. Daddy just—

Train's pullin' out any minute. Lookit all these folks around here. We can walk right into that crowd of 'em over there and get lost in it 'til the train goes.

And for a second she thinks she sees enough of a spark in Juss to go along with it, the way she could always get Juss to go along with things. But then they're all startled by the sound of a shell descending frighteningly close to them. It whistles to the ground and explodes perhaps a block away, and there are screams from nearby and panic. Another shell follows almost on top of it and lands even closer, just a hundred yards or so from the train. At the end of the platform a coach pulls up next to the tracks, and they can see what looks like several cabinet ministers, and then President Davis himself, step out and toward the caboose of the train. And Mary looks at Juss and sees the answer is no.

This is it now, sir, a man in uniform says to Mista Kittredge by the door to car number eight. This is gonna be the last train out 'fore the Yankees come pourin' in.

And Mista Kittredge pulls at Justinia's arm, leading her onto the train to where the Misses is already sitting down. Mary can see Juss flop down on the seat facing opposite the Misses, looking toward the back of the train and beginning to cry again as soon as she sees Mary. Then Mista Kittredge is calling to Mary, snapping his fingers and then reaching for Mary's bag when she is slow to follow.

That's all right, Mista Kittredge, Mary says, I can carry it.

Well, let's go then. I wanna make sure Oates told the attendant on that car up there about our arrangement.

And they walk through the confused crowd to the other end of the train, a cargo car just behind the coal bins. There aren't any seats in it, but Mary looks inside and sees well-dressed slaves sitting on their bags or on the floor, or on the large trunks stacked near the front of it.

That's it, Mary, it's all arranged, Mista Kittredge says. We'll see you in Danville.

He watches Mary step on the train, then he's off without waiting for a response, walking so fast he's practically running, all the way back to car number eight. The steam whistle blows three times, and Mary looks around at the folks in the car, all of them with sad looks on their faces like they're defeated every bit as much as the Confederate soldiers they saw marching down the street. None of them are talking, not to her, not to each other, just sitting there waiting to be taken to wherever it is their Massas say.

As the whistle blows twice more, Mary's heart starts to race, thinking back to the first time she ever rode on a train, back when she was something like these folks here, beaten, robbed of any spirit, being taken to that auction block in Raleigh. Only now she's not scared the way she usually is when those kinds of memories come to her. Instead, as she hears the steam pushing the locomotive wheels slowly into action, *hummph . . . hummph . . . hummph . . . hummph,* it's like the sound calls out to her, bringing her back before the train ride to the auction block . . . back to the rhythm of Gertie's heavy breaths, *hummph . . . hummph . . . hummph . . . hummph,* standin' there in the Deep River, with Mary beside her while she's catchin' her breath . . . *hummph . . . hummph.* And closing her eyes, she can almost feel the cool water trickling through her fingertips again, and the images of being carried away, just her and Gertie off to someplace where it'd just be the two of them and the little cabin by the stream somewhere . . . and freedom, pure and perfect as that water . . .'til it's almost like hearin' Gertie's voice whisperin' to her when she first set foot in Deep River and Mary wanted nothin' of it . . . and Gertie breathin' hard . . . *hummph . . . hummph,* just to stand still there in the water, but reaching out her hand to Mary . . . *C'mon, Chil', jus' that first step gonna be the hardes' one . . . hummph . . . hummph . . . then you be okay . . . Gertie ain' gonna let you fall . . . hummph . . . hummph.*

And when she opens her eyes, a step is all it is—sliding open the door—seeing the wooden platform beginning to run out ahead of them—the train moving quicker with every *hummph . . . hummph* . . . until the locomotive and the coal bins pass the end of the platform . . . and a smile on her face now as she holds tight to that bag in her hand and takes that step, feeling the wood of the platform beneath her feet and then a few little steps to catch her balance—and *hummph . . . hummph* . . . the train still pulling away and nobody seemin' to notice she's not on it anymore.

Then there's the deep breath of freedom to fill her lungs, and there are tears too and smiling besides, knowing what she's leaving behind. She looks up at the numbers of the cars as they pass, five then six then seven, until the hardest one of all to see go. And there's Juss starin' out the window still, not seein' Mary right away, but then, just for a moment, she can see Juss's eyes go wide and her hand come up to cover her mouth. But just before it gets there, Mary thinks she can see a bit of a smile startin' to form on Juss's face, the kind that comes just before the tears. And she knows they'll be plenty of those, but first that bit of a smile . . . something for her to hold on to and remember her friend by.

And know these last twelve years ain't all been for nothin'.

Ethan
cooperstown
april 4, 1865

The news poured into town the previous afternoon, and people celebrated the way they *should* celebrate such news. Not like it was vengeance being brought upon *those damn Rebs,* but like it was one step, one day, closer to the end of this whole damn war. Ethan hadn't been able to sleep for more than a few restless moments at a time, thinking all the while that it was as if the great walled city of Troy had at last fallen. And he could only imagine what it'd been like for Micah. So when he heard the creak of footsteps on the stairs the next morning, he knew it had to be him. And he waited only a few minutes, making sure that Aislinn wasn't stirring, to slip out of their room and join his friend on the porch.

Nice mornin', Ethan said, after he'd run the gauntlet and made his way to the front door.

I was tryin' not to wake anyone, Micah replied, still getting used to living with more people than he ever had before.

I'm gonna hafta talk to th'carpenter that fixed those stairs. Third one from the bottom's got a creak in it like you wouldn't believe, Ethan said. Shoddy work.

Yep—tough t'find good men these days, Micah replied, as they slipped into their now-familiar banter.

Ethan sat in the chair next to Micah, looking out over the

dark landscape with just a suggestion of light appearing over the hills to the east. Their two family histories seemed forever intertwined after the events of the past few months. Corrine and Isabelle had been staying here at the house along with Micah for going on a month now. They'd stayed in Brooklyn with Ethan's family for the first two weeks after they finally got a boat off Edisto Island. And now they were waiting on the better weather of summer, when there'd be more work for everyone and they could get a place big enough for the three of them.

So what're you still doing here? Ethan asked matter-of-factly.

Micah looked at him, a little perplexed.

Richmond's an open city, Ethan added, knowing what it would mean to Micah.

Micah looked away from him, back out over the hills, like he was allowing himself to dream a little again.

You figure I should see if she's still there? Micah asked.

Ethan pulled his head back and let his eyebrows crowd over his eyes.

You have other pressing engagements to tend to? he asked. I know the Hoffmans' chicken coop needs fixing, and the Richters are lookin' to do somethin' about th'leak in their barn, an' th'Wesleys want a porch like this one and–yes, I guess that's enough to keep a workin' man from goin' after the woman he loves. A woman it sounds like is worth chasin' to the shores of the Ever After, but sure, this makes more sense. Maybe you can fit her in sometime in July or maybe August, an' then just see . . .

And Micah'd already started laughing by then.

You think she's still there? Micah asked, hopefully.

Only one way t'find *out.*

And Micah nodded, looked out over the porch railing again.

Ten-thirty train's still runnin' outta Richfield Springs, Ethan said. Henry said we could take the carriage.

Mmmm, Micah responded.

'Til Ethan grew impatient.

Just how long you gonna keep that woman waitin'?

And the hopeful hint of a smile on Micah's face was all the answer necessary.

MICAH
RICHMOND
APRIL 12, 1865

His first steps through the streets of his former home are unimaginable. Maybe a third of the city gone completely. Other sections with pockmarked streets where shells landed. Buildings torn through or burnt to the ground. Like the Longley place, with nothing but three brick chimneys and a foundation to say there'd even been something there. And there's not the kind of lustful joy he might've felt to see such a thing not so long ago. Just shaking his head over and over.

President Lincoln visited Richmond a week before. All the colored folks swarming the streets to meet him. Reporter for the newspaper Micah read it in compared it to the Messiah being welcomed into Jerusalem. Said that if they had palms to lay before the President, they certainly would have. And he wonders if Mary had still been there for the excitement. Wishes he could've been there, too. Not so much to see Lincoln. Just that all the fuss made it impossible to get into the city. Took him eight days from Cooperstown. Every day maybe the one where Mary slipped away. Or maybe, if she was gone already, the day that little bitta thread that'd help him find her got swept away somehow.

It's mostly just Yankee soldiers and colored folks in the streets now. Plenty of smiles on all their faces now that Ol' Bobby Lee, like Ethan calls him, surrendered altogether. And the war's all over but for the last little bits of it. Killin' the ones so stubborn they won't stop 'til it's all just chimneys to mark what used to be. The whole land covered in the penance of slavery.

And as Micah walks to the Kittredges' store, he's relieved at least to see it's still there. Nothin' in it, and windows smashed in out front, but still there. And his and Mary's special meeting place around back left untouched. Then the walkway up to the house, and his heart up near his throat like it was first time he saw her. Thinkin' now that maybe she's still here after all. That maybe God could forgive the man he was enough to give him that one more chance. But then as he gets closer he can see Union soldiers walking out the front door. And more sitting on the front porch. Union flag draped from a window on the second floor like it never'd be if Mista Kittredge was still there. And the only hope he can see is the colored soldier standing guard by the door.

Beg pardon, Suh, he says, just to be safe. Might you know the family that lives here?

The soldier looks down at him. Suspicious.

Why you wanna know? He says.

I used to live here—well, not here, but in Richmond, Micah answers.

You run off?

Yes, two years ago.

From this place?

No, this is where my . . .

Where yo' gal live? The soldier asks, smiling now.

Yes, Micah replies, disappointed that this is the first colored soldier he's ever spoken to.

An' you run off wit'out her an' now you come back to fine her? An' you 'spect she be happy t'see ya when you run off on 'er like dat? He says, laughing louder with each breath. I lef' my gal in Carolina befo' the war, an' I ain't botherin' t'go back an' find 'er. I jus' find me anotha one.

Well, I had no choice. Micah says.

Well, you go an' see if dat gone git you anywhere wit her. And he can't stand up anywhere near straight any more from his laughing.

Micah starts to walk away. Gets maybe three four steps, then the soldier calls him back.

Hold on jus' a minute here—I think I know jus' where yo' gal is. He says, opening the door to the house and pointing back at Micah. You jus' wait there, an' I go get someone t'fetch her.

And the soldier steps inside for a bit. Talks and laughs with another colored soldier just inside the door. Then comes back out and stands his post.

You jus' wait right dere. He says.

And Micah can tell by the way he laughs to himself that it isn't going to be Mary. Then he hears the soldier inside the door talking.

I dunno, he just told me there was someone here to see ya.

The front door opens, and the soldier outside looks back at Micah.

This here yo' gal? He says. And stops laughing before he

can get started. Since it's clear straight off that they know each other.

It's Cora. And Micah feels more relieved to see her than he ever would've imagined being.

Well, you come back afta all. Cora says.

And Micah nods. Lets a half-smile come over his face. Is she here?

Now you two sho' got dis way of passin' each other comin' and goin', an' here's me gettin' stuck in the middle same as always.

And with the colored soldier standing there silent as a column, Micah and Cora talk only in essential details. Him about the North. About ending up in Cooperstown. Nothing about the Home Guard or Dunmore and the Embrys. And her about the end days here. How he'll be prouda Mary jumpin' off the train like she did. And how she left just three days before. Volunteered on a hospital train goin' to Washington. Didn't know where she'd go after that.

Looks like she done changed her mine back, Cora says. She gone lookin' for you!

MARY
NEW YORK
APRIL 24, 1865

It's been ten days here now, Gertie. I know I said I was gonna stay just long enough to sell the rest of the mournin' veils, but something happened the day I arrived that made me kinda shut down with fear. Like it was a bad thing runnin' off again. That's 'cause the day I got here was the day Mista Lincoln, the Yankee President, got shot. Killed dead by a man from the South, it turns out. And it's like there's no end to the death all around us.

You remember when I talked to you about seein' him there in Richmond, when he came just after the Yankees took over the city? All the slaves he freed lined up along the streets, and even though Micah never had much use for him, and the Kittredges thought he was the devil himself, I was happy to see the man, the President of this new country we're all fixin' to be a part of again.

That train with wounded Yankees got me as far as Washington. And it's my fault we ain't talked since then. Since I been thinkin' all about Micah, and what bein' in the North'll be like, and what's gonna happen to me—and thinkin' 'bout Juss too. Then Mista Lincoln gets killed like that and—I guess I was all kindsa caught up in this fear I got that maybe—I know it's foolish—but how both times I run off, somebody died. And I couldn't talk to you, Gertie. Not 'til now.

I sold all those thirty-four veils I had left with me just in these last two days, once I started comin' outta that sad kinda place I was in. It helped that Misses Corcoran runnin' the boardin' house I been stayin' at says that she needs another week's board from me or I gotta get out. So I sold ten veils yesterday and gave her some of the money, then sold the rest today in just about an hour or two. Three dollars apiece, the way Misses Corcoran said I should charge, insteada the dollar I been chargin'. And the reason why I sold all of 'em, even at three dollars apiece, is 'cause the train with President Lincoln come through town today. There was a parade—a procession

I guess is the better word—down Broadway. Then they laid his body out at City Hall for all the folks to see. So I went, Gertie. I felt I had to for how he helped end this war and have it give us freedom, even though I come to understand that it wasn't Mista Lincoln's to give—our freedom, that is. Folks can only take away freedom from other folks, not give it.

So anyway, I waited in line for three hours just to get the chance to walk by his casket and see him up close like that. His face looked like a hundred-year-old man's would be, all hollowed out and wrinkled. Death can't have helped him none, of course, but he musta had an awful tough time in this life, the way he looked. And I prayed as I walked past, askin' the Lord to look out for him. 'Cause I do believe he was an awfully good man, despite what the Kittredges and everybody in Richmond usedta say.

And when I come back here to the boardin' house just a while ago, I told Misses Corcoran where I been and she got a sad look on her face, then she give me back the money I already paid for the resta the week. She told me to get goin' on up to where I said I was goin', though she couldn't remember the name. And she wasn't bein' mean, just sayin' that I should go find that man I said I'd be lookin' for 'cause there ain't many men good enough to go lookin' for and she figured I'd better get up there 'fore some other gal stole him away. And so I said I'd go.

Tomorrow's the train up to Albany and then change for another to Buffalo, and then it's another across to St. Catharines, way up in Canada. But I'm scared, Gertie. Not of the runnin' anymore, or of the not knowin' if Micah'll be there, or if things'll be all right when I—well—I guess

I'm scared of all those things. But I'm most scared of all this not-knowin'. I'm tired of it. And if this is what freedom's all about, then maybe it ain't such a good thing after all. I just don't know anymore. And it's hard not hearin' from you, Gertie. My dreams've got turned off ever since I left Richmond. And it'd be nice to hear from you again. To know, whatever else's gonna happen, that at least you're still there.

NEW YORK CENTRAL RAILROAD
APRIL 25, 1865

Gertie's settin in her rickety old chair at her stitchin' again—an there's you watchin' her, same as always—ain't but a trickle a'light comin' from what's left of th'fire, an still she's pullin' that needle through, back an forth . . . an' you fussin' about same as always . . . lookin' outside the winda 'cause the rain's pourin' down so hard ain't no workin' inna fields today . . . jus' settin' inside tryin' to keep dry an warm an no playin' inna crick neither like on mos' days when they ain't no work . . . an you fussin' some more . . . askin' Gertie 'bout yo' Momma an Daddy some—tryin' t'see what they faces musta looked like . . . then askin' if you can throw anotha log on the fire and she says it's okay even though it's April already . . . an' when you do and the fire starts kickin' up some you flop down onta yo' bed an let it warm you on one side, then the otha . . . 'til you starin' right at Gertie an' seein' her stichin' only from the side that don't make no sense . . . and you ask her again 'bout what it's gonna be, an she just get a smile 'cross her face the way she sometimes do when you ask such foolish questions.

You gonna know soon enough, Chil', she says. You gonna know sooooon enough . . .

ST. CATHARINE'S, ONTARIO, CANADA
MAY 7, 1865

She had allowed herself to believe that he'd be here, ever since the dream on the train, when she was sure it was Gertie speaking to her, like she was sayin' *Keep goin', Chil', keep goin'.* It was that dream that helped her cross into Canada, certain he'd be here. And that dream that helped her when she arrived and didn't find him that same day, or in the days afterward, or find anyone who'd even heard of a man named Micah passin' through here. Twelve days later it was helping her believe still, though belief was wearing a little thinner these days, and she found herself feelin' more alone than ever before.

She'd arrived two Fridays ago and looked all around the colored settlement near Salem Chapel, then went into the few shops there and even stopped people on the street, asking if any of them knew of a man named Micah. Then, figurin' he might've changed his name for safety, she went into long descriptions of him and his skills as a carpenter, and still received not a single encouraging response. The next mornin' she was at it again, and every mornin' since, even speaking to the few white abolitionists from another section of town. And still she'd found nothing.

The old woman who ran the boardinghouse where Mary stayed told her about a number of other settlements stretching out over hundreds of miles along the Canadian border.

She said he might've gone to one of them, and Mary began to wonder if that was a possibility. Maybe circumstances had forced him to cross the border somewhere else. Maybe he'd married another woman before he ever arrived here. Maybe he'd never made it at all, gettin' swallowed up by the snow and winter in the Blue Ridge Mountains. No–she wouldn't allow that thought, she insisted to herself. And that was when she decided to look for work, figurin' this might be a *The Lord helps those who help themselves* kind of situation, like Gertie used to say. She'd work, and wait, and search, for as long as it took.

When the Sunday service at Salem chapel was done, she stayed in her pew a little while to let most of the crowd pass. Some of them, people she'd spoken to in the past few days, nodded to her as they walked by, and she felt encouraged that she'd be accepted here. 'Til eventually she stepped outside the chapel and down the several steps, and all around were people assembled into little groups and sharing a few words or some laughter before they were on their way home. And Mary stood there for a moment and took it in, realizin' that it was the first time in her life she'd seen such a congregation of colored folks, well dressed, cheerful, leisurely. It brought a smile to her face as she moved along, planning to return to the boarding-house. And then.

Mary.

Spoken in a deep voice, not as a question but a statement. And in the time it took for her to turn around, that quiet, determined faith that had allowed her to even conceive of such a moment surged through her once again. She *felt* it was him before she set her eyes fully upon him, then breathed in with a gasp when her sight could confirm it.

Without words, she stepped toward him, seeing the imprint of exposure and hardship upon his face–the time intervening written in lines across his forehead, but the hope still radiant in his kind eyes. And unable to do anything more than match his weary, relieved smile, she simply buried her face against his shoulder and became surrounded in his embrace. For this moment, and many more to follow, words would only seem like the unwanted wakeful moments after the sweetest of all dreams.

He was here.

16 *Frontsways*

Ethan
cooperstown
april 25, 1867

Seated here along the lake like this, on a rock big enough to serve as a chair with your feet stretched out to the edge of water, you can almost remember what it was like back then, back when the men and women who'd survived the hard life of the Old Country long enough to have crevasses runnin' the length and width of their faces would get to reminiscing in the way they used to do. And someone'd be sure to say, *Was it dat laahhng ago, sure it cahhn't be twenty years now . . . ohch how th'time pahses . . .* and you and the other children would look at them amazed that anyone could live so long to describe twice your own lifetime as if it were nothin' more than half a planting season waitin' on the new potatoes. But now, though there aren't any crevasses on your face just yet, twenty years doesn't seem like such a vast expanse of time after all.

The whole family is up for the occasion, everyone but Uncle Paddy that is, and him havin' to drive his ferryboat back and forth across the East River was excuse enough for remainin' behind. And who could blame him for wantin' to miss what was likely to be a funeral twenty years in the making. It's always been a day you try to simply get past each year, only *this* year, this twenty-year *anniversary* of the day, it seems as if time is determined to slow itself down in ways it hasn't since you were in the army. There's the sun to prove it, no more than an hour in the sky, even though you've been wide awake for three or four at least.

Mary was by the house just after first light, wantin' to see if Marcella and Aislinn–little Aislinn, dear love–would come along for the mornin' walk they sometimes take. And the surest indication of what a long day this'll be was the way you could hear Marcella whisper how she better not go along as well, as if the memorializing had already begun. Still, little Aislinn wasn't to be denied, and she and her Anta May set off not long before you did, with Marcella lookin' at you through beleaguered eyes and saying *oh yes, that's a good idea, yes you take a walk too . . . I love you . . .* as if you'd only been married four weeks and not as many years–and still you are smilin' at her on the way out all the same, just because.

You hadn't set out with a plan, but somehow the walks you take by yourself along the lake almost always end up here in the slight clearing where you sometimes come to talk to her. There's something about the shore of any body of water, even a lake or a river, that's made you feel through all these years like all you have to do is send off a whisper's worth of words and they'll be carried back across the ocean, all the way back to the Lane outside Enniskillen, and maybe she'll know you haven't forgotten. Not this day, or any other.

But you don't say anything right off, just watch the tiny ripples across the water and think of *how th'time pahses* indeed. Before long you can almost remember what it was like to be that young, to see twenty years as if it were twice a lifespan. And then, closin' your eyes to let the memory wash over you, it's as if you can hear the words again, with Father Laughton up to his old tricks racin' though *Th'LahrdismyshepherdIshall notwant* . . . as if his Protestant bladder was overflowin', and not in the good way it did during the less somber occasions. It's not the chill of that twenty-years-ago morning you feel, or the emptiness of the days that followed, but the helplessness of a boy trying to be a man . . . and all the ways you'd let your family down, let *her* down . . . the funeral Mass that wasn't fit for a stranger that'd died wandering the countryside, let alone her . . . with the too-small coffin . . . and the tiny slate laid flat on the ground left to the carnage of the overgrowth. And you begin to imagine what it must look like now, with the weeds and grass covering it a little more each year, suffocating the only thing that ever made her final resting place appear to be anything more than a patch of grass beside the decaying old church . . . until it must've become nothin' at all . . . nothin' even for the folks to walk past and say, *Oh poor lass, just sixteen what a pity, what a tragedy, musta been The Hunger.* And what of the promise you'd made to her that you'd never let such a thing happen?

The very thoughts of her now—of how you'd *failed* her—are tiny daggers of guilt and shame jabbing at the place deep within you where you've put all such memories away—until bitin' your lip or shakin' your head side to side can't stem the tide that bursts from within you in gasps of air and a few childlike yelps. The water's not stoppin' at your eyes the way it always does, but rollin' down your cheeks and off onto the rock big enough to be a chair as you bury your head in your hands that rest upon your knees. And the memories burst forth upon you, *all* the memories, tellin' the story of the connectin' years in disjointed fashion, each of them awash in the guilt, the shame . . . the helplessness.

There are your boyhood friends, mere lads from Red Hook who went on to become Excelsiors, to become part of the *Fightin' Sixty-Ninth* of the mighty *Irish Brigade*—then all of them to become maimed or dead. And you, with all your limbs intact and a treasure of a wife and daughter, and all your wits mostly about you, how was it *you* merited such a fate? What'd you done, other than *fail* them all? Where were you to help rescue Harry or Finny the way they'd rescued you at Antietam? Where were the words of comfort and consolation for Smitty, who'd left more than his arm behind at Malvern Hill—and you, the *Perfessor*, without so much as a sage word or two to explain it all—to explain the reason for all the suffering, even if you didn't know why yourself. There are the wounded lads in the hospital, their faces now as distinct as they were when you tended to them, *lied* to them, told them the arm or leg or the eye they'd lost would be all right, somehow—and all of them now just part of the barrage of vivid, anguished faces that mingle with your memories in flashes and spurts, becomin' now the grass-stained mouths back on the Lane . . . or the little girl who was the first to die on the *Lord Sussex*, then Mrs. Quigley who was the last . . . there are the runaways along the peninsula, left behind to their fate just like the battered souls on the docks at Newry and Liverpool . . . and there you are to *watch* it all again . . . powerless, helpless . . . as if you've been that twelve-year-old boy *all* your life—consigned to such a fate because you failed all those years ago to keep the promise you'd made to her . . . and what a cruel God it is who'd keep you alive through all of this, the way Suah told you on the dock in New York, no matter *what* the reason might be . . . until there's one last involuntary gasp of breath and the tears now abating . . . the stillness of the morning slowly easing the flood of memories to a more manageable tide . . . and your thoughts return to her. It's not her funeral anymore, or the imagination of what her resting place must look like now, or even the guilt of how you'd failed to live up to your promise. The memory that comes upon you in that weary moment is of the night before she died. And with your eyes still closed tight, you can almost see that tiny loft in Aunt Em's old cottage on the Lane, the place where you and she used to lie awake in the flickering light from what was left of a stale turf fire, separated only by the proud collection that had become your Library, and how you and she would imagine what books might pass through your fortunate hands once Mr. Broderick made another trip to London.

There's a steadiness to your breathing now, and the fresh memory that comforts you is of nothin' so trivial as the hope of being handed down another history of the English monarchs or even the great endowment of *The Iliad* or something more from Mr. Shakespeare. No, there you are, all of twelve years old with boyish dreams untainted by harsher realities still to come and full of plans for what your lives will be once the money from Da and Seanny arrives and you're *all* off to America. There's you, talking about being a teacher, a professor even, or a famous actor . . . or maybe you'll write stories to surpass even the ones that fill your tiny Library . . . and there she is, just as ever, listening to everything you have to say without tellin' you all the reasons it might never be so . . . no, she wouldn't do such a thing . . . instead, as you *listen* to the memory that fills your head now, it's as if you can hear her saying, *You could do that Ethan . . . sure ya could.* And then, in a voice not born from memory but hers all the same, you can hear her add to that familiar refrain, *But first ya gotta let go of it ahll, Ethan . . . let go of all the sorrow . . . you've got a worlda livin' left t'do, y'know . . .*

Anta May, Daddy! Looka Daddy!

Your eyes open in a jolt and you lift your head up from your cupped-together palms as if you'd been caught sleepin' during the Mass. There's grooming to do, wiping the remnants of the water from your eyes and cheeks and clearing your nose as best you can without being so obvious as to take out your handkerchief. And then she's upon you before you can even stand up all the way. You lift her and strain a little in straightening your back, and it's far more than a typical morning greeting, even for a three-year-old.

Surely there's something special for her to be on such an adventure as this and then see you there so far away from everything familiar. And she's got to tell you about everything they've seen so far, even the things she's seen countless times before on similar walks with you. But you don't mind, of course, and you smile at Mary as your daughter goes on for a minute or more in a flood of words with hardly a breath in between. When she's done and ready for some more exploration, she begins to wiggle free of your grasp, stopping only when you press your lips to her cheek and hold them there long enough to help you fight back the water that's gathered in your eyes again. And when she's off, there's just you and Mary there, the evidence of your boyish flood of emotion made obvious by what certainly must be the redness of your eyes. Still, Mary has a way of not making such a moment any more uncomfortable than it has to be, without ignoring it altogether either.

How *are* you, Ethan? she asks, in a voice that suggests all the understanding her own life has surely instilled in her.

Fine, fine, you say quickly, then blurt out a question you obviously know the answer to. You're out here every mornin' now that spring's here, I suppose?

Mmm, just about, she answers. It's my time to talk with Gertie.

And you're relieved in the silence that follows that she doesn't seem taken aback by the implicit awkwardness of the question, or feel the pressing need to ask about the plans for the rest of the day or details on your current emotional state.

Thanks for takin' her with you this mornin', you say after a few moments, and nod toward your daughter.

It's my pleasure, she says, *really* it is. There's something about the way the little ones see things—like everything around them has such special meaning.

It helps to have a short memory, I s'pose, you say, then worry that it might open the door to a deeper conversation.

But she just laughs and looks protectively over at Aislinn, who's busy brushing the palm of her hand over the azalea shrub as if by doing so she can make it bloom faster. And then Mary turns back to you with her eyebrows slightly pressed together and a slightly puzzled look on her face.

I was thinking this mornin' about something Gertie would tell me from time to time, she says, and then gazes out over the water as if letting the notion rest for a moment or two while she collects her thoughts into the exact words she means to say.

And just as you start to feel compelled to break the silence, she looks back at you and smiles.

I was always an inquisitive child, I guess you could say. And she nods over to Aislinn, smiles again, and adds, Sorta like someone we both know.

And you laugh, saying, *Inquisitive*... that's puttin' it gently.

I s'pose, Mary replies, but I think I musta been even *more* of a handful—especially for Gertie, with all she had to overcome just to get through a single day. And I had a memory just this mornin' . . . thinkin' about—y'know—what day it is.

And now you worry that the foolish emotions of the moments preceding will wash over you once again. But Mary looks back out over the lake to allow you to fight back the water that wants to return to your eyes.

I remember watchin' Gertie do one o' her stitchin's, she continues with her eyes still averted and her voice changing ever so slightly. An' I could only see the *back* of it, y'know, 'cause she didn't much like showin' it to anyone, even me, 'til it was close t'bein' finished. So all I could see were all these bitsa thread, all different colors, different types of material even, runnin' ev'ry which way—all of 'em tied off togetha in justa fit of knots an' tangles . . . just a mess, y'know? Didn't make *any* sense.

And you can feel her look over at you for just a second before looking away again, content to hear you mumble an unconvincing *mmm-hmm* for a response.

It didn't look like any of it could ever fit together, not into somethin' with any kind of *meanin'*, anyhow—an' I just *hadta* know how she made all th'pieces fit together—how she even knew what she was makin' an' what it was gonna look like in th'end. And I remember askin' her—*demandin'* almost, as much as I'd ever try to demand anything from Gertie, leastways—sayin' to her, Gertie, how you know whachu doin' in all that *mess*? But she just laughed a little and asked me how I was ever gonna see what it was she was makin' when I was all caught up starin' at just the knots an' tangles an' such.

Mary turns her gaze back to you now and smiles when she sees you looking back at her, unashamed to have the water in your eyes.

Then Gertie tells me . . . and it's clear as anything I can remember from those times I've been runnin' from all these years, Ethan . . . runnin' from all the sad memories of everything that got lost along the way . . .

And now it's Mary with the water in her eyes, but she carries on.

. . . she says to me . . . Don't none of it, the stitchin', the knots an' tangles an' such . . . don't none of it make any sense 'til you seein' it with all that mess fit togetha the way it's *s'posed* to be seen—'til you seein' it *frontsways.*

And she laughs a little, sniffling back the memories and dabbing with her sleeve at the water along her cheeks. Then she looks intently at you, as if she's trying to tell if you're artist enough to understand the real meaning behind her story.

Anta May! Aislinn calls out, then appears around the corner of the shrubs and points up the path.

I see a flowa, Anta May!

And Mary walks the few steps up to the clearing of the path, taking Aislinn's hand in hers, ready to be led to a bold lily or delinquent crocus or whatever other manner of bloom has your daughter in such a frenzy.

But she stops at the clearing to glance back at you for a quick moment, and understanding now, you think, it's long enough for you to say in a voice just above a whisper . . . Thank you, *Anta May.*

And she smiles . . . knowingly.

It's that evening in the dwindling light of the gloaming when the moment arrives to truly celebrate the founder of this gathering. Chairs are set out on the porch for Mam and Da, Aunt Em and Corrine, and Seanny, too, and here's the audience for the play to follow outnumbered by the cast and crew to perform it . . . as if such a thing matters to anyone at all.

Inside the screen door, Ethan and Isabelle and Mary and Aislinn put on their costumes, little more than blankets wrapped over their clothes in the fashion of togas, except for dear Aislinn, who giggles all the while as she steps into the large burlap sack filled with pillows. Marcella kisses her, then takes her seat at the piano, looking out through the window for Micah's cue. And as Mary and Isabelle gingerly fit Aislinn into the costume that would terrify less adventurous three-year-olds, Ethan can't help but giggle himself, with thoughts of how this day has turned into something only the distance of twenty years could make so possible.

When they are settled, Micah clears his throat and sets the scene for the audience gathered before him as Marcella plays the dirge of Beethoven's Seventh Symphony to set the mood. Ethan steps outside the screen door and onto the porch, enacting every emotion as Micah tells them of the perilous voyage of the great Odysseus, who left his home in Ithaca to fight with the vast armies of Agamemnon, alongside the mighty Achilles outside the walls of the fortress city of Troy . . . and so on and on. Oh, the many and terrible battles they did fight, Micah says, as Ethan takes his broom handle become sword and pretends to battle the mythical hordes sent to smite him. And there is such laughter amongst the audience that he begins to embellish the moment, the way he always did those twenty years ago.

Now Micah bellows out the description to match the crescendo of the music and laughter. Oh, the hardships they endured, through the death of so many valiant men on both sides of the seemingly unending conflict . . . and when it was done Odysseus was left to fight the god Poseidon, who endeavored to keep him from his home. Only when Aeolus did contain all the winds of the sea and earth within a cloth sack he gave to Odysseus was there hope of returning to Ithaca.

And here Ethan steps inside the screen door, picking up Aislinn wrapped in her satchel and giggling just the way the winds should. He walks back out to the porch, followed by Mary and Isabelle wrapped in their blanket togas, and following enviously behind him. Until Odysseus did grow tired, Micah says, and the music and the moment grow more still—all except the giggling winds set down on the porch before them.

His companions did conspire, sure that there was treasure contained within the mysterious satchel, Micah declares, and now Mary and Isabelle pretend to whisper and plot and move about. Until finally they open the satchel and the wind, uncertain at first, pops out of the satchel, and surveys the audience before their laughter encourages her own, and Aislinn pops her arms free, bursting, giggling, forgetting to be the wind until Isabelle reminds her, then blowing hard as she can toward the audience. Marcella scrambles her way up and down the keys to make the music of all the winds of the earth, and Isabelle lifts Aislinn up, the bottom of the sack still around her, and they spin all about the porch, Isabelle and Mary making the sounds of the wind and Aislinn mostly just reveling in it, along for the ride, making some sounds of the wind herself when she can remember to.

Then Ethan wakes up and throws his hands over his head. He rushes to contain the winds, taking them from Isabelle, as Micah tells of the ship being tossed all about on the waves. Mary's thrown off the porch first, and then Isabelle soon after. And Ethan holds on for dear life to the hysterical winds, stealing a look at the audience, boundless laughter and smiles from all but Seanny and Da, neither one of them having witnessed the original performance of this scene but knowing the significance of it all the same, and the two of them thinking maybe they could've somehow held back the tide of The Hunger all those years ago, if only they'd been there to do it. Now instead, it's their clenched jaws holding back the tide of the water in their eyes, anguished memories like Ethan'd known all too well 'til just that very morning. But then, Aislinn, the wind, seems to focus in on the two of them while Ethan holds her in his arms, and there's a slight tilt of her head, the way her father does sometimes, the way he'd emulated from her namesake once upon a time, and it's as if she knows all about it, somehow offering with a single kiss of her hand and the sweep of it over the audience there before her . . . at long last, redemption.

And the music begins to slow, becoming soft again, as Ethan twists a few more times and places the wind back on the floor before collapsing to it himself, exhausted, his arms and legs sprawled in every direction. And Aislinn, smiling at her audience for a moment first, falls across her father's chest and squeezes her eyes closed. No more of the wind within her.

Only laughter.

ACKNOWLEDGMENTS

Many thanks to:

Marly Rusoff, Michael Radulescu, Julie Moscow, Alison Calahan, Coralie Hunter, Sheila Klee, and Janet Biehl.

And the start of things:

Mrs. Pat Carter from Catholic University those many years ago, a wonderful writing teacher; Father Charles Kohli, a sage who made my family so much the better for having known him; and Peter James Troy, who instilled in me a love for the beautiful game of baseball, and more significantly even, a love for history . . . and the apparently genetic inability to pass a roadside historic marker without stopping to read it.

And Frank McCourt, Alice Walker, Alex Haley, Shelby Foote, Langston Hughes, e e cummings, Frank Capra, Ken Burns, Maya Angelou, and Junot Diaz, too.

And Most Essentially:

Carol Troy, who was there for every tangent and byway and found endless promise around every turn . . . and helped me to see it, too.

Jerrilyn Breslin, who shared the wisdom that it is sometimes necessary to fall in the ditch in order to see where the road is truly headed.